COF

Ian McKinley

COF

DOUBLE DRAGON

Chapter 1 - Understory

I was sitting in the tub, watching the sun sink slowly into the tropical sea leading up to its usual, but still surprising, final rush for the horizon. It looked so beautiful that I felt a typical rush of guilt as I recognized how lucky I was, not only a part of the small fraction of humanity that had survived the apocalypse, but one of the very few who lived in luxury. It clearly wasn't my fault that billions had died, but how many thousands, millions had died due to my actions or, maybe, my inaction. I had helped some, an extremely small number, who probably considered me some kind of saint. To a lot more, I was probably more of a demonic, murdering bastard from hell.

How would history view me, I wondered, assuming of course that we would survive as a species long enough for anyone to really care. Although I tried to communicate confidence that we should be OK now, with death rates dropping and birth rates soaring, I knew that the way that we had fucked-up the environment over the last century could come back and bite us at any time. Was extinction really on the cards or was this just the inevitable pessimism associated with advancing years and awareness of my own mortality? Only time would tell.

***

A discrete cough brought me back to the present, reminding me that I was supposed to be narrating my autobiography. A raven-haired girl - either Sue or Sophie, I could never tell them apart - was taking my dictation down on an antiquated solar-powered word processor. It was one of those things made to be sold in the third world for a hundred bucks US in the '10s or thereabouts. Of course, between the start of design and final production, hyperinflation had turned this into about ten thou; but it was still about a hundred turn-of-the-century US, if you calculated it in Mars Bars or some other real commodity.

Sue, or Sophie, was staring at me questioningly and I realized that musing on the source of her tool had caused the restart of my monologue to die stillborn. Happened a lot these days; old age certainly does not come alone, rejuv or no rejuv. "Sorry, where was I?"

"Rice cooker," she replied, her dark eyes flashing as they caught the last direct rays of the vanishing sun.

"Ah, yes, the rice cooker hypothesis." I switched to auto dictate mode and forced my mind back to the story of the collapse of civilization as we used to know it. I'm not sure that I really believe it, but it's such a great yarn that it deserves to be true. How many ends of the world have there been? It's such a common theme in books, vids and the old online games that you'd have thought that all options had been covered. Asteroids, plagues, wars, invasions of aliens. There were even Krakens, killer tomatoes, birds and demons in TV sets. But nobody considered the humble rice cooker as the vector of the apocalypse.

Well, true, it wasn't the cooker directly. Just that, according to documents unearthed during post-mortem work now going on in Japan, this seems to be the way that al-Qaeda inserted their virus into the global internet. Now, you have to remember that, by the early '40s, this Islamic terrorist group had been fairly well forgotten. Old fogies like myself remembered the early 9-11 and LPG attacks. However, after the US backed out of the Middle East, the collapse of the dollar caused more chaos than a bunch of mad ragheads in caves could dream of and Arab terrorism returned to being a much more domestic activity.

It was inevitable that some opening for hackers would exist. Security was always a big issue for communication in the various inter-, intra- and domestic micro-nets that evolved into the U, the universal ethernet. Nevertheless, despite gigabucks, anything that can be designed, can be designed around. For every white hat, there is an equal and opposite black hat. For decades this was the way that a large fraction of the rather incestuous communities of IT cops and robbers spent their time.

However the hack was actually done, the smart thing about the particular virus used was its combination of high speed of propagation and long incubation time. It was so small that it could spread undetected through the entire U within its nine month gestation period: achieving effectively 100% infection of every electronically interlinked piece of equipment. In 2041 that was simply everything more sophisticated than a soupspoon. Maybe even smarter, however, was its target: the Gödelization routine that was the basis of all memory units. Of course, you don't get these now; today it's back to the stone age of simple magnetic and optical digital storage. But, for quantum computers, Gödelization was really the cat's pajamas.

It was a couple of Indian mathematicians who came up with a practical manner of using QCs to both factorize truly huge numbers and break them down into a minimum-sized exponential expansion. Something to do with minimizing entropy. Or was it maximizing entropy? Whatever, it was number theory at its most obtuse. Gödelization, on the other hand, is just a simple way of coding information as numbers, the only problem being that the resulting numbers rapidly become mind-bogglingly gigantic and hence the back calculation to decode them is extremely laborious.

Combine Gödelization with a bit of quantum-level mathematical legerdemain, however, and you have the tool that revolutionized 21st century computing. The Exabytes of information in a major library could rapidly be converted into a gigantic number that was, in turn, reduced to a minute data string. Moore's Law was kind of forgotten about then as, in effect, both processing speeds and storage capacities were so large that they could be considered near as dammit infinite. This was a bit like invention of the transistor, only with more immediate applications. QCs could carry out calculations at gobsmacking speeds and the Gödelization trick made information storage and retrieval trivial. The math professors shared a Fields Medal, while the geek who patented the resulting software package became the richest man on Earth.

"Um... , Cof. This bloody thing keeps buggering about with Gödelization, putting wee dots over the o." Sue-Sophie was clearly unhappy.

"Just ignore it: it's an umlaut. We don't have them since the Germanic tongues joined ancient Greek and Sanskrit as dead languages. Along with French and all their bloody accents; just shows that there's some progress in the world, when you think about this at least! That toy you're using predates this giant leap for mankind. Anyway, where was I?"

"The virus targeted the Gödelization routines."

"Right, OK, here we go. The problem with the subroutines involved was that they had been bootstrapped by QC artificial intelligences... " It's all a bit mystical when you try to put quantum operating procedures down in plain text. The process that R&W came up with - the Indian guys were Rama and a bloke with a name about half a paragraph long, starting with W and ending in -sing - inherently allowed for the process to be self-improving as, apparently, whenever a quantum calculation had been done once, it never needed to be repeated. Incidentally, this little aside in their work proved unambiguously that no higher intelligences exist in our particular neck of the universe. Although this formally applied only to those using quantum computers within our light cone, the gutter press interpreted this as demonstrating that God did not exist, resulting in Rama being assassinated by a rabid Christian who took this badly and W-whatever disappearing into isolation in a military barracks somewhere in the foothills of Tibet.

Bootstrapping, the idea of lifting yourself by your own bootstraps, is nowhere better applicable than in QC. Advanced quantum computers need electromagnetic fields that preserve qubits for long enough to allow a calculation to be performed: fields so complex that they can only be practically maintained by advanced QCs. Basically, all you have to do is construct the first prototype and then it's a self-propagating process. Well, self-propagating with a bit of basic nanotech and given sufficient energy and raw materials. But with the huge number-crunching capacity available, muon-catalyzed fusion and directed transmutation become practical and hence you can build intelligence into just about everything.

Of course, just because you can, doesn't mean you have to. There's no physical law that makes you do it; just the Law of Commercial Drive. This is probably the most powerful force for good - or, more often evil - since the mid-20th Century. Take the telephone. This was once something that was very useful because it allowed you to talk to somebody when it was so urgent, or you were so lazy, that a letter wouldn't do. This was changed a little when a generation grew up with the things; then letters were a kind of emergency option when you couldn't get someone to answer the phone or you were marooned on a middle-of-bugger-all desert island. But technology then allowed mobile phones to do more things: act as calculators, diaries, cameras, music and video recorders, access the U. After a bit, commercial pressure built up to use all technology possible to cram more options into the smallest size Handy. It could, literally, sonic your teeth, holographically analyze your painful big toe and guarantee your girlfriend an orgasm. Oh, yes, and also allow you to talk to people. More than 99% of the services provided by this workhorse of the '20s and '30s were things that people at the beginning of the century hadn't even dreamt that they could ever want.

So this is where it comes to the rice cooker. You still remember that? You probably could have constructed a form of mobile phone that could zap rice with tailored microwaves, but purist Japanese would certainly not accept a substitute for a nice, big, solid rice cooker. Of course, like all other bigger service items such as air conditioners, hot tubs and toasters, the Drive ensured that all possible intelligence was built in, along with full two-way communication capacity. You never knew when you might need to reprogram your rice cooker because you were going to be a bit late home or had changed your mind about that curry and were going to have home-made sushi instead; the rice cooker could then liaise with the fridge and the U food-provider to sort out all the logistical details involved.

So, by default, every piece of equipment that could possibly be interlinked, was interlinked - and the linkages were often simply left to themselves to grow and mesh as was needed, under the directions of the ever-present QC controllers.

So the stage was set for a life of luxury for everyone on this somewhat shagged-out old planet. Of course, getting as far as 2040 with the huge population wave breaking at that time was, in itself, an amazing tribute to the power of the developing technology. Despite runaway global warming, exploitive mining of all major groundwater resources, pollution of land, air and water and population spread to even the most unsuitable locations, for decade after decade we managed to totter on the brink of multiple catastrophes. There were, indeed, some close misses, but disasters were contained and the final collapse never came. The support infrastructure provided by the directed efforts of unlimited computer power always managed to haul the coals from the fire. Everyone, or almost everyone, became complacent. Why not? The QC-driven artificial intelligences could solve any problem they were presented with. So why worry?

Another girl entered the spacious onsen and sat behind my hard-working secretary, A blonde: Helga or Heidi. Heidi, it was; a rusty relay in my cortex tripped and reminded me of her confused expression when I had laughed after she informed me that her brother was called Peter. One of my masseuse team. She was starting to work on Sue/Sophie's neck, evidently a very pleasant experience if the low moan was anything to go by.

Noting my distraction, the moan changed into a muttered "... and the Survivalists weren't in much better shape." Even with her eyes closed, the black-haired girl radiated amusement in the way she could read my questions before I had even get around to framing them myself.

"Yes, the Survivalists and a lot of other groups of varying degrees of nuttiness did their best to stay out of this joined-up world and retreated to their backwoods fortresses with their over-dimensioned arsenals and under-dimensioned libraries." Nevertheless, in general these weren't the types to stick to flintlocks when the latest smart rifles could shoot round corners, penetrate DU armor and had hundred shot magazines. Also, if you're living out in the boonies, you need a car: which meant a rather smart piece of kit after hydrocarbons were phased out as fuels in the early '30s.

Of course, there were some pastoralists who really did opt out - the Amish and a range of other God-bothers come to mind - but they were few and far between. They had to be. The option of opting out of all technology more sophisticated than a horse-drawn cart or plough was available only to very small communities that were privileged enough to have access to the large areas of land needed to support their low-tech lifestyles. With global populations heading for ten billion, there

13

simply wasn't enough space to have very many of these.

And then there was me. I wasn't the only one, of course, but there weren't a lot of folk wealthy enough to live their hobby of freezing time in the year 2025. Well, actually, I suppose there were plenty of people rich enough; it's probably fairer to say that there weren't many people weird enough to do such a thing. That's when I picked up my nickname - Cof. The Crazy Old Fool, that's what my neighbors called me. Actually, that was the polite ones. Crazy Old Fuck was probably more common, especially amongst the younger generation.

Heidi let out a very un-ladylike snort and broke into my monologue. "You're joking, Cof, aren't you? That's not really where your name comes from, is it?"

"Dead fucking right it is! In the early days, I must confess, I was a bit pissed off when I first picked up on the name they called me behind my back. Anyway, with time, I kind of took to it. Especially after the way things turned out. Anyway, it was a hell of a lot better than being called Herman."

Another snort and a giggle from my secretary. "Mmm, maybe you're right." The tall blond looked thoughtful. "Cof's definitely a slicker name than Herman. And we probably all agree that you're pretty crazy, like a fox. Yep - Crazy Old Fox - that'd just about sum it up."

Smart as shit, all these girls. They knew exactly how to play me: no sycophancy, but just enough casual banter, with the odd hidden stroke to my ego, to keep me amused.

"Yes, well, whatever. The key thing was that, by the mid '20s, I was rolling in dosh. It was all a bit of a fluke, really, because I started off as a lowly materials scientist, developing piezo-electric organometallic polymers for use in data gloves: you know for those old clunky virtual reality systems. I had produced a fantastic tactile membrane, which was not only incredibly sensitive, but also registered and simulated the sensations associated with contact with fluids. Unfortunately, this was just when QCs were bringing in immersion holograms and tactile force fields, so the entire project went belly up and, after a decade and a half of work, I was shown the door; with the patents covering my polymer work in place of a gold watch. The stroke of luck, though, was that I was living with my sister, who was completely addicted to masturbation."

Heidi's snort was even louder. "Come on, Cof, you're making this up! You can't tell us that you got mega-rich because your young sister liked to jack-off!"

"Just listen, wench, and you might learn something! Anyway, she's my older sister, even if a bit better preserved than I am." We were, I suppose, a very strange family. Our parents were both career managers, who seemed to have decided together that a nuclear family with one of each would be a good thing to have. It fit in with the house in

London, the flat in New York and the Villa in Tuscany. We had au pairs and housekeepers who looked after us and occasional visits from the Old Dears, when they could conveniently fit it into their busy schedules. So we grew up very close, with my sister, Andrea, taking the lead role throughout, even though she was less than two years older. We separated to go to University; I had seven years at Edinburgh while she spent nine at Heidelberg. However, after we graduated, she suggested getting a flat together in Oxford. We lived together there for about fifteen years.

"Masturbation!" My amanuensis called me back to the present from the beginning of a stroll down a long and winding memory lane.

"Yes, yes, I was coming to that. We grew up very close together..." As children we bathed together, slept together and went through puberty together. We had some very strange au pairs but one, in particular - Margit her name was - had a major influence on us. She was completely casual about clothing; I guess her family was solid German FKK. When working she wore short skirts and loose blouses, but never knickers or bras. When in her room after work, she never wore anything, even when we came to visit her, as we did with great regularity. I guess Andrea was about eleven or twelve when Margit taught her how to masturbate properly and gave her free access to a drawer full of sex toys.

Yes, my sis took to wanking like a dog to water. I think she also took to Margit, although it

16

wasn't for another decade or so before she finally gave up experimenting with boys and decided that she was 100% lesbian. At this time, remember it was at the end of last century, it wasn't easy for young girls to get their hands on porn. So, although younger, I got pressurized into purchasing the porn mags and vids that my sister craved. Not a problem for me, though, I quickly grew keen on those things, almost as much as she was.

"But this was, what, when you were in your teens?"

"Yes, but this is all background so that you can understand that, when we shared the flat, we didn't have the most conventional brother-sister relationship."

"What, you were shagging your sister?"

"'Course I wasn't. Apart from anything else, she's fucking lesbian to the core, as I told you. We just were very casual and relaxed about nudity and sex. She had her girlfriends stay regularly and I had mine. She was always flirting with my girls and, I must confess, I chanced my arm a couple of times with some of her bi pals. Yes, well, it might have ended up with three or more in a bed on a couple of drunken occasions, but I never had sex with my sister."

It did get a little bit strained when Andrea finally found her perfect girlfriend, the one she wanted to spend her life with. I thought it was finally time for us to set up on our own, but her partner, Tina, was a commercial pilot and actually spent more time overnighting around the world than

17

she did in the UK. So we had a two-phase life; I was gooseberry to the two lovebirds when Tina was at home and it was back to normal with Andrea masturbating to old lesbo sex videos when Tina was travelling the globe. That was the thing about my sister, she considered onanism to be a social thing. Thought it was really sad to be wanking alone, when you could be doing it along with others.

"Maybe something to do with the influence of your au pair, Margaret was it?" Heidi was clearly fascinated.

"Margit," I corrected, automatically. "You could be right; I've never really thought about it. It was just the way she always was."

"Yes, but I still don't see... "

"For Christ's sake, I'm getting there, woman. If you'd stop bloody interrupting I'd be able to tell the fuckin' story."

The blond rolled her eyes and mimed the process of zipping her lips closed.

"Right, well, I really felt it was time to go, but didn't have the heart to leave my sister on her lonesome. I first rigged up a two-way vid link, so the girls could share a lesbo vid and also see each other on a split screen, but it still didn't have the intimacy that my sister wanted. Then I got fired ... "

It was serendipitous, I suppose. I had patents to a material with no applications and a sister who was desperate for closer contact with her lover. It only took a couple of hours of programing to set up a prototype for interactive pressure transfer between two sheets of polymer and five minutes to talk

18

Andrea into giving it a try. It was successful beyond my wildest dreams: now when Andrea touched herself, Tina could feel every sensation - and vice versa. As soon as one of them became moist, the other could feel it directly. According to my sister, the realism of the contact was unbelievable and, although planned to help them when Tina was abroad, this quickly became a major component of their love life together, as they experimented with a wider and wider range of sex toys.

My first version resembled a very tight pair of diaphanous panties, but, for Christmas, I treated them to body-suits of the same material. Probably the best present I have ever given anyone: I don't think they emerged from their bedroom until the evening of Boxing Day. Just then I realized that I might have a commercial product on my hands. I contacted the biggest producer of marital aids, as they were then called, and the rest is history.

"You invented all those things, yourself?"

"Well, initially it was just the pants and body suits, focused on the female market. I admit that I was rather naive; I hadn't realized that self-abuse had such a huge customer base. But my commercial partner certainly did. Although the firm was based in Sydney, Australia, they assigned a product development agent to work with me as soon as we had agreed a contract. She was an Ozzie called Kelly and didn't at all look the part of a sex toy specialist."

Actually, she looked like somebody's mum. Dumpy and homely. I'm not at all what you would

19

call a shy person, but I confess I had problems at first even discussing our products with her. It just shows how wrong impressions can be. She was born for the job, being the possessor of one of the dirtiest minds that I have ever encountered. I had thought my sister had pretty wide experience of sex toys, but this was nothing compared to Kelly. The company she worked for had a massive catalogue and she appeared to have tried them all.

It was an extremely productive collaboration. She dreamed up the specifications and I did the actual design and programing. The most fascinating work I've ever done. Until then I had no idea of what people got kicks out of doing to themselves - and how keen they and others were to share the experience. It was easy enough to couple suits and toys to vid or holo links, the critical thing was that I had the patents on the magic polymer. Within a year, Kelly had her own design team and I was back to fundamental materials science: building in temperature functionality and improving textural sensitivity and mechanical performance. This was cutting edge stuff, a film as thick as a few coats of paint that could transmit the full sensations of being reamed by a twelve-inch todger.

"The very thought brings tears to my eyes," Heidi grimaced theatrically.

"So you've tried it yourself?"

The silence was broken by a giggle from my secretary. "You walked into that Heid. Folk rarely admit to it, but I guess everyone has tried some alternative options in secret at one time or another."

20

"Yes, I suppose that was something contributing to the huge success of the toys. In private you could try anything at all that you had ever dreamt of. It was the logical end product of an evolution that started with Paleolithic Venuses and dildos carved from wood or stone and took off with the first internet porn sites. Of course, it also helped that, by the '20s, the population explosion was really pushing demand on resources to breaking point and any option that could satisfy the natural human imperative for sexual gratification without risk of producing children was strongly supported by national governments, even if such support was tacit in most cases."

"But surely contraception is an easier solution to that problem."

"Certainly in a lot of developed countries but, even in some of these, there were religious taboos that limited application back then. But the real problem was what was called the third world in those days - Africa, Central America, Central Asia - where population growth rates were highest. Not only were there cultural blocks to acceptance of chemical contraception, the actions of some of the bloody aid agencies very seriously fucked things up."

"There was some mega riot somewhere: in Africa?"

Heidi had clearly forgotten that she was supposed to be staying quiet but, as my faithful scribe was taking it all down, this was probably as good a way of getting my story documented as any other.

"Yes, in the old Republic of South Africa. Some fuckwits in a US-sponsored charity decided that adding a contraceptive into local drinking water would be the best way to solve the problem of population growth. They couldn't have screwed up things better if fucking-up scientific population control had been their original intention. Not only was the action uncovered only after water had been contaminated in five major cities, but the contraceptive effect was racially selective for blacks and Asians and caused irreversible loss of reproductive capacity for both men and women."

The term mega riot hardly covered the response of the affected population and their neighbors: it was closer to civil war. Although the US link was exposed and resulted in the bombing of embassies and consulates throughout the African continent, blame was extended also to Europeans and the local white populations. The final death toll will never be known, but it was certainly many tens of thousands in Africa - and almost fifteen thousand in Washington DC as a result of weaponized cholera released into a reservoir in a revenge attack by black African terrorists. Typically, most of those who died in the States were poor blacks living in sordid ghettos, rather than the white fatcats and politicos who had been targeted.

"Contraception... " Sue/Sophie reminded me.

"Yes, well, as you can imagine, all this fuss led to a great reluctance to use chemicals that were

22

predominantly produced by Western megacorps and might be part of a plot to sterilize the populations of less developed countries. It was a bit of a global catastrophe but, for me, one with a silver lining. The kit we were selling was not only perceived as safe but also, due to its rapid initial spread through Europe, the States, Japan and Australasia, seen as an indicator of development and cultural sophistication. I remember in 2030, the year that the population hit nine billion, we estimated that our total sales had topped five hundred million. That's when I decided that I was rich enough to stop working and sold out."

"You sold out? That's crazy! That stuff must have been selling like hotcakes. There's even a fair amount of pre-QC kit that some of the staff here have, but they hoard it like gold dust. You must have lost a fortune."

"Well, I did sell my share of the company plus the patents for a small fortune. No, I should be honest here; it wasn't really a small fortune, it was actually a fucking huge one. Certainly it was unspendably huge for me. Remember, only a decade earlier I had been an unemployed boffin sharing a flat with my sister. But, after I hit fifty, I decided that there were other things I wanted to do with my life. Earning megabucks was too distracting, so I just took a bulk sum and decided to turn dosh into tangibles."

"So you guessed that things were about to go belly-up?" my secretary enquired. Unlike Heidi, she had clearly remembered the initial thread that had led to my diversion into the sex toy business.

"I hadn't the foggiest idea, to be honest. Well, predictions of the collapse of civilization were produced on a regular basis but, as a last minute solution always seemed to emerge, the rantings of global catastrophe Cassandras weren't taken too seriously. I suppose I expected that some kind of local disaster was inevitable, but not anything like what actually happened."

"If there is anything that explains my decision to set up this estate, it's probably that I'm basically an antisocial hedonist... "

"... with an inordinate fondness for young ladies!"

"... yes, indeed, with a desire to be pampered by beautiful women. And, thinking of this, it's about time I got out of this tub before I look like a prune... "

"... you mean, more like a prune!"

I clambered from the bath and posed in profile. "That's the only problem with the toys I produced, too much self-abuse and you go blind. If you weren't being regularly rogered by huge virtual dongs, you'd realize that your employer is a veritable Adonis."

Heidi smirked as she looked me up and down and then turned to pat down a thick towel on the massage table. "Not too bad, for someone of your advanced years," she conceded.

"Not bad? Not bad? I'll have you know this is the best kit that money can buy. I got this rejuv in

2035, when the technology got really nailed down. The entire shooting match is biological age thirty, and will be for decades yet."

"Shame about the brain though," Sue added. Based on that comment, it must be Sue, I concluded; blunt as baseball bat, that I certainly remembered about her.

"Yes, that was a bit of a miscalculation." I clambered onto the massive massage table and made myself comfortable, face down, while a huge towel was draped over my body. Heidi then turned up the lower edge and started to apply pressure to points on the souls of my feet.

A miscalculation, but also maybe a stroke of luck in my misfortune. Gluck im Ungluck, as they said when German still existed. There was no way that I had been going to let anybody bugger around with my brain until the procedures were mature and proven to be without long-term side effects. Early cortical rejuvenation was entirely biochemical and, to be honest, was a bit hit and miss. Some brain functions were certainly improved, but loss of blocks of memory was a common result. Then came the brain implants. These were much better targeted and, if anything, improved memory retention; but I just didn't like any invasive technique that involves a bunch of glorified mechanics guddling about within my skull. Finally, in 2040, biomechanical tuning using a combination of nanomachines and external EM control fields emerged. After swithering for months, I finally booked in for the three weeks of treatment required. It would have taken place in March 2041. The rice cooker time bomb went off on February 20th. So I was just too late for brain rejuv. Who knows if this technology will ever be recovered but, in any case, it probably won't be until it's too late for me. On the other hand, if Gödelization had been lost in the middle of treatment, I certainly would have been one of the billion or so people who died immediately as a result of this hack attack.

Chapter 2 - Building paradise

"So, then, how did you end up with this place?"

Heidi's question brought me back from a rather salacious daydream that had resulted directly from watching Sue strip off her cheongsam, evidently her only item of clothing, and ease herself into the hot bath, carefully holding her little notebook clear of the water.

Sue looked at me expectantly, probably wondering if I would force the narrative back to the hack attack. I thought about it for a moment and then decided that making a fuss was probably not a clever idea in my present position. As if reading my mind, hard thumbs pressed into my calves, causing my buttocks to clench involuntarily while the shock of pain forced a grunt through my gritted teeth.

"More chance than anything else," I admitted. "The one boundary condition was that I wanted to be well away from the UK, with its shit weather and rapid descent into third-worldhood. Since the beginning of the century, the country had been going continuously downhill. The climate was totally shagged as a result of the Gulf Stream beginning to stall: blizzards all winter and drought every summer, with a hurricane thrown in every couple of months to make things interesting. The educational system had been complete pants for yonks, turning out hordes of innumerate accountants, illiterate sociologists and bloodsucking, thick-as-mince lawyers. Maybe providing just enough for national survival when a major source of income came from financial services. But, when these went to the wall, the entire fucking house of cards collapsed."

"How did that happen? We still have money, don't we?" The high priestess of pain had moved onto my thighs and there was no way that I was going to try to get the tale on track now.

"Yes, money still seems to be the best way of organizing commerce, though barter was much more important immediately post-Crash. Anyway, in the '10s and '20s, more and more services were offered through the U and managed by smart software. OK, the tools we had then were nothing like as smart as the stuff that emerged a decade later when QCs really came to their own, but they were smarter than most of the wankers making truckloads of Euros for faffing about with other people's dosh."

"Do I detect a bit of sour grapes there, my lord and master?" Hard fingers were identifying the tender points on my left buttock that bore evidence to my poor performance in the dojo that morning. "Surely an Übergeek like yourself would hardly be bothered by the shady goings-on in the London money markets?"

An earlier suspicion became more concrete. I was now sure that Heidi was leading me on and probably knew as much as I did about the financial market collapse. I strained to remember; I was sure that somebody on my extensive staff had a degree in economic history or something similar. Was it Heidi or one of the redheads? The redheads, now: one was a personal trainer and the other a chef...

"Money markets... " Sue reminded me that I was supposed to be dictating my story, history, autobiography, whatever the hell it was.

"Well, it all seems a bit petty now but, remember, I was an overworked, underpaid boffin for most of my working life. It truly got on my tits every year when I had to read about the mega-bonuses the cunts at the top of the banking and insurance trees were paying themselves."

What made it worse was that it was evident to everyone outside the business that it had nothing to do with performance; all went well, they all got big payouts - things went awful and they still got piles of dosh. I loved every minute when these organisations finally fell apart and large numbers of the top shits got totally reamed. Actually, I think most folk worldwide did. It was only afterwards that, in places like England, the full consequences of a collapse of a mainstay of the economy became obvious. Typically, of course, this happened just when hyperinflation hit the dollar and the US imploded. It really should have resulted in a global recession but, somehow, the AIs kept things afloat. They could prevent people starving, but couldn't stop global restructuring. The countries with solid technological bases, natural resources or industrial capacity floated to the top and a lot of the old super-powers, who had lived for decades on the credibility provided by their former glory, slipped gradually towards to arse-end of the pecking order.

"So you were a poor economic refugee?" My valiant clerk was attempting to keep my musing to the point.

"Well, I was anything but poor, but I wanted well away from the hellhole that no-longer-Great Britain was rapidly becoming. I wanted sun and sea, political and economic stability. Mmm... and somewhere that I wouldn't have to worry about the latest catastrophe-de-jour, whether it was earthquakes, volcanoes, floods, plagues of locusts, whatever. With the Gulf Stream shift, the hurricanes that used to devastate the Western Caribbean had moved eastwards, mainly ending up hammering either the Northeast US coast or Western Europe. It's certainly an ill wind that blows nobody any good!"

"But why here?" Sharp elbows were grinding into my buttocks and lower back and my torturer was clearly determined to use her position of strength to keep control of my story.

"There were certainly quite a few options but, when I was searching the U for specific properties, this place caught my eye. The whole estate, with this main house and all the auxiliary buildings, was up for sale as a lot. I'd actually never been to the Caribbean at that time, but I liked the look of it and so I bought it without ever having seen it in real life. It wasn't actually planned as a villa: it was originally designed as a nudist resort, which explains the wall around the entire place."

"Although not the electric fences and anti-personnel weapons... " Yes, my scribe definitely was Sue, I concluded.

"Yes, I did add a few little touches of my own to keep the hoi polloi out. Couldn't have my beauteous staff being salivated over all day by the local yobos." But, of course, this was only a small part of the entire story. There's a backbone that I'm happy for my various scriveners to draft up for me, but there are bits that I plan to add later myself. Not that I'm ashamed of what I've done, but there are actions I've taken in the past that I have to think about very carefully before I can put them into words. The rationale for my defense system is one of these.

I closed my eyes and pretended to drift off to sleep. A good ploy, evidently, as the massage became gentler and more soothing. Yes, relaxation was the trick to putting my life in Barbados after February 20th into context. As I thought back on it, it was so different to the other major catastrophes that I could remember over my long life. As a young kid who was determined to be a scientist, I remembered the shock of seeing the first TV coverage of Chernobyl. Until then, I had a very simplistic view of science as taught in school: I thought it was founded on absolute truth that was passed on by omniscient teachers. We had been covering nuclear power that week and had learned about the science and technology that assured safety. My physics teacher had actually mocked the general public's ignorant fear of reactors exploding.

I never believed another teacher after that; probably why I did so well in materials science, where scientific gospel always seems to be playing catch-up with empirical technological advances.

Then we had 9-11, the Xmas tsunami and Fukushima: disasters covered live on TV and thousands of internet sites. It didn't make any difference if the catastrophe was fast and localized like the LPG attack on LA, or slow and global like the US dollar collapse; everything was covered by the full range of news media in real time. That's what made the Feb 20th Crash so frightening. The first that anyone - or at least any of the survivors - knew about it was when everything stopped working. And, what was most shocking part for a population accustomed to instant information on line, this also meant no news. No internet, no TV, no radio. Indeed, in most places, there was also no power: so even the scale of the catastrophe was unclear.

The immediate death toll, within the first hour or so of the hack attack, has been guesstimated as at least half a billion. This included all those in the air - or unlucky enough to be on the ground wherever the planes, airships, helicopters, rockets, whatever crashed. Then there were those near fission and fusion power plants, transmutation plants and other major industrial facilities that didn't failsafe, in high speed ground transport, undergoing medical treatment or simply living in areas where active control systems were needed to prevent flooding by rivers or seas.

About as many died within the next twenty-four hours. One of the major advances made possible by QC technology was large-scale wireless power distribution using directed electromagnetic fields. Wires and cables vanished from hand-held electronic equipment, houses and factories; replaced by EM fields generated by room-temperature superconducting magnets. The collapse of such fields when the computers went down led to vast amounts of power grounding, frying equipment and causing millions of fires. Of course, with no power supply, almost all fire-fighting capacity was lost. Many who escaped death in the blast of power that signaled the destruction of the AI control network, died from the fires raging through buildings in which electric doors no longer opened, lifts were frozen in place, fire engines were immobilized and water pressure vanished.

Naturally enough, the mega-cities were most vulnerable and were hit hardest during this phase and the subsequent Dying: a month during which most of the other four or five billion direct victims of this atrocity kicked the bucket. Starvation and disease killed most, although flooding, exposure and human violence also wiped out tens or hundreds of millions. We'll never know details; all we have is a little preliminary forensic archaeology and guesswork. That's the thing: not only did everything stop, but most records vanished as well. QCs went down and memories evaporated. Even if there were non-volatile backups, the Gödelized databases were now inaccessible and so completely useless.

In January 2041, Barbados had a population of just under 400,000, concentrated in Bridgetown and scattered through central and western regions. Nobody but the craziest of surfers wanted to live on the storm-surge ravaged Atlantic coast. By the beginning of March, I guess that maybe only about 40,000 or so had died, showing the advantages of our physical isolation and relatively low population density. Then cholera hit, starvation began to take its toll and fighting for remaining resources got really vicious after all traces of government control vanished. Within a month, Bridgetown was a ghost town and there were fewer than 200,000 left alive, mainly scattered in small communities and family-sized groups. These were particularly concentrated along the south and west coasts, where fishing complemented subsistence farming that was heavily focused on small market gardens and the remnants of low-intensity poultry and cattle raising that had survived the collapse of all automated systems.

I had lived on the island for just over a decade by then and my hobby estate was well established. Because QC developments had destroyed my original livelihood, I had come up with the neo-luddite concept of building a self-sufficient community that was completely independent of quantum technology: which meant more or less anything post-2025. Although far from primitive, such reliance on what were considered stone-age tools and services was considered extremely eccentric and was certainly very expensive to set up. Some hardware - solar collectors and heat pumps,

34

for example - could be found as junk. Non-quantum electronics were harder to come by and much of it came from museums or specialist collectors. An integrated set of software tools was even harder to obtain, but at least here I could do a lot of the cobbling together myself. I had to build my own workshops for integration and maintenance of all the electromechanical kit and employ a couple of staff that I had to send to an industrial history museum in Kyoto to get trained up.

Actually I shouldn't imply that I employed the staff. After I had decided on this idea of a QC-free community, my sister took over most of the practical logistics while I got into the more fascinating, for me, job of finding all the technical bits and bobs needed. Andrea had a degree in economics and an MBA, but was nothing like the airhead accountants that I usually encountered with such qualifications, which I attribute to her being educated outside the UK. She had managed a couple of big charities pre-Crash and, even following collapse of the British finance sector and much of the wealth that supported such charities, she managed to move smoothly to a Swiss-based charity that supported destitute women and children in England. When I begged her to help manage my rapidly growing fortune, she had been happy to oblige, although insisted that she retained enough flexibility to continue with charity work on a volunteer basis. All this circumlocution serves only to explain how my big sis ended up with the job of recruiting staff and thus why we ended up with an entirely female team.

As Andrea explained it, she had spent years working with charities that tried to combat the effects of active and passive discrimination against women, which always got worse when the economic situation deteriorated. She was simply responding with a bit of positive discrimination, favoring women if there was a choice. She insisted that this did not in any way lead to inferior qualifications; if anything, the opposite. I had to admit that she had been right in terms of quality of staff and her initial approach slowly evolved into a recruiting policy.

I should emphasize, however, that this didn't mean I was surrounded by a bunch of dykes and rabid carpet-munchers. I had never done an analysis, but guess that the proportion of lesbians and bis on the staff was probably not much different from the general population. If anything, any bias in that direction might be attributed to the large number of single mothers and victims of past abusive relationships. Most of the unmarried staff lived in an accommodation block that had originally been envisaged for resort staff but, nowadays, sometimes gave the impression of being a woman's shelter. In any case, it all worked very well and I was more than happy with the scenery provided by my team - being a fan of the female form in all its wonderful diversity of incarnations. Indeed, my current staff of about fifty seemed to cover a large part of this range, especially given the natural demographic of Andrea's target group and the fact that the Dying took a disproportionate toll on the old and very young.

In any case, my somewhat exotic community was well established by 2041. Even if the butt of many local jokes and viewed with great suspicion by the native Barbadians, it was accepted as a significant contributor to the regional economy and national tax income. Maybe some of this was a last remnant of the British colonial heritage: the bemused tolerance of the genuinely eccentric. We were thus quietly content and, in the Caribbean area, maybe amongst the last to even notice that 20th February would be the blackest day in recorded history.

The software time bomb went off at 15:00 GMT. Maybe it was just an arbitrary choice, but it certainly maximized the immediate impact on Europe and the USA, while initially sparing the sleeping populations of the Far East, Australia and Oceania some of the immediate impacts. Certainly, at this time, the USA was hardly a major regional, much less global, power. Nevertheless, given the history of interactions between the States and al-Qaeda, it may not have been completely coincidental.

I had been breakfasting at the time and noticed a warning on the old laptop I was doodling on that reported a loss of external com links. This was not a big deal; to buffer the sone-age software my estate used from being swamped by a QC internet that was about 10 generations more advanced, all external communications went through a data-transformer, the only quantum-based system I had on the estate. Unless I had really wanted to sever all links with the outside world, this was an inevitable compromise. Internally, we used top-end 2025 wireless broadband to give TB/s data transfer rates. In terms of storage capacity and information transfer rates, this compared with the 2041 U like scraping text onto clay tablets and moving them by runner would have compared to the internet of the late 20th century. A dedicated facility in my basement was assigned the translation job, which, as a side effect, provided an extremely effective fire wall. By the time any incoming data-stream had been filtered and compressed to the point that my internal servers could handle it, anything as subtle as a virus, worm or Trojan would have been swamped by noise. So we weren't cut off, but we lived in the electronic Middle Ages when it came to computers. Or, rather, I did and I inflicted this situation on any residents of the main estate. The staff accommodation was not as primitive; it would have been unfair for me to force them to forego the delights of fully-immersive interactive virtual communities just to fit in with my peculiarities. Nevertheless, even here QCs were used only for external links and not integrated with other tools and services, which were supplied directly from the estate.

So, the data-transformer was down. Not an unknown occurrence: a rapidly evolving U had to be interfaced with a primitive system caught in a time warp. I guessed that probably it just needed the filters to be turned up even further. I remember actually wondering to myself when this Red Queen's race would finally end, when the differences between my static microcosm and the outside world would become so great that they couldn't be bridged by such a lash-up. I had no idea that that this was not going to be a problem in the foreseeable future - if ever.

***

As with all survivors, the 20th remains seared into my brain. I may forget the names of half of my staff, but I remember having coffee in the conservatory as I struggled with the software for an automated composting and organic recycling unit. Fabricators and transmuters were compact and energy-neutral, but all relied completely on QC-controlled technology. Trying to get anything like the same recycling efficiency on the basis of wet chemistry and electromechanical sorting was clearly impossible, but the lesser goal of getting something that moved closer to my goal of self-sufficiency was realized, in its latest draft incarnation, by something about the size of a large garage that used about as much power as the rest of the estate put together. Nevertheless, my smartest software agents were combing through my in-house knowledge base looking for optimization possibilities. If at all possible, I'd crack this myself. Only as a last resort, would I contract the job out; when a QC AI would probably do the work in milliseconds. One way of looking at this was that I was wasting my bloody time. The other, my own view, was that this was a harmless hobby that helped to keep the old brain from clogging up - at least until I could get my much-postponed cranial rejuv sorted out.

***

It would have been about a couple of hours later before first mumbled complaints that the entire computer system in the staff barracks was down began to register. Again I wasn't very concerned until Lisa, my estate manager, reported that none of the externally resident staff had turned up for the shift starting at ten am: not a single one. Now our lack of communications was beginning to get annoying, so I dragged myself down to the basement to have a look at the data feed transformer. Everything was fine on the 2025 side of the system, but the QC was dead as a dodo. A single green light indicated that it had power, but otherwise it was completely inert. Now, for the first time, I began to feel a little bit worried.

The local artificial intelligence of a QC should have been sufficient to correct any imaginable problem, even in the extremely unlikely case of all electromagnetic links with the U being cut. I had never before heard of a QC flat-lining like this. The non-appearance of the staff was now beginning to look like part of a pattern. Could the U be down in the whole of St James Parish? All of a sudden there seemed to be an explanation: a massive electromagnetic pulse. Sometime in the mid '30s, a bunch of Tibetan nationalists had almost managed to detonate a nuclear weapon in Shanghai. I remembered that it had actually been designed and located to increase the size of the electromagnetic pulse, rather than blast or radiation. The consensus had been that this would have, indeed, maximized its impact by increasing the damage to QC infrastructure. It seemed to fit; you wouldn't even need an atomic bomb in the light of recent advances in portable power sources and ultra-high density capacitors. I reflected, sadly, that there seemed to be no development in technology that some bad bastard couldn't turn into a weapon.

It was then clear to me that, however the EMP was generated, chaos was inevitable. Everything automated or AI-controlled would be out of action. This not only meant no coms, but no power, transport or services. Water would be gone as soon as any local holding tank was drained and sewage would soon back up. It was certainly not going to be pleasant outside the estate.

I can remember all this going through my mind, debating with myself how we could best help by using the resources of the estate, when a major inconsistency in my interpretation of the evidence began to dawn on me. Everything within the estate was functioning perfectly, with the single exception of the QC in the basement. My electronics may have been old and clunky, but '20s kit would be just about as sensitive to an EMP as anything else. I didn't have military-spec hardened kit or ancient

41

invulnerable valves. How could we be fine if everything else was out?

I guess it was about ten-thirty when Andrea showed up with Tina in tow. She had a villa about a kilometer to the south, on the outskirts of Holetown, that she lived in when visiting Barbados over the winter; for some perverse reason she insisted on spending her summers back in a smart town house she had purchased in Oxford. Although my house was huge - originally dimensioned as a boutique hotel - Andrea had decided that having her own space was a good idea. Apart from anything else, most of her charity work was coordinated using U resources and, despite the way she humored her mega-rich little brother, she evidently thought the concept of my community was not only silly, but also rather pretentious.

Andrea and Tina had recently gone through full rejuvenations - my Christmas present to them - and thus looked to be in their early 20s. I was still getting used to their new appearances but, looking into my sister's eyes as she hurried into my study, there was no doubt that it was the same old dominant Andrea. There was also no doubt that, although she was doing a good job of appearing calm, she was very worried.

"It's a fucking zoo out there!" were, I remember, her first words. She then went on to describe waking up in a world where nothing functioned and, indeed, they had taken an hour to smash through hardened patio doors in order to escape from their house. That was something else

I'd completely forgotten: integrated security systems with a default lock-down mode. How many others were still trapped in their homes?

The women had climbed the gate at the end of their drive and walked to us along an almost completely empty road, the left side blocked by the walls and hedges hiding the many large, mainly foreign-owned villas along the stretch of coast that the locals called FCB - Fat Cat Beach. Closed craft shops and restaurants lined the inland side of the road, hiding the housing estates further uphill where the locals lived. At this time of day there should have been commuters heading for Bridgetown, staff heading for work in the resorts and hotels and kids setting off to school, but the street had been almost completely deserted. The few individuals or small family groups that they had encountered had the dazed look seen in the victims of natural disasters, but these locals had clearly enough concerns for each other and avoided any approach to obvious outsiders.

The only large group that they encountered had been clustered around an old 24-hour convenience store. The non-responsive robotic staff and vending machines were causing tempers to fray and it didn't look like it would be long before the kicks aimed at inert machinery got out of control and turned the crowd into a looting mob. Andrea and Tina had rushed past on the opposite side of the road and were breathless when they arrived at the estate - and almost in tears when Andrea's retinal scan had opened the main gate, the first sign of operational technology that they had encountered since awakening that morning.

I remember the silence in the room as my sister completed her report. I guess about ten of my staff were in the study by then - most unusually, a couple with kids in hand. I remember also an involuntary groan of "Fuck!" and the glare that I received from Tina as she cocked an eyebrow at a dazed looking boy about eight years old, who was staring at me with big blue eyes.

"Fuck!" I repeated, glaring back at Tina. "The boy's going to hear that a lot in the next little while, so he may as well get used to it."

"Fucked certainly describes the situation quite succinctly," Andrea intervened, "but doesn't help us decide what to do now. OK, bro, you're supposed to be the tech wiz. So tell us what the fuck's going on?"

Tina rolled her eyes in despair, as she often did when we cut her out of things. I quickly outlined my first EMP ideas, then as quickly shot them down. "So all your primitive electronic Lego is working fine, while real world technology has universally gone tits up," my sister summarized in a typically blunt manner.

"Seems that way."

"And it can't have been this pulse thingy?"

"An EMP that fried the QCs would have knocked my stuff down as well, or at least some of it. Even if we were lucky enough to be at the very edge of the pulse, then we should already have seen emergency services coming in from outside. It's

44

been more than an hour since whatever it was happened and you've seen no signs of anything but a few locals on the streets. This must mean we're near the center of the impact zone, so all my stuff should be buggered also."

"So it not only isn't a pulse, it's also something that's affected a large area," Andrea perceptively observed.

"Suppose it's got to be," I agreed, "but we've no idea how big until we get external coms. Could be several parishes."

"Or the whole island!"

"There's no way of saying. It's possible, but I just can't imagine what could have caused it. If it's that big, though, the consequences will be fuckin' horrific."

"So, how do we find out?"

"Go out on a bike and have a look? I can't think of any other option that doesn't go through the U. In the olden days we would have had phones, TV and radio, but that's all defunct now, usurped by effectively unlimited U bandwidth for inter-QC links. I think I've got an electric scooter in the garage somewhere. I could see if it still works."

"Maybe going out just now might not be the smartest of things to do, especially if you are on the only functioning transport in the area. I'd let things settle down for a bit first, before we rush out."

"What about the old bomb shelter?" The quiet voice caused us to start and I then realized that the study now contained about twenty bodies. It was one of the waitresses, another Lisa but, whereas my estate manager was Scandinavian blond, this girl was intensely black.

"No, Lisa," Andrea explained, "we don't think that we need to shelter from anything. That old thing must date back to the last century, when people were worried about nuclear wars. We don't have to worry about radiation now ... or do we?" she looked in my direction.

Before I could respond, the girl peeped up again. "That's not what I was meaning, Miss. We use the bomb shelter as a wine cellar now, but there's lots of the original shit an' stuff all still stacked up in there. I'm fairly sure that there's a radio."

I hadn't even known that there was a bomb shelter on the estate, although I could see the wine cellar on a map that I called up on my desk screen. "Seems reasonable, I suppose. I just hope it still works. Even if it does, though, who else in the world is going to have such a thing?"

"Ham freaks!" This time, to my surprise, it was Tina contributing input. "Amateur radio nuts. Build radios out of valves and transistors and shit and talk to each other in Morse and low quality audio."

"Why the hell would anyone want to do that?"

"Why the hell would anyone want to freeze time in the '20s? They're just nutters with a hobby; mostly male I would guess. You should understand them, if anyone can."

I was reminded again of why I had been so keen to move out of the flat when Tina moved in. "OK, I suppose it's certainly worth a try. I don't

suppose anyone here knows anything about ham radios, so I'll start a search of my knowledge base...
"

"Not needed, I can do it," Tina smirked. "Remember, commercial pilot, trained in the teens. In the early days, we had radio in planes and even emergency sets in case of crash landings. If your girl can take me to the shelter, I'll see if the kit's operational or not."

The next hour blurred a bit, with most of it spent trying to calm down employees with friends and family outside the estate. Andrea did her best to persuade everyone to stay within our walls until we knew more, but it was evident that several local women were determined to leave on the search for loved ones. We dug up some backpacks and loaded them with canteens of water and fruit and asked only that they didn't broadcast the fact that we had functioning services. As the day wore on, my original thoughts about how we could help had morphed into concerns about being swamped by refugees if the scale of the disaster was really as big as it appeared to be.

My study had cleared a bit and, probably mainly to keep their minds off things, most staff were working on their normal tasks when Tina and Lisa returned; the former looking grim and the latter in tears. Andrea was squeezed beside me while we worked together on an inventory of estate stores but, for the first time, this did not seem to annoy the pilot. Rather she simply seemed at a complete loss for words.

"OK, love, spit it out," Andrea eventually broke the pregnant silence. "It can't be that bad!"

"It fuckin' is! It's fucking well worse than bad. It's fucking... " This from Tina, who never swore, gave me a shiver that chilled my spine and braced me for some terrible news.

"It's fucking global!" she finally managed to get out. "I've raised sad bastards in Florida, Rio, somewhere unpronounceable in North Africa and Nagoya. Absolutely everything is out and the cities are burning. These folk have their radios and maybe a battery-powered torch or solar water-heater, but nothing else. According to them, there should have been thousands of broadcasters active, in an hour we could only find four. Much less than point one fucking percent. Shit! Shit! Shit!"

Andrea rushed from my side and cradled the two weeping women in her arms. While making soothing sounds she looked directly at me. Not a word was said, but our dialogue was unmistakable. As kids we had played war games and as teenagers we had spent many a drunken night discussing the approaching collapse of civilization. At the turn on the century, this had been a big topic: populations of third world countries were shooting ever upwards, resources were dwindling and climate change was finally accepted as a reality. What if our world went belly-up? What would we do? If we could escape into the countryside, how would we survive?

In a world of omnipotent AIs, this had vanished as a concern but, while I was planning my tropical enclave, we had reminisced on our old debates and the crazy ideas that we had discussed into the early hours. This was the essence of our silent communication; the catastrophe was unknown, but the situation somehow familiar to us. Even better, we had a starting point that was much more favorable than we had dreamed of three or four decades previously. And it was not entirely coincidental. I could never have imagined any event that could take out all electronics with the exception of my own intranet, but I had considered the possibility of some kind of natural disaster, even if the risk was considered remote. I thus had a lot of useful stuff lying around the estate, untouched for the decade that I'd been there, but possibly of great use in the coming days and weeks.

Chapter 3 - No man is an island

A voice whispered gently into my ear "OK, wakey-wakey! Turn over for me now, please."

I was completely disorientated by the shock of mental transition from my daydream of the horror of "the 20th" to the reality of the angelic blond who was hovering over me. Massage, that was it! "I wasn't asleep, just resting my eyes," I mumbled defensively.

"And snoring like a grampus," contributed my scribe.

"Not at all, just heavy breathing; inevitable result of thinking about your beautiful bare body," I retorted.

"Some chance, you old goat!" Heidi pointed, lifting the towel as I struggled to turn onto my back. "If you had been thinking about any of us in the buff, that poor little thing there wouldn't be as limp as it evidently is."

Sue was on tip toes to witness my humiliation, while the muscular blond ensured that I couldn't cover up the offending organ.

"May be a little thing at present, but in its full majesty it is indeed a sight to behold," I babbled, defensively. "In any case, you know, it's not the size, but the pleasure that it gives that counts."

"Do you believe that, Heid?" Sue enquired.

"Well we can easily check claims of its majesty." An oily hand grasped my penis firmly and started to squeeze it sensually. "Or maybe not... "

the rapidly growing erection was quickly released and a towel drawn over my body, "... seems to be on a hair trigger. Don't want this going off inadvertently and making a mess for the pool girls to clean up."

A hand playfully slapped the towel where my dick was acting as a tent pole. "Calm down now, Cof. Didn't you get enough last night? You were with the twins again, weren't you?"

"None of your bloody business," I retorted rudely, causing both girls to giggle. Must be a point for Heidi; I knew they kept an informal score on who managed to irritate me the most. "Anyway, where was I?" Definitely time to change the topic of conversation. If it stayed on the twins, the small tent would be approaching marquee dimensions before long.

"Setting up the estate, turning it into a fortress," Sue responded immediately, as if expecting the question.

"Yes, well, the essence was that I wanted a retreat where I could work on things that interested me at a rate that I determined, not one set by the exponential growth of the power of the U. I suppose this decision really resulted from the last project I worked on with Kelly. This was enhancing our membrane technology to cover smell and taste."

"I didn't know you could do that," my masseuse interrupted, momentarily slowing the circles her thumbs were making on the fronts of my feet. "I tried a few of these toys - in my youth that was," she added defensively. Her embarrassment at

51

having to confess this was clearly losing out to her curiosity. "Full taste and smell?"

"Yes, well we had all the tactile side of things nicely nailed down and, although AI-controlled force field technology was always moving forward, they just couldn't manage the sensations of liquid contact the way that our membranes could."

"Or penetration with... " the blond ground to a halt, having been carried away by the topic of conversation. To break the following silence, her fingers found a pressure point below my knees that forced me to groan.

"Or penetration," I conceded, "especially with larger objects." My snorted laugh turned into a squeak as pain shot through my thigh.

Safer back on the original topic, I decided. Or, at least, less painful. "Anyway, we were getting close to market saturation and developments were increasingly aimed at the high-end customers: the ones who'll pay premium prices for specialty items. Of course, it was Kelly that came up with the ideas, all I did was work on the required technology."

"So how did this work?" I think Sue was trying to save Heidi further embarrassment by asking the question for her.

"The spec was fairly clear. We had body suits that allowed transfer of all touch sensations between two or more participants. Video and sound was old hat, just a matter of preference: whether the clients preferred 2D, holo 3D or full immersion VR. The missing senses were smell and taste. What could we do here? We were going to have to build in some subtle chemistry and it would be very expensive, but the punters were prepared to pay a lot for this dream."

"Really, there were lots of people who dreamed of putting taste and smell into a wank suit?" Sue's question hung in the air as I surreptitiously glanced at my masseuse. Face like a tomato. Well, that question had fairly well answered itself.

"Anyway," I continued, "we needed a marginally thicker membrane with molecular shape sensors and a method of pre-impregnating tailored-release vesicles with a few key activators of the smell and taste receptors as, obviously, we couldn't simply reproduce the full cocktail of chemicals released during the various sex acts involved."

"Mmm... " Sue seemed unconvinced. "But, surely, that's very subjective. I've no idea how your tactile membranes work at a mechanical level, but touch seems a very generic sense. Like sound and vision, something that doesn't need to be tested on individuals. You could determine quality of these with a machine. But how do you do that with smell and taste?"

An extremely perceptive question; this girl really was one of the brightest of a bright bunch. "You're perfectly right. We can do a lot with our atomic-level understanding of molecule and receptor shapes, but direct testing with volunteers was a key part of the development program. It certainly wasn't like anything I'd done previously in the materials field, but fascinating nevertheless."

"I bet it was, you dirty old man," Heidi was back in the game and, for the moment, the massage was forgotten and her hands were unmoving on my stomach. "So you hauled a load of hookers into the lab and wired them up?"

"Well, it wasn't quite that easy," now I was getting a little uncomfortable. "Hookers weren't exactly the customers that we were looking. There are exceptions, but the vast majority of prostitutes are in it for the money, rather than the fun. And that applies just as much to male, homo, bi and all the other specialist purveyors of flesh. We were looking for something to please the connoisseurs of the porn market. So Kelly volunteered to do the beta-testing. Actually, not so much volunteered as insisted. It was, after all, her original idea."

"So your partner, who looks like somebody's mum, was being worked over in the lab by all and sundry, in real-life and virtual, while you looked on and took notes?"

Sue was far too perceptive for her own good or, at least, for my peace of mind. Nevertheless, I had mentally committed myself to be honest in this record. I may not rush into telling all the truth, but I wasn't going to duck hard questions or, even worse, lie.

"We didn't need such a wide range of volunteers. We had all the genetic markers for key receptors of a wide enough demographic to fill in details. All we actually needed were calibration points to tie down the minimum set of scent and flavor analogues that we were using, so we needed only a man and another woman."

There was a crack like a whip as Heidi slapped my stomach in delight. "And who was the woman?"

"My chief laboratory technician. Absolutely drop-dead gorgeous, luckily for me. I had actually fancied her since we started working together, but I have always separated business and pleasure. Well, at least, work and bonking."

"But not this time, eh?" Strong hand slid under my neck and along my spine and, pulling from below, dragging the shoulder blades backwards, causing my back to arch.

"This wasn't bonking for fun, it was science. Something totally different! In any case, we needed a good tech to set up all the instrumentation for Kelly. We had to get quantitative measurements to complement her subjective reporting. I must admit that I was actually too shy to even suggest it, but ten minutes talking to Kelly and Li... , um... " I coughed dramatically to cover my faux pas, "... um, our technician was raring to go."

"So the three of you managed to calibrate everything needed for all your specialist markets?" Sue was relentless, like a Doberman, when she got her teeth into something. I noticed my masseuse giving her a look of admiration.

I coughed again. "Well, yes, more or less. Everything that we needed for the calibration."

"So what would that involve? You can't leave your readers hanging."

"What the fuck do you think it involved? Imagine anything that a perv like Heidi here would want to smell or taste. Then bear in mind that Kelly was very much more sophisticated... "

"Or pervy?"

"Or pervy, if you want to put it that way. She enjoyed herself. We enjoyed ourselves. So what's the harm?"

"But the girl was an employee; wasn't that exploitation?"

"A volunteer, fully committed to the work. There was no coercion, none in the slightest. In fact, afterwards, she moved to technical management for another division and we went out together for a while. Actually, we lived together for six months or so."

"I knew it!" Sue bounced into the air displaying a pair of beautifully formed breasts as I craned upwards in surprise. Holding the small scriber above her head, she continued her dance as water slopped over the edge of the hot bath.

I looked at Heidi, who reflected my complete surprise. Neither of us had the foggiest idea what she was on about. Then the hammer fell. "It's Lisa, isn't it? The tech you're talking about. She's the one that runs this entire circus now. I knew she was more than just a normal employee."

I groaned as a light began to dawn on the face above me. "You almost said it once. Li - something. Could be Lisa I guess. She is supposed to be a really dirty beast. But there's also Liz, she's definitely bi."

56

"So how do you know that it's a Lisa and, even if it is, that it's our site manager rather than the other one we've got and at least two I can remember over the last few years?"

Sue unselfconsciously clambered out of the bath and placed her little computer on the bartop. She started counting on her fingers, apparently oblivious of the effect that her naked, svelte figure was having on my self-restraint. "OK, as Heid pointed out, you gave away the name beginning with L. Second, it's someone who's was with you in the early days, so she's got to be old, even if maybe not as ancient as you. Third she's a techy and forth someone who went into management. Fifth, someone who lived with you."

"But that's just a rumor," Heidi interrupted.

"A rumor that's never been denied. Anyway, when they're ever together, you can see that they've once been close."

"I thought she was straight lez, though."

"Jesus, living with Cof would turn anyone lez."

I tried to raise myself onto my elbows to defend my reputation, but the big blond pushed me roughly back in place, with a giggle that informed me that Sue had probably just scored another point or two.

"And, finally, she has an amazing fondness for her wank suit. She's got a special that nobody is ever allowed to touch, much less try. I bet it's one of the smell and taste ones!"

"God, you're so bloody annoying, I don't know why I don't just swap you for a Dictaphone."

57

Sue added a chalk mark to an imaginary blackboard and then posed in profile. "Dictaphone? Yes, that'll be right!" She grinned smugly and then added "And all this was supposed to explain why you were setting yourself up in Barbados."

I closed my eyes to avoid the very distracting view presented and struggled to remember where this latest diversion fit into my story. "Ah, yes, that was it. The last bit of work I did before I sold out. Did all the fundamental work... "

"... got into all kinds of kinky sex... " The massage was completed, but the blond was still keeping control of my body, maintaining a firm hold on my rapidly responding erection.

"Well, I certainly learned a lot there, no doubt about it. I'm not sure that I'd call all of it pleasant, but it was, sure as fuck, educational." I squirmed with a discomfort that was not entirely caused by the tight grip on my dick. "Anyway, that wasn't why I decided to jack it in."

"You were too embarrassed to work with what's-her-name - Kelly - anymore?" Heidi suggested.

"Not at all. That was quite surprising for me. One of the main reasons for my original reluctance to get involved was that I was worried that she might have a bit of a fancy for me and I didn't want anything to spoil our working relationship. We were actually very good friends, but she wasn't my type."

Sue feigned a gasp of surprise. "Not your type? I didn't think there was such a woman. She wasn't a tranny then, a chick with a dick?"

"Don't be daft. Kelly was a married woman, with a husband and a couple of kids. She was homely... I suppose maybe a bit plain, but basically really nice."

"... so a bit of a dog, then? Rough?"

"Definitely not! Homely!"

"Seems to be damning with faint praise."

"It's hard to explain. If you just saw her in the street, you'd think plump, middle-aged, maternal. If you got to know her, however, her personality shone through this facade. She was so crazy, funny..."

"... sex mad!"

"Yes, undoubtedly, randy as the proverbial sack full of ferrets."

"So, you did fancy her a bit?"

"Not at all. We were just great friends. I also met her husband and daughters several times."

"What was he like?" Heidi interjected, possibly feeling a little cut out of my interrogation. "Built like a bull I'd guess."

"You guess wrong! He was very slim - skinny, really. Small, blond and a bit camp. He was an interior decorator of some kind. I'm not sure, but I'd guess he was a bit younger than Kelly. In any case, they were a happy couple."

"And this wee guy satisfied all of his big wife's bizarre cravings?"

"As Kelly once explained it to me, there was sex with the man she loved and sex that was physical exercise to scratch a particular itch that she was inflicted with. Before she was married, she apparently spent a lot of her spare cash in the brothels of Sydney and surrounding cities. After marriage, she was happy to make do with her toys, with the full understanding of her husband."

"So, you didn't have a problem having some very dirty sex with her and then working together afterwards as if nothing had happened?" My scribe was again, valiantly, trying to pull the rambling threads of dialogue into the skein of a consistent story.

"Kelly convinced me that the sex would be purely physical and that my participation, rather than some stranger, would be her preference. She also made the point that the experience would give me a much better understanding of our clients, which I suppose it did. Especially as, for our calibration, we needed only to sample a small fraction of the experiences that would eventually be on tap. Deo Gratias for that!"

I paused for a moment, trying to see how I could get this tale back on track. "So, we got the calibration done. If anything, my working relationship with Kelly got even better and, although it was a little bit uncomfortable working with Lisa for a while, everything was fine when I was no longer her direct boss and we moved in together."

"Ha! That's it! Lisa, I told you!" Sue was doing a little victory dance around the massage table, still in her birthday suit.

"Fuckity fuck, for fuck's sake! OK, it was Lisa. Just don't say anything to her. Please!" I was begging now. This must be worth a bucketful of points to Sue.

"Some chance!" Heidi emphasized her statement with a painful tug of my slowly wilting erection. "I'm going to ask her for a shot of her tasty, smelly wank suit."

"I'll tell you what, keep all of this quiet and I'll let you borrow one whenever you want."

"Done!" Slow caresses indicated that my masseuse was very happy with the deal.

"What would I want with a smelly suit?" I groaned in response to the question. Sue! She could taste blood in the water and was now going to have her pound of flesh.

"OK, what can I bribe you with to ensure your silence?"

She bent over to whisper in my ear, a pendulous breast rubbing against my bare shoulder. "I'd just like one try of the suit, with the original calibration recordings."

"Fuck off! Go to fuck! Go directly to fuck! Do not pass fucking go? Do not collect fuck all!"

"That was a double negative," my tormentress observed, completely unperturbed. Her lips brushed my ear as she continued in a whisper. "Just one recording then, I select it."

I grimaced and then fought an arm loose to push Heidi back, the girl straining to hear what was going on. "Aaaa, shit! OK then, one - but I choose!"

"You're on!" Given the speed at which this offer was accepted, I realized that I could probably have struck a better bargain.

Definitely! The victory dance was continuing around the table until she bent to whisper into my other ear. "I suppose that I need some of my own calibration input though, Cof old chap, so just lie back and think of England." Two long fingers slid down my forehead and drew my eyes closed.

"OK, Heid, why don't we give our lord and master a nice thank you for the presents?" The towel covering me was whipped away and the tip of a tongue ran round my belly button and then headed south.

"Sue - you cunning bitch - what did you get?" Heidi was clearly annoyed, but her manual manipulations continued automatically.

"Mmm olive, extra virginal, I'd guess," came the rather indistinct response. "Always prepare for the unexpected, even in massages. What a clever chap!"

"That wasn't him, that was my idea," from an irate Heidi.

"OK then, not clever at all; just shows that you're a dirty bitch!" This was the end of the conversation, as her mouth enclosed the head of my penis.

"Fucking smart arse! Anyway, it's just part of the professional massage service that I offer. Bugger it! I suppose we'd better get the show on the road." Her second hand came into play and it was immediately evident that Heidi had lots of experience in the tantric side of her art.

Just how did this come about, I wondered briefly. All I wanted was some pre-prandial relaxation while I got started on my book. Well, no point in looking gift horses in the mouth, just go with the flow and enjoy it while you can. The rate at which these two vixens were going at it, it was going to be over quickly. My body arched in an involuntary spasm that slammed my head against the pillow. Short, but very, very intense.

***

After Heidi had carried out a perfunctory clean-up with a towel, I adjourned for a quick shower. After that, clad in a thin cotton yukata, I settled myself onto a thickly padded lounger constructed out of massive mahogany and stared vacantly out of the window that made up the entire west-facing wall of the onsen. The sky was darkening, still bright with faint traces of pink in clouds near the horizon, but this graded quickly into a deep blue with the first sparkles of stars or, more likely, defunct space stations.

"And the reason you gave up on your sex toy job... " I hadn't even noticed that the imperturbable Sue had slipped onto the neighboring seat. She was clad in some kind of diaphanous wrap that was about as concealing as cling-film. She looked directly into my eyes in a guileless manner that belayed our activities of the last quarter hour, but I could make out the slightest trace of a suppressed grin.

I tore my eyes away from her nipples and tried to concentrate. The old neurons just didn't seem to fire as rapidly as before and the synapses were distinctly treacly. We had discussed several factors that had nothing to with my decision. My relationships with Kelly and Lisa, the last development project, the calibration runs. Now I had to think of how to present the truth to Sue. Damage limitation was the name of the game; how could I present it in a way that would provide her with least ammunition for the future.

"... and the reason!" She wasn't giving up. Maybe this was really the reason I decided on a secretary rather than a Dictaphone, with the latter I'd be daydreaming by halfway through the first paragraph.

"OK, the reason I left. It was completely technical. Nothing to do with any of my working or personal relationships. It was the development work. The fundamental principles I got nailed down, as I explained in much more detail than I had originally intended." I glared at Sue, but it was water off a duck's back.

"All the other materials development stuff I had done myself. The tactile piezo-electric tailoring, for example, was real state-of-the-art science. I was working with the smartest of smart materials to get the mechanical range involved. From nipple clamps to... "

"Anal penetration by massive dongs?"

I pointedly ignored the interruption. "Going on from the original fluid sensation, I added thermal sensitivity, with really fine resolution. I had a team supporting me, but I led all the development personally, right up to transfer to the production engineers."

"Until the taste and smell variant?"

"Until then! I nailed down the principles, but I just couldn't get a working product. The marketing folk were going berserk. They had pre-advertised it and had a huge waiting list."

"Most of the kinky pervs on the planet."

Most of the extremely rich, kinky pervs. They were aiming this only at the very top end of the market, making exclusivity a hook for attracting interest."

"And jacking up the price."

"That too. Anyway, the point was that, after six months, I was getting nowhere. I knew that I had all the bits I needed, but I just couldn't integrate them into a robust product. So, finally, I let them transfer my entire database to a fucking industrial chemistry AI. Fucking thing... "

Sue waited for a moment, then gently added "... solved the problem?"

"Within a fucking day! And, just to add insult to injury, the bastarding thing came up with an approach so elegant that I'd have never found it, not in a month of Sundays. Fucking, cunting, glorified adding-machine!"

"So... " I could almost hear her mind ticking as this nymphet Sherlock Holmes put the pieces together, "... once again QC-based AI was displacing you from your work! That's why you packed it in! That's also why all this '20s low tech computing; it wasn't techno-fear or premonition that something like the 20th would happen, you just hated AIs and QCs!"

"Well, you can't really hate anything as insubstantial as an artificial intelligence and the quantum computers were only the tools that allowed software to reach the needed level of sophistication. So it wasn't hatred, just being very pissed off. I accepted that, for our terminally sick planet, AIs were a necessary evil. Really, they were the only thing holding the fucking top-heavy house of cards together. But they were too powerful, too capable. They removed the challenges for humans: the problems that we had to work really hard on to solve for ourselves. I'm sure that I could have cracked the materials development on my own. It would have taken years - and the final product wouldn't have been as good - but I could have done it."

I noticed my voice getting louder as I relived past anger and forced myself to calm down. A couple of deep breaths and then I continued. "So that's it in a nutshell. I had more money than I could ever spend and so I, for one, wasn't dependent on bloody AIs. I could choose to opt out and build my own little world where I would solve any of my own problems by myself. So that's how the Crazy Old Fuck's community came to be."

This seemed like an obvious place to finish this chapter, but Sue was still looking at me expectantly. I guessed she wanted more details, so went on. "Ending up here in Barbados was really just a fluke. I had originally envisaged something much smaller, a bit of a fortress of solitude kind of a thing. The problem was that, as soon as I started to look into the logistics of opting out of the U-connected world, I realized that it wasn't going to be easy. I wanted all services to be independent of AI management, so that meant building infrastructure from scratch. Starting with something planned as a holiday resort helped a little bit, but we needed our own power, water, comms, sewerage, security, everything. I'm OK in the lab and can hack software, but I'm not the kind of universal handyman needed here. So I started to build a team."

"This is where Andrea started recruiting girls."

"Exactly! From the idea of a few support staff, it was like Topsy - it just grew. It was a bit chicken and egg. The size of the estate influences the number of staff required to run it and, with my sister's policy of providing accommodation for those needing it, the number of staff, in turn, influences the size of the estate to house and feed them. I could have made it easier for myself, I suppose, by allowing staff quarters to be serviced externally, but that seemed like cheating. Kind of silly, when I say it like that, but I was writing the rules for myself at that time and the entire point of the exercise was to provide me with challenges that wouldn't be solved by AIs, things that I'd sort out for myself."

"So that's why we came to have the farm and all the hydroponics shit."

"And the staff to run them. A lot can be done with automation and robotics but, without AI controllers, you need people to keep the whole thing ticking over - and sorting things out when inevitable problems crop up."

"This almost seems too neat. You're providing probably the ideal environment, a kind of work therapy, for the kind of people who needed it most, women who had been displaced from the system."

"Not my plan and, actually, nothing at all to do with me. My big sis handled all of this and I'm not sure, even in her case, that it was all planned analytically. It just kind of evolved this way but, when you put it like that, I suppose it might be the reason why it all worked so well and why, despite their troubled backgrounds, we've had such success with our staff."

"Mmm... " the slim woman rose and plonked herself inelegantly on my lap. "Does that include me? Is this book you're dictating just make-work for a troubled woman?"

"Of course it is, you're the veritable epitome of a girl who couldn't survive outside in an AI world. Your intelligence is no good when even the dumbest of AIs is a billion times smarter and, let's face it, your interpersonal skills leave something to be desired."

"You seem happy enough with me," she objected.

"Only because I'm a complete masochist!"

"And I give good head!"

"Fair, I suppose, five out of ten. Maybe nine out of ten." I corrected rapidly as sharp teeth took hold of my left nipple. "So, I saved you from a life of giving blow jobs in a sleazy massage parlor in downtown Bridgetown."

"Or Andrea did."

"Yes, I suppose so. Actually, how did you get recruited in the first place?" For the first time I was actually on the offensive, turning the interrogation in the other direction.

"Didn't you know? Casting couch, of course! You don't think I only give fantastic head to men, do you? My cunnilingus is to die for. Ask Andrea!" The beautiful woman licked her lips salaciously.

"Um, I think that's too much information for the present. Anyway, this is definitely a good place to stop. Time for dinner!"

"Fine" The girl bounced lightly to her feet and shoved an errant bosom back into place. "When do you want to start tomorrow? It'll be Sophie doing the honors."

"Why doesn't she just join me for breakfast and we'll take it from there."

"Okeydokey, I'll let her know when I pass on this record. We'll do a first hack at editing this evening and download it for you to look at when you start at crack of dawn tomorrow. Just don't wake us before seven, if you have questions."

She was heading for the door when she turned and added. "I'll be back day after tomorrow, we can organize my present then."

"Your bribe you mean," I responded to a closing door. Now I had also to remember to have a flick through my old pornsuit programing files, to find the least damaging option. I wondered for a moment if I could fob her off with something else, but realized that she was far too smart for that to work. I levered myself up with a groan and headed upstairs to dress for dinner.

Chapter 4 - The days after

As I stared at Sophie across the table during breakfast, I wondered how I managed to mix her up with Sue. They both had long black hair, but Sue was bronzed while Sophie had a natural olive complexion. Also Sue was tall and well-endowed, buxom almost, whereas Sophie was minute: maybe one meter fifty and very slim. Sue was classically beautiful; Sophie was kind of cute, but her sharp features were far from any classical norm - eldritch perhaps. I suppose elfin would be the term that summed it up. Sophie was also one of the first to join their community after the QC meltdown. She had been a cleric of some sort, I seemed to remember.

The girl seemed unperturbed by my open inspection and had an air of self-confidence that contrasted with her diminutive build. She bit the end of a croissant, fastidiously wiped flakes of pastry from the corners of her mouth and washed down the mouthful with a sip of black coffee before she started on what was evidently a prepared spiel.

"Sue and I have gone through the first text block and reorganized it a little to improve the flow. Was it OK for you?"

Not wanting to admit that I'd forgotten to check my mail for the promised script, I decided to arm-wave. "I don't want to start mucking about until we've gotten a bit further into the meat of things. Let's leave it for two or three days. Anyway, I'm sure that you're doing a grand job." I was quite pleased with this spur-of-the-moment response. Not a lie, just diverting attention away from the question.

"So you forgot to pick it up, then?"

"How the fuck did you... " Now I remembered why I mixed them up: both so sharp that they could cut themselves.

"Sue bet that you'd forget and I bet that you'd try to bluff your way out of it."

"OK, now you've got one point each. So, what am I supposed to be covering today?"

Another sip of coffee, then she responded. "Well, we have threads that start on the technical basis of the apocalypse, worldwide impact thereof, this place pre-20th and the local version of the Dying. Actually, we reckoned that it would be good also to have some kind of inventory of what we have here, because it's not clear why it was so different from any other survivalist or luddite community. I guess we could fill that in from the estate database, but it would be good to get your take on it."

"I suppose that's the easiest bit, so why don't we get that out the way first." Sophie was already taking notes one handed on the little machine that Sue had been using yesterday - or maybe a clone of it. Anyway, it was clear that I could start while we worked our way through breakfast.

"Yesterday, I explained my rationale for setting this place up and the background for my desire for self-sufficiency. As anyone who lived through the beginning of the 21st century will tell you, it's clear that the most fundamental thing that you need is a reliable source of power."

"Mmm, maybe we need to backtrack a little here. I did live through the tens and twenties and it wasn't at all clear to me."

"Christ on a bike, what age are you? I would have guessed about mid-thirties." I stopped in my tracks, following a look that suggested that my Alzheimer's was showing. "OK, maybe not. You've been with us for, what, 15 years and you were some kind of qualified God-botherer... "

"Jesuit priestess!"

"Jesuit God-botherer, then. Training how to bother God seems to take an inordinate amount of time, so maybe you were in your thirties then. Anyway, you were still a baby at the time I'm talking about."

"You don't think God-botherers get rejuv? I was just past sixty when I first met you. OK, I know that you're older, but not by very much!"

We did have staff files and I made a mental note to have a look at them one of these days. I stared into the woman's eyes. Maybe there was an air of experience that could have come from all those years, but somehow not the weariness I saw in the mirror each morning. Slowly, then, like a lead brick in microgravity, the penny dropped. "Brain rejuvenation! You got a cranial while the going was good. You lucky devil!"

"Maybe luck, but actually based on Vatican policy. With the shortage of clerics, even after women were accepted into the priesthood in the late twenties, rejuv was encouraged - and funded - for all pastors over fifty-eight. I had the full Monty at fifty-nine, with a reset to physical thirty-five. Should be good for another couple of decades, according to the specs."

I sat back, cradling my mug of coffee, trying to assimilate this new information - and hide my feeling of intense envy.

"So, the fundamental requirement for power... " Yes, definitely, she was just as relentless as her fellow scribe.

"OK then, let's go over the basics. From the middle of the last century, it seemed inevitable that population growth would cause eventual breakdown of the entire global infrastructure. There was too little food, water, natural resources, suitable land... basically everything that you needed for a comfortable life came from an inventory that was inherently limited. In those days, one of the major constraints was cheap power and the ability to distribute it to where it was needed. By the 21st century, though, it wasn't so much cost that was limiting energy production, but more the environmental impact of use of the cheapest sources, fossil fuels. Of course, by the time that was recognized, the planet's climate was fairly well fucked. Nevertheless, there was enough technology available so that, anywhere that power was plentiful, all the other problems could be managed. Drinking water could be recycled or extracted from sea water, food could be produced in energy-intensive farms or hydroponic facilities, land could be protected from natural threats or remediated from past pollution. All you needed was energy."

"And this was clear, was it?"

"I think so. Of course, this solution could only be implemented on a global scale when QC-AIs were available."

"The necessary evil you mentioned yesterday?"

"I may not like them personally, but I'm sure that the growing population would have caused a major meltdown by the early thirties without them. As it happened, though, they only ended up postponing the day of reckoning by a decade or so and turned a catastrophe that would have been mainly regional and possibly short-lived into one that is global and may take centuries to recover from."

"So all we needed to do was produce enough energy?" Again a gentle nudge back on course.

"Well, a hell of a lot of other infrastructure was needed too; but after mini-fusion plants were widely available and complemented by solar satellites and deep geothermal, the food, water and other issues got quickly sorted out."

"That's fine for all these AI-controlled sources, but how do you provide independent power here?"

"A small nuke at the bottom of the garden."

"Don't be silly! You can't run one of those without QCs, everyone knows that. That's why we don't have them now."

"That's fusion you're thinking of, especially the muon-catalyzed kind. Although, I must admit even

75

conventional fusion is pretty heavy in terms of computational control system requirements... "

"But we don't have that kind of nuke," Sophie interjected, seeing me start to wander off the beaten track, "the kind they can make bombs from."

"Well you can make bombs from both fusion and fission reactions. Matter of fact, if you think about it, mankind has been pretty ingenious in terms of utilizing just about any energy source for explosives."

A cleared throat served to cut me off at the pass and herd me back in the desired direction. "Anyway, what we have is a small fission plant. I got it really cheap; it was a floating plant that had been constructed in Russia and was intended to replace the original one in Bermuda. They got it as far as Miami, then the order was cancelled - so it lay in a dry dock there for years. Nobody wanted anything to do with it; the beast was fully-fuelled and the costs of decommissioning would have been huge. I didn't actually pay anything for the plant itself; I covered only the transport costs and took over all future liabilities. If I had been a bit cannier, they would probably have paid me to take it off their hands."

"You're serious about this? You've really got a buckshee nuke on the estate and you don't have an AI-controller?"

"Yes indeedy. All I needed was an underground dry dock and all the switchgear and shit. That was what cost big bucks. The generating plant was also integrated into the barge complex. No AI controller:

actually no real controller at all. It's a twin, inherently safe, fast reactor unit. Pre-fuelled for a 50-year lifetime, but we run the units sequentially rather than in parallel, so this'll give us about a century. Somebody else will have to worry about a replacement, but it's so low tech that I guess that it might even be doable by then."

"This is mind-boggling. I've lived on this island for as long as you've been here and on the estate for the last fifteen years and I had no idea about this. You got a license for this thing?"

"Now, this is actually another advantage of AIs. When I moved here, all government functions were QC-based. So, when I applied to bring in a floating reactor unit, they simply did a safety assessment and set down the specs for the dry dock, the quality checks and all that shit. No blockages by Greens or other thick bastards who simply go rabid every time the word nuclear is mentioned."

"My parents were hard green, who were proud to have fought off the nuclear lobby in Northern Europe at the turn of the century!"

For the first time, my secretary was walking up a side path, rather than keeping me away from them. I couldn't resist adding oil to the flames, just to see where the wildfire would go. In any case, the book was for me: I could meander wherever I fucking wanted to!

"Exactly! Just the type of ignorant cunts that drove Europe back to the middle ages and did so much fucking damage to the planet. These would be the kind of fuckwits that caused one of the old medical techniques, originally called nuclear magnetic resonance imaging, to be renamed magnetic resonance tomography. Just because tossers like your Old Dears were able to convince the undereducated great unwashed - and thick-as-mince politicos - that nuclear was a synonym for dangerous."

Sophie was clearly taken aback by my tirade, but gallantly rallied to defend her parents. "OK, I'm just a theologian, but even I know that nuclear radiation is bad for you. We should try to avoid it as much as... "

"Yes, indeed, from your extensive scientific background, you have a solid basis to be a fucking theologian. Fuck me rigid! Your parents, who were teaching you this shit, were probably a flower-arranger and a ballet-dancer."

"Professors of sociology and ancient history!" she responded haughtily.

"Exactly! With the scientific nous of a telephone sanitizer and a color-therapy consultant. You'd get more sense from a bricky and a plumber! What the fuck did either of them know about nuclear physics, chemistry or radiobiology? Fuck all! Yet they considered themselves entitled to lobby for changes in national policy, in such a complex and highly technical area."

"You're being deliberately abusive now, Cof. You don't need to be a doctor to know that taking poison will kill you!"

"That's the point! That's exactly the point!" I was physically bouncing up and down on my chair.

"You know what to do with a poison - but only a doctor, or some other kind of specialist, can tell you in advance what's going to be poisonous. Unless, of course, you just go for the suck-it-and-see approach, in which case it's your next of kin that might inherit this information. If radiation was going to kill you, we'd all be long dead. You live in a world of radiation - all of the time. OK, get an unusually high dose and it may do you no good. But, most of the time you'll never even notice it's there."

"But we've got a reactor somewhere on the grounds. That's got to give a dose that's going to be pretty unusual!"

I stared for a moment at the ceiling and silently cursed Green parents, the Vatican, the educational system and all other organized sources of disinformation. This was one of the smartest girls: well I now realized that girl was the wrong term, one of the smartest matrons on my staff. Despite her talents, her education still disenfranchised her into her eighth decade. Now I decided that I was no longer jealous of her cranial rejuv. What's the point of having the old noggin rebored when it's been fundamentally corrupted by a crap education?

I recognized that it really wasn't her fault and tried to be less bellicose. "Look, put it this way, are you frightened of radiation and want to reduce your radiation dose?"

"That's a really stupid question!" I could tell that she was also fighting to calm down. "Everyone fears radiation and it'd be crazy not to reduce your radiation exposure."

"Are you sleeping with anyone at present?"

"None of your business! You're just trying to change the subject... "

"Stop tap-dancing about and answer the fucking question!" Despite my good intentions, I lost control of my temper again. "Are you sleeping with anybody?"

"I am! And if this is some kind of crap about the risks of sex at my age... "

"For fuck's sake, stop wittering, woman! We're still on exposure to radiation here!" An intake of breath served as a pause as I tried, once more, to regain my composure. "Right, to reduce your radiation exposure, stop sleeping with your partner immediately! I suppose an occasional bonk would be allowed, for the sake of your sanity, but keep as much space between the two of you as possible. As a matter of fact, keep well away from all people. And walls. And soil. And seawater: swimming wouldn't be a good idea."

"Now you're just being ridiculous. The easiest thing would be just to move further away from your bloody nuclear reactor!"

"Um, actually, of all the options that I've mentioned so far, that's the only one that wouldn't decrease your radiation exposure at all. The reactor is, I guess, about 500m from where you sit. If you were to sit here for a million years, the total exposure from it would still be negligibly small. You're getting a hell of a lot more dose from the radiation that's contained in your own body but, of course, there's nothing you can do about that. You'll

80

also up your exposure from moving closer to me. It's negligible, but vastly more than you get from the reactor."

Sophie sat in silence - a conceptual rug having been pulled out from the intellectual basis of her Weltblick. "You're totally serious on this, aren't you?" she finally managed to get out in a low voice.

"Yup! I'm dropping a background file onto that toy in your hand. It's all stuff from the house intranet, but easily verifiable if you check any kind of external source material."

She closed her eyes and grimaced. Then, to my amazement, it was like a switch had been tossed and we were back to the original path. "So, this reactor provides all our power?"

"And some. Remember, this unit was dimensioned for the whole island of Bermuda in 2030! Even on half capacity, we have more than enough power for all the needs of present day Barbados."

"So why don't we provide this power to all the poor bastards outside the estate?" The cleric, do-gooder side was evidently coming out.

"I'm happy to, but what I supply at present is extremely limited because most of them can't use it. There's no infrastructure for the kind of twenties power that we have on tap in the estate."

"But you say it's twenties level, we're now in the seventies! We lost a lot during the crash, but we've had almost fifteen years to build it back up."

"It wasn't the events on 20th February that did the real damage here, it was the prior decades of AI control, coupled to the Dying. When all QCs disappeared - as far as we can see for all time, or until something equivalent can be invented - this took down all of the infrastructure used to provide every support service. Every! Single! One! It was like going back to sometime before telegraphs, railways and penicillin. Now that would have been bad enough but, at least in 2041, we still had the old guys with experience in the pre-QC world."

"Folk like you?"

"Not at all like me! The men and women with real talents, who could run the industries that we had at the turn of the century. Remember, only a few decades ago there were no QCs and only the most primitive idiot predecessors of what would become AIs. Me - I made sex toys! Lot of fucking good that is when the lights go out."

"Not sure my girlfriend would agree with that," Sophie sniggered, lightening the mood for the first time since the session started. "Anyway, the Dying made recovery impossible?"

"It's all about critical masses of experience and infrastructure. You can't have a railway without rails. You can't have rails without steel, iron mines, transport infrastructure, etcetera. Every one of these components needs dedicated facilities, tools and a trained, experienced workforce. After the AI revolution, the facilities and tools were largely gone. After the Dying, the workforce was gone too."

"But all wasn't lost. We still have knowledge!"

"Greatly over-rated as a commodity," I countered. "We have all the knowledge needed to build a space station in the databases here in my basement. But how would we go about it? The civilization that we had in 2041 was based on a couple of millennia of progressive, stepwise technological development. Within seconds of the hack attack, it had all gone. I'm pretty sure that the bastards who planned this had no idea of the real consequences. They were probably fundamentalist ragheads who envisaged back-to-nature camel herding in a world freed from macdonaldization. They may even have had a chance to see their error up close, when plague devastated the cities of Northern Africa and the expanding Sahara, freed from AI controls, enveloped the rural communities. I've heard that a few sad nomads still exist in that wasteland, but they're a miserable remnant of what was once a Muslim empire."

"So, how can we help others? You surely don't just aim to stay cut-off from the outside world forever."

"Well, I can't say it was philanthropic planning but, if you look at the big picture, the best thing we can do is preserve our oasis of 21st century technology and drip-feed input that could accelerate regeneration outside. I overstated my case a bit on knowledge, most of the stuff from the 21st century isn't much good to anyone but us, but we've also stuff from the 18th, 19th and early 20th that's in great demand. We can help leapfrog dead-end developments and avoid technology that may come back and bite us."

"For example?"

"Um, let's see. Coms would be an example where we can maybe jump over telegraphs and landline phones, directly to mobile networks. They might be very clunky, based on transistors or simple integrated circuits, but the technology needed isn't too challenging."

"Once you have power?"

"Right, smart girl! You're not unsaveable!" My smile was met by a pixy grin. "We need to produce power and also be able to distribute it. But here we want to avoid the fossil-fuel trap. Getting back into coal would be easy, but this just sets us off again on a highway to environmental hell. A mixture of renewables, that's hydro, wind, solar and that kind of stuff, will do as a start. Then we need to get back into nuclear, when higher energy densities are needed."

Sophie did not look fully convinced, but I guessed that she'd do her homework before getting into this topic again. "So, we've got oodles of electricity and the only locally functioning facilities to use it, thus providing us with a life of luxury."

"I have actually started to supply electricity to neighboring communities, but what they can do with it is still very limited. Also, we certainly aren't the only ones with operative tech." I suddenly remembered one of her earlier questions that had been left hanging. "There were quite a few other groups that, for some reason or other, opted out of QC tech or, at least, had more primitive backups. These included survivalists of various forms: communities which became quite widespread in the

84

States and Canada after dollar hyperinflation. There were also God-botherers of diverse hues: everything from the Amish to pagan neo-hippies to mountain-top Buddhists. Also, very importantly, industrial museums and private collectors: crazy old fucks like myself. There weren't many as independent as me and lots went down during the Dying, but there's definitely a core scattered around the globe that, in time, will serve as centers of the renaissance. A bit like medieval monasteries, if you remember your Church history."

"Lots of the others went down - why didn't we?"

Now the hard question. One I'd been trying to formulate a tidy answer to since yesterday. I noticed that she had also finished her breakfast, so I waved Sophie to follow me as I wandered through to the conservatory. Rain was lashing against the glass, but the noise of it hardly penetrated the triple glazing, making it seem unreal. More like TV with the sound turned down than the real world. I settled myself in a huge leather recliner and tried to marshal my thoughts.

"Combination of luck and advance planning," I started abruptly, rushing to get it over as quickly as possible. "The luck is our relatively isolated position and the fact that, apart from a few locals, nobody had any idea of the potential of our estate immediately following the 20th. It was inevitable that, slowly, word would get out about a place that had been untouched by the catastrophe. However, coms were out, along with any transport more sophisticated than a bike, so this took a long time. Given the total loss of everything elsewhere, our existence was probably considered a myth by the time you got more than about 10 km away."

"The planning bit, though, was very important. Being somewhat paranoid by nature, I laid in a defense system when I took over the estate, although I didn't finish installation and activation until immediately after the 20th..."

When we first found out from Tina that breakdown was global, my sister and I both realized that we were in a potentially very vulnerable position. Even though we had no idea then that there would be no recovery, the fact that QCs had been down for hours meant that it would be getting bad now on the island, but likely to get a lot worse in the future. I had added a couple of strands of razor wire to the high wall at the sides of the estate grounds, but this had never been completed where it was visible from the main road, towards the back of the house. Even worse, the beachside border was established only by a line of fence posts. I checked inventory details for the rest of the razor wire and then sent a message to a couple of maintenance girls to get started on completion of the fence. Once this was finished, I would modify the alarms on the image recognition system supporting the security cameras, adding a link that would automatically electrify the fence in case of perceived threats.

"We had an electric fence?" The interjection brought me back to the present.

"Not had, have! And a number of EM tasers in strategic locations that I installed over the following months. Mainly non-lethal."

"Mainly?"

"Yes - fucking mainly. We've killed a few people who tried to break into this place. In most cases, though, they just got a very bad shock. When they tried human wave techniques, big groups, then we were forced to turn up the juice. A few kicked it."

"How many?" It was evident to this perceptive woman that this would be a number that I would know exactly.

"Over the last fifteen years, fifty-six for certain. There could be others whose bodies were taken away by their companions."

"Christ, Cof, fifty-six! That's almost the number of people living here now!"

"Exactly! And they were a small percentage of those who have tried to get in. If we had allowed it, we would have not only been swamped, our infrastructure would have collapsed and then nobody would have been any the better off. It happened in a lot of other places - the ones that were less remote or that couldn't be defended. We possess valuable resources that can, literally, mean life of death to those who control it. Typical human nature is to fight over it continuously, in most cases killing a lot more than fifty-six in the process, until eventually the facility is destroyed in the conflict."

"Why doesn't everyone living here know this?"

"The defense systems are run by Andrea and myself, with the support of our security team. These are far too safety-critical to be revealed to anyone else. We do the cleaning up, to avoid others having it on their consciences. But, awful though it is, the defense structure is the trivial part. There's one decision that's now tacitly accepted by everyone, but never discussed. The elephant in the room that nobody notices. That's the real killer."

Silence stretched painfully for a couple of minutes, then she whispered, "No entry."

"No entry, indeed! Over the years we've turned away thousands of men, women and children. Maybe half of them are now dead. Most of the rest are living in squalor; hungry a lot of the time and riddled with disease. Infant mortality may be 50% and, surviving that hurdle, life expectancy is maybe thirty or so."

"But I got in," in a voice so low that it was almost inaudible. "Why me?"

"Andrea brought you," I answered bluntly. "As I remember it, she found you in her house when she and Tina went back to pick up personal kit just before they moved in here."

Silence stretched again as I thought back to the first couple of weeks after the 20th. I tried to batten down the hatches, but it was very difficult with the local staff. They all had extended families that they wanted to find and bring in. The shock during the first day or two helped Andrea and me keep most of them on the grounds, but then we had to let them go out to search for relatives and friends. So we made a hard rule that, more or less, we've stuck to since. Staff could bring in only immediate family: husbands, partners, children. No parents, no cousins, no friends. It was hard, painful to enforce - but we had no option. Any exception would have broken our already taut community ties apart. Several cases ended up in tearful confrontations at the gates, where a decision was forced between bringing those allowed into the compound and abandoning the others, or leaving together in the face of our implacable refusal to bend our rules. Strong Bajan family bonds meant that, as often as not, the option of suffering outside together was the one chosen. There were also a few of our staff with international roots who decided on the evidently hopeless option of attempting to travel home to search for loved ones. In cases where we lost staff who were not replaced by the extended families that we now had, Andrea somehow selected their successors from outside. Sophie, I remembered, had been the first of these.

The short but intense rain shower was passing and first traces of a strong, watery sun were beginning to show through breaks in the heavy clouds. The brightening sky seemed to reanimate my scribe. "I suppose I must have known, somehow. Nevertheless, at the time, the situation didn't look too bad."

"That's right. Even after hours stretched to days, days stretched to weeks, everybody hoped it was some kind of temporary glitch. Something had knocked out local services, but help would come from neighbors. The remaining AIs would get it all sorted, they always did. We were lucky in Barbados, no big concentrations of people and lots of hobby gardeners and yuppified, low-tech organic farms. Some kind of food could be scrounged up, even in February - and water could be collected anytime it rained, every couple of days or so. The weather was warm, but not too hot. Think of what it would have been like in Tokyo, New York or London. These places had food reserves that would be gone within a couple of days. No water when holding tanks were drained. Freezing conditions, so no chance of getting food anywhere in the vicinity, even if moving through the chaos of a collapsed public transport system was possible. To add to their miseries, fires and explosions where active AI control systems failed, flooding where the storm surge barriers failed to operate. People were dying in their millions all over the globe."

"Sometimes I think it's amazing that anyone survived."

"People are tough, especially when it's life or death. They burned furniture to stay warm and melt snow, pets and zoo animals were barbequed, anyone with a bit of string and a bent pin went fishing... "

"And then cannibalism."

"Another elephant in the room that survivors never talk about, but certainly a factor that explains how so many survived, especially in the big conurbations."

"I think that was when I lost my faith." Sophie was clearly distressed, but intent to get everything

90

into the open. Catharsis, I guessed; just like the real justification for my book. "I was never very mystical, mainly entered the priesthood to help people."

"You don't need to be a signed-up God-botherer to do that," I observed.

"OK, maybe also a bit to piss-off my atheist parents. Anyway, I saw the way that the world held together despite all the Malthusian predictions of doom as a sign of some kind of benevolent God. Maybe not a bearded old guy on a cloud, but some directed, beneficent force that looked after mankind."

"So the bastard was having a day off on the 20th?"

"For a long time I just couldn't believe it was as bad it appeared. Much longer than common sense would allow. Classic denial! Then I heard about cases of cannibalism in Bridgetown. Bridgetown, for God's sake! I just couldn't get my head round it. Then the cholera started to spread."

No doubt about it, it was a good time to be an island with all long-distance transportation down. Sailing boats were island hopping, but we saw nothing of the plague variants that spread like wildfire through the southern landmasses. Bodies everywhere, no clean water, no medicine; it was completely inevitable and there was no possible defense. In the north, it was some kind on chicken flu. That really hammered western Europe, in particular. But there was no respite for the poor buggers that survived, either. In the northern summer, the plague moved north and the flu south. If God had wanted to make a clean start on the human part of His creation, He was certainly going the right way about it!

"I remember when it finally dawned that things weren't going to get any better. I must have cursed God using the most obscene language that I knew for at least an hour. Then I realized that this was where God had come from in the first place. When things happen that you don't understand, you can attribute them to a divinity. Saves you having to accept that it's blind fate. Shit happening. So I just thought, fuck God! I don't need this crutch anymore."

"Yes, it's not easy to accept your own fate, without hope of divine intervention or recognition. Anyway nature, not fucking Dog, has decided to turn off the rain for a bit. Fancy going for a swim?"

Sophie laughed, breaking the spell of gloom. "No way you're going to use me as an excuse to doss off. I can see Katya there dying to grind you into the deck."

I followed her glance and, sure enough, my personal trainer was waiting, wearing a robe and sandals, with a pair of goggles round her neck. No possibility of procrastination, so I pulled myself to my feet with a theatrical sigh. "OK, if I survive this, we can meet back here in about an hour and work on until lunch."

"Fine with me," she replied to my retreating back. "You kids play nice together!"

I stifled a retort. Had to think about saving energy now, as Katya will have heard about Di creaming me in the dojo yesterday and would be out to go one better.

*****

The gate to the beach was open and two guards, armed with heavy-duty tasers, were standing by an ancient Zodiac. It had been moved from the boathouse that lay beside the deep-water entry to the underground dry dock that housed my reactor and was now moored by the concrete jetty. Katya casually dropped her robe, apparently oblivious of the looks her naked body was drawing from the male guard. Suddenly he grunted in response to an elbow in the ribs and I grinned, remembering that this was one of the husband and wife teams that we gained after the 20th; Jack and Jill, they were called, or something else equally nursery-rhymish.

My trainer ignored the distraction and crouched to rinse her goggles, moving with catlike grace. I pulled off T-shirt and shorts and joined her, rinsing away the generous quantities of saliva that I'd been rubbing into my own goggles. She rolled her eyes dramatically, but we didn't need to say a thing. For years she had been trying to convince me that all you needed to do was rinse the non-fogging lenses, but I always insisted on the method that I had picked up when I started scuba diving in my late teens.

"OK, we're doing three k this morning, so it's breast stroke to the blue buoy first of all." She was originally from Oregon and pronounced buoy the American way - boo-ay.

"Breast to the blue buoy, righty-ho." I, of course, used exaggerated English pronunciation - boy - as always, just to be annoying. It was a ritual; sometimes I thought we were like an old married couple.

"Duck dive there and pick up the green weight belt - the green one!"

"Oh, come on Katya, it's about eight meters at the blue. How about fins, at least?"

"Stop being a bloody big baby. Weight belt on and backstroke to the pink buoy."

"I hate not being able to see where I'm going; how about freestyle to the pink?"

The slim blond thought about this for a moment. "OK, but then you pick up the blue weight belt."

"What's the difference?" I was always very suspicious when this little devil gave way to me in anything.

"Green's eight kilos and blue's twelve."

"And you'll have?"

"Black - six"

"That's not very fair, is it?"

"It's all relative to body weight." She stood in profile so that I - and Jack, or whatever his name was - could admire her slim, androgynous figure.

"But women are more buoyant," I complained, lamely, while trying to balance the options. My

94

backstroke was fast, but I had a tendency to drift far off course. Crawl was usually faster, but twelve kilos instead of eight would make a difference. "So what then?" I was looking for more time while I swithered.

"Drop the weight belt and crawl back to the jetty as fast as you can."

"Mmm... OK then, I'll go for the blue and freestyle."

"Don't you want to know what the penalty is first?"

"Let me guess, press-up for every second that I'm behind you?"

"Oh no, lover boy, that's only for the first ten seconds you're behind. It's then two per second up to twenty secs, three per second up to thirty, and so on."

"Shit! OK, then, I'll go back to the green belt and backstroke."

"Sorry, not allowed. Once you've chosen it's irreversible."

"Whose fucking rules are those?"

"My fucking rules!" she smiled sweetly. "Christ, Cof, we've been training together for a decade now and you still can't get it through your thick skull! The trainer is God and you are only a lowly mortal."

"Just after developing a consensus that God doesn't exist, I get proven wrong immediately," I muttered sotto voce. "OK, OK ... ten seconds start then?"

"Dream on! Now 5... 4... 3... "

I struggled to settle my goggles and, cheating to the maximum extent possible, was already in the air on "Go!" I kept the dive as shallow as possible, slapping the water painfully with my chest, attempting to build up as much of a lead as possible. It must have worked, as I estimated that I was about halfway to the buoy before I was overtaken.

This was the tricky bit, keeping up speed but avoiding getting out of breath, as that would make diving for the weight belt impossible. In fact, I was sure that Katya had slowed a little, keeping just far enough ahead that I could be tempted to race her. She really was a cunning bitch, I thought with a tinge of admiration.

Katya was now at the buoy and was treading water while she took a couple of deep, controlled breaths. For the second one, I was close enough to make out the prominent brown nipples on her small, pert breasts and I had to think of press-ups to reduce the risk of a costly distraction.

The nymph dived just as I touched the buoy; I grabbed a single mighty lungful of air before going straight after her. This was a calculated risk, I had to get the belt immediately or I was going to be in trouble. The girl was stroking strongly for the bottom in a relaxed, effortless manner, one hand holding her nose to equalize pressure in her sinuses. I grabbed the rope tethering the buoy in place and pulled hand-over-hand downwards, swallowing hard to clear my ears. My luck was holding, the belts were lying on the block of concrete used as an anchor.

Katya separated a slight tangle of the straps and had just lifted the black belt when I pushed her roughly to the side, crouched to grab the blue one and, pushing off with all my strength, shot towards the surface. I was gasping as my head cleared water and my ears were throbbing painfully, but I forced myself to calm down as I buckled on the belt and set off for the pink buoy that appeared and disappeared in the gentle swell.

The weight was pulling me uncomfortably deep and now was the time I really had to stay calm. Get a regular stroke that was pulling me through the water smoothly and think about something else.

I was going to have to say more about the isolationist policy that Andrea and I chose for - or forced upon - our little community. The logic was irrefutable, but the ethics of closing our doors and doing nothing while the surrounding country went to hell was still hard to defend. When cholera broke out, we used quarantine as an argument. This worked reasonably well because nobody had any real idea what was going on outside and, after the first week or so, the survivors became so frightened of disease that they retreated to their homes or their own little isolated groupings. Probably nobody on the entire island had an inkling of how bad it really was, except Andrea and me.

Already on the 20th, I knew how vulnerable we were due to our lack of coms with the outside world. The U was gone, so we could forget about international news, but a higher priority was to know what was happening in our vicinity. Within the estate, we used little pin-sized cameras for audiovisual monitoring and it didn't take much effort to tape small solar cells onto a couple of dozen spares. They originally had a range of ten kilometers, so the first few nights I set off under cover of darkness to set them up at locations that would let me check on developments in general and, in particular, give advance warning of anyone who might be heading in our direction. These worked perfectly and, by the time of the cholera outbreak, I had an aerial on the roof that extended their range to over twenty k and, on night time excursions on my mountain bike, had extended coverage right into the middle of Bridgetown, the port and even population centers on the south coast as far as Oistins.

Most evenings Andrea and I would scan highlights picked out by my pattern recognition software, so we followed in detail the horrors associated with the collapse of Bajan culture, of basic civilization - and did nothing. I know it hurt Andrea a lot and, indeed, she did start a little, secret aid program of her own. We dropped off supplies at night where she considered that they would do most good. In general this was relatively safe as, especially when unlit by a bright moon, the nights were completely dark and everyone stayed locked up in their homes.

I did, however, get ambushed once while cycling back from such a delivery. No doubt the light on my bicycle acted as a flame for the ragamuffin moths. A cricket bat out of nowhere knocked me off my bike and, as I lay dazed on the tarmac, a flurry of boots and fists pummeled me to the edge of unconsciousness. All of a sudden they were gone, along with my bike, and I was left to stagger the three k back to the villa. A couple of cracked ribs and mild concussion, so I got off lightly. We cut back on our Samaritan work after that, restricting it to communities close by.

The loss of the bike was annoying, but the lamp on it was potentially more worrying, as it was a rechargeable of a type that might be recognized by some of the older survivors as proof that a power source must be available somewhere. I increased surveillance in the area where I was attacked and even slipped back to place a couple more cameras when my ribs felt sufficiently healed for a nigh-time foray. Even after a decade on the island, I had a great deal of difficulty following the strong Bajan dialect of the local gang on the occasions that they were close enough for the inbuilt microphones to register. Nevertheless, I picked up enough to realize that their boss, a heavy built man in his thirties who seemed to be called Darcy, was keen to trace the source of the bike.

It wasn't long before they had picked up rumors and set out from the base they had established in an abandoned shopping mall in Warren, heading for Holetown. Darcy might only have been the leader of a gang of thugs, but he was anything but stupid and must have done his homework before setting off. While I was busy beefing up our conventional defenses, he wrong-footed me by heading straight for the old Holetown police station, where one of my hydroponics technicians lived with her family in a fishing community. Although the community was twenty strong, it was mainly women and children when Darcy arrived, the men being at sea. His eight vagabonds with their machetes were easily able to control the screaming mass for long enough for him to identify Irene and drag her off. This kidnap team then rendezvoused with the rest of his gang, about two dozen men with a half dozen, very rough, camp followers. Andrea and I watched this live on our video monitors, unable to lift a finger to help.

The gang brazenly marched along the main road to the estate, but were clued-up enough to stay back beyond the range of our tasers. He certainly had some good source of local information. I still remember the way he dragged the crying woman forward by her hair and demanded that we put together an offer good enough to save the girl's life. He didn't wait for an answer, but called two huge men forward, who held the struggling girl while he brutally raped her. Andrea was beside me in the control room, alternating between cursing the perpetrators and the women of the gang, who were now cheering on one of the hulks who had taken over from Darcy and was now anally raping the semi-conscious woman.

"We've got to offer them something." I remember Andrea broke down, the first time I had ever seen that happen. "We just can't... " We looked into each other's eyes and knew, logically, that it was impossible. Darcy wasn't going to settle for one payment, no matter what we gave him. If we gave

100

way now, it'd set a precedent. Darcy would simply get greedier and greedier until he had run us into the ground, or some other gang took note of the easy pickings and took over the racket. I was already flicking through my inventory list as I threw a slave headset at my sister. "Get wind directions and speeds! At this time of day, with the sea breezes, it'll be touch and go, but I don't see that we've got an alternative.

As always, when under pressure, she understood exactly what I was doing as if she was able to read my mind. By the time that I had struggled to the back courtyard, after ordering security staff to their positions and everyone else to the basement of the main house with a bogus warning that there might be some shooting, Andrea was there with a couple of guidance units locked onto the estate micro-gps. Our headsets and data-glasses were slaved to the control center, so we could follow - in much too much detail - the progress of the third rape of our poor technician. Immediately after the mortars were locked on, I set a pattern of airbursts upwind of the unruly mob. At first the quiet pops seemed to go unnoticed in the hubbub of the shouted encouragement for the brutal show, but then the first victims of the anesthetic gas began to collapse and the scene became complete bedlam.

The mob initially ran away from the sounds of the gas shells, which took them towards our walls and into the range of the tasers, which I had now turned up to lethal levels. Actually, to levels far beyond lethal: the first victims spasmed horrendously as their hair and clothing burst into flame. This then caused the rush to break to both sides of our entrance drive, where they had to try to fight their way into dense undergrowth, thickly planted with crown-of-thorns bushes, a brutally barbed shrub originally imported from Madagascar. Anyone who made it through that barrier would have left a lot of skin behind. Within two minutes, the only bodies to be seen in the entire area were motionless on the ground.

Allowing another minute for the gas to completely disperse, we strapped on taser pistols and, each armed with a baseball bat, then cautiously opened the gate and hurried over to examine Irene. She was extensive bruised, seemed to have lost a couple of teeth and was bleeding from her anus and vagina. I lifted the prone form as gently as I could and carried her towards the gate. Out of the corner of my eye I could see Andrea prising the machete from Darcy's limp fingers. "Bring a blow torch," she shouted as I pushed my way through the gate.

It took me a little bit of time to load up the small electro-buggy with kit. Irene was in the care of a couple of security guards who, despite their pleas, I forbade to leave the estate and come to our assistance. By the time I drove out, Andrea had pulled groups of bodies together. The rapists were in one pile, another fifteen or so men in a second and five women in the third. The men had already been stripped of their trousers and underwear and my sister was currently struggling with the very tight jeans of one of the girls.

As I arrived, she waved at the other women. "Finish this," she grunted and, picking up the machete, rummaged in the buggy until she found the small plasma torch. I could have turned away, but considered that this was a team effort, whatever way she wanted to play it. There was a lot of blood with her first victim, Darcy, as she slashed his wedding tackle free, cutting deeply into both thighs in the process. The bleeding stopped with a hiss and the stink of roasting flesh as she cauterized the cuts with a flash of plasma, leaving a band of seared flesh about 10 cm wide. The other two rapists were handled in a similar manner although, as she got the hang of the razor sharp machete and the industrial blowtorch, the amount of collateral damage decreased a little.

Without exchanging a further word, I finished getting the trousers off the gang whores and collected self-tightening ties - usually used for bunching cables - which I used to bind the hands and feet of Andrea's castrati before lugging them onto the bed of the buggy. Darcy and his two hulks were the heaviest and the ones in worst shape. As I started to load the next batch, I noted that my sister had limited herself to removal of their testicles although, with the violence of the machete cuts and the intense burn zones of the torch, it looked doubtful that the remnant penises would be much good in most cases.

By the time I caught up with the Butcher of Holetown - the name became legendary, although most people actually thought it was me - she had reached the first girl and was poised indecisively, with her tools held loosely in her blood drenched hands. The gas was beginning to wear off and first groans and cries of pain could be heard from the pile on my transporter. The woman who would be her first victim then opened a pair of bloodshot eyes that widened comically in abject terror as she noted the blood dripping from the huge knife onto her flabby mahogany thighs. She lost control of her bladder at that point and my sister looked down with disgust as a spray of urine was added to the gore that already soaked her jeans.

Completely inured to bodily fluids at this point, like a soldier with some kind of battle fatigue, I gently moved my sister aside and started binding the women and adding them to the top of the pile. Only when the battlefield had been cleared was my sister suddenly galvanized into action. She strode purposely to where she had started her bloody work and bent to retrieve the products of her handiwork from the ground. Returning to the buggy, she roughly pulled hair to identify the three older women, the ones who had been loudest in urging the rapists on. With slow deliberation, she pinched their noses in turn and, when they gasped for air, crammed one of her grisly souvenirs into the proffered mouth, then jamming it closed while they choked in horror.

I thought at first she was going to force them to choke but, in each case, she relented after a few seconds and allowed them to spit and vomit to attempt to clear their mouths from this foul intrusion. She then clambered wordlessly into the cab and we ran over to add three frazzled corpses to a pile that was now beginning to writhe in a very unstable manner.

Then, it was over. We drove the buggy halfway to Holetown and chucked the screaming or inert bodies onto the road with the same lack of care. The men were either unconscious or in extreme agony, but the hags were more sullen. As we started to draw away, one of the younger ones couldn't resist a final goad. I remember the exact words "Fucking hell bitch, next time we gonna have twenty fuckin' huge black lads gonna rape the arse off you!"

Andrea leapt from the cab before I even had a chance to brake and strode back towards the girl who, in abject terror, was trying to worm herself towards some of the screaming men. My sister looked for a moment at the bloody machete, then hurled it towards the undergrowth. The black girl looked relieved, but only for the moment before the plasma flame was jammed into her groin. The scream was the loudest of the entire day - and the one that has stayed with me longest, the crux of the nightmare that still occasionally wakes me bathed in sweat.

I had a sudden shock as I swum into a shoal of pale blue fish that exploded in all directions, a shell-burst of silvery reflections. Shit, I was almost there,

105

three more strokes and I touched the buoy and, with the other hand, released my weight belt. Suddenly I felt as if I was floating in the surface microlayer, so buoyant that I could be in the Dead Sea.

A slap pushed me aside and kicking feet just missed my face. Fuck, that was Katya back in the lead. One quick glance to line up on the pier and then it was head down, full speed, holding nothing back. We always had the penalties when Katya triumphed, as she inevitably did, so I had a real incentive to pull out the stops. Even sweeter, was the promise of the prize - I could have my evil way with my trainer, anything I wanted, if I could only beat her in one of the races. I could never really work out whether it was the threat of pain or the dream of pleasure, but it certainly made me work harder than any other training session.

About 500m and I had pulled up neck and neck. My heart was ready to burst and blood was pounding in my ears. The voice of reason in the modern, surface layers of the brain was developing good logical reasons to back off a bit before I had an infarction, but the deep, primitive, animal core didn't give a shit. Now 300m to go and I was definitely ahead; maybe only centimeters, but that smooth, hairless body was finally going to be mine after a decade of wet dreams. About 200m and I was sucking air like a jump jet, vision beginning to blur. Katya seemed to be catching up again and, as I risked a glance, I caught a mouthful of seawater. I coughed as it burned my throat and snorted as some seemed to manage to make its way back up my

106

nose. I was drowning, ready to vomit, but my arms were still powering on and, if anything, my legs were kicking even more frantically than before.

My trainer's feet were now level with my head and I found some final store of energy for the last sprint. My lungs were bursting, but I wasn't breathing any more. Just head down and powering through the water with every muscle screaming in agony. A glimpse of a tight pair of buttocks: I was pulling back! Two more pulls though the water and then, to my amazement, the buttocks vanished. I had just a millisecond for the surprise to register before I crashed into the jetty with an impact that almost rendered me senseless.

With some survival reflex I managed to catch a hold of the wooden planking above my head while I tried to gasp for air and be sick at the same time. It was several seconds before sounds registered at all. "7... 8... 9... "

"I'm here," I coughed, "stop the count!"

"Nope, you need to be back standing on the jetty. 13... 14... "

Kicking with all my remnant strength, I managed to pull up far enough to get an elbow over the edge. Another wrench and my belly was scraping painfully on the rough wood surface. "19... 20... 21... "

"Fuck, this just isn't fair," I managed to gasp before spewing saline bile onto the boards. "25... 26... "

A final push with legs that felt like jelly and I swayed upright on "29!" I hovered in place for a second then, like a cartoon character, toppled backwards into the water.

As I surfaced, spluttering, a little hand reached down to grab my wrist and, with strength that seemed incompatible with her diminutive physique, hauled me back up onto the jetty. "Actually, that wasn't too pathetic. If you had just gone straight up the ladder you would have been about three or four seconds behind. So, now you've got five minutes to catch your breath," she started the stopwatch function on her little wrist diving computer, "then only fifty-seven press-ups and we're done for the day. Wasn't that fun?"

I turned away to retch more acidic bile into the crystal clear Caribbean, no doubt adding to the fun experienced by this athletic sadist.

***

After a shower I felt somewhat better, although my body still ached as if I'd done ten rounds with Muhammad Ali in his prime. I dreaded to think what I'd feel like tomorrow morning, or more likely the day after, when the muscles that I'd overstrained made themselves known. Definitely a hot soak this evening and, maybe, a gentle massage.

Sophie was waiting patiently in the conservatory, peering at the small screen of her electronic notebook and making notes with fingers that blurred over the keypad. Lifting her hands free with the flourish of a concert pianist, she smiled wickedly at me. "You look nice and refreshed now, ready to start?"

"Just let me get a drink first," I poured from a thermos flask containing an isotonic cocktail based on grapefruit juice that was Katya's own special recipe. It was always ready for my return after yet another humiliation. I gulped down a half-liter glassful, feeling the cold fluid sooth my raw throat. Then I poured a second glass and settled back into my favorite chair.

"Now, we can continue with the infrastructure we have here... "

"No, I'd been explaining - maybe trying to justify - our exclusion policy and the lengths we took to enforce it. You're certainly aware that I've been tiptoeing around something else here... "

"Yes, Sue and I discussed it last night - but we didn't want to force you, if you really were so uncomfortable with it."

"It's an important part of the entire story and I was thinking about it while I was playing nice with Katya. I'll run through it quickly, so it might be best if you don't ask questions until the end." I caught a raised eyebrow, so added "... and I won't go off on a tangent here, I promise."

"Fine with me, fire away!" Again the pianist with hands raised, ready to strike the first cord at the slightest twitch of the conductor's baton.

I then told the tale of Darcy and the Butcher of Holetown. I didn't pull punches, but dropped Irene's name, as she still worked in the hydroponic greenhouses, having recovered amazingly well from her ordeal. One very seriously tough lady, that one! I also played down my sister's role. I made it clear that Andrea and I were fully responsible for the choices made and actions carried out that day, but wasn't more specific. I'm sure that, if played to a general audience, 99% of the listeners would assume that I was the one with the machete and the blowtorch, but with Sue and Sophie that would be a harder call.

After the narration Sophie sat quietly for a minute or two, clearly trying to assimilate the gratuitous violence of it all. Then the question I was waiting for. "Why?"

"The way I told the story made it seem as if it was all very spontaneous from our side. It was a surprise and it caught us off guard, but something of this sort wasn't completely unexpected. In fact, it was probably inevitable. Our advantage was general planning, generic threat evaluation. My sister and I were old hand war-gamers, remember. True, there's a hell of a fucking difference between a game and real life, but we knew what had to be done, not just for our own sakes, but for the sakes of everyone else living here. If you want to understand us though, you also have to realize that, by this time, we knew that we were sitting on a treasure trove that could be essential for catalyzing local or even regional recovery. Hyperbole, maybe, but true nevertheless."

"Why?" The repeated question made me recognize that I was avoiding the direct answer, protesting too much, ducking and diving.

I took a deep breath and let it out with a sigh. "Andrea and I had been watching not only Darcy, but also some of the other gangs that were coming together like weeds amongst the regular communities. Most survivors were living from hand to mouth, which is easier to do in a small group or family, by working together, sharing. The gangs were, in terms of total numbers, a small fraction of the total population but, due to their propensity for extreme violence at the drop of a hat, they terrified, dominated and exploited much larger groups. Complete parasites that served no purpose at all, not even the pretense of a protection racket, just gangster terror. The gangs, of course, preyed also on each other, with the most violent and vicious floating to the top, like the turds that they were."

A raised eyebrow hurried me on. "This meant that, sometime or other, they would target us. The only way to ensure that this didn't become a constant plague, was to hit so hard that it was clear that we were, by far, the meanest fuckers on the whole fucking island. Totally stupid, but it's the Law of Gang Warfare."

"But the castrations... You had already electrocuted some of the gang, killed them. Wasn't that enough?"

"Not at all! Killing a few of these cockroaches has no effect. If anything, the opposite: it encourages them to come back for revenge. They are surrounded by death, day in and day out. They drowned in it during the Dying. How could we frighten them just by killing a few? Even if we killed them all, slaughtered the whole gang, it wouldn't be long before the next one had moved in to claim their territory and the whole zoo would start again."

"So the castration was premeditated?"

"Made a lot easier by the rape, but it was what Andrea and I had already identified as the best deterrent."

"But why?"

"No, I've done enough for now. I'm going to have a coffee. You may be an ex-Dog-botherer, but you're smart enough despite that. Consider it an exercise for your Jesuit logic. Why did we castrate those poor bastards?"

My secretary wasn't happy about being put on the spot like this, but she rallied bravely. "Castration: the ultimate fear of men... " This time it was my raised eyebrow that caused her to rethink her string of argumentation. "Well, fear of men who value their virility, probably less of a problem for celibate monks and grandfathers... "

" Yes!" She slapped her brow as the answer crystallized, forming from the over-saturated solution of hints that she had been provided with. "The gangs: they're all dominated by alpha-males. The toughest, the most virile. That's even what the rapes are about! The leaders of the pack show off how well hung they are by sexually violating their victims. As you said, even the women they drag along with them get caught in this web of insanity. The bitches at the top encourage this form of sexual domination, they benefit from it."

112

She stopped and looked at me. Something was changing; I don't know what she saw in me in the past, but it was going to be different from now on. "You and Andrea worked all this out in advance and executed it in cold blood, keeping the details from the others."

"The locals all know about the Butcher, although it has almost become a myth, a story to scare young children on stormy nights. Irene and her community, in particular, know all of the gory details. But it's in everyone's interest to keep it vague; this makes it more frightening and keeps unwanted visitors away."

She was mulling over this as I added, "... the bottom line is that, in a civilized world, the smartest tend to control things while, when civilization breaks down, it's the toughest and most violent. So, if you're smart, when shit hits the fan, you've got to convince everyone that you're also the toughest and most violent on the block. The naturally tough and violent reinforce their control on a daily basis. We, in a completely premeditated manner, assured our position with an atrocity that is still spoken of throughout the entire Island. The Butcher of Holetown: we haven't had a single gang come within five kilometers of the town since then."

Silence again drew out while Sophie scanned her notes. "Ah, I knew there was a loose end. What happened to the gang members after you left them on the road to Holetown?"

"It was a couple of hours before the men folk of the rape victim's community returned and gathered up some support from their neighbors. You can imagine their surprise when the rescue party came upon the gang, trussed up in a pile on the road. They were all in a pretty bad way by then, lying in the sun with flies crusting horrific wounds. Even the untouched women were pretty messy. I think I mentioned that I bound them up with self-tightening ties and so, the more they struggled, the tighter the ties became, cutting deeply into flesh."

"And... "

"I can show you, if you want. We recorded everything that was in view of our videos."

The black haired woman shivered. "No thanks. Just briefly summarize what happened."

"The kidnap party had caused injuries, slashed a couple of women and children, and... " I had to be careful to avoid use of Irene's name, although it was very probable that my scribes would work it out for themselves anyway, "... a woman was missing. As you can imagine, they weren't in a forgiving mood. The men were battered to death where they lay."

Another taut silence. "And the women?"

"The one who had annoyed Andrea was dead. In her agony, she had forced the ties around her wrists so tight that she had torn through veins and bled to death. The other four women were carried back to Holetown. I guess what saved them was the fact that they weren't in the original raiding party."

"Then what?" Sophie was pale and looked as if she might be sick at any point, but was fighting through to the end.

"About then, I showed up with the rape victim in the back of a bicycle rickshaw. She worked for me, so I was known and, although there was some disgruntlement, I think most people simply tried to forget that we existed. I said nothing, just left. I had, however, explained what had happened to the woman who, although doped to the eyeballs on painkillers, was perfectly lucid. She could explain what she wanted to her community.

"And what happened?"

"She decided to describe exactly what we'd done and why we'd done it. Said she agreed with it completely. Then, one by one, two men; her husband and her brother I think they were, cut the ties on the women's ankles and she used one of these barbed harpoons, the ones used for spearing fish from the shore... I don't think you need to know more details."

Now she really looked ready to spew, but managed to gulp, "No!"

"There was no shouting encouragement, like the gang during the rape, but all the adults in the community watched in silence. It was almost like some kind of pagan sacrificial rite," I continued relentlessly. "After that, they simply cut their victims' hands lose and dragged them to the southern town limits. Two of the women bled out there. One managed to stagger to a nearby Church, where a resident Christian commune treated her for a couple of days, until word came through the grapevine of who they were sheltering. A sister commune had been raided a month earlier by

115

Darcy's gang, so they handled her like true Christians."

She was forced to rise to the bait "And?"

"They crucified her! Must have rotted on that cross in the cemetery for a month."

"Christ!" She swallowed hard and then went off in search of a glass of water.

Returning, with slightly more color in her cheeks, it was clear that the analytical brain had continued to function despite the body's discomfort. "That makes four. You got five of the original six women in the gang, so presumably one managed to escape the gas. But one seems unaccounted for."

"Your arithmetic is impeccable. The last one seemed much smarter than the others; first thing she did when dumped at the edge of the village was to bind herself up with a nappy-kind of thing made from banana leaves and bits of her shirt. Last seen limping towards Bridgetown. No idea what happened to her."

"But she must have been the one that spread the story. You said that the Holetown people don't talk about it, so she'd be the one that made it into a legend. Unless, of course, some of the gang members you didn't catch hung about to watch the whole thing. Although that doesn't seem very likely, surely they'd have helped their friends after you first dumped them on the road to Holetown."

"She may have done, but that really wasn't necessary. As I said, we had vids of all the very nastiest parts of the action and then used the goriest of images for a poster. Made about a hundred of

116

them and, over a couple of nights, nailed them up all over neighboring parishes. The message was sharp and to the point. Don't die like Darcy: Don't fuck with Holetown! Since then, nobody has."

Sophie flicked through her notes for a bit. "I think that's complete. If anything, maybe a bit too much gory detail for my taste. But, somehow, I get the feeling that there's something else. There's something about protecting our little retreat that you're not talking about."

"Very perceptive, but I've covered everything relevant to the period when we were surviving the 20th and the Dying. This other event came much later. Anyway, how about lunch?"

Fingers were flying over the keyboard. I sighed: another scabrous cat out of the bag, they'd pursue me mercilessly until I'd revealed all. Something else that I'd have to think about very carefully in advance.

Chapter 5 - One step at a time

After lunch, I spent three hours in my study, checking in with my partners in Renaissance projects scattered around the globe. So little time and so much to do! Radio was the key link, especially for a group like this who all retained computing technology of some kind. As far as I could make out, I was probably best set up in terms of technical hardware - although nobody was too open here, as we were well aware that we were sitting on goldmines and, although we were all well separated, radio was hardly a secure medium. Some of the remote military bases and research teams in places like the Antarctic seemed to have been able to cobble together operating computers from informatics rubbish heaps, but they had generally lost most of their supporting databases when volatile QC memory evaporated.

The real star, however, who really made our collaboration possible, was a geek genius living in the Falklands, who was running a completely home-made system. David had squirreled away electronics by the truckload as these were displaced by QCs; stripped them down completely and reassembled a veritable Frankenstein's Godzilla of a computer. Not a match for a QC, but it ran an AI that was the closest to one I had ever heard of. David and his AI bootstrapped an acoustic coupler by using ancient code buried in some Microsoft Easter Egg that existed buried in most old source code - ignored by software evolution like a vestigial tail. This allowed simple audio signals to create code that, in turn, improved the translation of audio signals into code and so on until we effectively had our own communication internet and were able to directly send each other small files and databases by radio - a few Gigabytes or so.

As had I emphasized to my scribes, I'm a paranoid bastard by nature, so I set up an old 2015s stand-alone work station for this link - physically isolated from the rest on my estate intranet. I remember the first email I received from David. *Cof, you are a cunning Old Sod! Good on you! Can't be too careful!* That's the problem with geeks, they can't help fucking about with other people's kit, even if it does them no good. It's just in their nature.

My key resource was my database. There were lots of other pre-QC databases scattered about, but they tended to be abandoned archives that were frozen in time in the '10s or '20s, or even earlier. Lack of updates on '30s and '40s knowledge wasn't important - more problematic was accessing material in outmoded formats and recovery of corrupted data from the fragile magnetic and optical storage media used. This could be a full time job for a team of IT-archaeologists, but nobody had the time or expertise to waste on this.

My database had been continuously updated until the 20th, to provide me with an in-house alternative to the U. Although containing only a minute fraction of the amount of material in the QC-AIs, it was a carefully selected fraction, stripped of dross and aimed to provide a comprehensive overview of any topic that my smart search engines considered might be of interest to me - which covers a fairly huge range. More importantly, all the information it contained was in a standard format and fully searchable by the smartest non-quantum knowledge management tools that were available in the '20s.

This gave me my niche. I could provide customized databases on any particular topic and, with a lot of help from David, we could translate them into a format useable by whatever bastardized chimera of a computing system our partners were using.

Especially for the others, such output was gold-dust. It provided them with a product that could be bartered for food or services in whatever part of the globe they lived in, becoming increasingly important when the region went through the transition from simply fighting for survival to beginning to rebuild. This went relatively quickly in places like the Caribbean, Australia and New Zealand, but took a hell of a lot longer in countries dominated by megacities - the Americas, Europe and, in particular, East Asia.

Naturally, it was David who invented e-money. As he pointed out, some members of our group were mainly suppliers of knowledge and others were users, which wasn't very fair. As separation made barter clearly impractical for us, we needed some way of keeping track of accumulated debt, so he produced a simple bulletin board where transactions could be specified and an agreed e-credit recorded. Positive balances of credits could then be used for further transactions. It wasn't long before David and I were credit millionaires and most of the others were in the red. They didn't really care though because, after all, it was only play money.

Then David moved the bulletin board to his newly created International Bank of Stanley. The video authentication he provided was just another example of his virtuosity as a hacker, but he had demonstrated real cunning by also setting up a small community with a stand-alone computer and radio link whose only job was to run the computer system tracing credit transfers; in effect, acting as honest brokers. For this, they got a commission of 0.01% of the transaction. Interestingly, every transaction was accessible - no banking secrecy here. I think this was David's way of ensuring that we trusted the system - as everyone knew he was perfectly capable of building his own back door into any computer software.

I remember being completely flabbergasted by the rate at which the IBS took off. It seems like the Falklands, being both remote and blessed - as it turns out - with very low tech infrastructure, survived the 20th better than almost anywhere else worldwide. Very biblical somehow - the last shall become first; a town at the arse end of creation becomes the technology transfer and commercial capital of the world overnight. The Falklands had suffered very little chaos resulting from the QC collapse, possibly the result of a history with long periods of being cut-off from the rest of the world. There was no Dying; no famine as, apart from anything else, they had more sheep than people - and no resultant epidemics. What they did lose, of course, were the banks. In the 2040s these were a tightly interlinked, AI-controlled network that was used to distribute resources rather than, as was the case at the turn of the century, pour gold into the pockets of the already mega-rich to the detriment of the poor.

Barter is all very well but, for any civilization above stone-age level, some kind of money is needed. When electronic banking vanished on the 20th, this left a huge gap which had to be filled before reconstruction could get properly underway. David, being way, way smarter than the average bear, picked up on this. The problem with a bank, though, is that it needs collateral - the basis for confidence that your credits stored now will be repaid in the future. Traditionally, this was handled with gold - huge quantities of this useful metal did nothing more than lie in vaults to ensure the customers' peace of mind. Well, there wasn't much gold in Stanley and there were many more useful things that could be done with a highly conductive metal than stockpiling it as inert ingots. So David set up the IBS on the basis of the value of the fundamental knowledge that we had already begun to trade. Within days his credits were being used for trade in potatoes, turnips, sheep and homebrew. Within a week, the Government of the Falklands had negotiated a block of the bank's server for the department of finance and the first post-Crash taxes came into existence.

I'm sure David must have had the Falklands Government over a barrel because, somehow or other, he forced them to have the same complete transparency as the rest of his banking system. In a very nice twist, taxes were not levied on the individual transactions - only the commission that the bank made. This avoided any incentive for traders to avoid tax by using an alternative method for handling commercial transactions.

Because it suffered so little and it was such a tightly-knit community, setting up the main IBS in Stanley was relatively easy. It took me almost a year to set up the first branch office in Holetown, but this clearly had to be a priority when the trauma of the Dying had subsided and first moves towards reconstruction were being made. The hardware was simple enough - a small laptop, a radio and one of my button video cameras, all powered by a solar panel. The tricky bit was setting up the software for retinal identification from the rather crappy image quality provided. I'm sure David could have done it in no time, but this was a good project to challenge my programing skills. I brought in an apprentice to help - actually one of Irene's sons - as he was being groomed to run the bank after it was finally established.

Although David was, formally, completely independent of the IBS, he was the one I had to haggle with to nail down the logistics of establishing a branch office. I had, originally, considered setting up my own Bank of Barbados - but was convinced by David that this would set a very bad precedent, going down the road of competing national economies, rogue money traders, etc. If it was IBS, then how would taxation be handled? After much toing and froing, we finally settled on a standard tax rate on bank transactions in Barbados being split 70:30 between the Governments of Barbados and the Falklands. Now I had a bit of a problem: at that time there was no Bajan Government.

Although, during that first year, I focused monitoring efforts on my own Parish of St. James, I did have a couple of surveillance cameras in Bridgetown. Spending a bit more time on these feeds - and with a bit of input from Andrea, who spent increasing amounts of time outside the estate as things slowly normalized - I was able to determine that a group, mainly comprised of past members of the police, coast guard and fire service, seemed to be taking a lead role in slowly bringing some kind of normalcy to the town. Although hardly a Government, with the lack of a better choice, I decided that they would be as good a core as any to begin to take over this role.

My approach was cautious, constrained by my usual paranoia. A volunteer - this time one of Irene's cousins, who was employed as one of my security guards - cycled into Bridgetown with an ancient, solar walky-talky that I had found in the bomb shelter. She boldly muscled her way in to the old coast guard office, which was used as their base, and made herself generally unpleasant until she managed to get an interview with the acting commander, a fireman called Nigel Smith, who had also served as a magistrate pre-20th.

Nigel had known of me and my community before the Crash and had picked up on rumors of developments in Holetown afterwards, but hadn't put the two pieces of the puzzle together. When I introduced myself on the radio and explained that I was already setting up international banking links, he was smart enough to realize that I must have a lot more working infrastructure than he had in the whole of Bridgetown. Thereafter, an hour was wasted with bluster. He demanded that I put my facilities under official control - for the first time that I had heard of, tacitly equating his group to the Barbadian government. He was, of course, not pleased at all at being told to take a flying fuck to himself. Then came the threats: his ability to take whatever he wanted by force, if it wasn't handed over peacefully. I then mentioned Darcy, which had the desired effect. My ambassador, who was present throughout, reported that his black face turned noticeably grey at the mere mention of that name.

Having gone through this first phase of strutting our stuff to establish pecking order, I then gave him the good news - that I was contacting him with an offer to pay tax. The entire concept floored him for a bit, but, after I spent ten minutes giving him background, he demonstrated how quick on the uptake he was by asking if, as a resident Bajan, this meant that I'd also be paying tax on my amassed credit. This caught me unawares, and, for the first time he took the initiative. If this banking idea was going to take off, then he would need money to pay to set up the government. At present, I was the only one in the Island with credits, so I would, some way or another, have to contribute to the national coffers. I tried to explain about the tax on Holetown banking transactions, but his derisive snort made it clear that he saw through this ploy. Such a minimal taxation rate would take a long time to build a functioning budget.

We tap-danced around for a bit and finally settled for a one-time payment of 10% on all my income to date and, in lieu of confiscation of my infrastructure for the national good, a 75% discount on all services that I provided for the Government. I put up a token fight on this last point and managed to tie it to a commitment from his side to include Holetown within the police umbrella that was being implemented in Bridgetown. In fact, I had been prepared to offer support for free, as it was in my best interests for Barbados to get back on its feet as quickly as possible. The sooner that we achieved more equality in standard of living, the less I stood out as an anomaly - and a potential target for those who felt that I had a disproportionate share of the cake. Nevertheless, I recognized that Nigel's idea had a lot going for it: something that is paid for is always valued more than anything you get for free. I provided credits as tax and got them back for knowledge and infrastructure support services. Any positive balance could be used to supplement payments to my staff, which was entirely in the form of goods until then. I would just have to be very careful how I used my large international budget surplus before trading got properly established again.

The other concession I had to make was to set up an IBS branch in Bridgetown. Nigel insisted that this was needed for a location that had already recovered enough to be once again the biggest population center on the island - and also to run the new government accounting system. He couldn't be expected to rebuild when he had to do everything involving finances over a walky-talky or by cycling down to Holetown. Thus Barbados came to possess also the second branch office of the IBS. Within a year it was the center of the new Caribbean trading network and, even today, in terms of total transactions, it is second only to Stanley.

***

By the time I finished my database searches and other administrative chores, strained shoulder muscles were beginning to ache and I decided it was time for another hot bath. I'm not convinced that these really do any long-term good, but they certainly reduce the pain for the time that you're soaking. Or, then again, maybe it's just that the shock of the hot water is sufficient to overwhelm the pain receptors - so the agony is all still there, you just don't notice it any more.

My bath was a traditional Japanese onsen, with hot water from a three kilometer deep borehole on the grounds, which was already in place when I bought the estate and thus dimensioned for simultaneous use by a significant number of resort guests. I had, for some original reason that I've forgotten now, introduced the Japanese bathing ritual, including the really stupid low stools that you sit on while performing your pre-bathing ablutions. Two complete soap-downs, from head to toe, followed each time with a rinse using buckets-full of scalding water. Only then did I allow myself to slowly ease into the steaming pool.

The pool itself was circular, about six meters in diameter and waist deep, constructed from some kind of black, volcanic rock. The sun was, again, setting, but today it was hidden behind a line of clouds that fringed the western horizon. The edges of the clouds that concealed the glowing orb, in the center of my view through the picture window, blazed with actinic brightness, laying down a glowing path over the sea that led directly to the bottom of my garden.

I had washed and was already ankle-deep in the onsen before noticing the small figure, kneeling on the ledge that ran around the edge of the pool, with only the dark silhouette of a head evident in the glare reflected from the sea. The water seared my body as I slowly progressed down the steps into the pool, pulling against the handrail as if strength would, somehow, help me resist the heat. I waded slowly to her side, while Sophie turned languidly in

128

the water, easing her elbows onto the sides of the bath and floating almost horizontally before me.

Since the '10s and '20s, sexual mores have been fairly relaxed in most parts of the globe - a consequence of the second sexual revolution resulting from cures for AIDS and other sexually transmitted diseases. Of course, there had been still Puritanism associated with Christian and Muslim religious fundamentalism in places where such cultural curses were endemic, but the power of such cults had diminished greatly in the world of plenty ushered in by the omnipotent AIs and, as one of the few silver cloud linings, had lost even more ground after the 20th. Survival was something that you had to do for yourself; those who wasted effort begging help from a God tended to be the ones who didn't make it. Also, when your sellable skills mainly involve the ability to endlessly reinterpret bastardized manuscripts originating from barely literate reporters of actions from the Middle East of two millennia ago, then you're hardly going to be welcomed with open arms into communities trying to scrape an existence from the ashes of the collapse.

Such musing was helping to divert me from the automatic physical reaction to my view of Sophie's naked body. She had almost no discernible breasts, just the smallest convexity of her olive chest, topped with dark brown button nipples. Her mons was completely hairless, with only the trace of a slit to differentiate her from Barbie doll asexuality. Especially here in the Caribbean, I had seen 10 year old girls with more developed characteristics of the adult female. Perversely, however, this made her very erotic in some kind of way. I had a sudden flashback of my sister's room when she was in her teens - covered with photos of Annie Lennox, in pinstripe suits, dinner jackets, uniforms. The fascination of the androgynous: hard to rationalize, but amazingly potent.

My blatant inspection of her body seemed only to amuse my secretary. "Haven't you ever seen a naked woman before?"

"Seen more naked women than you've had hot breakfasts" I retorted, before suddenly remembering that that this woman was very much older than she looked. "Or maybe not," I amended weakly, "but a fair amount of bare woman-flesh anyway."

"So, what's so fascinating?" She was slowly paddling with her feet to maintain her horizontal position, offering titillating glimpses between her slender thighs.

"Well, I've never seen you naked before," I answered honestly. "A bit limited on the tits front for my taste, but I wouldn't crawl over you to get to the Flynn." I had often wondered who this mysterious Flynn was, featuring in a line I picked up from my University days in Edinburgh. Must have the search engines take a look! I posted a note for myself in the rather cluttered and untidy notice board that seemed to serve me as a memory these days.

Sophie turned back to her original position and typed something into the small machine that was lying on a folded towel at the side of the pool. "So, we need to fill in some personal background now. Your sister set up this villa with a female staff, which must have put lots of temptation in your way. However, you said before that you made a point of avoiding relationships with your staff. How does this all work out?"

I gradually lowered myself onto the ledge beside the elfin form, feeling the scalding water rise up to my chest. I closed my eyes and resisted the temptation to rub my shoulder against her flank. So, how does it all work? Funnily enough, I'd never thought to analyze it myself - it was a situation that just evolved.

"Before the Crash is easy to explain" I started slowly, feeling my way gently, like the tentative probing of a cavity in a back tooth with my tongue. "I had my staff and I had a range of girlfriends; there was no overlap at all between the two groups. The latter included some that were local and some international, who I first met during travel or in U chat rooms. Some girlfriends stayed overnight, some stayed for months, but I didn't have anything permanent - not like Andrea and Tina."

"You couldn't find a substitute for Andrea?" Even with my eyes closed I could hear a teasing smile in the question.

"I didn't need a substitute. We still were, still are, best friends and, even before the catastrophe, we saw a lot of each other. Our relationship is intimate, but not sexual. I didn't go for girls that were like my sister, but equally I didn't avoid those

131

with any particular resemblance. If you could characterize my past girlfriends, the main characteristic would be diversity. Race, color, shape, size, academic background, interests - about as broad a cross-section as you could imagine."

"Anorexic, super-model types? Being mega-rich, you must have attracted them in droves."

I rolled my eyes behind closed lids. I bet these bloody women had run a profile before they even started putting together their questions. "OK, well maybe you can imagine a broader cross-section than I was thinking of. I don't go for very skinny women, or very fat ones either. Slim and trim is great, but I also appreciate the attractions of more generously built women, the comfort rather than speed kind of option. In fact, I'm not so keen on some of the more common ideas of beauty - the harsh symmetry you find on catwalks or the Playboy plastic voluptuous."

"God, you're getting quite poetic here Cof - is this you protesting too much?"

"Just another rant, something that used to get on my tits in the old days. So where was I?"

"Your wide range of girlfriends, even including slim ones - presumably with very small tits." The laugh in her voice was almost a giggle.

"Yes, lots of girlfriends. Usually one at a time, although I did strike lucky on a couple of occasions with girls that were happy to share."

"Like the twins?"

I ignored the interjection and tried to slide towards safer ground. "At the time of the Crash, my romantic interest was a Columbian girl, Anna-

132

Maria, who lived in New York. She was an agent for holiday home projects on the Island, selling or renting them to the Manhattan jet set. She spent about two weeks a month in Barbados and stayed with me whenever she was here."

"So a 50% girlfriend was sufficient?"

"We didn't have much of a romantic relationship - it was basically sexual. Whenever Anna was about, we fucked like rabbits. If she was back in New York, I had occasional one night stands - just as she certainly did in the Big Apple. It was completely relaxing. Thinking about it, we must have been together for about nine months, which may be a record for me."

"You seem to be scared of close relationships."

"I don't think scared is the right word. I just don't rush into things. You know, the old marry in haste, repent in leisure kind of thing. I suppose that, if you were being Freudian, you'd probably say that Andrea fulfilled some of the needs for companionship and support; the maternal roles, which might otherwise have encouraged me to attain them via a long-term partner or wife. I honestly don't know. In any case, I was content and most of my relationships functioned well and eventually ended amicably. Many of my female friends are ex-lovers."

"What happened to Anna?"

"Fucked if I know!" My response was a bit harsh, but this was still a sore point. I took a deep breath and continued. "She was unlucky enough to be in NY on the 20th. Over the years I've tried

133

everything I can to trace her, but nothing, nada. At least seven large aircraft went down on top of the city and God knows how many smaller ones. High speed monorails crashed and two fusion plants suffered catastrophic loss on containment. The parts of Manhattan that didn't burn down were flooded by the first storm surge thereafter. On the 23rd, the entire state of New York was hit by a blizzard that lasted three days. The percentage mortality before any epidemic breakout must have been about the highest of any megacity in the West. Not really surprising that she vanished without trace."

We soaked together in silence for a couple of minutes before Sophie decided it was safe to press on. "So, what happened after the Crash? How did things change?"

"Everything was total chaos for the first couple of days, but I was one of a small number of men locked in with a bunch of frightened women. In fact I was the only single, eligible man: the others were all husbands or young sons of staff. There was a lot of comforting, clinging together for support. The families had each other and many of the women banded together, but there were those that looked for solace in the arms of a man."

"So this was all a premeditated act of charity?"

"Don't be silly, you know it wasn't; especially in the early days there was no planning and I had as much in need of comforting as anybody else. In fact, as time went on, I probably had a better idea of just how bad things were and how precarious our situation was, so I certainly needed opportunities to de-stress, chill-out. With the benefit of hindsight you might say that we were sitting pretty, living in luxury while the rest of the world went to hell in a handbasket. But, at the time, we hadn't a fuckin' clue. For all I knew, it could just be a matter of time before my firewalled computer system went the way of all the rest. We had defenses, but we had no idea what the capabilities of anyone who attacked us might have been. Somebody with a handful of serious weapons - a couple of bazookas or heavy machine guns, for example - could have walked all over us."

"Remind me to get you back on weapons later, Cof, but now we're discussing your love life. You started sleeping with the staff on the 20th... "

"The trauma of the Crash - and its aftermath - forged lots of intense relationships between the survivors. It also changed cultures, especially in the areas that were hardest hit. Barbados got off lightly, but the effects can still be seen. For the enlightened times of the '40s, this part of the Caribbean was considered rather backward; taboos against public nudity, brothels illegal, homosexuality frowned upon and stuff like that. Look at it now, prostitution is a major source of tax revenue around Bridgetown docks and the nearest beaches are packed with naked hookers of both sexes. One industry that doesn't seem to have come back is the manufacture of swim suits, as you can see on any Holetown waterfront... "

"Sleeping with staff!"

"I was coming to that! It's just important to note that a lot changed when our AI-controlled world vanished, things that went deeper than the physical effects of the Crash. So, I comforted some of the girls, women. In some cases we simply clung together in bed. In others we had wild, outrageous sex - reacting, no doubt, to the deep biological drive to propagate in times of threat. Men, spread your seed while you have a chance! Women, get pregnant, so the male has a vested genetic interest in protecting you! You can interpret it retrospectively however you want. We knew only that we had strong needs and no reasons to hold back, because who knew what the future had in store for us?"

"So it was like when they had power cuts last century - the lights went out and nine months later a baby boom. So there are now a lot of Cof-fathered rug-rats running around?"

"They'd hardly be rug-rats now, they'd be in their teens" I pointed out, pedantically. "Anyway, I'm happy to say that I'm confident in being still without issue - both legally and de facto. It was only after I began to accumulate my fortune that I noticed - or, to tell the truth, Andrea pointed out to me - that I was becoming more attractive to women. I hadn't been poor before, working away as a single research scientist, but this is a process that only seems to kick in when you get seriously rich. Thereafter, your pulling power for a certain class of women becomes directly proportional to your wealth."

"Gold diggers!"

"Exactly! Of course, in many cases they're easy to spot. If women - or, on a few occasions men - come out of the blue and start chatting you up, it rings alarm bells. But sometimes it's more subtle, maybe the women involved actually respond completely unconsciously to their growing awareness of just how much dosh you have. So you learn to take precautions. In my youth, I assumed all girls would be on the pill and my precautions were mainly associated with avoiding picking up a nasty disease. By the '20s, this was no longer a risk, so love was free, like in the old, hippy days after the contraceptive pill was invented."

"Then you got caught out?"

"Probably would have done, if a friend - actually more of an acquaintance, he really was a total wanker - hadn't been taken to the cleaners by three women, all with children genetically proven to be his. Had to pay a fortune in maintenance. To add insult to injury, the next he heard the three were living together: they were apparently lesbians who decided that they wanted to have some kids and came up with this plan for killing two birds with one stone, getting the kids plus a bit of funding into the bargain."

I couldn't help laughing again at the story. "The stupid cunt had been boasting for months to all his mates about this session he'd had with three hot nymphs, totally into everything dirty, especially girl on girl. We had assumed that they were actually hookers, but he swore that he never paid for sex."

137

I snorted inelegantly, remembering reading all about it on a chatsite. "By God, did he pay for that sex. He would have been cheaper renting a top-end brothel for a decade. I learned from his mistake though: went to the doc for a chemical vasectomy first thing."

"But that won't be reversible now!" Sophie sounded surprisingly concerned.

"Remember my paranoia! I wasn't going to have anything done that I wasn't sure that I could reverse - alone, if necessary. One little pill and I'm back in full operational status."

"And you haven't been tempted?"

"Not in the slightest! But, anyway, to get back to the story; this is why I can be sure that there wasn't going to be a batch of babes containing my genes for intelligence and beauty appearing around November 2041."

"And modesty, you forgot modesty."

"And modesty!" I agreed, immodestly.

"So... " the girl - woman, I had to keep reminding myself - seemed to be checking her notes "... your relationship to the staff changed after the 20th?"

"Well, when you sleep with someone, whether you have sex or not, it's a fairly irreversible change in your relationship. You can't unsleep with them and, unlike the earlier case with Lisa... "

"Our Lisa, that is?"

"Fuck, Sue promised she wouldn't tell a soul!"

"Well, think about it; she couldn't not tell me, could she? We're working together on this bloody masterpiece and we have to integrate all the input we can get. You're not going to censor it, are you?"

I thought about this good question for a moment. "That would be rather silly, I suppose, as my original purpose was to have a complete record of my experiences and my personal take on the apocalypse. Maybe I could go over it once it's finished and see if there would be any point in making an abridged version for wider distribution. You or Sue should remind me about this later."

"Nul Problemo: I've flagged it so the reminder will appear as soon as a complete text is logged. Now, back to shagging your staff."

"Whether shagged or unshagged, just then I didn't have the option of transferring staff to another division, as I did with Lisa. Or even to another employer, as would be possible in the olden days or, I guess, maybe even again now. For our first couple of years as an effectively closed community, we had to accept that we were locked up together and adopt an alternative way of living and working together. I tried to ensure that I didn't treat anyone that I had been intimate with any differently from the others. There have been a couple of uncomfortable situations over the years but, by and large, it's all worked out very well."

"But don't you think you flaunt it a bit, wandering about in the altogether when you're the only eligible man on the estate?"

"I try to be careful about that but, really, it was more of a problem pre-Crash, when the local Bajan girls were a bit more prudish. Andrea carefully

139

vetted them and tried to ensure that the women who were likely to encounter a naked Cof were the ones who wouldn't be bothered - or would only laugh at my feeble, pink body. There were plenty of jobs in the labs, hydroponics, office or wherever, where the worst that they'd have to encounter is me in shorts and a vest. So, even before things changed, it wasn't such a big deal; most of the locals considered me half mad anyway. There was one time, though, when an extremely tight-arsed God-botherer, but a wonderful cook, got transferred upstairs when the maid that usually does my room was down with some bug. Walked into the bedroom and through to the en-suite to find me in the bath with my sister. I thought she was going to have apoplexy." I couldn't help laughing as I remembered the look on the poor woman's face. Age has slowly blurred some images, but that one's as crisp as it was two decades ago.

"Good God, Cof! In bath with Andrea - that's pretty kinky?"

"And why would that be?"

"Well, it's a bit intimate, isn't it? Naked bodies touching... "

"At this very moment we're in a bath together" I pointed out. "We're naked and... " I moved closer so that my arm was in contact with her flank, "... our bodies are touching."

"Yes, but that's different. We're not ... " She seemed suddenly at a loss for words but, interestingly, I noticed that she didn't move away. "Well, anyway, this is all getting off the main issue - don't you think that you actually entice your

140

employees into your bed, encourage their attention?"

"Mmm, maybe I do. It's not deliberate or planned, but I certainly don't discourage relationships; not like I used to do in the past, anyway. Most of these are fairly superficial anyway; just physical, relaxing sex, nothing more to it. We may also be close friends, but it's not any kind of romantic, long-term partnership. We can keep at this level for years, but often the woman finds someone else, someone that they build up a romantic relationship with. In most cases they stay on as staff and we stay friends, but we just don't bonk anymore."

"So, no long-term regular relationships with anybody who works with you?"

"No, none."

"What about the twins then?" I finally opened my eyes and, through the diffuse pink glare of the setting sun, could make out a satisfied smirk. The hunter hearing the sound of the trap snap shut.

"I almost said that they don't work for me - but of course they do, though on a different basis from the rest of the girls, women."

"They both work on the search engines, some sort of programing. Why's that different from anybody else?"

"OK, we're now going confidential. You can record this - and, I suppose, discuss it with Sue - but nobody else, please."

Sophie noticed that I was looking directly at her, so she just nodded silently.

"Right, the twins' programing work isn't their job, it's their payment - or at least, part of it." I grinned at the woman's evident confusion. "They're paid for services rendered and, maybe in some way, I decided on this option to reduce some of the problems with my relationships with other staff. They come from some unpronounceable part of what was once the Soviet Union; a country so chaotic and riddled with corruption and ethnic conflicts that it was still a fairly rough place in the '40s, despite the best efforts of the AIs. They identified Barbados as a retreat for international playboys, so came here to ply the oldest profession. Actually arrived on 1st February 2041 but, despite a lack of any local knowledge, had enough street smarts to make it through the Dying and, eventually to get established in Bridgetown where... "

"Hookers! They're prostitutes?"

"Executive level companions and consorts, I'd call them. That's what they're paid for. But, you know how this place is - I thought it was better to bring them in nominally as computer support and just leave any other roles they may have open to speculation. The funny thing is that they're both smart as shit and are actually getting into the programing side. I'm training them up now as a partial payment for their services. With the way AIs bootstrapped their own development, computing is a bit of a lost art nowadays, so I'm sure they'll do very well for themselves when they retire from their current line of work.

Sophie seemed still to be perturbed. "Do you think it's alright to pay for sex then?"

"Why not? Here it's an open transaction with no strings attached; just what I'm looking for at present. Would that be very different from picking up any of the hundreds of girls who'd give their left arm to live in a place like this? I could call them girlfriends, but it would still be sex in exchange for the lifestyle I can offer."

"Umm... " she was clearly unhappy, but couldn't see an obvious counter to my argument. "Well, how did you select them? It's not like you could look them up on the internet or a telephone book at the time that you recruited them." The sarcasm on recruited was palpable. "That was about five years ago, I guess."

"Yes, just over five pleasure-filled years, half a decade of disgusting, commercial three-in-a-bed sex!" I glanced to the side to check that I was winding her up successfully; very successfully if the way she was hammering the keyboard was anything to go by. "Anyway, as usual, it was Andrea who selected them - who actually came up with this idea in the first place."

"Your sister pimped for you!" This idea seemed to be more shocking for my scribe that the revelation that the twins were ladies of the night.

"Pimped! Now there's a word I haven't heard for a long time. If you mean helped organize a mutually beneficial relationship that has probably contributed significantly to the harmony in this little cloister, then the answer is yes. But this isn't the

143

usual connotation of the word, implying exploitation of the girls and commercial gain for the pimp. Talk to the twins sometime; they certainly don't give the impression of being exploited in any way. In fact, to me, they seem happy as pigs in shit."

"But they have to say that to you. You're their employer after all."

"As I said, have a chat to them. They're open and honest about their jobs and my slight deception about their work description wasn't to protect them, just to avoid disturbing some of the less worldly of my entourage: like yourself, for example."

She rose directly to the bait, turning to glare at me and revealing that her nipples were notably erect, seeming somewhat out of place on her tiny breasts. I wondered if it was anger or the proximity of my naked body that was causing the effect, sincerely hoping it was the latter.

"I'm not at all prudish and don't really give a shit if you feel that you have to pay for sex. It just seems to set things up for exploitation of women who were in a vulnerable position after the Crash."

I felt a bit guilty then for teasing her, so I responded in a conciliatory tone. "I agree that lots of people, in particular younger girls - and boys - have been exploited, and this will probably continue as long as there is an imbalance between the rich and the poor. Helping to accelerate recovery is the best possible way I can think of to help those at the bottom of the heap. As I explained before, we're physically restricted here - we just can't bring a load of outsiders in to share the luxury that we have here. Equally, it would be masochistic for us to degrade the standard of living that we have, just out of solidarity with the rest of the world. So what we can do is support technology transfer and help physically with getting a working infrastructure that is at least the level of late 20th century. I, personally, think that the world may end up a better place if we are clever in the way we set things up."

"Three questions then... " the analytical mind had conquered emotions again I noted. "... firstly, you supply information at a price; you were very rich beforehand, but now you're one of the richest people on the planet. How is that helping equality?"

I lifted my hands out of the water as I started to respond, but received a matronly slap to indicate that Sophie wasn't finished. "Secondly! You say that you're doing all you can to help, but there must be lots of tools and gadgets that we use for trivial purposes - cleaning the pool or cutting the grass - which could be invaluable outside. Why don't we lose just a little bit of luxury to contribute to an increased quality of life outside? And thirdly, most importantly, you and some other geeks who survived the apocalypse with functioning hardware are now making decisions that will influence the entire future of the world. Who gave you the right? What happened to the democratic process?"

"Three very good questions; I'll have to think a bit about them. Actually, I suppose there are four questions, if you include the one about democracy? That's the only one that's easy to answer.

145

Democracy is a luxury that you can have in times of peace and plenty. Otherwise it's just plain stupid. It's like all the shit about referenda - letting the public decide if you will have nuclear power or a tax on aviation fuel. Most big issues are far too complex for the idiots in the street to make any sensible decision about them. The whole thing then becomes a battle between spin-doctors and advertising agencies. Not a very good way to run things. Look at the old US system for electing presidents if you want to see how fucked up democracy can get. Not just one Bush, but two of the useless wankers."

"You're ranting again, Cof! You really don't mean to say that a dictatorship or hereditary monarchy is preferable to a democracy, do you?"

"That's exactly what I do mean" I ranted. "Well, the dictatorship anyway. Inbreeding is never a good way to select for brains, look at the Bush imbeciles for example."

I caught a hard stare and tried to tie my raving to the original question. "Benign dictatorship, though, just the thing you need when times get tough. Or, under war conditions, a tight military Junta. It's not called that, of course, but look at the countries that were very good at war - Israel or Afghanistan - run by tight military groups who were well separated from any democratic control. On the other hand, look at the ones that were crap. The US of A immediately springs to mind; the most powerful land on the planet after the middle of the 20th century and they got scrubbed in every conflict they got into thereafter. Super-power technology against jungle-bunnies with machetes or ragheads with flintlocks - and the Yanks got completely humiliated, time and time again. Why? Because they had a democracy that messed into all top layers of the administration and a democratically elected commander-in-chief."

"So you'd scrap it all, set up a plutocratic Brave New World?"

"Not at all, the public can have all the democracy they want, but only after we get things basically sorted out. Here the we is defined simply as those who possess power at present. They're a self-selected bunch, but with proven abilities: they not only survived a catastrophe of biblical proportions, but they moved to the top in the process. They are exactly the people needed to get things working, not some complete tosser that people will vote for because he has a great smile or she has a strong position on woman's rights. We can't afford that now; they would only fuck things up! We're so vulnerable, even now, that one idiot would probably be enough to set us back years. After everyone has electricity and running water and our medical services function again, then we can consider having elections. I guess that, if we can get a generally accessible internet and some form of TV up again, the public will eventually get organized and make their demands known."

"Why do I feel that this is all too pat? At present, you and your buddies are having fun playing global strategists. So, as soon as you are asked, you'll give it all up and meekly hand over the reins to whoever is chosen by the public - the great unwashed as you previously called them?"

"Well, honestly, I don't think we'll have a choice. After things get back to a certain level of organization there'll be police, armies, bureaucrats and politicians. They'll demand control and will have the power to take it, if we don't just hand it over."

"And you don't have any back-up plans? Plots hatched with your pal David?"

"David's all set up anyway. If they had elections in the Falklands tomorrow, he could get himself elected emperor for life, if he wanted. But he's a geek; he'd shit himself at the thought of having administrative responsibility. He'd much rather be behind the skirting board than sitting in state in the throne room."

"But that's you too! You don't want to be King of Barbados, or even the whole Caribbean for that matter. Then you'd have responsibilities, you wouldn't be able to pick and choose which hobby projects you play with."

"It's a fair cop, guv!" I tried my best, but still rather rubbish, imitation of a Brit wide boy. "Note this down as another point we've to come back to. Nevertheless, much though I'd like to chat further, I see my leather-clad Domina is waiting by her instrument of torture, so it's time for me to get a sound thrashing. I guess this must be me exploiting another poor, defenseless woman!"

Katya had been standing silently by the massage table for the last ten minutes, evidently

148

fascinated by what she was overhearing. She smiled at us as I extricated my lobster body from the pool. "Not leather: a miracle, breathing, self-cleaning fabric of the kind that we can't make any more. I'm hell'va glad that it's almost indestructible. But what's this about exploitation? Old Sophie there think we don't get paid enough? What'd we do with more credits? There's just about bugger all outside that's worth buying? You need more coconuts and bananas, Sophie love?"

It was bad enough me goading the small woman, but she wasn't going to be slagged-off by a personal trainer. "We were talking about physical exploitation, Cof's manipulation of some of the more vulnerable bimbos on his staff."

I quickly dried off and clambered onto the table, metaphorically keeping my head down. There had been a bit too much emphasis on bimbos for it to be anything else but a direct insult.

Katya was completely unperturbed. "It's all a matter of self-respect, I suppose. If you consider yourself an abused slave or servant, then that's what you are. For myself, this is just a hobby. I originally trained to be an accountant but, by the time I graduated, it was a profession that had gone the way of tanners and candlestick-makers. Andrea brought me in to manage the financial side of this ark, which took about fifteen minutes a day before the Big Bang and vanished again thereafter. Now I help organize logistics. I like to work out and it's much more fun if I can torture Cof at the same time."

149

Sophie was now on the defensive. "But now you're massaging him. A bit menial for someone with your background, wouldn't you say?"

"You've got to be joking," the trim blond laughed, "this is the highlight of my day. I have an hour to inflict as much pain as I like on his flabby bod. There's lots of girls would pay money to change places with me."

"Do you find that an erotic experience?" Now there was less aggression in my secretary's voice, more curiosity.

I smirked at the question and was rewarded with a slap on my left buttock that sounded like a gunshot and was seriously painful. "Lovey," I could tell Katya was smiling even though I was face down with my eyes closed, "if I could get your naked body on this table, that would be an erotic experience!" I would bet that my masseuse would be leering theatrically at this point. Another slap, to my right buttock this time. "This useless hunk of manflesh, however, is a mere plaything that allows me to burn the latent sadism out of my system."

"Latent? You really sound like a dominatrix."

"Everybody needs a hobby!"

That seemed to have killed that conversation, I thought, as Katya started on my shoulders, strong fingers instantly finding the muscles that had been abused during my swim and starting to ease out the resultant knots. It was painful, of course, but despite her claims to the contrary, she was the gentlest of my massage team. I would, in fact be happy for her to work me over more regularly, but these massages came only after her own training sessions. As she explained to me, *if I break it, I fix it*, although this seemed to apply only to my body and not my self-respect.

I wondered how much the perceptive Sophie had picked up. My trainer had also been taking the piss with regard to her sexual orientation. I knew that she'd had a boyfriend in Holetown for the last couple of years and I'd heard rumors that she was actually now living in a threesome with two guys. If she was, good on her: she was certainly fit enough for two, or probably more, come to think about it. Anyway, although we were close friends and I was spending increasing time with her in her accountant role as I developed plans for the IBS, we never discussed personal matters. It wasn't a taboo subject or anything, just that we always found more interesting things to discuss.

Although occasional shocks of pain ensured that I didn't drift off completely, the soothing manipulation of tired muscles sent me into a sort of daydream. I was still thinking of the unanswered questions, but these were leading to flashbacks to the chaotic months after the Crash and, especially, the terror of the Dying.

It was all related to one of the hardest questions for me: could I have done more? Of course, when I looked back with the benefits of hindsight, there's probably lots more help that I could have provided without risking my little community. At the time, however, we had little idea about what was happening in the outside world. We were all frightened and Andrea and I decided that we had always to err on the side of caution.

The outbreak of cholera was a direct consequence of catastrophic failure of the sewerage system and contamination of much of the drinking water used in Bridgetown. If I'd known that then, I could have knocked up an industrial water sterilization system and, maybe, enough solar panels to run it. Apart from my ignorance, at that time very few people were aware of our existence. The little bit of surviving administrative infrastructure vanished when people started getting very sick and dying in droves. I've gone through it in my head dozens of times; I had the technology to save a lot of lives, but not the manpower - or womanpower - to implement it safely. Maybe, after Darcy, I could have used my notoriety to group my neighbors within the parish together and start implementing some of the projects that, as it was, came only years later. But here Sophie was definitely right. This isn't the kind of thing that I do. I can plan things or put together the kit to make ideas work, but I hate actually going out and dealing with people. Deep down I might be a cross between M and Q, but I'll never be an 007!

Chapter 6 - Yardy trouble

It was only day three of my literary project, but, when Sue appeared at the breakfast table, it seemed like a routine was already established. I had considered making a record of the destruction and rebuilding of civilization for a couple of years now, but the activation energy needed to sit down in front of a computer or dictating machine or whatever to get things started was just too much. This option, working with two scribes as my sister suggested, was actually turning out to be fun. True, I was being forced to go to places that I really didn't want to, but maybe that would be an important contribution to the value of the final product. The first couple of days had been an experiment; putting a toe in the water to see if taking the plunge would be sensible. If I'd ground to a halt - or got pissed-off or bored - I'd have simply jacked the whole thing in and started on something new. There was certainly no shortage of interesting projects to work on.

After introductory pleasantries over a first cup of coffee, Sue came straight to the point. "We now have about a dozen threads that we could pick up on but, personally, I'd like to know more about your little Renaissance group. Just what are you up to and how do you see things developing globally over the next decade?"

Blunt and to the point. Somehow I didn't expect anything else. A silent sigh, a sip of black coffee and then I started to break the question down into digestible chunks. "OK, how about the group first, what I would like it to do second and my view of how things might go over the next few years third?"

"Sounds fine to me, although this second bit makes it sound like your group functions democratically. That can't be true, surely?" She was smiling as she raised this question.

"Not at all; you couldn't get further from democracy. But I'll get to all that after you've got some background on the group members." She made a sign of zipping her lips that I remembered from the day before yesterday and settled down to listen.

"The first incarnation of the Global Contact Group, as some insisted on calling it, was simply the individuals with radios who passed on information on local conditions to each other. These were mainly ham radio nutters with some local power source, usually rooftop solar or something similar; simple and robust. In the early days this group had constantly changing membership, mainly losses as the Dying decimated populations and gave survivors more critical concerns with day to day existence, making hobby radio too expensive a luxury. We did, however, get a few new additions, some of these being teams or communities that retained - or managed to rapidly cobble together - some working infrastructure and were now searching for similar oases of technology. This is the basis that really evolved into what is often called today the Renaissance group, although a basic radio communication network still exists that acts as a major conduit for international news, especially from the regions that were hit hardest or had no surviving technology hotspots."

Now I was on auto-pilot, tracing the way in which some members of the unbelievably diverse groups that managed to establish international telecommunication links ended up evolving into a global cabal who were making fundamental decisions that would influence how the planet dug itself out of the pit that it was presently in.

A single example : English. Anybody possessing working computers that were any way 21st century had smart translation on tap. It probably was one of the applications resulting from AIs that did most damage to civilization, set it back years. Translation on tap, not only from one stupid language into another, but even from incredibly daft local dialects into others that were equally useless. This is where democracy is nothing but part of the problem. Get a bunch of politicos sitting around a table trying to sort out international languages for communication. You can be sure that vested interests, complemented by a vast amount of arse-covering, will ensure that nothing sensible ever results.

One of the first meetings of the Renaissance team led to the simple operational proposal that we work exclusively in English, thus avoiding all the shit with side-conversations going on in Spanish or Mandarin. It took us about ten minutes to agree this. We then set up the IBS, with services in English only. Dave and I, as the biggest suppliers of knowledge, not only set all support in our mother tongue, we also offered only commercial translation of other languages to English, not vice-versa. So now, only a few years later, we really do have an international language and a very high power team committed to keeping it this way.

This, finally, got too much for Sue and she couldn't help breaking in. "For fuck's sake, Cof, that's not your call to make. All these fantastic languages that could end up dying... "

"Fucking absofuckinglutely bang on! All these beautiful, but fundamentally useless languages will either die or persist as local voodoo that lets the locals take the piss out of visitors. They won't clog the path towards getting the fucking planet functioning again. Jesus suffering Christ on a bike! Half the tossers remaining on this poor forsaken globe can't even speak, read and write one language properly. Why make it more difficult for the intellectually challenged? One single language - the most bastardized that we currently have - English. Time will quickly eliminate all the nonsensical spelling and stupid grammar from the core British variant, especially as it has to incorporate more and more words and concepts from other cultures. You'll end up with something like Esperanto, but user-friendly, because it will emerge from a consensus of the Hoi Polloi, rather than the research project of an anal professor of linguistics."

"You and your pals have the right to just take it on yourselves to eliminate French, German, Cantonese, Arabic... ?"

156

"Of course: because, if we didn't do it, nobody else would have! Let's face it, it's all total touchy-feely shite! Why the fuck, if we have one planet, do we need more than one fucking language? The fact that hordes of the fucking things persisted into the middle of the 21st century is a triumph of jingoism over fucking common sense. You, as one of a very small percentage with the capacity and interest to master more than one tongue, may have a vested interest in keeping this polyglot albatross around our collective necks. But, from a practical viewpoint - saving lives rather than the quality of the polyphonic church music - what does even a second language contribute to the betterment of mankind?"

Sue wiped a hand over her face, apparently trying to drag up a logically argument to support a case that she believed in with all her heart. "That could be technically sound, but ethically... " She was clutching at straws, and knew it.

I almost felt sympathy while I ground my way through the rest of the argument, but not enough to hold back. "Fuck ethics! We lost at least five billion people in the Crash and the Dying. How many of them had such strong ethical principles that they would have supported an abstract idea rather than their own continued existence? Maybe 0.1%, being on the generous side. Now, if the ethical concept was as abstruse as the preservation of a second class language, who'd die for that? A few sad-bastard professors of linguistics, but nobody whose genes would contribute to the pool. Best rid of the stupid cunts, is what I'd say!"

"I wouldn't try to argue that getting this post-meltdown can of worms sorted out absolutely requires a single international language, but it'll certainly go a lot faster if we have one. I pushed it, the others agreed: maybe because I've got better databases than they have, but now it's a fait accompli. Did I do wrong? Mightn't this have saved lots of lives and maybe prevent even more loss of life in the future? Tell me I'm wrong!"

Realizing that she was on shaky ground here, Sue moved the topic of my rant. "Apart from enforcing English, what other global dictates have you up your sleeve?"

"More important than English is certainly the IBS. A single world bank and a single currency. No money markets and currency traders anymore."

"Yes, I can remember how you felt about them."

"More importantly, though, we can use the bank to facilitate trade. If we can get the Falklands and Barbados models widely accepted, all taxation will be standardized and run through local bank offices. Transactions can be inspected by anyone, which instantly eliminates a lot of dodgy practices. No trade tariffs or protectionism, a simple, easy open way of keeping track of debits and credits that is available to all regions as soon as they manage to emerge from the barter economy that the Crash drove them to."

"This is all a bit too pat, Cof. The spiel sounds like you've used it before, probably to cover your tracks on some bit of skullduggery that you're up to. Out with it!"

I pursed my lips and was about to explain further, then stopped myself. Why should I do all the work? I was the boss and was supposed to be having fun. "Maybe it'd be more interesting to see if you can work it out for yourself. I think you actually have all the pieces now: take the input that I've given you this morning and use it to determine our cunning plan."

The raven-haired woman first looked annoyed at my tactics, but then smiled in a somewhat feral manner as she accepted the challenge. "What do I get if I work it out?"

"God, but you're a mercenary bitch! OK, if you work out the entire plot, then I'll answer any other question that you want. If you don't get it, I'll just move on to another one of your loose threads and this will hang here until you and Sophie crack it yourselves."

"Deal!" she responded immediately: a bit too fast for my liking. I couldn't see how, but my scribe's wide grin seemed to indicate that I'd been suckered once again.

Now there was a frown of concentration on her brow. "So you've identified universal banking and one language as major contributions made by your group, whose very name indicates that members are dedicated to rebuilding a new, improved civilization from the ashes of the old. If you think of the way that the first Chinese empire of Qin was established, a single language and currency were critical

159

components. There were also standardized weights and measures, but we had that kind of stuff well established worldwide last century and this, at least, hasn't been lost. There was also the Great Wall, but, for a unified planet, there's nobody to keep out. What else? Emperor Qin also built roads to allow rapid transportation of goods and his armies, with standardized axle length of wagons and chariots, if I remember correctly. He also set up a system that led to the bureaucracy that administered the Middle Kingdom for two millennia."

A smile made her already pretty face glow, transfused with the beauty of satisfaction from an intellectual challenge mastered. "Administration! That's what it must be. You're trying to lever in a world government!"

I smiled back. "That was very quick! Yes, we agreed that a sensible goal is to eliminate the old national governments, the entire idea of national identities if we can. One planetary government, complemented by local or regional administration for districts of a sensible size, certainly small enough that any administrators needed are well known to the public they serve and vice versa."

"Nice idea, Cof, but it won't catch on. People are proud of their national identities."

"Total crap! National identities are concepts forced on impressionable youths by people who want to manipulate them, get them to join an army, pay taxes that allow superfluous levels of administration to exist, support a football team. That's the role of languages and dialects: to separate population groups, limit their communication and build up rivalry. If we have an effective local admin structure - set up using only English - then we only need one level of government above that to provide standardization and oversee issues that transcend local boundaries. A single world government: why not? One set of laws, rules and regulations that avoids duplication of effort and maximizes efficiency when we need to get things done."

"All good arguments, but will the people accept it?"

"If the Crash had happened earlier in the century, probably not. National governments were just too strong and had indoctrinated populations into believing their absolute necessity. A decade of AIs changed this a lot. The huge global problems, most of which could be ultimately traced to overpopulation, demanded international solutions. The success of the strategies devised by the Artificial Intelligences was rapidly eroding the roles of national governments. If the AIs hadn't been wiped out, I'd guess that national governments would, in any case, have died a natural death by the end of the century. We're just hurrying the process on and replacing the benevolent global dictatorship that the AIs provided with a more simplified one of our own."

"World domination! Your team doesn't lack chutzpah, I'll say that for them."

"Maybe so, but we've taken the job because, at the present time, there's nobody else to do it. We do recognize our limitations, though. As you commented before, we're a self-selected group that, by its very nature, tends to be technical. We can solve technical problems and plan optimized strategies for global government, but we don't have the experience to form a legislative body, even with all the support of our knowledge bases and smart search engines. We still need to hack out an implementation plan, but the general idea will be to set up a paid legislation team, selected on the basis of their qualifications, who will work together with our unpaid technical support group. Eventually, when it becomes practical, the legislators could be elected and actually meet together rather than communicating by radio and our proto-internet."

Sue remained silent while I spent an hour outlining the various options that we had considered and the systems we had tested already. Our main concern was to avoid the mistakes of the past and the fundamental dichotomy of politics: the types of people who wanted to be politicians were exactly the power-crazed, untrustworthy, inherently corrupt types that were unsuited to the job. So, initially at least, make this a paid rather than elected job and recruit the best people we could find. We'd certainly not end up with the most ethnically- and gender-balanced team, but this didn't really matter as long as they got the job done. The critical issue was to ensure that they were transparently honest, to assure public confidence. Here again we simply set up the communication links so that all were open, recorded and could be inspected by anyone at any time. No meetings in camera or lobbying behind closed doors. Of course, our single language policy and open bank records would also help a lot here.

When I eventually ground to a halt, Sue looked a stunned. "I always knew that you were a megalomaniac, but didn't quite realize the scope of your hubris until now" she muttered.

"Is there anything you need clarified? You've been unusually quiet."

"It's a bit too much for me to get my head round at present, so let me take a rain check on that. I'll go over this script with Sophie first and then get back to you."

"Fine." I stretched and bones creaked from sitting to long in a single position. "How about a run before lunch?"

"Who're you training with?" she asked cautiously.

"It's Di today, so running will be safe enough. Just don't let her get you into the dojo. She's discovered some kind of Russian thing, Systema or Spetsnaz Sambo I think it's called. It's brutal in any case."

"So what will the running involve?"

"It's too hot to do much outside, so we'll start in the gym on running machines. Then it'll be some short, sharp reps along the beach."

"OK, why not! I'll just go and get some kit."

"See you in the gym in ten minutes."

***

163

Di is a very unlikely-looking personal trainer. The kind of adjectives that would come to mind when you see her - especially, as now, in spray-on, garish, pink lycra - would be bounteous, curvaceous, well-upholstered. But certainly not sporty. She looks like she might be a cook. In fact, her other job is head of security. Apart from anything else, she has black belts in at least half a dozen martial arts, most of which I had never even heard of until she painfully introduced them to me.

Large breasts, thighs and a well-rounded belly would tempt you to assume that she was flabby. That would be a serious mistake; the generous layer of adipose concealed muscles of steel. She could easily bench-press double my best effort and she ran like a machine. Once, for a laugh, we put the running machines on maximum gradient and tried for six minute kilometers. Ten kph sounds bloody slow, but it's painfully fast on a 15% slope. I died in about five minutes, just about fell off the machine. When I could finally stand again, I had a drink and went for a walk to calm down. I came back about fifteen minutes later and she was still chugging away. Tough or what?

It was six minute kilometers again today for warm up, but on a 3% slope. I was in the middle, with Sue on my left and the formidable Di on my right. Our machines were slaved to Di's, so we had no choice when the gradient went up to 5% after ten minutes. The trick, as for swimming, was to stay as relaxed as possible. Try to make strides as long and smooth as possible and then think about something else. I had originally worried that Sue had planned to continue my interrogation during training but, even if that had been her intent, she was soon panting so much that this was no longer an option. After a couple of minutes at 5%, Sue was puffing so hard that Di relented and dropped her speed to seven minute kilometers. I made the mistake of starting to object about the unfairness of this - and had my speed upped to five point five. Why, I cursed myself, do I never learn? Do Not Provoke Your Trainer. I tried to nail this mental post-it onto the middle of my stupid forehead.

I was getting close to the point of deciding that I was going to have to beg for forgiveness when the gradient dropped to zero and it actually felt as if I was coasting downhill. Speed went up to 12 kph, then gradually ramped up, ... 13... 14... 15. I was starting to suffer a bit, but it still was not anything as bad as the slower pace at 5%. Then the speed ramped down and soon we were at walking pace for the interim cool down.

I had almost stopped sweating when the machines stopped and Di led us down to the beach. Sue vainly attempted to escape, but was sternly told that, if you started a training session with Di, then you finished it. I suspected that this would be the last time that my secretary would join me for any of my daily exercise sessions.

The exposed sand of the beach extended about half a kilometer between two rocky headlands. A 200m stretch had been marked out: simple lines scratched in the sand showing the start and finish.

Straightforward enough; repetition sprints with two minutes recovery between them. Sue didn't look too worried, even when it was explained that one of these minutes would be spent doing jumping jacks, if you finished more than three seconds behind Di. Sue was tall and slim and Di was, well, Di-shaped. I guess it looked like a fairly sure thing, if you didn't have a lot of experience in running in soft sand. We took off our shoes on the lawn - beach runs were bare foot - and I attempted to help by advising Sue to aim for the firmer sand near the water's edge. She evidently thought I was trying to con her so, for the first run at least, she did the exact opposite - and finished a good fifteen seconds behind the pink leviathan.

We did ten reps; I had jumping jacks after six of them and Sue after them all. Latterly, she wasn't even attempting to race: keeping up some kind of running speed was a defense mechanism only, to ensure that our trainer wouldn't impose further penalties. When we finally finished, she collapsed against me, an arm around my neck. "Cof, you bastard, you knew this was going to happen!"

"I didn't know, but I must confess that I did hope!" I smiled and suddenly felt a lot fresher. The cool breeze of Schadenfreude. "I always feel better if someone has had a tougher time than me in one of these sessions" I admitted.

Suddenly an evil grin appeared on her sweaty, sandy face. "Of course, I've still got a free question that you've got to answer" she reminded me. "That should be something for you to ponder over lunch."

166

Maybe encouraging Sue to do the run wasn't such a clever idea after all. A real recipe for indigestion. Don't Bait The Scribes. Yet another mental note to self, which would probably obscure more important ones buried below.

***

Sue joined me for a light lunch of flying fish fingers: a true Bajan delicacy, especially when washed down with a glass of ice cold Chablis. The wine was a rare treat, an attempt to butter-up my nemesis, who smiled smugly throughout the meal. She certainly had something nasty up her sleeve.

We took coffees through to my study and settled into deep leather swivel chairs, the kind you used to get in the boardrooms of Fortune Five Hundred companies. "OK", I started, eager to hear the worst, "fire away."

"You told us all about the Darcy thing, but there was something else, wasn't there? Some other threat to our community that you and Andrea handled."

This was about as bad as it could get. "Could be..." I responded cautiously.

"... and does this have anything to do with the two fingers that are missing on your sister's left hand?"

"Fuck!" my response was involuntary. I couldn't make out how much they knew and how much was inspired guess work. Well, I suppose it had to come out sometime - I just wished that I'd had more time to get my story straightened out.

"I take it that's a yes." The smile definitely reminded me of a cat that's been at the cream.

"Yes, fuck! It's just a bit complicated. It could easily sound like over-reaction. You had to see it in context."

"You're waffling, Cof dear. Just get on with the story, you can put in your excuses later."

I sat back and closed my eyes, willing myself to be calm. Not easy when I ever think about this fiasco. "Right, it was about six years ago, just when things were starting to settle down and we could see progress with rebuilding. That's when the Yardie trouble started."

"Yardie?"

"Jamaican - but the term is mainly used now to refer to the gangs that came out of the Island."

"Jamaica, that's where about six years ago... "

"Look, do you want to hear the story or not?" I knew I was being a bit ratty, looking for an excuse to stomp off in high dudgeon, thus avoiding having to go into some painful territory.

Again the lips were silently zipped closed, so I had no choice but to continue. Well, something like this really had to go into any record of the apocalypse, although it would certainly need to be significantly censored before it could be considered for general distribution. I squirmed a bit, but the obvious way forward was to get the story down and then worry about sanitizing it afterwards. Trying to censor it in real time just wouldn't work.

"OK, back to just before the apocalypse. At that time, the gangs of Jamaican thugs who were responsible for a lot of drug trafficking in the Caribbean, and also places like England, were really suffering. The AIs were blocking loopholes and even the smartest of the gang-lords were feeling the cordon of control tightening around them. At the beginning of the century, and even before that, I suppose, organized crime had been very fast to take advantages of new developments in technology. As the primitive internet evolved into the universal U control and communication system, gangsters not only employed a host of geeks who specialized in electronic crime, but also used it to support their other, well established criminal activities: sale of illegal porn, prostitution, drugs. By the mid '30s, however, the police AI systems were closing all this down. In response, the gangs went back to low tech, replacing high-tech weapons that could be shut down remotely by knifes and old-fashioned sawn-off shotguns, smuggling drones with sailing ships, internet telephony with couriers... "

I suppose it is a reflection of the power and the flexibility of the human brain that, despite a decade of world control by the AIs, crime still wasn't stamped out. Probably the main contribution towards reducing crime was removing the abject poverty that was a breeding ground for much of it, but direct head-on conflict with the major established criminal organizations - Mafia in both its Italian and Russian incarnations, Triads, Yakuza and all the others - had little direct impact. In fact, the way in which criminals were forced to rely on pre-AI technology to avoid detection by the nanny U, placed them in a good position to be able to continue in the chaos that developed when QC controls melted down.

Major criminal organizations have always tended to follow the concentrations of populations, so they were hit just as hard as the general public by the QC crash and subsequent Dying. The gangsters may have avoided technology for their illegal activities, but they liked the luxury that could be provided in their home lives as much as anybody. As a few of the mega-cities began to slowly recover, organized crime was inevitably re-established. We've had many long discussions about how the IBS could be structured to make it difficult for mobsters, but so far we haven't come up with anything that would have more than a mild nuisance value.

A discrete clearing of Sue's throat acted to guide me back on route. "The gangs in rural areas weren't hit so bad and, as you would imagine, amongst the best off were those on Caribbean islands: the largest and most powerful being the Yardie gangs based in Kingston, Jamaica."

Jamaica is much larger than Barbados, with a similar solid agricultural basis that provided the basis for rapid recovery. However, it had also a much higher population with much of that urban: for example greater Kingston originally had a population of almost two million. The larger towns and cities had a high initial death toll, setting the

170

scene for a series of epidemics that were catalyzed by the tropical heat, including cholera, typhoid and malaria. Nevertheless, the tight-knit Yardie gangs managed to persist throughout this period and, by the time that recovery had begun, had taken effective control of the Island. Although there was inevitable bloodshed during initial turf wars, gang leaders eventually got organized and started to coordinate their activities, something quite novel for these mobs who, in the past, were known more for their reckless violence than any ability for sophisticated crime.

I was running out of general background and could see that Sue was getting impatient. "So, by the late '40s, Jamaica was a state run by Yardie warlords. The country was medieval in terms of its brutality, but provided a huge power base for the gangs. By that time, tentative inter-island trading was being established and the Yardies were already expanding from their past dealing in marijuana and crack cocaine to plundering of shipping and coastal communities, re-establishing pirate lifestyles that had been eliminated from the Caribbean centuries before."

"And this is going where?"

No way I could put it off any longer. "By the beginning of the '50s, Yardie ships were all over the Caribbean. Mainly concentrated in the north, but regularly seen around Barbados and St. Lucia. Mostly drug smuggling, but ships disappeared mysteriously and remote communities were raided, which was attributed to the Yardies although, by then, they weren't the only pirates in these waters."

Another warning cough over my bows, forcing me to tack round to address the original question. "That was when Andrea was kidnapped."

"What? Six years ago? I've never heard about that." My scribe was clearly perturbed to find such a large gap in her knowledge.

"Only members of the security team were aware that Andrea was missing for a bit, but they don't know any details. Nobody does, except Andrea, of course, and Tina."

"Andrea was kidnapped... " Sue was keen to hear the story.

"As things got better outside, she was spending more time actively helping with reconstruction: training people, finding out bottlenecks in projects and determining if we could use any of our kit to help. Our workshop and lab, in particular,... "

"We can get more of that later. Andrea was kidnapped... " The woman was relentless.

Another heavy sigh and I forced myself on. "One day, she just didn't return. I didn't notice anything in particular, because she and Tina had by then started spending some nights back in their own place, which they'd set up as a kind of low tech hideaway. It was Tina who started to really worry and got me to set up an image recognition scan on all my video monitors. The only match I got was a distant image in the port of Bridgetown, of all places. She was accompanied by five large black men with long dreadlocks. She didn't seem to be under duress but, as I maxed the resolution of the image in slo mo, I noticed how she bent as if to tie her shoe lace, but actually untied it as she glanced directly at the camera. Seconds later she was walking again, shoelace trailing, and vanished from our field of view."

"I remember Tina, who was standing at my side, being perplexed by this strange behavior, but it sent a cold shiver up my spine. Andrea had spent enough time with me checking these video feeds; she'd know roughly where the cameras were in Bridgetown. She'd also know that, if I was looking for her, I'd use my search engines on the video feeds, looking for any sign of her or anything that the smart software would pick up as anomalous behaviour. She had given me both."

"But, if she was being kidnapped, why wasn't she struggling. Even if someone in the area didn't help her, it would be even more certain that your search would pick it up."

"That's the reason for the cold shiver! It was clear to me that there was a message in the fact that she wasn't struggling... "

Sue quickly spotted that she was being tested and responded with a small frown. "Mmm... struggling would get you onto her quicker, but not struggling communicates a message - or maybe it's just too dangerous. These guys have made it very clear that they're not to be fucked with, so anything beyond tying a shoelace is too dangerous."

"Exactly, either too dangerous for her to attempt or, maybe, a warning to me. In either case, I

173

was scared shitless. This wasn't somebody threatening the estate, when I had all my resources here to hand, this was someone who had targeted my sister and had taken her out of my reach. I was almost in tears."

"It was already dark by then and I was all for cycling into Bridgetown to look for her. It was Tina who stopped me, convincing me that I hadn't a hope against a team of thugs. I didn't back down because of fear, though, more recognition of the sheer logistical problems of finding my sister at night, especially as she may well have been aboard a ship by then."

"Here I need to give you a bit of background - only a small diversion, I promise." A reluctant nod, so I continued. "I've already told you that Andrea and I were very close and, I suppose, rather strange. As school kids, we didn't have many friends and spent most time together; looking after each other or, in most cases, my big sister looking after me. Even though we went to a reasonably good school, there was a lot of bullying and we were obvious targets because we were different, weird. It was Andrea who came up with the strategy of completely over-reacting in such cases. If anyone tried to push me or her about, she went completely ballistic - punching, biting, kicking - regardless of how mild the provocation. We got into trouble for that a few times, but gradually the bullies learned to leave us alone, we just weren't worth the grief."

"As we got older and the bullies got tougher, inside and out of school, we got tooled up. There were a lot of young guys - girls too - carrying knives in London at that time. My sister managed to obtain a truncheon-sized steel bar that she carried in her school bag and got me sorted out with a bottle of .88 ammonia."

"You're kidding me, Cof! You carried ammonia to school?"

"Dead right! Andrea and I worked it out quite rationally. Andrea was big and strong for her age, so if we were threatened by someone with a weapon, she would handle them."

"Andrea? Our Andrea?"

"Only happened once. Junkie tried to mug us one time when we were coming home from school. We were in our mid-teens and I guess he was in his early twenties. He was a bit wasted, but was armed with a Stanley knife - you know, those things the Yanks call box cutters." A vacant stare, but I ploughed on. "Anyway, razor-sharp thing with a small blade. He had only started to list the stuff he wanted us to hand over, when Andrea walloped him over the side of the head. He went down like a sack of potatoes. Thing is - and this is my point here - we didn't run away crying to the police. We coldly and methodically kicked seven shades of shit out of the stupid cunt as he lay squirming on the deck. He ended up in a coma. When the police found him, they thought he'd been worked over by a gang. But it was just Andrea and me."

"And you, did you ever use your ammonia?"

"Well, we reckoned that if we were up against a gang, metal bars, knives and stuff like that wouldn't help a lot. If anything, it would probably only ensure escalation and make things worse for us. The obvious solution would have been a firearm, as there were very few guns in our area of town, but we couldn't think of a way to get one. So chemical warfare seemed the answer. Even if there were quite a few people threatening us, a spray of ammonia at about head height would blind some and put the rest out of action. If we held our breaths and ran like hell, we had a good chance of getting away."

"But did you use it?"

"Kind of... "

"What's this kind of shit? That's like being kind of a virgin: either you are or you aren't."

"Well, I didn't use it against a gang. There was, however, a builder's yard that we passed each day on our walk to and from school. It had a massive Doberman guard dog that barked at all the passers-by, particularly smaller kids. Every couple of weeks, the gate to the site would be left open and the dog would be on the street, forcing us to do a long detour to avoid it. One day the gate was only slightly ajar, so that we didn't notice until it was too late. The brute threw itself at me - I guess they always pick on the runt of the pack - and bit the arm I was using to protect my face, slavering all over me at the same time. It retreated when Andrea screamed at it, battering it with her schoolbag, which allowed us to retreat back home. Our housekeeper called the cops, but they weren't very interested. The arm of my blazer was a bit ripped, but the dog's teeth hadn't actually broken the skin. Andrea herself phoned the cop shop the next day and was told that the builder had assured them that the gate was always closed. The dog was only to protect his property from vandalism, much of which was due to local kids. If I was bitten, it was because I was trespassing - and, if it happened again, the builder would press charges."

"I'd hazard a guess that you two didn't take that well."

"Dead fucking right we didn't! Two nights later, we sneaked out about three in the morning armed with a kitchen knife, a bottle of vinegar and a steak stolen from the kitchen, the beef being liberally dosed with about thirty or so powdered sleeping tablets purloined from our au pair. This was complemented by a pair of bolt cutters and a bottle of barbeque lighter fluid from the garden shed. When we got to the yard, we hurled the steak over the fence in the general direction of the Hound of the Baskervilles. It didn't even bark, just wolfed down the meat. I guess the builder probably kept it hungry to make it mean. About a quarter of an hour later it was down, so we used the bolt cutters on the chain on the gate and walked in. Andrea clinically hacked at the face and flanks of the unconscious beast, then poured vinegar onto its wounds, causing it to writhe despite the level of its sedation. I poured lighter fluid into the cabs of the two parked vans and then hurled the bottle of ammonia through the window of the portacabin that was used as an office. It must have smelled like a thousand cats had pissed in that place. A couple of matches in the vans and then we walked off home."

177

"You just got away with it?"

"Well, the builder and two firemen were bitten by the pain-crazed dog, before the builder managed to shoot it with a shotgun that he had in the boot of his car. The gun turned out to be unlicensed, so he was arrested by the police, who had finally shown up on the scene. He was bailed out after a couple of hours in the clink, then arrested the next night while attempting to fire bomb a rival company, the owners of which he was convinced were behind the attack on his site. I think he got a couple of years for attempted arson: the place he was trying to set on fire was next door to an orphanage!"

"Christ on a bike. And this was for a bite that didn't even break the skin."

"Yes, exactly. Our motto was bastardized version of one used by some Scottish regiment - *wha daur fuck wi' us*. I think this explains the Darcy thing a bit."

"And the Yardies... "

"That as well. If I had gone after a group of five big lads who had my sister, I wouldn't have been carrying a big stick, I'd have had something a lot more lethal."

"But you didn't go after them?"

"Not immediately. They came to me. Tina and I had been up all night, even though there was nothing that we could do except scan video feeds from empty streets. Early next morning, I was contacted by radio. Someone with a strong Rasta accent simply commanded me to exchange a box that would be delivered to me for a laptop set up for secure communication via a radio link. If this exchange didn't occur, further boxes would appear."

I stopped to wipe my brow. Despite the air conditioning, I was sweating heavily as I remembered that day. "I had a very bad feeling about this terse message, so I got a small solar palmtop set up with the required links. About two hours later, a boy cycled up to the gates, covered in sweat and looking completely terrified. A Bridgeton lad who'd been raised with horror stories of the Butcher of Holetown, I guessed. I went to meet him, accompanied only by Tina, although I did have automatic defenses armed for the unlikely case that he was a Judas Goat aimed to entice me into the range of a support gang who had managed to evade my video surveillance."

"I clearly remember the small cardboard box. It was completely ancient, marked *fuses, 5 amp*. It was held closed by a piece of tape, which I easily slit with a finger nail. I opened it with bated breath, trying to conceal the contents from Tina. It held two fingers that I couldn't help but recognize. I simply handed over the palmtop in its canvas carrying case and hustled the fraught woman back into our enclosure. As the gates closed behind us, I silently handed over the box, then took my sister's lover in my arms as she broke down in tears, screaming, cursing, crying as her heart broke. Up to that point, over the many years that we had known each other, our relationship had always been cool, guarded. She clearly resented the closeness of our sibling bonds, recognizing that, despite the fact that Andrea clearly

179

loved her, there was a special link between us that she could never share."

"And you were jealous of her sexual relationship with your sister?"

"No, not that - or, at least, I don't think so. Maybe just the smallest bit of a feeling that Andrea had less time for me when Tina was about. But anyway, that changed the moment that we saw those fingers. We then had only one aim: to get my sister back and ensure nothing else happened to her. For this we would work together, with no reservations. We've been very close ever since. Of course, the trauma of... "

Sue seemed to suddenly realize that she had been leading me astray. "OK, but what happened with the Yardies."

"It was a full seven days before we had further contact from the kidnappers. I was a bag of nerves the entire time, but wasn't spending it sitting on my hands. I had my search engines tracing all the background on kidnappings in general, and Yardies in particular, that I could find on my databases. I also used the radio network to get a better picture of recent developments in the Caribbean, although I was aware that it was quite possible that my opponents would be able to listen in to me. I also went over the full inventory of kit that I had available, sorting out appropriate packages for different scenarios. While I got that lot together, Tina sorted out the plane."

"The plane? You've got a plane?"

"Had! Had a plane! I was able to take off un-noticed, but we were spotted landing. There was no way I could cover it up, so I donated it to the Bajan government; this saved them the process of confiscating it. Anyway, this is getting ahead of the story, don't you think?"

A silent nod, so I went on. "We got the email with video attachment a week after Andrea was taken. The message was short, sharp and to the point. I can recite it verbatim. *I will give instructions, you will carry them out. Or there will be more boxes.* The video clip showed Andrea sitting on a terrace beside a swimming pool. She held up her left hand, showing the professional-looking bandaging over the stumps of what had been middle and ring fingers. The sound track was faint, but she was reciting what must have been a rehearsed speech. The gist was clear: this was not a team to be messed with, do as I was told or the consequences would be dire. She finished with *Don't hold back, Cof.* I was sure that this was something that she had added herself; apart from anything else, she never called me Cof. The ambiguity would be missed by anyone else... " I looked at Sue and raised my eyebrows.

"Well... " the now familiar pause as she wove disparate threads together to try to picture what would emerge, like the pattern from cross-stitch. "If kidnappers were making demands, they would automatically assume that *don't hold back* would be an entreaty to pay up, to do as told. Following your previous anecdotes, however, this could also be interpreted as an encouragement to over-react. Best form of defense is attack, sort of a thing."

"Exactly! You see my old brain isn't completely rusted yet. These diversions did serve a useful purpose."

"But you didn't go through all this skeleton-hunting in the old cupboards of your childhood just so I could answer your questions. There's more to it than that. More than you've told me so far. Probably what happened when you didn't hold back, I'd guess."

"You're indeed a hard woman, no trust in your soul." But also, I added silently, completely correct.

"After contact was made, it was negotiation time: first via email then, when things got a bit more heated, via direct radio link. It was quickly clear that I wasn't dealing with some thug who'd lived his life in the Kingston slums, but someone both very bright and well educated who'd taken advantage of the Crash to establish himself as a feudal warlord. He called himself Raz and would sometimes speak in a Jamaican accent that was so thick as to be unintelligible. Nevertheless, especially when we were haggling, the accent would sound a bit more South London and his vocabulary implied university level education. Anyway, it was clear that this was someone who'd not be easily conned and who'd respond to any attempt in that direction with the ultraviolence so characteristic of the Yardies... "

He had done his homework and, although clearly not aware of what exactly was available in our little community, knew both that I had a lot of functioning technology and also had a good idea about the value of my databases. His demands were clear: he wanted it all, the estate and everything in it. He also wanted the contents of my IBS account. If he didn't get it, he was going to hack my sister into little pieces, which I could watch on video, if I doubted him in any way.

I wasted a lot of time trying to haggle him down. This wasn't because the extent of his extortion made any difference to me, just that I guessed that it would be what he expected. In any case, he didn't budge an inch. Not even the slightest pretense that he would allow me to keep some of my possessions. This must be the way that he had established himself as tyrant of his particular horde: sheer implacability. After he had made his mind up on something, he wouldn't budge. Not much chance of a Jamaica containing people like this ever evolving into a democracy, I remember thinking to myself.

With our relative positions thus established, we came to the harder part of arranging the handover. Here I had bargaining chips: both my physical control of the estate and my close relationship to the IBS founder. This ensured that Raz had to be able to convince me that I could take really take Andrea back if I kept my part of the bargain, but ensure that I still felt myself sufficiently threatened that I wouldn't try to double-cross him as soon as I was out of his sight.

The final agreement seemed a feasible compromise. I would sail to Jamaica and take possession of Andrea there. When this transfer was complete, I would radio home and everyone would leave my estate, which would be taken over by Raz and his gang. I could then take Andrea to my ship, while Raz checked that the infrastructure and software was OK. I guess, for this, he must have a smart team of programmers on hand who could ensure that I hadn't left any time bombs in the software. I would then transfer my IBS funds and would be allowed to sail off wherever I liked. We spent lots of time nailing down fine details, then set the date for the exchange in eight days, which should just about allow me enough time to sail to Jamaica, but not enough extra for me to attempt something major, like putting together a mercenary support force.

Sue had been squirming in her seat for a bit, like a child desperate for a pee who, at the same time, doesn't want to leave for fear of missing out on something. Finally she could restrain herself no longer. "You actually agreed to this! You were going to hand over everything!"

I had to actually think about this for a bit. "Actually, I suppose I would have, if there had been no other way. I couldn't have let harm come to my sister if there was any possible way of avoiding it."

"Despite the harm that would be done, the resources for rebuilding lost if this place was taken over by a gang of thugs?"

"Despite all that. Andrea and I put all this together and, when the cards are down, it's fundamentally up to us - to me in this instance - to decide what to do with it. Rebuilding and bettering the lives of millions are nice ideas, but they're fundamentally abstract. My sister is totally real, so she takes precedence."

Sue was clearly having problems digesting this, but said no more on the topic. I decided to put her out of her misery. "I had to think about your question, because it was a moot point. I had absolutely no intention of handing anything, anything at all, to those bastards. They had mutilated my sister and were threatening me. In fact the Yardies were nothing more than a wart on the arsehole of humanity. Remember what my sister told me - don't hold back! Well I sure as fuck didn't intend to!"

"So you just went head to head against Raz and his entire army?"

"Yup!"

"Alone?"

"Tina was with me."

"And you weren't worried about the odds?"

"We had an equalizer."

"And just what was that?"

"A small vial of weaponized Ebola."

The woman went white as a sheet. I'd heard this expression before, but never seen it in real life. She looked like she was going to pass out. "Fucking Christ! Jamaica, six years ago! That was you?"

"I'm afraid so."

***

185

Well, I thought to myself, that wasn't so hard after all. Then I looked at my scribe, who was breathing deeply as if she had just been punched in the gut. I suppose it must be a bit of a shock when your employer confesses to genocide. Denying access to my estate after the Crash of the 20th could be seen as murder, but a kind of passive sort that was more a by-product of my desire to protect me and mine. The real killers were the hacker bastards that caused the destruction of the QCs in the first place. Darcy and company represented a more active case, but clearly revenge on individuals, response to an attack that they initiated. It would take a bit more work to defend my actions in Jamaica.

I stood and stretched. "Time for a break. Fancy a swim with Katya and me?"

Just a shake of her head in response. No banter today. I padded out without a further word, leaving the woman to try and make some sense out of what I'd told her this morning.

My mood was lightened by Katya, who was waiting for me on the jetty, already stripped down and apparently oblivious to the tropical downpour that was lashing down on us. "You're late," she noted, "so that means that you're going to be carrying two kilos."

Only a couple of kilos, Katya must have had a very good morning. I grinned in relief, remembering the weight I had been carrying two days before. I stripped my soaking clothes off and threw them beside the hut where my rather unamused security folk were sheltering. It was difficult to tell due to the rain on my swimming goggles, but it looked like Jack and Jill again.

The rain felt good on my bare flesh as I stood beside my trainer at the end of the jetty. "What're we doing today, Oh Brutal One?"

"Very simple: out to the black boo-ay and back."

"The black boy, fine," I responded, on cue. Then I peered into the rain again. "Actually, not so fine. I can't see any buoy out there."

"Of course you can't. It's a couple of klicks out and I'd guess visibility in this weather can't be better than a couple of hundred meters."

"So, we wait for the rain to go off?" I inquired hopefully.

"Don't be so soft. It's going to be pouring for ages yet. Here!"

I automatically caught the small item she flicked at me, seeing that it was a digital compass on a strap. "You have got to be joking! There's no way I can navigate with that thing."

"You don't really need to. You just need to head straight out from the end of the jetty here: that's due East. Hold the straight line for two k and you should be able to see it."

"If I don't need it... " I started to remove the compass, but it was then firmly clasped in place by a delicate, but surprisingly strong, hand.

"You don't need it to get there, but you have to take a wrist band from the buoy and swim back. If the weather hasn't cleared, you'll need to know

exactly where due west is. Hence the compass."
Almost as an afterthought she added "... of course,
if you can't find the buoy after an hour, you'll need
the compass to get back anyway. But you certainly
don't want to do that."

"I don't?" I knew this wasn't going to be good.

"No race today, so no penalties... " she smiled
at my look of relief, "... except if you don't come
back with an armband. Hundred press-ups. Of
course, if you do something silly like come back
within a hundred minutes or so with no armband,
that'd be two hundred."

I caught myself before I could object - feeling,
for once, that my mental post-its had remained in
view at a critical time. I contented myself with a
theatrical groan instead.

***

With my weight belt snugly in place, I waited
for Katya to set us off. Unlike our last race, I didn't
want to be in the lead. In smooth seas, my trainer
swam straight as an arrow and she was a demon at
estimating distances by counting strokes. Being well
aware of my limitations in both regards, my plan
was simple: stay glued to Katya's heels and let her
do the navigation for me.

As I expected, she was aware of my ploy and
set off at a brutal pace. I knew, however, that she
wouldn't be able to keep this up, especially when we
emerged from the shelter of the headlands and
caught more of the swell. All I had to do was go fast

188

enough to ensure that I kept her in sight. Sure enough, as we started to get thrown about her speed dropped off and I was able to close to within a couple of body lengths, so it was easy enough to keep her in view despite the swell. She tried to draw me out a couple of times, going into a sprint for a few tens of meters, but this always died when she saw that I wasn't going to rise to the bait. She had actually slowed to the point that my head was almost level with her feet, when, all of a sudden, she put on a serious turn of speed. I glanced at my watch and noticed that we'd been swimming for thirty-six minutes. Could she have seen the buoy? Being bang on with dead-reckoning under these conditions would be little short of a miracle, but the timing was very suspicious. I abandoned all caution and set off after her at racing speed.

Sure enough, this time her speed didn't drop off. Either she had spotted me, which seemed unlikely the way that she was swimming, or the previous sprints had simply been feints to set me up for this sucker punch. After five minutes in this heavy sea I was beginning to feel the strain, but the figure ahead of me showed no sign of slacking off. Three more minutes and I was beginning to get light-headed and realized that I was losing track of my guide. A calculated risk then: I went on to breast stroke, which allowed me to follow Katya's progress much better, especially when I was on the crest of a wave at the same time as she was. It was only the second such wave combination when I not only saw the little blond, but also the buoy that was directly in front of her. How much luck was that: to immediately hit the target bang on?

I glanced at my watch again, having difficulty believing that even someone as good as Katya could have kept a straight line over two kilometers of such a swell. Then it dawned: there was no way! She was following some kind of location signal, and probably had another on the shore. A roar of rage gained me a mouthful of seawater, but I felt electrified by wrath. Head down, I sprinted for the buoy.

I reached the buoy, grabbed the blue rubber wrist band hanging from it and glanced around to find my cheating bitch of a trainer. She was about thirty meters away, setting a good pace, but no longer sprinting. Powered by fury, I crashed after her. We raced for about one and a half k, until I could start to make out the jetty emerging from rain that was now easing to drizzle. I immediately slowed into an easy breast stroke and let Katya pull ahead, noting that her pace dropped off as soon as she noted that I was no longer on her tail.

Typically, by the time I clambered on to the jetty the sky had cleared and she was sitting, still unclothed, in a padded deckchair, basking in the light of a watery sun. She looked amused as I stormed up to her. "You cheating bitch from hell! You were on a beam, in and out, straight as a nail. Me, what do I have? A fucking compass!"

Her grin widened. "Yes indeed, you did well!"

"Fuck that! It's just not fair!"

190

"Fair? Fair?" She was giving me a stare as if I was an idiot child. "Since when does fairness have anything to do with it?"

"When we're racing... "

"... but we weren't, that's the point. You're very competitive but, in a race situation, tend to concentrate on brute force and ignorance. Today's exercise focused on strategy."

Now I was beginning to feel like an idiot child. True to idiot form, I kept on going. "So the whole compass thing was a bluff?"

"Not at all. If you hadn't worked out a suitable strategy, it would have ensured that you could find your way back to a beach. In addition, just in case, it's got an inbuilt tracker, so we'd be able to find you."

"Well, I suppose that'd save me walking back."

"Don't be daft, if you got back to shore, then finding your way back here is part of the exercise. The tracker would be used only if you didn't make it back to land, to help us find the body."

I was flabbergasted, finding it difficult to decide whether to take the laughing woman at face value or not. Then I had a pleasing thought. "Well, at the very least, I don't have a penalty this time."

"Wouldn't have had, had you not referred to your beloved trainer as a cheating bitch from hell, if I remember correctly. You did well today, so I'll settle for fifty push-ups, soon as you like. Ah... Ah... Ah... you didn't do that well that well: the weight belt stays on. Go for it!"

Notice to idiot self: if instructive post-it found on forehead, do not remove until the fucking training session is well finished.

***

I lunched alone but was not at all surprised that, when I wandered through to the conservatory afterwards, both of my S-scribes were sitting together waiting on me. They looked at me as I entered, each of them with obvious confusion on their faces. Sue took the initiative. "Before we start again, Cof, we just want to be sure that you're not winding us up. We know that you have a very bizarre sense of humor and wouldn't put it past you to take the blame for a natural catastrophe just to make some strange point or other."

"Look, girls, ... ladies," I caught Sophie's frown. "I can assure you there is nothing I'd rather do more than move blame for this. In my defense, it wasn't planned to be quite such a big deal and, in retrospect, it may even have done more good than harm. Nevertheless, it wasn't worked out in so much detail. Maybe it'd be best if you just listened to the full story and made up your own minds afterwards."

I realized that I was wittering a bit and tried to force myself to calm down. Two silent nods from the secretaries and then I started. "We can get all the background Ts crossed and Is dotted later; what you want now is the whole truth about how I responded to the kidnap threats... "

192

"The critical thing at the beginning is to understand the psychology of the kidnapper: all my searches came up with this as a critical issue. There are psychos who are going to kill the victim regardless of what ransom is paid and others who end up in a kidnap situation by accident and are only desperate to get the victim returned safe and sound as early as possible. For people like Raz, however, kidnapping is only a tool: if the goal could be achieved easier by bribery or direct force of arms, he would go in that direction. When he has started, however, a Raz-type will do anything to achieve his goal, which he sees in terms of the larger picture of his global ambitions. So, if he gets what he wants from the kidnapping and sees a benefit from seeming fair, he will honor his side of the bargain. If, on the other hand, he wants to emphasize his ruthlessness, he would be quite prepared to gratuitously kill both his kidnap victim and whoever is providing the ransom."

"He may have a university education, but there was no possibility of having a rational discussion with him. You either gave in and hoped that he would see some reason to be Mister Nice Guy in this particular case, or stood up to him and were subject to the calculated brutality of his response. Of course, the other option was to appear to give in and stab him in the back at the first opportunity. I considered that I had no option. I had also to take into account that he was the center of a vast network of organized crime that wouldn't take kindly to one of their top dogs being taken out. Apart from anything else, it's fundamental to the technique of bullying: you can only control people, if you can subjugate everyone below you in the food chain. If there are exceptions, folk who won't be bullied, your credibility is lost and the entire house of cards collapses. Raz knew this and it governed his entire approach. I knew it too, which meant I needed to take out the Yardies as an organization."

At this point, it looked like Sophie was going to interrupt, but a nip on her arm brought her back under control. I continued relentlessly. "With the way in which the transfer of Andrea was set up, he expected that I was going to have to rush to kit out a yacht of some kind and sail to Jamaica. As I previously mentioned, however, I planned to appear on the scene long before I was expected... "

I originally bought the small four-seater turboprop for Andrea and Tina. There was absolutely no reason to go for a vintage Cessna, but Tina flew commercial jets in her day job, where pilots were mainly present to make the punters feel safe. All the real technical stuff was done by smart software. Only the vintage planes flown by collectors were exempt from the QC control systems, so this thing was forty years old then and had originally run on oil-based aviation fuel, until it was converted to a bioethanol mix. It was fitted with long-distance tanks and its official range was two thousand kilometers, but Tina reckoned that, with prevailing easterly tail winds, we could make it to Jamaica in a single hop: we just had to get as much weather information as possible, to reduce the risks of hitting anything that would cut down our very small margin of error. Coming back, winds were likely to be less favorable and, although we wouldn't have the extra weight of the drums that we'd need to carry in order to refuel in Jamaica, we would, hopefully have Andrea with us. A refueling stop was thus needed to be on the safe side, so we decided on Montserrat, effectively uninhabited since the last volcanic activity in the '20s.

We could thus kill two birds with one stone: load the plane up with the maximum load of fuel in drums as cargo. Drop off some in Montserrat on the way out, with a top up of the tanks to widen our margin of error for getting to Montego Bay, apparently the area of Jamaica where Raz was holed up. Given the popularity of classic planes before the crash, it was quite possible that either the small airfield at Montserrat or Montego Bay international airport would still have some biofuel but, considering the post-Crash value of any kind of high energy fuel, we certainly couldn't bet on it. Better to take all fuel with us and hope that there were no scavengers who would plunder our reserve depot before we could get back to it.

It made logistics easier that we were taking only minimal kit with us. Everything I needed fit into a small shoulder bag. Only additions were a few beers and sandwiches to keep body and soul together and we were ready to go.

I remember wondering if it was going to be possible when I got my first look inside the small plane. Even as a vintage, there had been a number of obligatory '30s-level electronic navigation, communication and control aids that had been added. Over the last couple of days, Tina and a couple of my technicians had ripped all this stuff out and replaced it with a magnetic compass, a few maps, a pair of optical binoculars and a mechanical fuel gauge. It all looked very Heath Robinson, but Tina seemed happy with it, which was good enough for me.

We took off from the deserted Grantley Adams airport at six o'clock in the morning, the day after Raz had imposed his ultimatum. Flying for maximum fuel economy, we were in Montserrat two hours later and took our time unloading drums of fuel, rolling some into a shed at the side of the potholed runway and using the others to top up the tank. We sat together on the tarmac, sheltered from the sun in the shade of a wing, and went over our plans again and again, checking for loopholes or any ways of improving our chances of coming out of this in one piece. It was late afternoon when I removed a small container from my bag; the DLC coated titanium seemed frail, but you would require serious tools to cut through its thin walls and this would set off the explosive charge that would vaporize the contents. However, the cap popped open as it read my thumbprint and I removed two small blue lozenges, leaving a third green one for later.

Tina was clearly terrified, but she immediately swallowed the pill, washing it down with a small mouthful of lukewarm beer. I dry swallowed the other and we were committed: back into the plane and off to Montego Bay.

The sun was setting as we landed, the little plane lost on the huge runway dimensioned for the wide-bodied international commercial jets of the early noughts and '10s. Although it wasn't clear how many people had seen us, we taxied blatantly to the western end of the landing strip, where a shanty town lay between the deserted airport and a small harbor containing a dozen or so fishing boats and, incongruously, a couple of ocean-going yachts. The latter had clearly been luxury ships at one time, but now, although clearly functional, they looked distinctly dilapidated.

By the time we had switched off the engine, the plane was surrounded by a swarm of semi-naked children, their parents staying more cautiously at a distance. I remember that moment like it was yesterday. Tina looked at the smiling faces and, for the first time, her resolve wavered. "I'm not sure I can do this Herman. Maybe there's another way." She was clearly rattled: usually she copied my sister and called me by my childhood nickname, Ham. Herman was generally reserved for when she was extremely annoyed with me.

I had to swallow hard before I could reply, unable myself to look directly into the children's eyes. "Omelet, eggs, Tina. There isn't another option. In ten, fifteen years these kids will be part of the same mob of thugs who took Andrea and who terrorize half the Caribbean."

"But they're children now!"

197

There was no answer to that, so I simply opened the door of the cabin and we were committed.

**

The children parted before us as we marched up to a group of four youths who were standing to one side, with a clear respect distance between them and the rest of the villagers. "I've got something for Raz" I simply announced, which immediately took a lot of tension from the air. A plane arriving was an amazing event, but if it was a delivery for their gang-lord, it somehow made sense to them. The tallest and oldest of the group replied in an accent so strong that I could make out only about every third word, but the gist was that we would need to wait for transport. I told him my name and said that I was earlier than Raz expected, so he sent one of the younger guys off on an antique motor scooter to sort things out, while he ordered some of the villagers to help us with our refueling operation. With children competing to operate the small hand pump that transferred fuel from the offloaded drums into the tank, the work was soon done. We then adjourned to a shack at the water's edge that served as a bar.

The pub seemed to offer only rum - available straight or in combination with different fruit juices - or a homebrew beer that looked like tepid dishwater, or typical traditional English ale. My minder, Winston he was called, looked at me expectantly as I entered this establishment, clearly wondering what the owner of a plane would be worth. I rummaged through my shoulder bag and pulled out a credit card-size digital camera. I snapped a photo of a child who was sitting in a corner, rolling huge spliffs, and showed the result on the small display on the back. "Solar powered with a 500 Giga chip. I guess the barman here would be happy to take this for a round of drinks."

A smile showed Winston's set of perfect white teeth. He took the camera and hollered something to the effect that the drinks were on him. In any case, the bar was soon bedlam while everyone in the village appeared to be clambering for drinks. Without asking what we wanted, he handed Tina some kind of rum cocktail and passed me a beer. To my amazement it was actually quite drinkable despite its difference from the ice cold lager prevalent in the Caribbean before the Crash; Jamaican Red Stripe, Bajan Banks, Trinidad Carib... The taste reminded me of some of the smoky brews once found in the Thames valley, something like Brakspear's Old.

As I tried to take my mind off what we were doing by musing on beer, Tina was fighting off the amatory advances of Winston. I wasn't sure what the attraction could be; I now like Tina a lot, but she is certainly no beauty. A kind of acquired taste, I guessed. By contrast, the huddle of hookers at the far end of the bar, most of whom seemed to be in their teens or early 20s, included some drop-dead beauties. I cursed myself for inadvertently using this term, but forced myself to inspect the girls one by one. All shades of skin color from light mahogany to coal black, features showing pure African genes or complex mixtures with sources from Europe, South America or Asia. Every one was quite lovely in her own way.

My eyes were beginning to sting a little from clouds of ganga smoke that were building up. I decided to rescue Tina, interrupting Winston to ask about the bar prostitutes. I was rewarded by a frown from Tina, who clearly hadn't picked up on my ploy. Winston, however, was happy to describe the services that the girls would perform and emphasized that they were much cheaper than the whores in the Montego Bay or Kingston docks. However, he apologized that there was no time, unless I just wanted a quickie against the wall of the shack. My transport should be available at any moment and, as soon as his mate got back, he would be on his way to Kingston.

This was an unexpected development, which caused me to realize for the first time just how little control I had over the consequences of my planned raid. It appeared that the two yachts were owned by Winston and had been at sea, pirating, for the last couple of weeks. They had come in to this harbor simply to exchange booty and crew. Winston would sail one ship back to Kingston, while the other would go on to Negril via Montego Bay. The ships would be reprovisioned and, after a bit of R&R, sail back to rendezvous here before their next expedition.

200

I cursed myself for not having considered this option, but I realized that it wasn't something I could have foreseen and, even if I had, it probably wouldn't have stopped me anyway.

My black mood was broken by the arrival of an old Land Rover, which farted up to the bar with the sweet reek of ethanol-based fuel. It stopped with an explosive backfire that momentarily silenced the bar, then led to peals of relieved laughter. Four huge thugs poured out of the back and, without a word, hustled us into the car. Less than a minute later we were bumping along a potholed road at reckless speed, which felt like about a hundred kph, although it was probably only sixty.

We travelled in silence for half an hour, skirting the city of Montego Bay and heading west along the coast road. I was able to make out the name Round Hill on a weather-beaten sign, just before we turned left up a steep hill and arrived at a beautiful villa. Still without a word, we were marched into a huge room, constructed entirely of shiny, polished mahogany. Through picture windows, I could see a pool on the patio that I recognized from the video I had seen. This was where my sister was being held.

Ignoring our retinue, I dropped into a huge, overstuffed sofa and waved Tina to my side. We sat for about ten minutes before Raz appeared, clad in lurid silk shorts and vest covered with dragons and swords that looked like they might have originated from a Thai boxing team. I hardly noticed him, concentrating more on my sister who he was leading by the arm. She was wearing rather grubby, camouflage pattern shorts and T-shirt but, otherwise, apart from her crudely bandaged hand, looked fine.

Raz slumped into an armchair the size of a throne, which made even his two meter frame look small. He was clearly not pleased by my unexpected appearance. "What the fuck you doin' here, man? You's not supposed to turn up on my fuckin' 'land till next week. What you fuckin' at?"

"Bit of luck, that's all," I responded calmly. "I had this old plane in a hanger but didn't know if it would fly or if we could get fuel. It did, we could, so I'm here. I miss my sister a lot," I wiped tears from my eyes with a handkerchief, "and I just wanted her back as soon as possible." I stood and walked to Andrea, took her head in my hands and kissed her wetly on the mouth.

This first seemed to startle Raz, then he laughed, plainly delighted. "You sick fucks! You like that Caligula bastard, you make it with you sister. Andrea, bitch, you ain't no Andrea. You fuckin' Drusilla, you ho'."

I simply smiled back. "Raz, old boy, you'd better watch it: your classical education is showing. Anyway, I'm now here to collect my sister. We'll just be going now, if you'd be so kind to run us back to our aircraft. Toodle pip!"

I took Andrea's uninjured right hand, waved at Tina to join us, and turned to leave.

The tall gangster was bemused. "Wha' de fuck you sayin' man. You ain't goin' any fuckin' whea, ain't fuckin' taking nob'dy wit' you 'til I say so. Don'

202

even t'ink 'bout fuckin' wi' I an' I. Jus' one lickle t'ink 'bout fuckin' an' you machet meat , fuckin' dead'r 'n dead!"

"Not how it goes, Raz old chap." I was baiting him now. "You see, you have already fucked with me. You have very seriously fucked with my sister. We're not, not at all, the kind of people you want to fuck with! You ever heard of the Butcher of Holetown?"

His brow furrowed, evidently at a loss to work out what I was raving about. "Some fuckin' Bajan monster story?" he hazarded.

"Not a story - history, and we're the monsters."

For the first time, the educated thug looked a little worried. "Ya, you a monsta, but dat don' do you no good wen I an I's boys t'ick on de groun'." He gesticulated with his pinkie. "I jus' gotta lif' dis lickle finga an you's fuckin' dead."

"Too late, you see we've already killed you. You just don't know it yet."

Now he was starting to look worried: either I was completely insane, or I had something up my sleeve. Something that he hadn't thought of. The patois almost vanished as he struggled to guess what I could be up to. "I got 'bout fifty fellas on the ground here. There's maybe five hundred could be here in ten minutes. You got the power to take 'em all out?"

"I already have. Take a look in the eyes of one of the blokes who brought us up from the airfield. Tell me he's not already dead."

Raz slowly drew himself from his chair and moved towards our guards, who had moved back towards the walls while we were talking. He roughly pulled the nearest one towards him and peered into his face. "Eyes a bit bloodshot, nothin' much there. These fellas like to drink... "

"Not a trace of blood in the corner of the eyes, sweating a lot, a bit of a tremor in arms and legs? These guys are maybe frightened of you, but is that normal?"

I glanced at my watch and, as if pre-programed, one of the other guards vomited spectacularly. The bloody mess just missed the others and sprayed over a thick wool rug. The man gulped and, holding his mouth, fled from the room. Raz turned to look at me in amazement, only to turn back as the man he had been inspecting gulped loudly and ran after his buddy, a brown and red mess already beginning to seep from his shorts. Moments later we were alone in the room.

Raz hesitated for an instant, then raced back to his chair, pulling an evil looking gun from a concealed pocket under the arm. I smiled annoyingly when he waved it in my direction.

"What the fuckin' hell is that voodoo shit? What the fuck've you done?"

"Ebola. Weaponized Ebola. You've heard of that, surely? You must be old enough to remember the Miami attack."

The look of abject terror on his face gave me my answer. The natural outbreaks of hemorrhagic fever in Africa were bad enough, but the scenes when the weaponized version was used in a major city made Dante's Inferno seem like a Disney comic. The virus completely destroyed tissue and organs, resulting in a horrifying, messy and extremely painful death.

The Yardie boss was shaking, his eyes wide, but his gun was still centered in the middle of my chest. "You're a truly mad fucker, but if I'm going to die, then I should shoot you all as fast as possible. You thought that one out?"

"Of course!" I tried to act as cool as possible, although I could feel nervous sweat trickling down my back. "These!" I opened my hand to show three pills, two of which I passed to the women. We had all swallowed before Raz had time to react.

"What the fuck you up to?"

"Well, it's clear that, if we're spreading Ebola, then we should be very ill now as well. These pills are the antidote. The weaponized Ebola is incredibly contagious, but only for twenty-four hours, then it self-destructs. Telomere shortening or some other kind of genetic-engineering hocus pocus. Everybody already infected by then will die, of course, but it won't spread further. Anyway, all we need is one of these every hour and we're completely protected. Miss an hour and the damage starts. You can stop it when you take a pill, but the harm already done is irreversible."

"So you gonna give me some of them pills?"

"We've a supply for ourselves hidden on the plane and another two dozen in the village, the place where we waited for the pickup. You drive us to the airfield and then I'll tell you where they are. There's only enough for you, though, so it might not be too clever to take any of your bodyguards with you. If any of them realize that there is only enough for one person to avoid a really excruciating death, then you may find they're not so loyal to you anymore."

He was silent for a minute as he considered his options. "How do I know that you're not fuckin' with me here?"

"You don't really, but you don't have a lot of options. In any case, I've already set up a demonstration of the effectiveness of the pills."

"How's that?"

"Remember when I kissed my sister? We're not lovers, you know; I was just making 100% sure that she was also infected, probably marginally before you would have picked it up from the air or contact with your guards. You saw that she took a pill at the same time that we did, before any symptoms started to show. Check on her when you start to feel ill." I looked at my watch. "You've got about thirty minutes before it starts to really hit your internal organs."

The gangster was suddenly galvanized into action. "You, you bastard, stay close to me. A single wrong move and you're the first one full of holes." We rushed out of the house and past the Land Rover to where a huge, white Mercedes was parked. A driver and guards were ordered out of the way with a barrage of curses and I was waved behind the wheel, while he clambered in beside me and the

206

women piled into the back. "Get us there fucking fast, you evil cunt!" he commanded and, without further encouragement, I shot down the driveway in a spray of gravel.

Naturally, I had done no driving at all during the previous nine years and, indeed, little enough before that. Even though it was an automatic, I struggled with the old car on the terrible road surface, but kept the speed up as high as I could, being well aware of the gun centimeters away from my ear. In fact, after I got over about a hundred, driving became easier as the car planed over the potholes and I relaxed a bit when I realized that there was almost nothing other than pedestrians and a couple of bikes on the road. The sky was darkening and the car's blazing headlights were clearing a path for us, so I opened the throttle wider, aware nevertheless that there would probably be injuries as people were forced to throw themselves out of our path.

It seemed no time at all before we screamed to a halt by our plane in a cloud of burnt rubber and I checked my watch again. Twenty minutes: not at all bad under the circumstances. I switched on the internal light and glanced at Raz. Silently I turned the central rear-view mirror in his direction so that he could see his reddened eyeballs. I then pointed at Andrea: her pale blue eyes were completely clear.

"OK, now this is how it's going to play." I had to keep the panicked man moving and prevent him from getting a chance to gain any shred of control. "You don't trust me and I don't trust you. We leave the women here and I take you to where the pills are. You take one and, when it's OK, I leave. I need to take another in about half an hour, so let's get on with it."

As we passed in front of the car, engine still running and full headlights on, I noted something more than fear in the man's face. It was a hatred that was manic in its intensity.

Walking through the village would have built up the levels of his fear again, though. It was dark, with light only from a few candles and a couple of guttering fires on the beach, but not dark enough to hide the shapes strewn about. Some were immobile, but most groaned in agony. One or two screams came from the far side of the shanty town, but the victims hereabouts were too far gone, throats and lungs too damaged to allow anything but animal noises to express their pain. The most frightening thing, however, was the smell: which was unbelievable hideous.

The bar on the beach was reasonably well lit by a number of candles, but this epicenter of the original infection was almost deserted, the customers undoubtedly heading home when first symptoms started to hit bowels, bladders and guts. It took only seconds for me to locate the small plastic bottle located in the rotted stump of a palm tree and I pulled it out and showed it to my nemesis, noting the bloody tears that were beginning to seep from his eyes and the distinct tremor in his gun hand.

I poured pills onto the palm of my hand and held them towards him. "As you'll see, there's twenty five here. I wasn't sure how long we'd take and I guessed that you'd hardly be likely to trust me; I mean these could be arsenic or strychnine or some kind of shit. So, you chose one and I'll take it. You can then have the rest."

I moved my hand closer to his peering eyes and he silently pointed to one of the identical pills. Like a starving man, he watched as I slipped it onto my tongue and swallowed, taking care to ensure that I hadn't palmed it or tried some other trick. While his attention was fully on me, I threw the remaining pills in the air.

With a screech that sounded like that of a beaten cat, he made a grab at one that was passing his ear. His instant of satisfaction when he caught it was replaced by a real scream of pain as my steel toe cap lashed into the side of his knee. I was easily able to pull the gun from his sweaty grip as he fell backward. Just out of sheer badness, I booted him in the groin with all my might and left him squirming in agony, crying openly as he searched for pills in the sand, fag ends and vomit coating the ground.

I jogged back to the plane, trying to inhale through my mouth. By the time I got there, the engine was already revving up. We flew back and that was that.

"The trip back wasn't exactly as easy as I made it sound" I added, finally, realizing that I was being a bit unfair. "Our second landing on Montserrat, by moonlight with a half moon and a partly cloudy sky, was touch and go. Only a pilot as good as Tina could have done it - and you've got to remember here that she hadn't flown at all for five years. Anyway, the landing was rough, but good enough that, after refueling, we could take off as soon as we had waited long enough to ensure that the Ebola carrier phase had burned out."

"We had quite a reception committee when we landed in Barbados, but we said nothing. We simply handed over the plane to Nigel, who was present with half of his force, and took bicycle rickshaws back home. Actually, now I think about it, I did say something to Nigel. I told him that I expected that there would be fewer problems with the Yardies now."

***

The two women sat in mute shock. Sue was the first one to recover. "How many died?" she asked in a small voice.

I wondered if there was any way to soften the blow, but knew that there wasn't. "Nobody really knows, but Ebola killed somewhere in the order of a hundred thousand. I specifically chose my approach to minimize the risk of spread into the major conurbations. My original target was Raz's entire gang, but I knew there'd be collateral damage. I'd hoped to keep this down to a few hundred, but I was well aware that it could get into the thousands. I couldn't have guessed that boats would be leaving

210

our landing point at the optimal time to spread the outbreak to Kingston and Montego Bay."

The woman both looked dazed, so I guessed it would be as well getting all the details out of the way. "The death toll wasn't restricted to the direct effect of the Ebola, though. It was like the Crash all over again, rotting bodies in the street, secondary epidemics, famine resulting from local decimation of the workforce. Then, outside Jamaica, there were the consequences of the loss of the Yardies' power base. Like the pirates of old, Yardie gangs had taken over towns and villages all over the Caribbean. When their home towns in Jamaica were wiped out, they lost much of their ability to terrorize and the locals rose up and took their revenge. Yardie ships were then, all of a sudden, prime targets for other pirates and also for the remnants of local coast guards. I guess, all told, this would give an additional death toll in the thousands, but here I have no apologies: this was only a bunch of criminals getting their just deserts."

"In the old days, even if you did something like this during a war, you'd be prosecuted for genocide, a crime against humanity." Sophie pointed out.

"As far as I'm concerned, I was at war. I'm sorry for the huge loss of life, but the Yardie culture was damaging our efforts to rebuild and I've no regrets about totally destroying it. We've got to balance the lives lost in Jamaica - communities who were living well from the proceeds of piracy, violence, drug dealing and terror - against those that were saved in all the islands that were their targets

211

of their crimes. So, I'm sorry, but I can certainly live with myself as far as this is concerned."

Sue seemed to be trying to keep detached, flicking through her notes to check for gaps or inconsistencies. "One point here," she looked me directly in the eye, challenging me to be honest. "You said that you left Raz alive, with the pills. That doesn't seem like you. You didn't just shoot him, did you?"

"No way was he going to get off as easy as that. He was going to spend his last hours in total agony, but driving himself on to try to find pills amongst all that shit on the beach. That was the death that he deserved."

"But what if he'd found them all? Weren't there twenty-four?"

"There were two dozen alright, but finding them wouldn't have done him any good, unless he happened to be short of magnesium. Even if that was the case, the state that he was in, mineral shortages would have been the least of his worries."

"Magnesium tablets: but how could that help Andrea? Or did you have other tablets hidden?"

"We didn't need any tablets, the whole thing was a con. The weaponized Ebola that Tina and I were loaded with made us carriers, able to infect others, but completely immune to it ourselves. Genetically engineered Typhoid Mary types: only more so in terms of how contagious this stuff was. When I was tonguing my sister, I was actually passing the third biowarfare lozenge into her mouth, giving her immunity, but without being a carrier.

We didn't need any protection, although an extra bit of magnesium certainly does no harm. I take these all the time to stop cramps during sport."

The women looked at each other. Sue seemed to be the silently elected spokeswoman. "Right, I think we'd better stop there. Sophie and I'll look through this stuff and get back to you later."

"This evening?"

Another wordless exchange as they looked into each other's eyes. "Maybe tomorrow would be better," Sue reported.

"Fine, see you then." I got to my feet and headed for my study.

Just before I got out of range, Sophie called after me. "A last point. Andrea. What did she say when she found out what you'd done?"

"Wha daur fuck wi' us!" I replied, leaving a shocked silence behind me.

***

That evening, after a solitary bath, while Katya was working on the knots in my shoulders and neck, I wondered if this was getting to be too much for my scribes. I had actually enjoyed narrating my stories in a strange kind of way and found it cathartic, excavating some of the memories that I had boarded up in the depths of my hippocampus. Nevertheless, they had forced this neural archaeology to move faster that I had expected, so I didn't have a chance to properly prepare myself or, maybe more importantly, prepare them for the surprises in store.

Having seen their reactions, it was clear to me that I would have to be very careful with this biographical record, especially considering how it might backfire if read by others. Anything that I did decide to make generally available would need to be very heavily edited.

I groaned as a knot moved, sending a shock of pain through my right shoulder blade. Pain, I thought, God's way of reminding you that you're alive. I tried to think of my story from their viewpoint. Did I sound like a Pol Pot or Mengale; trying to concoct feeble justifications to cover the fact that, fundamentally, I was just an evil bastard? Raz had called me an evil cunt; which was quite something coming from a brutal madman like him. But maybe we were really just as bad as each other. He was evil all of the time, but on a more normal scale, if you can have normal scales for psychopaths. I did nothing to hurt anyone most of the time; in fact I went out of my way to do good. When I was riled, however, I was capable of atrocities orders of magnitude worse than a Raz or Darcy could dream of. I really hoped the girls would persevere; I'd really like to hear what they thought, how they would balance the good and evil that I was responsible for.

Chapter 7 - Paranoia

I breakfasted alone, becoming gradually gloomier as the day perversely brightened, the shadows in front of the house shortening as the sun climbed behind my back into a cloudless Carib sky. I finished a second cup of coffee and was just about to head for the lab to dabble with room-temperature superconductors, trying to find an appropriate candidate for fabrication with the materials and technology available on the island. Then the girls bustled in and I inexplicably felt better; must be really serious masochism, I self-diagnosed, because both women looked serious.

Coffees for everyone and then we headed to the conservatory; I hoped the view of the beautiful day might help to cheer them up a bit.

Sue again took the lead, starting as soon as my bum touched leather. "There's lots of stuff that we need to clarify in order to make sense out of what you've given us to date. What we've decided... " she looked at her partner for confirmation, "is to try to tidy up all the technical loose ends first. After we have that, then we'll try to get more background on your justification for your actions. Does that seem fair?"

"Eminently! The ball is in your court." Looking closely, I could see that both women looked haggard - I guessed long discussions into the night and little sleep. These would probably not be questions that would be easy to answer.

"Fine, number one: how on earth did you manage to get a hold of weaponized Ebola?"

I relaxed a little; tricky, but this one was not so bad. "The guy I contracted to set up the security system for this place. I needed a geek with '10s and '20s experience and found a guy who had worked for paranoid sheiks in the Middle East at the time that the oil bubble was bursting and Islamic terror was turning away from the spastic US of A towards the local elite who lived in the ultimate of western decadence, surrounded by a destitute population. I had to hold him back, he'd have not only electrified the fences, but also surrounded them with minefields. Anyway, he suggested that, like the sheiks, I might want to invest in a bit of MAD."

"Mad?"

"Mutually Assured Destruction. You know, from the old Cold War."

"The nuclear deterrent?" Sue was catching on.

"Exactly, weapons too terrible to use. If both sides have them, the stalemate prevents hostilities breaking out. A bit of a loopy philosophy - and extremely dangerous if anyone doesn't play by the rules - but surprisingly effective based on historical experience."

"Well, there wouldn't be anyone to record history if it hadn't worked," Sophie commented dryly.

"Yes it's all very quantum, a many worlds sort of a thing... " I caught a glance from Sue, "... but that's not important here. The thing is that several threatened oil zillionaires decided that this was what they needed: a defense against the surrounding populace that made any form of armed uprising against the elite fundamentally futile, as the insurgents would be guaranteed to lose everything in the attempt."

"Bio-warfare agents?" guessed Sue.

"Exactly! They're completely illegal, banned by international law and God knows how many different conventions, but still available on the black market."

"But why the hell did you want them? Did you feel threatened by the community of Holetown?"

"Of course not! But remember, these were pre-QC defence systems. With anti-terror AI sensors everywhere, such a release of a genetically engineered virus would be spotted in any halfway civilised area within minutes; even in the middle of bugger-all - somewhere like the Nullarbor or Gobi Desert - within an hour or so. It would then be immediately neutralized and all efforts made to trace back the source. This was a completely defunct weapon system and anybody possessing one was happy to be rid of it. My security guy noted that my entire system was pre-QC, so convinced me that this could be a good insurance for an uncertain future. It cost almost nothing, so I thought, why not? Never ever believed that I'd actually use one, but having the ability to make a high stakes threat seemed like a useful thing to have. And so, in fact, it turned out."

"Use one, you said." Sue again. "What others do you have?"

I groaned. This was one of the harder questions that I had wanted to avoid and I'd led them straight to it myself. "Well, it was a bio-warfare package - ex-Russian or Israeli I think - so it had a range of application vectors... "

"Cut out the Geek-speak!" now Sophie. "What've you got in your cellars?"

"Another Ebola, 48 hour strain; Anthrax, 24 and 48 hour versions. Plus about half a dozen non-lethal strains - various 'flus. Of course, here, non-lethal is relative. Still probably a 5 - 10 % of the most vulnerable, particularly the young and the old, might kick it, but nothing like the 95% plus you'd get in the center of a weaponized Ebola or Anthrax outbreak."

"Jesus, why do you hang on to this fucking stuff?" from Sue.

"If you had non-lethal options, why use a nightmare disease like Ebola?" simultaneously from Sophie.

I raised my hands in despair. "I thought we were covering the technical stuff first and were then going to come to this touchy-feely component later? Anyway, let me answer your questions in turn. So, having seen how the application in Jamaica ran out of control, why not destroy all my stocks? Two reasons. Firstly, I've already found a use for this stuff that I could never have envisaged when I bought it, so maybe other uses will emerge in the future. The world's a much more dangerous place now than it was when I was setting up this little tropical retreat in the '30s, you know. Secondly, it

218

did get out of control when I used it last time, but I know better now and, if I'm forced to go for a bio-war option again, I'll try to be more careful."

"You'll try... "Sophie exploded, but I drowned her out by raising my voice almost to a shout to talk over her.

"And, it's just occurred to me, thirdly, I know that I'm not the only one possessing this kind of shit. MAD may be a crazy concept, but it's a fuckin' lot better than being at the mercy of a lone nutter with unilaterally assured destruction"

Sophie was again trying to break in, but I waved her down. "Now, the second question has a more technical basis. Why did I use the most terrible bio-war agent in my arsenal? I actually used my Knowledge Management MAA tools to look at all the options for a wide range of scenarios. The original analysis is still on file somewhere; I'll dig it out and send it to you. The big problem was that Tina and I were alone against what was effectively an island with a population of a million or so that was on a war footing. The gang warlords had complete control of Jamaica and were intent on expanding their hegemony over the rest of the Caribbean. Even if, with a minimal intrusion option, I'd managed to get Andrea back intact, they wouldn't just sit back and accept this as a fait accompli. They would mobilize against us personally, and probably the entire island of Barbados, until they'd reasserted their dominance. I had not only to get Andrea back, but also hit them so hard, in such a terrifying manner, that they would stay well clear of us in the future. It comes back to the MAD argument; with the entire resources of Jamaica behind them, there was no way that this estate could resist a prolonged attack. But, if they saw how over-dimensioned my response would be, they'd be crazy to even think about messing with us again."

I thought for a moment about how to make this case. "Here again, I have the original attack plan on file. Our analysis suggested that wiping out an entire gang, along with hangers-on... "

"... and innocent families in the vicinity" Sophie couldn't stop herself adding.

"... and families, friends, acquaintances in the vicinity - whether innocent or not - especially if done in a horrible and terribly painful manner, would do the job. This is the technical justification. However, if I'm honest, all the options with non-lethal agents increased the direct risk for Tina and me - and the chance that we wouldn't get Andrea back. So, even if my KM tools had suggested another option, I'd probably have gone for the Ebola anyway. It's such a terrifying disease that anyone infected has little chance of behaving rationally."

"But isn't that the most dangerous situation that you can have? How could you predict what Raz was going to do when he learned that you'd infected him with a deadly plague?" Sophie was perplexed.

"You've got it back to front! As soon as I turned up uninvited, the logical thing for him to do would be to immediately start torturing Andrea and Tina until I gave him everything he wanted. I was in the lion's den; my only advantage was that I had him confused - I seemed to be rushing into his trap. Thereafter, I had to keep him wrong-footed; seeing your buddies bleeding from the eyes, vomiting and shitting themselves, will do that for most people, even tough bastards like him. As soon as he knew he was infected, I had him over a barrel. The challenge was to offer him hope. To allow him to think that there was a cure, that he could maybe turn the tables on me and get his revenge. It was a calculated risk on my part, but the trickiest part was getting the gun from him and, even if I'd failed, Andrea and Tina would have been free."

"You'd have sacrificed your life for your sister?" Sophie asked.

"I sacrificed a hundred thousand or so other lives; one more or less wouldn't change the equation."

It was quiet for a bit.

***

The girls went into a huddle while I stood and stretched, wishing that it was already time for my exercise session. Anna today, so it would be hard. Nevertheless, only physical pain, not the mental anguish I went through at the hands of these ladies.

Sue again. "We'll leave your biological arsenal for now, though we might come back to you again on that when we're filling in the touchy-feely stuff. Anyway, next question: apart from the reactor, bio-war viruses and an airplane, are there any more

221

surprises hidden away here. Things that most - or all - of the residents wouldn't know about?"

Another tricky one. Play for time. "Well, I have a nuclear submarine with a few cruise missiles on board, a couple of tanks, a stealth bomber, a squad of women commandoes trained by the SAS..."

Realization dawned on Sue's face. "Cof! You bastard! Stop taking the piss!"

I fell back into my chair, laughing like a hyena. I hadn't seen anything so funny for weeks. "God, your faces!" I spluttered. "Submarine with cruise missiles, stealth bomber, you didn't bat an eyelid! Christ on a bike, I'm an eccentric for fuck's sake, not a wannabe global dictator out of a James Bond movie!"

Sophie wasn't putting up with this mockery. "Look, mate, from what we've heard so far, you're only a Persian cat short of a Blofeld, so don't fucking push it!"

"Sorry" I apologized insincerely, ruining it with a snigger, as I fought to control another burst of laughter.

"Forget sorry, answer the question!" Sue was not going to be diverted.

This was as much time as I was going to get. Give them a full inventory on site, I decided, making sure to start with what they already know. "Defense; I've already told you about what we have on the fences - the electric wire and the tasers. The security guards also have tasers."

"Non-lethal?" Sophie was going after the fine detail.

"Usually. They're programmable. If the threat gets serious, then we can up the power. The range will go down but, in a pinch, they can be lethal up to a hundred meters or so. OK, that's the tasers. We also have the video surveillance that I set up."

"And it hasn't changed in a decade?"

"Expanded a little. I gave a monitor and some cameras to Nigel and he has distributed them in key sites: mainly in Bridgetown and the South Coast. I didn't actually tell him that I can access the feeds on all of these, but I suspect he guesses."

"So that's it for video surveillance?"

"Terrestrial, yes."

Sophie pounced like a hawk on a field mouse. "So what about extra-terrestrial?"

I rolled my eyes heavenwards. Couldn't I control my big mouth? Answer the question with the minimum of words and don't add anything that's not specifically requested, I silently commanded myself. Anyway, I had to answer. "Over the last few years David has managed to patch into and reprogram some obsolete satellites. I can now access some of the feeds; from some of the old SPOT satellites, for example. Compared with what we had pre-Crash, the resolution is poor and coverage patchy. Some of us with relatively good hardware - myself, David and some of the research teams - are now using the satellites for high bandwidth data links. We can now move a lot more information about than we could using radio."

The ex-Jesuit now had a gleam in her eye. "Over the last year, you said. So you couldn't access the satellites six years ago?"

I squirmed. "No, I couldn't" I answered truthfully, if not completely honestly.

To no avail. "You couldn't - so who could?"

I shrugged and realized that there was no way around a full answer. "One of the research teams who survived in Northern Canada was a bunch of atmospheric scientists doing work on aurora, solar storms, cosmic rays and that kind of shit. Although AIs could certainly have solved all this stuff if they were but asked, this was academic research and was set up to use some of the many satellites that had become redundant for their original purposes in the '30s. Like any university lab, they had all the latest QC support, but also generations of old computers; these guys are like pack-rats. They had satellite links within a year and were soon working with David to establish a wider range of services. The scientists establish links with the appropriate sputnik and David reprograms it to communicate with the kit available to us, rather than the huge radio-telescopes, microwave arrays and high power lasers they have in Canada."

"So, to the point, what did you have six years ago?"

"As I said, I didn't have anything myself, but David had. When I explained the situation I was in, he did some spot video searches for me, produced a couple of high resolution static images of the landing strips at Montserrat and Montego Bay to check that landing was feasible. He also set us up a low res GPS."

"So this is answering a question I had listed for later" Sue interjected. "I wondered how you knew to go to Montego Bay rather than Kingston."

"Based on the information that I had, we were able to pull an image of a Jamaican ship leaving Bridgetown port just after my sister was kidnapped. A week later it docked at the village by the Montego Bay airport, I guess to avoid the bother of getting through the sprawl of downtown. There was no coincidence to where we landed and what we did thereafter."

"This also explains how you were able to find the Montserrat airfield at night."

"The GPS was pretty rough - resolution no better than about fifty meters - but made finding the airstrip easy. Landing on it was, however, another matter entirely. I was shitting bricks, I can tell you. We were bouncing over potholes that we couldn't see, never sure if one of them would be deep enough to smash the undercarriage."

"If you had all this information, couldn't you see the yachts at the harbor. Wait until they had left before you landed?" Sophie was evidently still chasing the idea that I could have minimised the impact of the raid, if I had just been more careful.

"You've got to remember that, here at the house, I could only get images from Canada via David. Anything I had would have been a day old. Everything in the plane was lashed together in a rush; the nearest we had to communication technology was the GPS. So I had no way of knowing that any ships would be there. Even if I had known, I'd have no reason to suspect that they would leave just after their crews had been infected and before symptoms would have caused them to postpone sailing. So the answer is clear: I had information that helped me plan the attack, but nothing that could have been used to provide me with a better plan. I now have a lot better tools at my disposal but, to be honest, I'm not sure that even these could have changed things. It was bad luck, that's all."

"Who else has this technology?" Back to Sue.

"It's pretty restricted to the Renaissance group. Nobody else has the hardware to access it. I supply some satellite survey output as a service to Nigel and the unofficial Bajan government, so he knows something of what I can do, although I have never provided him with formal specs. Anyway, the capabilities are expanding all the time as David and the Canadians get their teeth into it."

"OK, let's move on - what else have you got here?"

There was no way that Sue would stay diverted for long. I had to finish up the inventory. "The computer hardware and the knowledge base are the most valuable fundamental resources that I have. Nevertheless, I also have top-end integrated materials and electronics fabrication laboratories: the absolute best that was available before QC-based systems took over. This was hardly a great expense; after AIs could be integrated into control systems, anything without this option was instantly obsolete. I had thought that the electronics lab would be useful to handle any repairs or replacement kit I might need - despite the fact that '20s hardware was very robust - and the materials lab was just a playground for me to dabble in my hobby projects."

If Sue had been a dog her tail would almost be wagging off. She knew she was onto a hot lead, but couldn't yet work out what direction it was going in. "These labs seem a bit of an anticlimax, having dragged out your other dark secrets. You kept them to last, though, and you don't look very comfortable. Right now, what can they make?"

"Just about anything" I answered quietly.

"A cure for cholera?" Sophie inquired.

"Takes a while, but it was doable; that's why nobody on the estate died during the post-Crash outbreak. I introduced it into our drinking water."

"But people were dying in droves outside! You looked after us, but left the others to die?"

"I had no fucking choice. I have a specialist lab, not a fucking pharmaceutical production plant! I first protected everyone here, then extended the net to the external communities where local staff lived; giving them drinks to take home that contained the tailored vaccine. Nevertheless, the key to cholera treatment is rehydration and avoiding the contaminated water that is the source of the problem. That, I could do little about; certainly not beyond our immediate neighbors. Regardless, after we had sorted out those closest to us, Andrea distributed assistance more widely; but by then the main outbreak had fairly well run its course, probably because the raw sewage had been flushed out of the drinking water supplies. We did what was possible, within the constraints of our production capacity and the priorities that we had set."

"OK, that was the cholera outbreak, but surely you could do more to provide high tech aid to the survivors, at least here in Barbados."

I glared at the heavens in frustration. This woman was smart, but so conditioned by growing up in a technologically integrated world, where the latest advance or must-have goody needs only to be manufactured and it will work. The infrastructure was taken so much for granted that it was completely invisible.

"Yes, that's entirely the fucking problem: high tech I can do easily, but that's not what's needed. The folks here need low tech: clean water, sewerage, electrical power, transportation so that trade can be established. Maybe a little mid-21st century know-how will help to get this up and running, but the big step is going from prehistoric hunter-gatherer to late 19th century or early 20th. Until we get there, all this high tech shit helps not a jot."

"But you're expanding your own systems!" I could feel Sophie's fundamentalist social equalizer mindset beginning to get on my tits, but tried to moderate my response.

"Of course I am, because I've got the technology to utilize this stuff and, if applicable, use it to help others. In the entire Caribbean - discounting outliers like Bermuda and the Florida Keys - I'm the only person with this ability. Probably 99% of the survivors will just have to sort things out on their own. I hope I can help the rest, but it will be on my conditions."

"Sorry, Cof, but who appointed you God when nobody was looking!" Sophie was looking seriously distraught.

"There are no Gods, Sophie, I thought we agreed that." Apart from sadistic personal trainers, I acknowledged silently, but didn't want to muddy the waters any further. "All we have is pragmatism and common sense. Go back to the database this evening and search our history archives. Find me one example of an open democratic process that ever helped anyone to respond to a major catastrophe. It just doesn't work that way, no matter what our philosophical, ethical or religious desires would like to happen. I didn't manipulate events so that we ended up in this situation; indeed you can easily argue that it is all luck, rather than judgment. But look at what we have now: after a decade this house is a center for activity in rebuilding which, if a certain Crazy Old Fuck hadn't set it up and defended it, wouldn't exist today. It is impossible to prove, but I am convinced that if Andrea and I had passed over responsibility for this place after the breakdown to someone in authority or, even worse, tried to make decisions by consensus, then it would be totally fucked by now. Nobody can run it as well as we can; so, even now, I'm not prepared to hand over any aspect of its control. Maybe this'll change in a decade or so, but not in the next few years."

Sue evidently decided to intervene before we came to blows. "Your labs, you've used them to support reconstruction?"

"Well, not initially. As you can imagine, in the early days our concerns were entirely on defending our fragile little community. So we produced video cameras, solar cells to power them, that kind of stuff. The electric fence, tasers and crap like that we had already installed, but the lab was invaluable for repairs after the early attempted incursions, before the raiders learned better. We made up walkie-talkies for communication with outside communities and tailored laptops for the IBS branches and other support that I agreed to provide to Nigel."

"Couldn't you have made up an antidote to your Ebola bioweapon, something that could have avoided the collateral damage, even if only the children and girls in that village, who seem to have affected you so much?" Sophie couldn't stop digging into this catastrophe, looking for a way that I could have avoided it or, at least, reduced the number of innocent victims.

"OK, you've got me down as a mass-murdering psychopath." I was rapidly losing my temper. "You may be correct: the mass-murdering is historical fact, it is only the psychopathic bit that's up for debate. However, I've never deliberately killed anyone who was not a direct target, trying to minimize collateral damage in any way possible.

We may have seemed gratuitously brutal, but this was premeditated: all in order to avoid future conflicts, which would result in worse bloodshed."

I hesitated for a moment, to allow this to sink in. "I could argue this until the cows come home, but the bottom line is that tailored bioweapons - or antidotes to them - aren't something I can just run up in my lab. If they were, I wouldn't have needed to purchase them in the first place, would I? Standard cures to natural diseases are hard enough. So I didn't, and still don't, have synthetic bio-war genetic engineering on line: either offensive or defensive. All I have is what I originally purchased."

Sophie looked chastened, but Sue continued in her typically relentless manner. "The plane, did you fabricate that?"

"No, don't be silly! I told you that I had already bought it for the Andrea. I fabricated the GPS unit to replace all the worthless QC shit that we ripped out, but that was it."

"But you could have?"

"Yes, given enough time, I could have built a plane; but it's a pretty useless thing on its own. Without distributed landing sites, fuel, navigation systems and stuff like that, it's just a box with wings. It didn't bother me in the slightest to lose it. I hoped we'd jump over the entire heavier-than-air history of aviation and leap ahead - or stagnate in time, according to which fortune teller you encountered. Not that I'm building balloons in my

231

back garden, but I'm trying to encourage the infrastructure that'll go in that direction."

"You're doing it again" Sophie objected, "unilaterally deciding what is best for mankind."

"For fuck's sake woman," I looped out, "you're supposed to be a cunting Jesuit! Or, at least, a fucking cunting ex-Jesuit! Had logic been dropped off the curriculum when they decided to include women? Reckon it was too much for their poor little brains? Don't give me this total shite politically correct gobbledegook - be a fucking rational, thinking human and, instead of platitudes, tell me how I could have done better! I may have fucked up. I probably fucked up. But don't give me aphorisms. Give me one fucking single, specific example of how I could have changed a past decision to produce an outcome today that would be assuredly better!"

Sue was out of her chair and came to my side. "Calm down, you daft bugger, you'll give yourself a heart attack! You and Sophie are just provoking each other; you're the one with the chemistry background, you should recognize an autocatalytic runaway reaction... "

A few moments of silence and then she bent over me and looked directly into my face. "... that now seems inevitable given Sophie's background. You set us up! You could have produced this record by yourself or by drafting-in anyone capable of managing a Dictaphone. Nevertheless, you set it up using an antiquated typed input and selected Sophie and me to work on it. It's now clear why you

232

selected a cleric, or ex-cleric! For absolution! You had to explain all of this and someone had to agree that you did the right things, that all of your excesses were justified. Does this explain why we ended up doing this?"

Sophie was looking completely gobsmacked and I must confess that I felt a bit light-headed myself. I had never planned anything more than some kind of bibliographic record, consciously at least. Nevertheless, Sue's arguments were very compelling. Why had I chosen to have physical scribes rather than simply dictating my story to smart software, which could easily do all of the checks that I had created as a job for these women? Why did I actually choose Sophie who, compared to most of the residents of the estate, I'd had little contact with in the past? In fact, why Sue? I have always known that she was probably the brightest individual in the community - including Andrea and myself in that comparison - but her vitriolic personality had kept us from ever becoming close. If it was a simple document that I was producing, I seemed to have selected mega-overqualified support staff.

Sue had given me time to work through the impact of her deductions, but seemed to have been reading my mind in the process and she belatedly added the single question "... in fact, even if it explains Sophie, what am I doing on this rather crowded Freudian couch?"

A good principle is that, if all else fails, run like fuck. "Good question. In fact, several good questions, observations, whatever. Unfortunately it's training time, but we'll get back on this straight afterwards. Anyone for high impact aerobics with Anna?"

I scuttled from the room, relieved to see the girls had other concerns than an hour of physical torture. An hour where the pain could be ignored, while I tried to work out exactly what I was doing with this fucking history project.

***

Anna's aerobics were popular with a lot of the staff and half a dozen women were already in the gym when I showed up. Our trainer was sprawled on the floor, legs widely spread apart and her body flat on the floor between them. Her back was curved to raise herself onto her elbows while she fiddled with the palmtop that controlled the music system. Although she appeared completely relaxed, just looking at her almost brought tears to my eyes. If I even attempted to get into a pose like that, I'd give myself a double hernia.

I moved to my usual position in the far left corner of the mirror-walled room. Out of Anna's direct line of sight and right below one of the vents feeding cold air into the exercise area. The gym was filling up and the levels of noise increased as more conversation groups formed. Anna and I seemed to be the only ones doing pre-class stretching although, probably, the woman was completely oblivious to the fact. As I worked to loosen up calves and thighs, I had an opportunity to admire my instructress's tight body. The girl was in her late teens, slim, with small conical breasts and a compact but well-rounded bottom. Her skin was jet black and her short hair was, currently, died a copper color so that it looked like rusted steel wool. Her delicate features indicated some Mediterranean genes in her makeup, but her skin and bottom were entirely out of Africa.

The noise level dropped as Anna flowed to her feet and outlined the plan for today's class. She made it a matter of honor that every class was different, just as her music always varied, an eclectic mixture of jazz, pop and dance ranging from contemporary, self-recorded Bajan reggae to bee-bop from the mid-20th century. Today's session would be a straightforward, high-impact cardio block followed by stretching and cool down using small balance pads. We were invited to strap on wrist and ankle weights for the first block; blue for boys and pink for girls, as she put it. As the only male in the class, I couldn't avoid taking the heavier weights; as I expected, Anna and about half of the other women also selected blue.

There was no opportunity for any wool-gathering during the cardio block, full concentration was required to memorize the rapidly evolving combination of moves while avoiding bumping into anyone as we raced around, taking full advantage of all floor space available in the gym. Just when we seemed to have the full sequence down pat, it was time for carambolage: we were split into two

235

groups, set facing each other, and had to run through the combi again, intermeshing our moves together. It was a tribute to the experience level of the entire class that, after a few initial collisions, we were able to carry out the entire sequence three times without mistakes - or, at least in my case, with mistakes that were too minor to notice.

The cool down was ideal for daydreaming, however, as having your mind on other things helped reduce the pain as hard-worked muscles were stretched to their limits. Now I could think about Sue's accusation. Was I really looking for atonement; was that the subconscious purpose behind the entire exercise? It certainly explained my choice of Sophie, if I was looking for absolution from my literary act of contrition. But why then Sue? Was this a masochistic desire for my ploy to be exposed? The hard, analytical Sue was certainly the person to do this. I tried to remember how I came to choose these women. I had been talking over the idea with Andrea and then we simply flicked through the files of all staff that had recently logged an interest in doing something new. I seemed to recall that the only criteria we used to rank them were vague: intelligent, analytical, focused. These were qualities that we agreed would be necessary to keep me on track, given my well-known tendency to go off on tangents whenever telling stories of any sort.

Now the best bit of the session: the final relaxation, a kind of yoga meditation. I could now distinctly recall looking through the prioritized summary files. Sue and Sophie were well clear of the pack and I was delighted when Andrea reported that they'd both be happy to have a go at this. Andrea always handled these things, because I worried that, sometimes, staff might feel pressurized into agreeing to do something for me because it was difficult for them to turn me down face to face. Andrea, however, could approach them much less formally and ensure that it really was an informed consent.

By the time I had nailed this down, the class had finished and I was freshening up in the shower, trying hard not to be distracted by the views in the unisex changing room. There were curtained-off cubicles, but, like me, most of the women ignored them. I was now feeling ready to face up to Sue. Her analysis had been impeccable and her conclusions so plausible that she had begun to make me doubt myself. I know that the mind can play tricks on itself, especially as it ages, but it seemed to be clear that this wasn't the case here. It was simply a coincidence that Sophie was an ex-priest; I chose the best team to ensure that the project ran to plan; there was no ulterior motive, conscious or subconscious. At that point Anna entered the shower room, surrounded by a gaggle of chattering women, all appearing to be talking simultaneously. Time to escape from the noise, I decided - and better make it quick before the physical consequences of the expanses of brown and black flesh on display became obvious.

***

I thought I was going to be alone for lunch again, but Andrea showed up to join me, interested to know how the book was going. Recently she had been spending more time back in her own villa, which she was setting up as a school for training coordinators for her various charity and reconstruction projects. A strong believer in the teach someone to fish approach to providing aid, she focused on self-sufficiency in the projects and staffed them with those who would otherwise need support, such as single mothers and their children.

I reported on progress in only the most general of terms. My sister had decided that she didn't want to look at any early drafts, wanted to save herself for the first complete manuscript. She then overviewed the status of her projects and we drifted into a detailed discussion of how the resources that I had available could be best used to assist. As usual, the limiting factors were the capacity of my fabrication facilities and limited stocks of some required raw materials. The latter could be handled by making up lists for the scavengers, who showed great ingenuity in finding anything I needed from the ruins of facilities that have been derelict since the crash. The former was more fundamental and always came back to the same strategic question: should I use the labs to clone themselves and thus double my throughput or did other products have priority? The problem was that the cloning operation couldn't practically be run in parallel with any other work. It was also a big job, not only blocking all production for about six months, but requiring that specific raw material stocks were built up before hand, considerably limiting the projects that could be considered for an extended period beforehand. Again, as usual, we agreed that we couldn't yet afford such a disruption, so cloning was again shelved.

Tina arrived in time for a coffee; apparently she was teaching navigation to trainee pilots. Barbados now had a second plane and two small airships. Our old Cessna was still flying, but could be considered space age compared to the 1940s DC-3 that had joined it. The plane had been found in a private museum in St Lucia and readily traded to Barbados because nobody local imagined that this relic - well over a hundred years old - would ever fly again. Although it required almost complete rebuilding, the machine was so primitive that much of the work could be done in a mechanical workshop assembled by scrounging tools from hobby engineers around the island. Only a little help was required from my facilities, mainly associated with the conversion required to run efficiently on the aviation fuel being produced: a blend of ethanol and biodiesel.

The airships were home-made, based on a 2010 design that I had ripped-off from a military project that I found in my database. The wooden frame and the Kevlar-like polymer fabric were produced in the airfield workshops and the only direct material inputs from my side were a coating that made the fabric gas-tight and the catalytic converter to

239

produce hydrogen from alcohol. Propulsion, at present, was based on a copy of the DC3's original Pratt & Whitneys, but a move to smaller, lighter options was planned as soon as workshop experience and tools had improved sufficiently. Personally, I hoped to leapfrog over all this IC stuff and move to fuel-cell driven electric motors, but I hadn't yet found an efficient enough ethanol-air fuel cell that could be fabricated with present Bajan technology and certainly didn't want to block my own production facilities for something that was so clearly non-essential.

My musing ended abruptly as I received pecks on the cheek from both woman and they wandered off together, hand in hand. My scribes had clearly been waiting for my sister to leave; no sooner had they disappeared than a couple of heads poked round the door to the hallway. "Your study, OK?" Sue was clearly keen to start.

"Why not?" I refilled my coffee cup and headed after my interrogators.

***

As soon as I had settled down behind my desk, I thought it was best to clear the air about the way in which I had selected them to work on the project. I quickly summarized how the process had functioned and posted them copies of the actual ranking that had been produced. "So, Sue's analysis was very convincing; so convincing, in fact, that I began to worry that I might have biased the

240

selection, even if I hadn't been aware of the fact. But, there you have it - luck of the draw rather than conspiracy."

Sophie looked relieved, but Sue didn't seem 100% convinced. In any case, it appeared that they had decided to move on from this topic. Sue took the lead. "We didn't get finished with your Renaissance group, but this seems very closely related to another loose thread: your views of where we are headed in the future. As before, we'll try to get your technical ideas down first, with your motivations later."

"I'm not sure that these will be easy to separate in this case, but I'll give it a shot." I closed my eyes to try to remember what I had already told them and, of the rest, rank it in terms of its likelihood to stir up trouble. "Right, let's look at the most technical bit. I think we all agree that we need to establish working technological infrastructure as quickly as possible. To assure health and build up to a someway reasonable standard of living, we need to use existing accommodation and make it livable by supplying power, water and sewerage. For Barbados, there would be strong arguments for distributing the surviving population in rural areas where food is easier to supply, but this actually requires much more extensive infrastructure, so we will have to accept that a significant fraction of the total population will remain in - or move back to - urban areas. With our reduced population, we should be able to downsize these significantly, however."

"Isn't that a bit premature?" Sophie wondered. "The rapid population growth rates of the late 20th and early 21st century had started to drop off, but there's been quite a baby boom in the last few years."

"Yes... , well... , we really hope that this will get sorted out soon. It was over-population that was the fundamental cause of this problem in the first place, so a high priority is to make contraception readily available... "

"You cannot be serious!" Sophie exploded. "The global population has been reduced by billions, hundreds of millions more are living on the edge; the slightest natural threat, drought, flood, whatever and they'll die in droves. And what are you working on? Fucking contraceptives. Are you fucking out of your fucking tiny little mind?"

I almost exploded straight back at her, but some evil side to my character held me back, so that I calmly taunted the ex-God-botherer further. "Righty Ho! You've got strong opinions here, so I suppose you've done the sums to support them. In my position, it seems that you'd be using all resources to build the population up to previous levels. Now why might that be?" I've never been quite sure what dripping sarcasm sounded like, but it's probably much like my voice then when goading poor Sophie.

Sue sat back and folded her arms. She was leaving her partner on her own on this one. Sophie took a deep breath and fought to calm down, knowing that she could only make progress in such an argument with logic, drawing on the fundaments of her Jesuit casuistry training. "We had a global population of almost ten billion a decade and a half ago. I don't know what the latest estimates are - but we're probably, what, less than 4 billion now. Doesn't that mean we need to rebuild our population as well as our other infrastructure?"

Sue rolled her eyes, but left it to me to loop out. "Where the fuck did that little leap of logic come from? We totally shagged the planet by inflicting it with 10 billion people who all expected to live a life of luxury. The only reason that the entire shooting match didn't go tits-up earlier was exponentially increasing technology, which managed to stay ahead of an exponentially increasing population for more than a century. Then - maybe it was inevitable - there was a hiccup. The whole fucking house of cards collapsed, as it had to."

"A hiccup! A fucking hiccup! How in Christ's fucking name can you call the entire apocalyptic fucking nightmare of 2041 a fucking hiccup?"

I was now at my most annoying. "My but you certainly swear a lot when you're talking shite! Is that a Jesuit thing?"

"Cof, you smartarse cunt... "

"Sophie, Sophie," I drowned out her interruption, "think for a minute, instead of spouting politically correct manifestos. In order to maintain ten billion in the lifestyle to which they had become programed to expect, we had to hand over the reins to electronic intelligences. We lost all control of our destinies. There seems to have been two potential futures; the system crashes, as actually happened, or it doesn't and, in that case, by now mankind would be lotus eaters. There would be hives full of drones living in contented luxury, but nobody would be challenged, solving problems for themselves, working... "

"So, you're saying the Crash was a good thing?"

"Fuck, yes! Better a few billion alive, even a few million alive, than many billions just existing in a form of suspended animation!"

Oops! This was the ultimate taboo. It was like saying that the holocaust massacre of the Jews had its positive side because it reduced the incidence of big noses in the population or cut the cost of soap. The act itself was so obscene, that any positive by-product could not be discussed in polite company. Could you ever argue that genocide was anything other than evil? What about world wars, then? Famous generals were responsible for killing as many people as Stalin or Pol Pot, but the fundamental immorality was hidden under a coating of jingoism.

I had actually never really looked at it this way before, but, all of a sudden, a lot of the issues that had been bothering me over the last couple of decades just came together and crystallized into a new Weltblick. I never expected the Crash, I didn't plan explicitly for it but, looking back, I wouldn't argue that it was all bad. All bad? There were strong arguments that it was the best thing that could have happened. Sure, it would have been better, with the wisdom of hindsight, to have avoided the

244

population explosion and associated environmental destruction occurring in the first place. But wasn't that what we were trying to do now?

Sophie's shock was wearing off. "Come on, Cof, you don't really mean that do you?"

Sue answered before I could even start to formulate a response. "Of course you do! You, deep in your bones, are completely convinced that over-population was destroying the planet. You relate to the people that you know, but the rest are just ciphers. You'd do anything possible to protect this community - and part of that is allowing, or encouraging, population to drop to sustainable levels. In Barbados you're already using very limited resources to produce contraceptives. In the rest of the world, you and your renaissance group will just stand by and let people die in areas where you consider residual populations to still be above a sustainable level. Could that be a summary of your plans for the future?"

I was speechless for a bit. Then I managed to spit it out. "Couldn't have put it more succinctly myself!"

***

Sue took this better than I expected, but Sophie was outraged. "That's barbaric, evil. People have already suffered so much and even now, after a decade and a half, they're hanging on by the skin of their teeth. Any you, with all your fucking resources here, you intend to do fuck-all to help them!"

"Not quite as black-white as that, but you've got the general gist," I was again struggling to stay calm. "The key thing is that, although I have a lot of resources in relative terms, when considered in absolute terms, compared to global needs, they're negligibly small. As I discussed with Andrea over lunch, not even enough to do a tenth of the high priority jobs we've set out for this island. I can - and do - supply information to anyone who requests it, which includes quite a lot of folk in the harder hit areas... "

"And charge for the service!" Sophie spluttered.

"And charge standard rates, but it's all funny money for these areas. They generally have nothing hard to trade as yet, most of their income is simply from supply of news: reports on developments in the remnants of the megacities, warnings of new epidemics, stuff like that. In the future, when things settle down a bit, they'll be able to utilize the large resources that they do have to establish trade with areas that suffered less."

"What do they have for resources?" Sue inquired with a frown. "Most of these kind of places - Japan, Europe, China - used up all their own easily accessed natural resources long ago. Until the AIs brought in technology optimized to reduce demand, these were the sinks for world mineral production."

"And so... " The secretaries frowned as they realized that I was setting them another test.

"The ruins of the cities, they mine them!" Sue got the answer first, but Sophie's nod indicated that she also saw how this would work.

"Yes, for scavengers there are vast quantities of useful materials that can be obtained from the cities themselves, or even from the old dumps and disposal sites around them. In most cases this will be a much easier job than attempting to mine the low grade, deep or relatively inaccessible ore bodies that have been left over after the ravages of the last century. Recovery will be fastest in lower population density areas with good agriculture and fisheries. Eventually, however, access to materials will limit technological development and so the old cities will be mined."

"This seems like exploitation." The ex-priest was still unhappy.

"Of course it's exploitation, but just in the reverse direction of the colonial, first world exploitation that's been going on for centuries. What goes around, comes around: it's almost biblical. Or maybe Gaia-esque. The important thing, though, is that we're trying to set up a basis and an incentive for international trade, even though it won't develop for quite a while yet. What we don't want is a repeat of the colonial annexation of resources or, indeed, the wholesale rape and pillage so characteristic of expanding empires: be they Norse, Mongol, Macedonian, Spanish or British."

"Or Jamaican?" This was like an open sore; Sophie couldn't resist probing it.

"Or Yardie! One way or another, we would have had to do something about them, if they had continued to expand at the rate that they were going."

"So this is why you're hanging on to your bioweapons? Waiting for the next threat, when you will use them in a fully premeditated manner."

"I wouldn't exclude the possibility, but our goal is to reduce as much as we can the probability of situations like that arising in the first place. Build up technology in the more fortunate areas, but try to constrain re-establishment of nationalism. Encourage inter-dependency by establishing trade and extend that to the post-Crash wastelands as soon as is practicable."

"It doesn't seem fair, though. You're concentrating your efforts on those who have most and effectively ignoring anyone at the bottom of the heap."

Sue was again staying out of the debate and I watched her carefully as I tried, yet again, to explain the facts of life in the real world. "Apart from my personal feeling that charity starts at home and my refusal to put my friends in this estate at risk for the sake of those I don't know - and might not even like - in a far off land, you have to think of practicality. Logistically, I still have problems helping out in Bridgetown, fifteen kilometers away. How on earth can I help anybody still surviving in the ruins of Tokyo, Shanghai, Sao Paulo, New York or London? Am I supposed to build a ship, put all my kit on board and sail around the world saving people. Even then, how would I get to all the inland disaster areas? Beijing, Mexico City, Chicago and the rest. The problem is not only too big for me to contribute anything directly, it's also too far away. Although you think what I'm doing is unjust, justice and fairness as concepts are not only unhelpful at the present moment, they're counter-productive. Think about practicality before mouthing off on what should be done. Then you'll realize much of what you're suggesting is, to be frank, fucking stupid."

Sue was fighting to keep her face bland, but there was a smile threatening to break past the current trace of an upwards curl to her lips. "So, maybe I'm fundamentally an evil madman, but there is method in my madness. We're lucky enough to be in Barbados, which has the potential for rapid recovery to the level of a functioning late 20th century technology. Barbados is situated in the Caribbean, which can also recover quickly if bootstrapped by Bajan resources. The Caribbean renaissance can then be extended to Central America. A bit trickier, possibly, but, as the region with technological infrastructure grows, the process is autocatalytic."

"So when will you get to the States, Europe, Japan?"

"Us? We probably won't. Remember there are quite a few other places where technology exists. Some of these may have difficulties growing due to remoteness and the struggle to survive: the Antarctic, Northern Canada, for example. Others have the same, or better, potential for recovery that we have: like Australia, New Zealand, some of the Mediterranean islands. These will also serve for centers of stepwise regional recovery."

"You're tap-dancing, Cof! When can the really badly hit areas expect help?"

"Not for a long time. They will have fallen furthest and will be hardest to bring back up. Just take a single example; one that I have, naturally, been following with some interest. England: a developed country, completely dependent on advanced technology with a largely urban population. Pre-crash population about sixty-five million, present estimate about a tenth of that. The cities are almost completely abandoned. There are no more engineered barriers to the ravages of the greenhouse climate; extensive areas are flooded during the summer rains and coastal areas are hammered by the combination of increased sea-level and massive surges from the regular hurricanes. The winters now more closely resemble those in Scandinavia; the Thames freezes over two years out of three. In some ways it is amazing that even five or six million people can live under these conditions but, to use your term, they are hanging on by the skin of their teeth. Summer mortality due to disease and winter starvation is keeping the population in decline, despite a greatly increased birth rate. Some technology has survived, but only in very remote areas: mainly small islands. Unlike here, however, the survivors are living in the conditions of the Dark Ages: closer to the 10th Century than the 20th. Technology can't grow naturally there. They will just have to wait until the rest of the world has recovered to the extent that large-scale support can be provided. A best-case scenario might be in another twenty years or so; less optimistic scenarios could be more like forty to fifty years. If the climate keeps degrading due to the inertia of the Greenhouse effect, there may not be many people to help by then."

Sue finally joined in. "This is what your Renaissance group is all about then? This is why you want to eliminate nations, set up world government and a single currency, force regional development; it's all to provide the components of your best case scenario. You really have it all planned out!"

"I really wish we had. There are a couple of us that have fairly similar ideas that run along those lines. Others - the majority in fact - are more concerned about getting through today and tomorrow in their own area, rather than what might occur in the wastelands in a few decades time. So we focus mainly on day-to-day problems, but provide a gentle and continuous push in the direction in which we would like to go. It's all a bit like the proverbial herding of cats."

"So this is driven by yourself and your mate David?"

"We're part of it, along with some Canadians and some Kiwis. To be honest, it's actually the New Zealanders that are the long-term planners here. They were originally some kind of marine research establishment, based in a middle-of-nowhere place called Napier. They're rebuilding fast, again with a lot of help from David. They have been running a lot of wargame simulations, apparently it's similar to the analyses they did of fish population dynamics, to determine how best to prevent development being hindered by empire-building or regional conflicts. I think they're keeping a wary eye on their larger northern neighbor."

"Australia? Isn't that a bit unlikely?" Sophie asked.

With a nod of my head I passed the question to her partner. Sue seemed less sure of herself here than was normally the case. "Oz, stable democracy, rich country with a relatively low population density. Large concentration in big cities, though, so probably hit reasonably badly by the collapse of February 2041. Although the center is desert, especially after the Greenhouse droughts, there is a lot of good agriculture and fisheries along the coast." She was clearly thinking out loud, working her way through the problem in a logical manner.

"Um... if any technology at all survived, I guess they could recover quite quickly. In terms of expanding beyond their national borders, there are plenty of surrounding islands that would be fertile ground for regional renaissance, based on your Caribbean model. I can't think why the Napier bunch would worry about them moving on to develop an empire of the Pacific Rim, however."

"What about Australia's pre-Crash role in Pacific Rim and Asia-Oceania politics?" I hinted.

"What role? After being part of the British empire, they were in a Pacific dominated by the Yanks and the Japanese in the latter half of the 20th century and the Chinese, Indians and Asian Tiger economies in the 21st... Ah, so that's it! National inferiority complex. They're making sure that history doesn't repeat itself by building an Empire of Oz when the opportunity arises!"

"That's what the Kiwis think and they know the region," I agreed. "I guess resentment has been building up for decades as the Japanese bought up prime Ozzie real estate and built their exclusive resorts for retired salarymen, the Americans postured in the Pacific with nuclear powered and nuclear armed subs and ships and the Chinese strip-mined mineral resources and shipped everything back home without even local processing. I imagine it wasn't much fun being considered the beach-bums of the region, getting minimum wage as a result of the plundering of their mineral wealth, which they could then use to buy high technology luxuries manufactured in China, Taiwan, Korea or Vietnam."

"It's all a legacy of the past, but could guide the direction of development if rabid nationalism re-emerges. A strong Australia is a risk, increasing the chances of unproductive competition and, eventually, possible conflicts. A strong Australian region, on the other hand, could network with New Zealand and the Falklands and serve as a focus for regeneration of much of the southern hemisphere. It does make some kind of sense, you know."

"Those Kiwis are certainly smart cookies: know about a lot more than fish! The problem is that it's a Prisoner's Dilemma kind of situation. If everyone opts in to the world government option and

253

cooperates on regional development based on trade, ignoring old national borders, then we have, by far, the most favorable scenario for rapid recovery. If even one powerful country cheats, goes on a national land-grabbing spree, it can cause the entire scheme to collapse and even degenerate into open warfare before rebuilding moves much further on than it is now. This is one of the worst case scenarios. So you can see how precarious things are, we're at a tipping point in history and it could go either way."

Sophie looked serious, but seemed less perturbed than she had been previously. "So, if things are so critical, why are we hearing about it now for the first time?"

"Two questions back at you. How am I supposed to inform people about stuff like this? There's no generally available TV, radio or internet. The newssheets that are starting to appear now cover only local news. I could sit down and explain the situation to individuals, but you've seen how long it takes to provide enough information to make sense of things. Then, even if I could inform everyone, what could they do about it? Don't you think that most people still have enough to worry about, without bothering themselves on account of other threats that may take a decade or more to develop?"

Sophie sat in silence until, eventually, Sue felt obliged to respond. "I think you've made your point. Even if we have some fundamental disagreements on the value of democracy, at the present moment

254

we're limited by the practicality of communication. It might even be true that, even if it was practical, the general public could contribute nothing and this knowledge would only be something else to give them ulcers. Despite all that, I think our basic concern is that you're part of a very small clique. You emphasized that we are on a knife edge, exactly the point where minimum effort can have maximum impact. Don't you worry that your group is too small and too inexperienced for you to be confident that you are making the right decisions?"

"All the time" I admitted. "It's one of the few things that keeps me awake at nights." A pre-emptive frown in Sophie's direction warned her off using this comment as an excuse to bring up Jamaica yet again. "It isn't quite as bad as it seems, though. We don't have free rein and have to argue major actions through the full Renaissance group, which covers a much wider range of opinions, ideas and vested interests. Probably more important, our clique doesn't develop plans based only on the knowledge and experience of the individuals involved. We have the essence of the entire amassed knowledge accumulated during recorded history in my database and my smart search engines; David's AI and the Kiwis' war-games software to allow us to make use of it."

"Isn't that even more dangerous, giving such responsibility to machines?"

"What do you think mankind did sometime in the mid '30s?" Sophie was bringing me to the boil again. "The entire job of running the planet was given to machines, to AIs."

"And look what happened!"

"True: that's the danger of a technological monoculture. Nevertheless, if we hadn't gone that way, overpopulation would have caused an ecosystem meltdown a decade before the Crash. Even without insane population levels, if we want the benefits of technology, we need to be able to use knowledge efficiently. We use the term renaissance, but this isn't the 15th century; even a Da Vinci couldn't grasp a small fraction of the knowledge in a single technical sub-discipline, much less overview entire topical areas of hard and soft sciences. We need to use the appropriate software tools for the kind of analyses that we're carrying out: there's simply no other option. As opposed to the global AI control, however, humans set up the questions and make the final strategic decisions. The tools only support this by making sure that we've considered all relevant issues and, in particular, historical precedents. We don't have the luxury of being able to repeat mistakes that have already been made in the past."

Sue glanced at an old analogue clock on the wall of my office. "Well then, that's maybe a good place to break for now. Do you want to have another session before dinner, while you're soaking your aged bones?"

This was definitely a good sign that the ice that seemed to have built up in our relationship was melting. "Definitely: whenever suits you. Maybe join me for dinner as well?"

"Possibly, never know your luck" responded Sue, drawing her fellow scribe to her feet and off in the direction of the door."

"One last question" Sophie managed to get in, as she was being pushed out of the door. "Do you discuss this stuff with anybody else at all, or do you make your decisions alone?"

The girls paused at the exit to hear my response. "I discuss everything with my sister. Andrea and I don't always agree, but we always manage to find a compromise. It's a system that works."

As Sue dragged the door closed I could just make out Sophie's muttered "Fuck! The Butcher of Holetown; now that'll make me sleep a fucking lot better!"

***

After a long afternoon spent dabbling in the materials lab, I finally got into the bath just before seven. The sun had already set behind some horizontally layered clouds in a glory of orange and pink; now there were only the slightest traces of laminations of a scarlet so deep that it was almost purple in the charcoal grey band of cloud on the horizon. Above this, the first stars were starting to appear.

The two women were sitting on stools at the bar, wearing matching loose black robes. They had their heads together, poring over the screen of their computer. Heidi was also present, lying on the massage table. She appeared to be asleep, but I noticed her eyes flickering in my direction as I entered. Trying to eavesdrop, I assumed with a smile; this explaining why my scribes were conversing in such hushed tones.

As I slowly started to force myself into the scalding water, Sue stripped off her robe and came to join me. Five minutes later I had managed to ease myself onto the ledge facing the massage table and had Sue's body bracketing me on one side and Sophie's legs on the other side, where she sat naked on the edge of the bath, laptop - appropriately enough - on her lap.

"Time to fill in more background details," Sue announced, rubbing her shoulder against mine by way of encouragement. "Why don't we get away from the global stuff for a bit and get some more down about local developments. You've said that you plan for Barbados to be a center for revival of the entire Caribbean. It's a nice idea, but how will this work in practice?"

"That's a good question. In many ways it's easier to plan long-term global or regional strategy, which is always a bit vague in terms of exact details, than short-term local development, which is focused almost entirely on sorting out fine details. This is something that Andrea is much better at than me. The trick seems to be to coordinate initiatives that have the support of individuals with a vested interest. This may look like a hodgepodge of hobby projects, but seems to work better than trying to impose a rigorous top-down structure on things. Whenever we note gaps, or particular assistance is needed for high priority initiatives, then Andrea and I tend to get involved; my sister on the admin and liaison side and me sorting out technical support, which I can do either directly or using my Renaissance group contacts. Of course, when needed, I repay this by helping them out in their local projects." As I expanded on examples, I could feel narration going into autopilot mode.

It was two weeks until the 15th anniversary of the Crash and the Renaissance group members all had particular milestones that we wanted to have in place by then. Two years ago I had managed to scrounge up enough cable - and, even more importantly a couple of old guys who once worked as electrical riggers, back in the days when that was still a manual job - to supply mains power again to all the communities in and around Holetown. Until then, electricity was spotty, based on local generation. The process was autocatalytic, once the basic system was in placed, others could be trained up as electricians. Then we can focus on helping the scavengers that supported them, scouring the hinterlands for abandoned electrical equipment that had, somehow or other, missed being recycled into QC based wireless power systems.

For the 20th this year I was planning something much more ambitious, putting a grid electricity supply back into operation in Bridgeton. If I could get it up and running, it would be the most extensive in the world in terms of population served.

For someone who considered only the recent history of the 21st century, Bridgetown's prominence might seem anomalous indeed but, from a wider historical perspective, it was maybe not so strange. In the 17th and 18th centuries Barbados was a hugely important nexus of the British Empire and then Bridgeton was, for a while, the most important colonial city: a sophisticated hub for administration, trade and industry. Apart from its deep-water harbor, the fertile soil, accessible aquifers and attractive climate led to fortunes being made from agriculture, particularly sugar cane.

Roll on to 2056 and the attributes that led the British to value this island so much are exactly the same as sought by anyone wanting to recover from the ashes of the QC Crash. Indeed, the Caribbean Islands were generally recovering much better than elsewhere due to the benefits of relatively low population densities and isolation following the 20th, good infrastructure for agriculture and fisheries, a beneficent climate and the ability to rapidly set up transportation links using sailing ships.

Many countries were still at the level of transportation by foot or, if very lucky, horseback or bicycle. Barbados always had sailing ships and these were now complemented by a number of boats with engines powered by ethanol, used either in internal combustion motors or fuel cells. Ethanol was now a major commodity and represented one industry where Barbados was well to the fore. In the '10s and '20s, sugar farming had come back into vogue as a source of biofuel. This bubble burst in the '30s, when AI power sources made all forms of hydrocarbon burning pointless. Nevertheless, it lasted on here longer than most places and there were many remnants lying around when they were needed again in our Mad Max post-apocalyptic world.

What I was trying to do was to use the functioning tools that I have here to help build back a standard of living that may not be early 21st century, but at least has the main components expected in the middle of the 20th. Radio we have; this was fairly critical for re-establishing the larger conurbations. TV looks a long way in the future, but possibly could be jumped over if we can find a way to produce simple projection video devices hooked up to some form of internet. We will, no doubt, eventually start to produce new material but, in the interim, there are several databases like my own with archives of more than a century's worth of past production. Everything from Gone With The Wind to decades of Coronation Street. If you need something contemporary, then go to a theatre or concert hall or to any of the small pubs and bars that feature live music.

"... massage now?" The question broke through the unstructured rambling that I must have been spouting. Actually, the more I thought about it, there was little or no integrated planning of the local reconstruction, it was all reaction to initiatives of others. Even my electrification scheme was really driven by Nigel; if he hadn't pushed for it, I probably wouldn't have gotten round to it. I tend to get lost in interesting materials technology problems - low temperature superconductors, hydrogen production catalysts - rather than working on the issues that are actually of top priority, which might be a low tech transformer design or easily fabricated plastics for insulating copper cables.

As I clambered onto the massage table, I happened to have a beautiful view of Sophie as she bent forward to discuss something with Sue, who was still in the bath. The thread of my musing vanished as I burst into laughter, snorting inelegantly as my awkward position caused me to choke.

All three woman looked at me in amazement, obviously baffled. "I've heard of wearing your heart on your sleeve," I spluttered, "but not on your right buttock!"

Sophie clearly picked up was I was referring to and turned to glare in my direction, but the other two women were still at a loss. Given that Heidi was standing above me, I estimated that, from her angle of view the rather rough tattoo would look only like a black cross within a red circle with a red diagonal bar crossing it. Could easily be something Goth or Heavy Metal. From my lower position, I could make out the script below - *Jesus Christ - No Thanks!*

Sue, of course, had instantly - and correctly - interpreted her partner's reaction. "OK, let's all see your bum. May as well get it over with now, or Heid here will be following you into toilets and changing rooms until she finds out what you're hiding." This was a bit unfair as it was clear to me that Heidi was still clueless about what was going on.

"Fuck! Cof, you will fucking suffer for this!" The small woman clambered to her feet and proffered her tattooed cheek to the women in turn.

Sue burst out immediately in a fit of giggles, but Heidi was still lost. "A tattoo on her arse - so what? I've got one as well!" With that she pulled her shorts and knickers down to show a tattoo just over the crack of her backside. The Gothic text was a little hard to read, but it was evidently *Abandon hope all ye who enter here!*

Sue and I both burst into howls of laughter and even Sophie couldn't help smiling. "God, Heid," Sue managed to get out, "you are a true gem. I bet poor old Dante is turning in his grave at a rate of knots at present. A Divine Comedy indeed?"

"So who's Dante - a comedian? There's a comedian plays Holetown called Davenport... "

We were all still guffawing as Heidi started on the fronts of my feet and calves, causing my laugh to transmogrify into a squeal of pain. My masseuse had no idea what was going on, but she knew we were making fun of her. She was now going to get her revenge on the single tormentor who was under her power - me. I grunted loudly as an elbow ground into my left thigh and again even louder as the action was repeated on the right. Sue and Sophie had both picked up on what was happening and this was amusing them further, making poor Heidi even more confused and annoyed. I then realized that I had used the term autocatalytic several times over the last couple of days, but always in a more abstruse context. Here was the analogy that put the process in contest for a non-scientist; the girls laughed, which made Heidi annoyed and hence hurt me more, which amused my scribes even more, which really pissed Heidi off,... That's autocatalysis! If I ever had to lecture materials science in the future, I'd keep this example in mind but, given that autocatalysis typically results in runaway reactions, I was actually more concerned about some inherent damping level being reached before I ended up in traction.

***

I literally fell of the table when Heidi announced the end of my massage with a slap to my buttocks that echoed around the onsen. About half way through, the two scribes left, removing the tormenting goads to my physio. I then spent a bit of time explaining the Divine Comedy; the girl was smart enough to pick up the background quickly, but I knew she was a bit sensitive about the breadth of her education, particularly when confronted with Sue and Sophie, who many found rather intimidating. A bit like me, I suddenly realized. In any case, the final work over my back and shoulders was much gentler and helped to finally provide the relaxation I associate with massages. When I tried to stand, however, I found out how hard the initial work over on my legs had been; they were like jelly and buckled comically as soon as I put weight on them.

Heidi supported me as I got back to my feet and walked out the worst of the damage. Although I insisted that I was OK, she helped me to the shower, then stripped off to join me in it, gently rubbing soap into my legs as I repeatedly went onto my toes to stretch out the muscles. It was clear that she was prepared to soap up further, but I decided that discretion was the better part of valor here, especially as I probably had two dinner guests waiting on me and at least one of them would be able to discern the reason for any late appearance.

I was hurriedly tying a yukata before I rushed towards my bedroom to dress when a small voice stopped me in my tracks. "The tattoo, you know, I don't really mean it."

That really gave me something to think about. If Heidi was offering what she appeared to be... Definitely not the best time to think about such things, I decided. When in doubt, procrastinate. "Excellent, Heidi, let's talk about that next time. Anyway, I'll send you a translation of Dante's master work and we can have a think about your tattoo."

"Brill, Cof, it's a date. Do you want to... "

I beat a hasty retreat before I dug myself deeper into a potential quagmire.

265

***

I was my usual informal self for dinner, smart white cotton shorts and a light, cream linen shirt, so I felt positively under-dressed when the ladies appeared, about two minutes after me, in full length dresses. My eyebrows raised instantly in surprise as I admired their outfits; in both cases very smart but hovering on the edge of openly provocative. Sue's dress was a simple full length black silk gown, with splits in both sides of the skirt that extended up to her waist. High-heeled shoes showed off her long legs to maximum effect while the plunging neckline presented her full breasts to the extent that it looked certain that her nipples would pop out at any moment.

Sophie's outfit was a presumably deliberate contrast. The white sheath covered her from neck to ankle but, above the waist, it looked as if translucent paint had been sprayed on and actually revealed, rather than hid, her body. Although it was impossible to spot exactly where the transition occurred, this bodice morphed into a layered skirt that was more transparent than translucent, but had enough layers of fabric to deceive the eye. One moment it looked as if she was clearly wearing no underwear, but the next it was impossible to tell; she could have been clad in Bridget Jones knickers for all that I could positively swear to.

After we had settled down and aperitifs were served, the initial tension melted away and we settled down to a light, insubstantial conversation which certainly helped me to relax. The first topic was music: appropriate background to complement the meal. Here I confess to being a total philistine, always surrounded by background muzak, but rarely motivated enough to over-ride a random shuffle from the database in order to select even a specific genre for a particular dinner.

Partially due to my own ignorance, but more to encourage the competition between the girls - the Mensa equivalent of a catfight - I encouraged them to show off their best recommendations. Surprisingly, Sophie first chose a light medley of late 20th century pop while Sue selected some 19th century Portuguese polyphony. As we worked our way through a light gazpacho starter, a Mount Gay rum granite to clear out pallets and then flying fish fingers with hot Bajan sauce and island bean risotto, blocks of contrasting music were played and compared. Simon & Garfunkel's Bridge over Troubled Water was set against a section from Nicholas Lens' Amor Amor. Bob Marley's No Woman No Cry, a rather provocative choice from Sophie that, nevertheless, didn't lead our conversation anywhere near Jamaica, was followed by the Flower Duet from Delibes' Lakme.

Gloria, the cook of the evening, came through to sort out deserts and I complemented her on the menu; the local food was always good, but this evening had been even better than usual. As I had guessed, the wine had been a laboratory synthesized copy of a late 20th century New Zealand Cloudy Bay Sauvignon Blanc. The distinctive grapefruit

267

tang had been exactly duplicated, but there was still a mysterious lack to the bouquet that distinguished the laboratory clone from the real thing. Nevertheless, perfectly drinkable. The women were easily talked into sticky toffee pudding, but I held out for cheese and biscuits instead, selecting a Camembert copy that also owed its taste and texture to advanced food chemistry and engineering rather than the quality of milk from French cows. The ladies were sticking to the white wine but, feeling well a glow of contentment from this excellent meal, I decided to treat myself to a half-bottle of a real 2020 Chilean Pinot Noir. Although my wine cellar was now seriously depleted, in general the contents had not been chosen for long aging and hence most of the remnants were getting to the point where they needed to be drunk before they started their inevitable decline.

For the end of our meal, the secretaries had agreed to move from the comparisons of pop and classical music to various forms of crossover. When Sophie described her first choice, Apocalyptica - a rock group composed of a bunch of manic, classically-trained Finnish cellists - playing Nothing Else Matters, a ballad by the Heavy Metal band Metallica, I could only imagine that it would be hideous. To my amazement, and evidently Sue's as well, the piece was enchanting. Sue thought for a bit, then responded with Classical Gas performed by violinist Vanessa Mae.

I had been a fairly passive observer for most of the meal, interrupting the musical debate only occasionally to ask questions that probably showed my ignorance more than anything else. It had been like having a private cabaret right at my table, made even more fun by the provocative dresses that the women were wearing. I really must do this more often, I thought to myself, suddenly realizing how often I'd dined alone in recent years, outside of the occasions when Andrea and Tina visited.

We moved on to coffee and, instead of the shorter pieces of music, an orchestral version of Jean Michel Jarre's Oxygene was playing. I could sense a slight shift in the air, a feeling that, finally, I was going to find out why the girls were so dressed up and being so pleasant to me.

I was having a first delicate sip of my double espresso when, typically, Sue came straight to the point. "Well, I think Sophie and I now have a lot better idea what's going on; we've talked it over and we've agreed to give it a go - assuming, that is, that we haven't disqualified ourselves over the last couple of days."

"You what?" I responded, gormlessly, having not the slightest idea what she was talking about.

"Yes," Sophie giggled, "we were fairly sure that you hadn't cottoned on yet. Nevertheless, we saw that Sue's original analysis was bang on when we checked how you came to choose us. It didn't take long to put the pieces together after that."

"But that's rubbish! I rechecked the search criteria myself. Sue was so convincing, that I was really worried that I'd unconsciously biased the

269

selection process. But it's kosher - exactly the way I remembered it."

"The search is very convincing, but it was fixed from the start. No matter what criteria you used, you would have ended up with the two of us." Sue laughed. "We tested it! Sophie set up a search for two argumentative, torn-faced bitches - and guess who came to the top of the pile?"

"Yes, well, I'd have expected that," I goaded them automatically, still trying to make sense of what was going on. "Didn't you try any criteria that don't fit, like gentle, caring, respectful... ?" I was rewarded with a playful punch on the arm from one side and a rather painful kick on the shin from the other.

"We tried a half dozen combinations, but always the two of us came top of the list."

"Maybe you're just the best two that were available at the time."

"Your trainer Di is one of the women looking for new challenges. We used black and fit as criteria, and we still came out on top. Sophie here is a little bit brown, but think of Di and look at me!" She spread her arms wide, exposing a cleavage of creamy white skin and ignoring a pink nipple that popped out. "Black! I'm whiter than Di's teeth and she's like the ace of spades!"

"That just can't be right" I objected. "Those search routines are completely bog standard. It'd take some serious hacking to bias their output."

"The routines are fine, it's the personnel files that are fixed. Interestingly, the editing is only on

270

the archived versions that were used for this search."

"But I never touched them!"

"Of course you didn't"

"Then who did?"

Sophie was about to answer, but Sue stopped her with a finger to her lips. "Now your turn for a course exercise. You have all the data you need. Who fixed the files?"

I thought for a couple of minutes and then it became crystal clear. "Andrea! My bloody sister!"

"Who else? Of course, your bloody sister!"

***

I sat, flabbergasted, as Sue explained the details. It was quite cunning really; for the exercise, the only change made to the two target files was to add in a wildcard in the ratings section. This meant that, regardless of the search criteria used or the scoring system, Sue and Sophie would score top marks. I could imagine some technical applications where such a wildcard might be applicable, but I'd never thought it could even be applied to personnel files. Nevertheless, there was no doubt that, if anyone on the estate knew that this kind of skullduggery was possible, it would be Andrea.

"OK," I conceded, "you've nailed down the how. What about the why?"

"Now that we've had a chance to think about it in detail, we can make more sense of the whole thing. It's even cleverer than I had originally

271

guessed; I suppose that's because your sister was responsible rather than, as I first assumed, yourself." Sue managed to get these back-swipes in even without thinking about them.

"It's killing two birds with one stone. The first bit, which I already picked up, is catharsis. You've obviously been brooding about a lot of things that you've done in the past and it's been healthy for you to air them."

"But I have discussed all of this, many times and in detail... " I started to object.

"With Andrea!" she completed for me. "Andrea is your partner in crime in all of this; you both fundamentally agreed on all of your past actions. She can't be your confessor, who forces you to justify your actions. That, as I deduced, was primarily Sophie's job. Even though she's given up with God, you know how it is - you can take the girl out of the Church, but not the Church out of the girl."

Sophie looked like she was going to object, but Sue crashed on. "Of course, you weren't in need of Christian absolution, but the ethics and morality of your war crimes needed to be discussed, so that you could clearly make up your own mind. Did the end justify the means or was this heinous and criminal over-reaction? Sophie got under your skin - I could see the way you were going at each other, so neither of you can deny it. This forced you both to bluntly present your opinions, in turn making you examine the bigger picture with the benefit of hindsight."

272

"But I was perfectly happy before I started with this book project. I didn't feel any need to justify anything I've done in the past."

"That's where the subconscious bit comes in. I suspect your sister knows you better than you know yourself."

"You could be right there" I conceded.

"And, I have to be blunt here, you're not getting any younger."

"What?" I stood and posed in profile. "Look here, the body of a young bull!"

"Due to rejuv," she agreed. "But that's only the body. It contains the brain of an aging cephalopod!"

As I've said before, Sue's not one to pull blows. "I didn't have Sophie's work-over," I acknowledged, "but that doesn't mean I'm senile. The physical rejuv gets rid of a lot of the contributing factors for mental aging. I've no chance - well, to be honest a negligibly low chance - of Alzheimer's or any other kind of auto-immune cerebral degradation."

Sue let me finish, the delivered the coup de grace, putting me out of the misery of trying to make the problem go away due to wishful thinking. "You have the physique of somebody about thirty-five years old, but does your mind function as well as it did when you were actually that age, that'd be about forty-five years ago?"

There was no away around the question. I had accumulated a vast amount of experience over the last few decades and there were some areas where I could, more or less, function as effectively as in the past. But this was cheating; I was using my

273

awareness of decreasing capabilities to focus my efforts in areas where my reduced concentration span or speed of uptake would be less noticeable. I may not have the detective bent of Sue, but I was fairly sure that, in my prime, I'd have spotted my sister's machinations earlier and wouldn't have required to have the whole thing explained to me.

"Cof, you're wandering again!" Sophie pointed out, almost kindly.

"Not this time, just facing up to a hard truth! Sue, you're completely correct; the old brain is firing on fewer cylinders now and, as a result, performance isn't up to earlier specs. I do think that I'm not yet ready for the scrapheap, though. Well, what about this rebored body? I could get a job as a gigolo."

"As long as you're still sufficiently in control that you don't drool!" retorted Sue cruelly, getting a glare from Sophie. I got the distinct feeling that the ex-Jesuit was beginning to feel sorry for me. Then again, inspecting the way a pair of prominent nipples were displayed through the fabric of her bodice, maybe it wasn't pity that she was feeling at present. For a moment, this helped me recover a bit from the impact of Sue's brutal analysis on my self-esteem.

"Anyway," she continued, "we're not saying that you're totally useless, gaga or anything like that. Just getting to the cranial age when more time is spent on introspection, brooding. We've spent some prime time together over the past few days; tell us it isn't so!"

I simply shook my head. I could have tried to waffle, but I'd only be emphasizing her point on my decreased intellectual capabilities. "Right, so this goes back to the original point you were trying to make. Remember it?"

"God, this is real salt in the wounds! In your previous life, you were probably patrolling a concentration camp with a Doberman. Yes, I remember the question, was I unhappy or broody? I didn't feel as if I was, but, with the extended time period over which I was losing my marbles, I wouldn't have necessarily noticed a change, would I?"

"See, given a boot up the arse, there are enough neurons still functioning for you to work such things out and, at least for the moment, we don't have to pack you off to the compound with the poor old bastards that need to be reminded to put their trousers on in the morning and then reminded again to button-up their flies."

"And this book project helps here? How exactly?"

A grin from ear to ear. "Course exercise number two; you now have all the information that you need to answer your own question." She looked at her wrist. "This gives you a chance to prove to us that you aren't really a senile old tosser who is kept afloat only by a devoted sister and a shit-hot computer support system. You have three minutes, starting now!"

"Fuck! OK, I can live with the fact that, as I slowly move into my dotage, I spend more time

275

dwelling over my extensive memories of the past. I am painfully aware that, with time, details begin to fade and, now that we don't have granny AIs watching and analyzing our every move, when these memories are lost, they will be gone forever. I want to have a record for my own purposes but, especially because of the global significance of the Crash and the role I ended up playing thereafter, I also wanted something that could form a source for analysis in the future - assuming that we don't fuck up again and manage to complete the process of driving Homo Sapiens into extinction."

"Two minutes!"

"The fact that I'm even concerned about providing a record for the future indicates that, despite my previous protestations, I still worry about what others will think about what I've done. Because some of the actions that might lead to greatest censure, maybe the ones where I'm not sure that I took the best course, are unknown to all but a select few, I guess it was good for me to present and justify them to a critical audience. I may not have been aware of this need, but clearly Andrea was. All of this, in a nutshell, backs up your earlier analysis, but doesn't show me how this project will stop me wetting my bed and slavering into my porridge."

"One minute!"

"If it's not what I'm doing that's critical, it must be what you two are doing. Which, now that I come to think about it, relates also to your new-found confidence and turning up for dinner tarted up to the eyeballs."

"Are you objecting?" Sophie asked, pointing nipples like a couple of huge acorns in my direction.

"Don't distract him!" Sue commanded. "Forty seconds!"

"By going through all of this stuff with you, you're now closer to me than anybody, with the exception of my sister." I felt sweat running down the side of my face as I fought my way through this puzzle. "You've managed to get a huge amount of information out of me in a very short time, keep me on track, reanalyze discrepancies: some that I would never have noticed without you. We make a good team! That's it! We're a team!"

"Actually, you were two seconds late finding the answer but, as you were interrupted," a glare in her partner's direction, "I'll give you the benefit of the doubt. You may be an old git, but you still have your uses if you work together with the pair of us. You needed to recognize, to openly admit, that help was needed and then concede that we were the right ones to complement you. Andrea clearly set it all up and, when you do your homework like we have, you will see that this isn't a spur of the moment thing - she's been setting this up for a long time."

"How can that be? I may be starting to fall of my perch, but this is relatively recent. I started planning the book when I first noticed that my memory wasn't all it had once been, but that's three, four - max five years ago. Of course, if you consider that a long time... "

"No, I think here we're talking about a concept that's been taking shape for over a decade or more, probably first ideas coming soon after you and Andrea put this little survivalist enclave together."

"OK, I may now have the mental powers of a very dumb Irishman - according to a Norwegian friend of mine, that's just above those of a smart Swede - but I can't see how my sister could have foreseen the need for this book so long ago."

"Almost certainly not, Paddy! But she's maybe smart enough to identify the inevitable problem caused by physical rejuv in a world where the cerebral follow-up is no longer an option."

Andrea and Tina had received standard rejuvs: a full service for all parts, physical and mental. It was only Luddites like me that went for physical only, because I didn't trust AI's guiding nanobots through my cerebellum. She knew I finally had a cerebral booked, but then the Crash intervened. Despite all the global chaos, it was completely typical that she would identify a long-term potential problem for me and immediately start looking for a solution.

The women watched in silence as I slowly pulled together the threads that validated their interpretation. "Yes, you're almost certainly right," I finally admitted. "She's not only smart enough, but also dedicated enough to scheme on such a timescale." I felt an old man's tear trickle down my cheek. "She does it because we love each other and she's always been my protective big sister. Is that so bad?"

"Not bad at all!" Sophie moved to my side and put a consolatory arm around my shoulder. "It

278

would, however, have been nice if she had let others into the plan. You, for example... "

"Us, more importantly" Sue interrupted. "You'd have probably forgotten it all anyway when your brain turned to marshmallow, but we were key components of her plan. We had the right to know."

"Maybe you just evolved into your roles. Andrea could well have had a long term plan and then, when it was time to implement it, simply have chosen the best folk available for the job." I was straining to defend my beloved - but inherently conniving - sister.

"Aye, right! This would be credible if you hadn't spent a lot of time with the personnel files, which your invitation to check your records gave us access to. These records are what convinced us that Andrea has not also been plotting this for a long time, she had us penciled-in for our roles from the start."

"The records show you that? How? Has she been regularly assessing how your input would keep me from going doo-wally, assessing when your input would be optimal."

"It's a bit more subtle than that," Sophie entered the conversation. "We've not only carefully examined lots of personnel details in your database, we've spent time examining the tacit knowledge base available: staff gossip, if you prefer. Incidentally, did you know that, of the eligible women who lived in this madhouse in the years after the Crash, we seem to be the only ones you haven't slept with?"

"Or, to be more precise, had sex with," Sue corrected pedantically. "We suspect that your sister may have had a hand in this, although we haven't quite worked out details yet. In any case, it's a situation that we're going to rectify tonight."

"Both of you?" I was struggling with too much new information to fully take in the last comment. "That's a lovely offer - and I'll definitely take you up on it sometime - but I have an appointment with the twins tonight and, even with this body of a bull, they're just about too much on their own."

"Worry not, your beauteous and incredibly smart future partners have things fully under control. The twins have a night off. Not, of course, before briefing us on your particular kinks..." Sophie grinned salaciously.

"Perversions, I'd call them," Sue added with a matching grin. "By the way, I also found your old materials development test files while I was searching the files that we now have access to... "

"That stuff's nothing to do with... "

"Maybe not - but remember that you still owe me a prezzy and I just wondered what the range available might be like. You've certainly been a dirty old dog, in your day!" She grinned and licked her lips suggestively. "In any case, it should be an interesting night!"

Now how the fuck did my sister manage to instigate this, I wondered, as the women dragged me to my feet and off in the direction of my bedroom.

Chapter 8 - Team sex

Over the last six decades, my sex life has evolved in a strange manner. Although my teens were definitely dominated by masturbation, Andrea helped me to make contacts with girls just as, whenever needed, I helped her make the first moves towards guys that she fancied. In England, at that time, there was a lot of prudishness and, because of AIDS, fear of sex. Thanks to my sister's instructions and the background checks she carried out on potential girlfriends, my awareness of the female body and knowledge of how far they would like to go avoided much of the usual juvenile fumbling and awkwardness. Problems getting and holding on to girlfriends were mainly due to the perceived weirdness of Andrea and myself as a pair and the way some girls regarded my sister as competition for my affections.

University was the first extended period that I spent separated from my sister. Compared to most students at Edinburgh, where I worked though both bachelor and doctorate degrees, I was relatively affluent and hence a natural magnet for friends: especially in the bar. I had a series of longer-term relationships, each lasting six months or so. I had my own rented flat - again a rarity in Edinburgh - so I had flexibility for regular encounters with girlfriends who lived at home, in halls of residence or in shared flats. In a couple of cases, they moved in and we lived together for a while. Somewhere around about half a year seemed to be the natural lifetime of these relationships. We either grew apart to the point where we decided amicably to move on or, sometimes, the girl started pushing towards formalizing our relationship with marriage or, at least, engagement. It wasn't that I was afraid of commitment, just that my plans were for travelling the world after graduation and I didn't want to be tied down. These particular affairs usually didn't end so well. Maybe the fundamental problem was that they weren't love affairs: they were friendship and sex affairs.

Typically, despite my grand plans, I got a job offer that I felt I couldn't refuse immediately after graduation. Instead of travelling the world, I returned to England and was soon sharing a large flat with my sister. Just after that, our father committed suicide. The background was never quite clear, but we suspected that it was because he had been diagnosed HIV positive. Considering the amount of time he spent on business in the Far East, it wasn't really so surprising. What was very surprising for us, though, was that our mother took it really badly despite how little time they spent together and the very limited extent to which they displayed affection to each other - or to us, for that matter. We were perplexed when, following the funeral, she resigned from her job and, after living as a recluse in the New York apartment for a year, finally upped-sticks and disappeared off to Rio de Janeiro. We did hear that she eventually set up

282

house with a 20 year old gigolo, but lost contact thereafter.

Given the remoteness of contacts with our parents in the past, these events had little effect on us, except for the fact that a substantial inheritance from our father's estate allowed us to buy the flat that we had been renting and set us up as comfortably well off, by the standards of Southern England. I was working in research laboratories, surrounded by nubile technicians and secretaries, while Andrea worked for a range of charities that seemed to be staffed entirely by sincere young women. It was a happy hunting ground for both of us; especially as my sister had now come out openly as straight gay and hence our close relationship no longer seemed quite so incestuous. Then, as the ultimate icing on the cake, a cure for AIDS was announced and the sexual floodgates burst in the second Summer of Love. It was certainly a good time to be an eligible bachelor.

Until that time, my sexual repertoire was based on conventional, good, solid British bonking. A variable degree of foreplay - generally related to how drunk or sober we were at the time - followed by sex in the missionary position. The Joy of Sex was used as the manual for a bit of variation, particularly by my more athletic or flexible partners, who were looking for opportunities to demonstrate their physical prowess. It was all simple, straightforward and eminently satisfying.

My growing wealth as I moved into the sex toy business seemed to counter any detriment that might have arisen due to the dubious nature of the industry that employed me. In any case it certainly didn't make it any harder to find sexual partners. Maybe it was the sex industry cachet - or just that my sister was getting known - but the one thing I noticed was that I was meeting more girls who proclaimed themselves to be bi-curious. As I noted before, this led to a couple of occasions with rather drunken groups in Andrea's bed. Nevertheless, apart from that, I didn't have any real encounters with kinky sex until I met Kelly.

Initially these encounters were more academic than anything else; Kelly's ideas on what products should be developed forced me to do some background to check exactly how these would be used. An eye-opener indeed. Nevertheless, until Kelly, Lisa and I did the exec suit calibration to test the new smell and taste functions, this didn't impinge directly on my sex life. I was certainly less easily fazed by some of the wilder boundaries of sex, but I didn't have direct contact with anyone - other than Kelly - with tastes running in those directions. The calibration run, naturally, couldn't even cover a small fraction of the uses to which, with my new awareness of the real world, I was sure that the kit would be put. Nevertheless, we covered the essential functions that were the basis of the clients' expectations. I may not have understood why anyone would want to have two people pissing on them, but I found out what it felt like. More importantly, Kelly, our connoisseur of sex in all its deviant forms, was able to confirm that smell and taste sensitivity of the suit polymers was sufficient to accurately distinguish different sources of urine. This is a facility that 99.9% of the sex-toy clientele don't require, but Kelly assured me that the specialist deviants would pay big money for this. I remember losing out to her on a bet on this very point; the suits sold like ultra-expensive hot cakes.

We might not have touched hard-core perversion, but we skirted the fringes. After that experience, conventional British bonking seemed a bit tame. It's the usual thing, I suppose; there're lots of things that you're perfectly happy without but, if you try them once, a life without them seems bland. I've heard that heroin is like that. It became the drug du jour when physically non-addictive variants became available, but it is inherently impossible to avoid the psychological dependence that such an altered lifestyle can cause. Users thus aren't addicted in a strict biochemical sense; they just have more fixes than is good for them. Chocolate is exactly the same in this regard.

So, Lisa and I started seeing more of each other after the initial psychological barriers had been broken - smashed - by Kelly. Our previous inhibitions were lost completely and we experimented with a wider range of options. Probably an important factor was that, most of the time, our sex life was completely conventional. Just for special occasions we'd try something unusual, bizarre, perverse. Lisa took the lead in most cases; I'm sure my scribes would attribute this to me responding to something that resembled the dominant influence of my sister. Maybe that was the explanation; whatever, I was a willing participant and our relationship outlasted most I've ever had and, in fact, was the longest that I'd had up to that time. After a while, however, the experimentation was getting to be, for me, too much of novelty for novelty's sake rather than something that we actually had fun doing. This was especially the case with the group encounters.

Lisa saw the group as the challenge; different combinations of males, females, others... The possibilities for sex grew exponentially with the size and diversity of the group, but this involved a purely mechanical focus on the physics of coupling, with all associated foreplay. If you considered the personalities of those involved, however, the larger and weirder groups involved a natural bias that resulted in participants that were increasingly bizarre, but in a strangely similar manner. This became more marked as my partner moved gradually into S&M circles, beyond the simple role-playing of bondage into a darker and, for me, unpleasant world. I'd happily pass on the S and, despite my proclivity for being humiliated by female trainers in my sporting life, I don't need anybody hurting me to get my rocks off in a sexual situation. There was no tension, however, as we were able to discuss sex in a completely open manner: again something we picked up from Kelly. We simply separated when the differences in our interests became too great, but this allowed us to re-establish our past working relationship. We've been working together for a quarter century since we formally split up and our past intimacy, in all its strange incarnations, hasn't caused us a single problem.

When I moved to Barbados, there was yet another change in the way my relationships developed. As a rich eccentric, I had many girlfriends over the first decade I spent here. These included international contacts - both from my previous life and from the jet-set who regularly visited when tourism still existed as an industry - and island girls. With time, I built up a definite preference for the latter. It wasn't just the fact that they were so beautiful in so many different ways, but also due to their simple and enthusiastic approach to sex.

Bajan girls cover the entire spectrum in terms of shades of skin and physiogamy. The dominantly African roots gave rise to girls who could be pure blood Bantus or Zulus, but also mixtures between African stereotypes and Europeans, Asians and native South Americans. A study of a thousand variants of the perfection of the female form. It's the exact opposite of the old Playboy-type image, forcing all racial stereotypes into a cosmetic engineering mold that makes them all look like enhanced Barbie dolls, with actual vaginas rather than the smooth expanses of plastic between their legs. Then again, US mainstream porn didn't go much into explicit presentation of the details of female sexual organs, so the Playgirls may actually also have had standardized mid-West America wet-dream cunts to go with their customized pneumatic tits and cheerleader faces.

In my early years on the island, I once estimated that there were probably about 50,000 women who would fall into the envelope that I would consider sexually attractive, although this excluded another 25,000 who were certainly attractive enough, but young enough to put me in jail. Of these 50,000 - excluding identical twins - there wouldn't be two that had the same combination of features; facial, corporal and sexual. It was a wonderland of endless interesting variety and a complete contrast to the mono-cultured mid-Atlantic looks driven by the media and, especially, the fashion and cosmetic industries.

So, I spent as much time as possible with island girls, if only to enjoy their appearance when I could be in their company. Despite the formidable competition - the island guys are, according to all my female sources, every bit as attractive as the women - a rich foreigner has unfair advantages that allowed me to tempt many of these beauties between my sheets. Despite both their rather puritanical culture and a lack of sophistication, the enthusiasm and athleticism of sex with them made it a total delight. Maybe it was a reaction to my experience with Lisa, but this seemed to be exactly what I was looking for. Initial one night stands often gradually extended into longer relationships.

My last girlfriend was, however, an exception to this trend. Nevertheless, Anna was a spectacular mixed-blood Columbian who would have easily passed as a Bajan from her appearance. Then the 20th February threw everything up in the air again.

Immediately after the Crash, I was the boss, alpha male, father confessor, surrogate for lost fathers / sons / brothers / whatever. I had experienced the majority of the female staff cry on my shoulder - metaphorically or physically - over that period. Physical contacts were unintended, but inevitable. Quite a few of these led to sex, which, for some particular women, was repeated on a number of occasions. I admit that I did nothing to discourage them and, in some cases, certainly encouraged the move into my bedroom. It may have been unscrupulous but, under the conditions at that time, I quite frankly didn't give a thought to the morality of what I was doing. Although the relationships involved were occasionally intense, there is no way that they could be mistaken for being romantic.

After about a year or so, things were normalizing - or, at least, getting close to what we consider normality. I still had regular encounters with women who had a shared interest in occasional sex without ties, but gradually weaned-off more needy females, wherever possible helping them to establish supporting relationships with either other staff or with outsiders from the communities being re-established in the vicinity of Holetown. It was about then that I began to feel a bit dissatisfied, as if there was more that I wanted, but I couldn't articulate exactly what. After much discussion with Andrea, I tried establishing relationships with a

289

couple of girls from Holetown and the surroundings, but on these occasions I always felt that it was a form of exploitation: we had so much in our estate compared to the surrounding communities that girls could hardly refuse any offers from me, even if they were mediated by my sister.

This rather unsatisfactory situation continued for a few years, during which time I even went so far as to try to re-establish a physical relationship with Lisa. This didn't work well for either of us, I couldn't get into her domination-driven role playing, while she had moved much more towards Sapphic relationships, although more than prepared to add any other sexual component to the mixture. We were both happy to call the experiment off after about six months and, again, it had no impact on our ability to work well with each other.

Then my sister found the twins. I was initially shocked by Andrea's suggestion that I employ a couple of hookers to supply my sexual needs, but she was able to convince me of the inescapable logic of it. I had a healthy sex-drive; one that was associated with my body's apparent physical age rather than the number of years that my brain had accumulated. The problem I was having with my relationships - both with staff and girls from the neighborhood - was my concern that I was exploiting them. The occasional encounters with women whose independence gave me no concerns about exploitation were too seldom to satisfy my needs and, by their very nature, these were the interactions that I couldn't force. It was a classic Catch-22 situation.

It needed a bit of Andrea's characteristic lateral thinking to find a solution. Link up with a prostitute; there was certainly no shortage of them in post-crash Bridgetown, as it slowly recovered and began to re-establish its role as a major Caribbean port. Although there were many desperate women working the lower levels of the oldest profession, there was also a small number at the top end, for whom this was a deliberately chosen occupation. My sister checked them out and quickly selected the twins; not only because they had been executive escorts pre-Crash and thus clearly hadn't been driven into selling their bodies by the desperate conditions after the U collapse, but also because they worked as a pair and hence this avoided the risk of the isolation that might be suffered by a lone girl under such circumstances. Another factor, which I only came to appreciate later, was that, despite their physical appearances which would suggest ages about seventeen or eighteen, they had clearly gone through extremely costly rejuv treatments. Even Andrea was never able to determine their actual ages, but we guessed that they must be roughly contemporary with us. Their depth of experience and long established familiarity working together in different set-ups undoubtedly contributed to their rapid integration into our little community.

Not since Kelly had my love life, or, at least, the sexual components of it, changed so rapidly.

These women were complete professionals, who not only enjoyed but were also immensely proud of their work. In the good old days they had serviced the great and the good. Politicians and pop-stars, media personalities and clerics. They catered for every taste, as long as it wasn't dangerous - for either themselves of their clients - or against the law of the land. They provided gratification for men and women, cross-dressers and transsexuals, individually and in groups; in all cases with equal enthusiasm. Given the very depressed market in a post-apocalyptic world, it wasn't surprising that they took up Andrea's offer of a life back in the 21st century. Nevertheless, it was professional pride that made them encourage me to expose my hidden fantasies and bring them to life in the bedroom.

In actual fact, most of the action didn't take place in the bedroom, although they often slept together with me there afterwards. A standard bedroom was too confining for professionals of their caliber. On their instructions, I converted an adjoining sitting room to their specifications. This was a sexual playroom, a marital arts dojo. They annexed a neighboring bedroom for themselves, but I never slept there; indeed I never entered that room. There were always rumors about what went on in there; they looked after it themselves, so the maids never entered it either. I had no interest in this, which was a great benefit of our completely commercial undertaking. Over time we became great friends, but there was never any aspect of romance. I could have whatever other relationships that I wanted; indeed they actively encouraged me to widen my experience. In their case, what they did with their time when they weren't with me was entirely their own business.

The twins were identical and called Natalie and Natasha - Nat and Tash. I have no idea to what extent it may have been cosmetic, but they appeared physically identical in every detail - and over the years I have explored and compared these details in extenso. Except when they were playing different roles, they tended also to dress identically, which was a source of considerable confusion. Based on talking to them, some claimed to be able to tell them apart - my sister was one - but I was never sure. Like everyone else, I soon gave up and simply called each of them Twin.

They were not exactly beautiful, certainly not in a conventional manner. Medium height, blond hair, green eyes and slightly sharp, Slavic features. Trim athletic figures with breasts that seemed only slightly over-proportioned. Passing one of them in the street, I'd have noticed her as pretty, but not breathtaking. Together, their radiance increased considerably. It wasn't just the anomaly of their identical appearances; they simply looked more complete, symmetrical as a pair. Of course, as soon as it came to some kind of erotic setting, they had a head start. There was something so inherently exotic, kinky about twin sisters who did everything together that my first encounters with them left me drained before they were even halfway through the foreplay. Seen together in their working outfits, they

293

were so breathtaking that beauty didn't come into it. They were at a level somewhere beyond such simplistic classifications.

They have been working for me - on me - for more than five years, but the novelty shows no sign of wearing off. Unlike Lisa, they seem to have no particular preferences and sex with them would be characterized in terms of its huge variety, rather than anything else. Sometimes one of them will take the active role, while the other will be an observer or passive assistant. Other times they are both fully active, either frantically going at it hammer and tongs or else so slowly that the tension of being held on the edge for extended periods of time cuts like any Domina's whip. Or else I am forced into the passive role, observing or only gently assisting while they have uninhibited sex with each other.

Fetishes and kinks are covered too, explored gradually in a step by step manner, exposing desires repressed by cultural taboos and pushing the boundaries of what can be classified as pleasure. Expeditions into the realms of alternative sex are, however, only occasional treats; spice to add an edge to more conventional fare - if, indeed, sex with identical twins could ever be considered conventional. Nevertheless, after a few years I was sure that Kelly would have been proud of me. I certainly hadn't reached her level of encyclopedic experience of perversion, but I was no longer the neophyte who had responded to her ideas with such wide-eyed innocence.

***

My musings on past encounters had been initiated when I was wakened by the first brightening of the dawn sky, bringing enough light through the curtainless windows that I could make out the faint shapes lying huddled together on the left side of my huge bed. Despite all my experience, I had never encountered anything quite like last night. In terms of sexual repertoire, there had been nothing that I hadn't already covered with Kelly and Lisa or the twins. Nevertheless, I had never had such uninhibited sex arise in such an unexpected manner.

The women had led me to my bedroom, where they were plainly surprised by its conventional fitments. Sue was strangely quiet and it was Sophie that spoke up "That's funny. From talking to the twins, we thought this would be different. A bit weirder." She turned to her companion. "Do you think those little bitches were taking the piss?"

This question broke through Sue's moodiness, causing her to laugh. "A very appropriate turn of phrase there, Sophie! Cof, where's all your pervy kit hidden?"

Without a word I led them to the double doors, which I threw open dramatically to show them the play room.

"Fuck me!" Sophie gasped as she wandered into the room, inspecting the various fitments.

Again Sue smiled. "Love, but you certainly have a succinct way with words! And, by the look of some of this kit, it's going to bring a tear to your eye if our boss takes you up on your offer." She lifted the largest sized dildo from a rack and waved it in her friend's direction.

The ex-Jesuit was now searching through cupboards. "The twins say there's some good champagne here. Industrial copy, of course, but fit for purpose. Where is it?"

I showed her the fridge beside the jacuzzi. "Help yourself!"

"Great. Here, Cof, make yourself useful by opening that." She handed me a condensation-frosted bottle. "And 3 glasses, just the job! What's this funnel for?"

I looked at Sue, who silently crossed her eyes, causing us both to burst into laughter.

At that point Sophie caught on. "Mmm, chilly," was her only comment as she held up the glasses one by one for me to fill.

Sue now seemed to have finally relaxed and took over as usual. "OK, Cof, this is how it's going to work. Your sister has seen fit to keep us from any intimate contact with you, so we have just decided to check if we've been missing out on anything," she looked me up and down with a critical eye, "unlikely as that may seem."

Now she was a little bit hesitant, but, after a moment's pause, rushed on. "For me it's a bit difficult, it takes me a while to get turned on... "

"I don't remember that," I interrupted, "I thought that you were the self-proclaimed blow-job queen?"

"Oh, that! That's no bother. I don't need to be turned on to give a bit of head. Probably best when I'm not, in fact, I get the job done more efficiently." A large mouthful of sparkly was gulped down. "No, it's when I want to have sex. I need time to get warmed up and I'm a bit hyper-sensitive during this time, I don't like being touched by anyone else. I need to watch for a while, then I'll join in when I'm ready."

Sophie set her glass down on a Y-shaped bondage table and started to remove my clothes. "I, however, need absolutely no time to get my juices flowing. In fact, I've been wet since we talked to the twins before dinner. The fact that Sue's going to be watching us only makes it even better. She took my free hand, lifted her skirt and shoved my fingers between her legs. She was certainly telling the truth, the thin panties that I encountered were soaking.

Sue stepped out of her dress, confirming my earlier suspicions that she was wearing nothing under it, and clambered onto a wondrous device that was currently configured as something resembling a gothic gynecological examination chair. She turned it so that she was facing us and then raised her feet into the stirrups, reclining with a feral look on her face.

I was now naked and Sophie lifter her glass, drained it and placed it on a shelf on the wall. This allowed her to flip the table into a vertical position. Although it was all fairly simple, the former priest's familiarity with such kit was disconcerting. I remember that she had mentioned that she had gone rather crazy after she lost her faith and was now beginning to guess what that might have entailed.

The white-clad woman was now in full control, pushing me roughly backwards until my back made contact with the leather-clad surface and then forcing my legs apart, to be strapped to the arms of the Y. "Hold on a bit, girls," I finally complained. "This is all a bit fast. We usually don't get to this stage without a lot of foreplay."

Sophie couched down in front of me, looking up into my eyes as she rubbed my erect penis against nipples that were attempting to burst though diaphanous fabric. "But Cof, this is the foreplay! Just wait until we get around to the real action, then you'll know about it."

I glanced over at Sue, who was squeezing her own nipples, while staring hungrily at Sophie's chest. To think that I had dreaded that dinner might lead to an irreconcilable breakdown in communication with these women. I hadn't dreamt that sex would even be on the agenda - and certainly not moving in this direction and at this speed.

Sophie then turned her back on me and, standing between Sue's raised legs, peeled off her bodice, skirt and then, finally panties. Without touching, she was clearly examining the woman's fully exposed vagina. Moments later, she was back beside me, returning the table to a horizontal position and then clambering on top, facing away from me as she slipped wetly onto to my erection without further ado. The smaller woman was looking at her taller partner as she gave a running commentary of what she was doing and what it felt like, just like the soundtrack of a cheap porno video. Slurping noises bore witness to how well lubricated she was, but the resultant reduced friction helped me to hold back from the edge of premature ejaculation and enjoy the fun.

The reduced sensation was also evident to Sophie after a while. She then lifter herself clear and directed my dick into a much tighter orifice. Her grunt was matched by one from our hitherto silent observer; continued slurping noises indicating not only that Sue's masturbation had changed focus, but that it was having the desired effect. I was back on the edge when Sophie suddenly raised clear, scrabbled round to face me, and then re-impaled herself. Sue then clambered on the table, straddling my head and leaning forward to bury her face in her partner's groin.

I could just make out Sue's muffled voice. "I bet you drank champagne when you calibrated your kit with Kelly and Lisa!"

I was momentarily disconcerted, thrown off by this apparent non-sequitur. How could the woman possibly be reanalyzing my book input at a time like this. Then the answer dawned. And this was still supposed to be foreplay! I came, for the first time of the night, almost immediately afterwards and the table got very wet.

***

Sue was stirring and I took the opportunity of catching her in a relatively vulnerable, unprepared state. "Good morning to you. And what would you fancy on this fine morning? Buck's fizz? Toast and marmalade? Bacon and eggs? Totally wild, obscene sex?"

I was answered by a heartfelt groan. Too much champagne, possibly. Many claim that champagne doesn't give hangovers but, as is the case generally, it always depends on how much you have imbibed.

"That sounds like a request for vitamin C," I responded cheerily, aware that my happy disposition was probably doing more harm than good. "The very dab for you," I handed over a glass of grapefruit juice, freshly squeezed and always available when I awoke - with just a trace of champagne to give it a bite.

Sue struggled through the drink, then let rip with an almighty belch.

"Ever the lady" I laughed. "Just have to watch that you don't waken up your partner in crime here."

Sue leaned over and slapped a bare bottom. Not a trace of a response. "Did you see the way that she was drinking last night? If she doesn't die of alcoholic poisoning, she'll probably wake up feeling like shit sometime around mid-afternoon."

"I didn't keep a track of the intake, but the consequences were hard to miss," I responded with a grin. "Just as well that that room is the most mechanized in the entire house. Even then, the robots will be pushed to have it returned to its original state by now."

"No sense in having a place like that and not using it." The woman was clearly unfazed by my references to the debauchery of the previous night.

Time to stop pussy-footing about, I decided. "So what was that all about? I can easily understand that my tailored physique drives the young girls wild... "

"... a more accurate statement might be that your vast wealth encourages stupid young girls to prostitute themselves!"

"... whatever, the young girls are wild in any case! But you two have shown that you're not impressed by that kind of crap. Despite that, out of the blue, you decide to seduce me. Not just the quick bonk, or even a decadent menage a trois, but a night that would make brothel-keepers in Berlin blush. You two - you in particular - don't just do things like that on a whim. What am I missing now?"

Sue rolled her eyes, but continued calmly. "Fine, but first I need another glass of whatever it was that you gave me just now, maybe with less fruit and more alcohol."

As I scurried to comply, Sue started in her analytical voice. "We got a bit sidetracked, so we never really got into discussing the second reason that Andrea set up your little literary project. She had chosen us to play a role supporting you, but we could only do so if we had an overview of the real history of events over the last fifteen years. Every sordid detail, not just the sanitized versions that we could pick up on our own, or through controlled information channels. The book project was perfect, especially with us as your inquisitors. I doubt if there is anyone - apart from your sister, of course - who has a better overview than us of where our little oasis of civilization sits now and how we got here in the first place."

"I've been thinking about this while the two of you were sawing logs; Andrea's manipulations seem to be evident and planned well before it had even occurred to me that she had anything to worry about. I know my sister and it's all completely credible. But this doesn't explain what you two are up to."

"It couldn't simply be that you're so sexy that we couldn't control ourselves?"

"Well, let me think about this." I put on a theatrical frown of concentration. "Mmm, your IQ appears to be larger than your shoe size and you're certainly not polite enough to be mistaken for gold diggers. So, that's not the explanation," I concluded.

"Well, I see your remaining intellectual capacity still outstrips your inflated ego; that's got to be a good sign."

"Was that, by mistake, a backhanded compliment?"

"If it was a complement, it was certainly a mistake."

I had to concede defeat. "Fine: mental ability of a mollusk, or whatever it was... "

"A cephalopod!"

"Whatever. I give in! What's all this about?"

"Obvious to anyone of even the meanest intellectual capacity, this was the casting couch. We were checking you out to see if we could work with you."

"Isn't this usually done with discussions, interviews and all the HR shit?"

Sue thought for a moment, giving the appearance of trying to work out a way to explain the charm of Shakespeare to an illiterate child. "Well, think about the last few days. You've revealed to us personal information that you would normally have restricted only to your very closest confidantes, actually probably only your sister. This was because we were merely scribes, secretaries. Your sister had manipulated things so that we could be set up in this role. It seems, however, that we're expected to move into a more active role in the future; but to do so, we need to be accepted as something different by you. We will probably remain employees, but you need to think of us more as partners and less as functionaries. This could have evolved naturally over an extended period of time, but we've the feeling that there's something coming up, something that led Andrea to accelerate the initiation of the book project. We just moved things on by taking control of your sex life and demonstrating that, if needed, we can do anything that your sister can do. This is something that you not only need to accept intellectually, but believe viscerally."

"Well, you've certainly done lots of things that I'm sure my sister has never even contemplated."

"God, Cof, you're so bloody naive! There's not a thing that we've done with you that we haven't already done with Andrea and Tina. Do you think we were saving ourselves as virgins while your conniving sister was developing her convoluted plans? They may have a solid partnership, but they've been living together for almost forty years; don't you think they need a bit of spice now and again?"

"Sorry! OK, you've also been into outrageously dirty sex with my sister and her girlfriend. It still doesn't answer my question. Why the alt sex scene last night?"

"Because you have to believe that, despite our backgrounds, we're not bound by the taboos of the past. We disagree with a lot of what you've done," she hastened to add, grabbing a slurp of her drink and handing the empty glass to me as an evident request for a refill, "but there is no doubt that we can only move forward by adapting to the new boundary conditions that we're faced with."

She stopped and again patted Sophie's pleasantly rounded buttocks. "You know that Sophie was once part of the religious infrastructure that you hated so much and are now planning to eliminate. Nevertheless, I think that you've almost accepted that you need her ethical solidity to balance your fundamental amorality. You tended, nevertheless, to regard her as a little flaky, out of touch with the real world. I suspect that you'll treat her a bit differently after last night!"

"So that's what it was. Establishing yourselves as credible partners in my eyes."

"Only partially, the other part was you establishing, for yourself, your own limitations and your needs."

"Don't I do that often enough with the twins?"

"That's different; as you previously emphasized, prostitution is a commercial deal that benefits both sides. But the twins are there to provide pleasure, not criticism. You need both. We've no intention of putting your hookers out of a job, but you now know that we can be as uninhibited as they are. You need to be completely open with us, just like we'll be open with you. If you can finally see that it's time for you to gradually start spreading the load of running the Caribbean part of the Renaissance, and you accept that we're the ones that you can trust to support you, then I guess Andrea's plan has succeeded."

"Do you think my sister could have foreseen last night?"

"I don't see how she could have. For Sophie and me, it just came to us as the right way to move things forward. I wouldn't be surprised if she had expected us to end up in bed at some time or another, though. I really doubt that the past relationships that Sleeping Beauty and I have had with Andrea and Tina were completely coincidental."

"Well then," I stretched with a yawn, "I guess the bed bit is over now. Time to get started."

305

"What's the rush?" Like an eel she slid on top of me, ending up straddling my thighs. "You completely drained? Slow recovery type?"

She slowly and deliberately leaned over and, while staring into my eyes, slid a hand between her sleeping partner's legs. "Seems not," she answered herself, feeling my response as she delicately licked her fingers.

"I thought you didn't get turned on like this?"

"I don't, but you certainly do. Don't you remember? I'm the BJ queen!" She then proceeded to demonstrate that her claim was well justified.

***

The two women joined me for lunch. Despite Sue's prediction, Sophie appeared bright eyed and bushy tailed. As we grazed on meze, Sue outlined the remaining text blocks that were needed to complete the documentation project. Quite a few of these they could actually fill in for themselves by focused searches of the house database, now they knew what to look for. A key area was, however, my worries about the future; ideas of things that could go wrong and possible ways to pre-emptively avoid them. Suddenly a lot of the annoying questions that remained unanswered began to line up and a pattern began to emerge.

I gradually realized that Sue had gone quiet and both women were frowning at me. Sophie was first in. "Cof, was that you having a senior moment there? You were miles away."

306

"I guess the sex last night was just too much for him," her partner sighed. "Burned out a neuron and now he's got nothing left to build a synapse with."

"Stop babbling, women! I've cracked it! I've found the last piece of the jigsaw!"

"Senile dementia," Sue concluded. "Probably your fault, Sophie, shouldn't have sat on his face like that last night. Starved his poor brain of oxygen."

"Me! I thought he was going to drown when you..."

"For Christ's sake, don't you want to know why my sister gave me the nudge to start this project off now?"

There was instant silence. "I think we have already sorted out the how and the why of all this, but there's still the question of why now? It could simply have been that I was showing increasing signs of falling off my mental perch, but the timing is too neat. As Sue convinced me this morning, this project was aimed to bring us together, but we had to learn complete openness, to fully trust each other. Last night was your initiative for a move in that direction, but this was all a bit platonic: if that term is usable in the context of decadent sex. In any case, it's not working together to solve a real problem, which is the actual proof of the pudding. I'm now sure that it's not a coincidence, because there's been a local crisis building up where I've got to make a decision about what to do pretty soon."

"Ah!" Sue looked very pleased, seeing confirmation of the final part of her theory. "So we, as a team, need to work together to solve it!"

"Nope, not at all!" I enjoyed the looks of surprise turning towards annoyance before I continued. "This is the casting couch for me. The acid test of whether you can hack it or not. My role is to provide you with all the background I have. Yours is to develop the plan and then implement it."

Sue appeared to be working out how this would fit with her view of the future, but Sophie had more practical concerns. "This can't work, we can't do it without you. We don't have any experience in this kind of stuff."

"There's only one way to get experience in making hard decisions, by getting your hands dirty. Learning by doing it."

Sophie looked ready to argue further, but Sue beat her to it. "No, love, Cof's right here, for once. We've got to test ourselves. I've been preaching at him, telling him that he needs to know his limitations and be open with us about them. The same holds for us; except in a very academic way, we've no real idea what our limitations are under relevant circumstances. I'll bet the problem that Andrea has identified is exactly the kind of thing that will provide this sort of test." Her tone indicated clear admiration of my scheming sister.

"Yes, I think you're right. We're having problems with Nigel. Grab coffees and we'll go to the study where I can provide you with all the background. Then you can decide if you feel up to it or not."

***

Taking my time and answering questions as I went, I gave as comprehensive an overview as possible of the growth of the de facto Bajan government and Nigel's key role in this process. His combination of experience in both politics and emergency services placed him in an ideal position to establish and lead the ad hoc group that attempted to impose some kind of control on Bridgetown and start the process leading to rebuilding service infrastructure. I had, of course, helped him to consolidate his administration which, as the banks became established and trade built up, naturally evolved into a kind of national government. Although he was supported by a small executive team, this was effectively a dictatorship, but one ideally suited for the conditions of the time.

Over the last decade, however, this government had been showing worrying trends. The executive was originally composed of Nigel's colleagues, selected on the basis of their abilities. With time, however, they were being replaced by members of his extended family, who appeared to be characterized more by their unquestioning loyalty to Nigel than anything else. Also, as the economy grew, increasing amounts of the budget were flowing, directly or indirectly, into his family accounts. The fraction of government expenditure going to the police and the coast guard was also increasing, making them look more and more like the core of an army and navy. He even had the beginnings of an air force.

Individually, any of these indicators was worrying. Together, they led to the conclusion that, as is so often the case, power was having a corrupting influence and Nigel was setting himself up as the head of a new dynasty.

With the way that the IBS operated, it was impossible for Nigel to conceal his manipulation of the budget from anyone, like myself, who wanted to examine it. Nigel certainly knew this, but evidently felt sufficiently confident that his position was above reproach. Probably this was a result of his eldest son, Winston, taking over as head of emergency services, the new integration of all paramilitary forces.

"Well, that's it," I concluded. "In the early days Nigel was a key part of the solution to rebuilding Barbados, but he's now increasingly becoming a part of the problem; not only slowing things down and blocking progress, but setting up structures that could destabilize both the island and the entire region. So, what are you going to do about him?"

"That's the broad brush background," Sue responded. "To go further, however, we need more details. How large are individual paramilitary units? How loyal are they? What do the people in the street think about his administration? That kind of stuff."

I stood up and pointed at my chair. "You've got access to all my resources here. Not only the databases that you could get into before, but the video cameras, satellite feeds, everything. If you want, take a couple of bikes and run down to Bridgetown, get a feel for what it's like on the ground." As I headed for the door I added, "I'm available any time you want me but, for the moment, I'll let you get on in peace. Toodle pip!"

***

After leaving the women with their challenge, I headed directly over to my sister's villa. It was noticeable how she had been avoiding me since the book project really started to get going, and now I finally knew why.

A retinal scan allowed me access to a side gate through the high wall that surrounded her property. Typically for late afternoon, Andrea and Tina were sitting on the west-facing patio, drinking iced tea. They reclined together on a sofa, feet up on stools, Tina snuggled in the crook of my sister's arm as they enjoyed the pleasant warmth of the February sun. I looked down at their naked, hairless bodies as my sister squinted up at me, the sun in her eyes. "Drop your kegs and come and catch some rays," she suggested, patting the free space beside her.

As commanded, I stripped off and lay against my sister's other shoulder, feeling the gentle caress of a warm sea breeze on my naked skin. I sneaked a glance at the naked body beside me. Absolutely fine, I could admire the view, but there was no sexual reaction at all. A lot of other taboos might have gone out the window, but programing against incest was sufficiently hard wired that it functioned on a completely subliminal level. Then, however, I had the distracting image of Andrea and Tina working out with Sue and Sophie. The physical reaction was immediate.

With typical perceptiveness, apropos of nothing, Andrea asked, "How did things go last night?"

I looked over, but she was lying in the same position, eyes closed, the question apparently completely casual. Tina, however, was grinning like Alice's Cheshire Cat, giving the game away.

"As you already seem to know, I had a very pleasant evening. Instructive I'd even call it. In fact, the last few days have been pretty damned instructive." I was trying to sound annoyed, but my sister was a past master of defusing my wrath before I could even get properly warmed up.

"Good, I'm glad. You needed a bit of variety. The twins are great, but a change is as good as a holiday for you. In actual fact, the happy hookers came over here last night to celebrate their surprise vacation. A jolly time was had by all." The slightest trace of a smile touched her lips as her hand slid down to rub Tina's right nipple.

"Ah... so that's how you know about last night!"

"Well, Tina was also talking to one of the maids. She thought that you'd had a particularly debauched night with the twins. The twins,

312

however, spent the entire night with us, getting into some very perverse lesbian sex." Index finger and thumb were now starting to squeeze the nipple. It looked quite painful, but, from the sound of the resultant small groan, it was having a pleasurable effect. "Ergo, you were getting a good seeing to from your secretaries. I guessed it would probably go that way, but it went a lot faster than I expected. Sue's idea?"

"I think so."

"It's always the case," she sighed. "We select people who are very bright, because we need their intelligence, but they're exactly the ones who are smart enough to spot manipulation and bloody-minded enough to oppose it as a matter of principle. Just as well that I expected her to do something like this, so it's well within the envelope."

"You don't think you could have let me in on this from the beginning?" Even to myself, I seemed to have a whine in my voice.

"Come on, Ham, you know that there're things that you're good at and others where you're complete crap. In the science field you're shit hot; head and shoulders above the wankers that you used to work with. The conspiracy and double-dealing side you rightfully leave to me. It was really important that you weren't conning those women; you were all victims of your evil big sister." She then cackled, her evil witch impersonation that she used to scare me as a young child, and pinched her lover's nipple viciously, causing a squeak of pain.

"Oops, sorry sweetheart!" She bent to kiss the abused flesh. "Sorry about that, getting a bit carried away. Anyhow," she turned back to me, "I take it that you're a team now and are ready to gird up your collective loins and go sort out the bad guys?"

"Not quite, they're going to sort out the bad guys, I'm going to watch."

For the first time, my sister seemed surprised, discomfited. "Are you sure about this, bruv? Nigel's very smart and could easily turn nasty if he felt threatened. Your partners need to be tested in real life, but throwing them at Nigel, alone, might be a bit extreme, even as a baptism of fire. Shouldn't you maybe... "

"Nope!" I interrupted. "You schemed to test all of us. They turned the tables and set out to test me. So now I have to test them."

"All of our arses are on the line here," she pointed out. "The girls fuck up and we're up to our necks in shit."

"Comes with the job. Anytime critical, I'll be with them; but I'm not going to interfere unless things get completely out of control. They won't do things the way we would, but that's why you chose them in the first place. If I start actively participating in this, I destroy the impetus for them to take the initiative. You know that's how this game has got to be played."

I got a hug that made me glow. This was the recognition that I was right and my dominant sister was, for a rare occasion, going to back down. "Of course, Ham. This is what it's all about. The

314

problem is that, when it comes to the crunch, it's very, very hard to let go of the reins, to pass the power onto others, when we've had it in the family so long."

"Exactly - which is Nigel's problem in a nutshell!"

"Yes indeed: there, but for the grace of God, go the both of us. If Nigel needs to be stomped on, we can't do it and gain acceptance if we're doing exactly the same thing. It's like the way the Yanks lost all international credibility at the beginning of the century. Pontificating all over the globe about terrorism, arms control, the environment, drugs, human rights, financial controls - when they were amongst the world's worst offenders in all of those areas. After a few decades, US diplomatic incompetence became expected, but the hypocrisy still got seriously on everyone's tits."

"You know, sis, you ramble on almost as much as I do - and you don't even have a degrading cortex as an excuse." I then yelped in response to a painful nip on the chest. "No, seriously, this whole book thing has been a bit of a revelation. Even during the long chats we've had together, we've never tried to integrate the entire picture or to look at how we would bring more people in to take over responsibility from us. I feel more positive about things than I have for years."

"Excellent. Well, if you're happy, I'm happy. In fact, I'm so happy I'm going to give this nymph an orgasm that'll bring tears to her eyes." She was now working on Tina's left nipple, twisting and squeezing in a way that was causing her lover's back to arch. "You want to watch?" She raised her eyebrows salaciously as she opened her legs to allow her friend's fingers access.

"Mmm, love to, but I think I'll take a rain check on that while I can still get into my shorts."

I heard a muttered "Spoilsport!" as I quickly scrambled into my clothes and headed back in the direction of home. Although having an observer seemed to add piquancy to their foreplay, it looked like they were going to be well past that phase very quickly.

***

I was rather disappointed to receive a message that my new partners would not be joining me for dinner, but this was tempered by the arrival of the twins. They dined with me irregularly, based on some kind of arcane pattern that I had never been able to decrypt. The women were dressed as schoolgirls tonight, in uniforms that I had never before seen outside the fun room. During the dinner they pestered me continually for details of my activities of the previous night, teasing out confessions one by one. My knowledge of their true physical ages was completely subverted by their role playing, they were completely plausible as a couple of precocious fifteen or sixteen year old Lolitas.

I was completely ensnared in their web, feeling embarrassed about the actions that I was describing to such young girls, but ultimately being unable to refuse them anything. When I baulked at providing intimate details of our more perverse moments, they bribed me with items of clothing. It was a tribute to the twins' mastery of the staged choreography of such games that they both ended the meal wearing only small pairs of white panties, dampened to transparency at the crotch, and school ties.

I cracked at that point; no possibility of even getting back to the bedroom. I ripped off my trousers and had sex with both of them, one after the other, on the dining table, spilling wine and coffee on the white linen tablecloth.

When the twins eventually got me to bed, I was completely drained. I don't even know if they spent any time in bed with me, I was sound asleep as soon as my head hit the pillow.

Chapter 9 - A cunning plan

Sue and Sophie were already at the table when I turned up for breakfast next morning. I hardly had time to seat myself before Sue got straight to the point. "Cof, when can you set up a meeting between us and Nigel?"

I poured myself coffee while I thought about the question. "Depends, I suppose," I mused out loud, "what you want to meet him about. As he is effectively president, or dictator, of the island - I think he still calls himself chairman of the provisional administration - he tends to be pretty busy and is difficult to get in contact without going through several layers of underlings."

"What if you pushed him?"

"Well, he's certainly still very wary of me, though definitely not as scared as he once was. I guess he feels a lot less vulnerable now that he's less dependent on support from me; I'm the cheapest option but, if necessary, he could get his technical database access elsewhere."

"So, if you urgently requested a meeting?"

"I'd imagine he'd try to fit me in as soon as possible. Apart from anything else, I don't go out often; he'd be curious about what I was wanting from him."

"And you could bring us along with you?"

"No reason why not? But what reason would I give for wanting to see him in a meeting that required two secretaries?"

"You won't require secretaries. The meeting will be about setting up a new University of the West Indies based on resources that you're going to donate. We're your paralegals who are going to nail down the associated details."

"Won't he be likely to end up with a big team of his own at such a meeting?"

"As a worst case, we can live with that. Nevertheless, we doubt that he'll have more than one or two family members with him, max."

Sophie now came in with her input. "If we present the donation as a combination of funding and equipment - hardware and databases - the temptation will probably be too great for our beloved chairman. He won't want anything as valuable as this escaping his control. We're fairly sure that he'll try to set up a member of his extended family as chancellor, head of the senate or whatever. He's fairly sure of his position, but I don't think he'd like any potential future rivals to know about a plum cash-cow like this."

I thought a bit about the plan. "Yup, it could work. I'll contact him now to see if I can set an appointment. By the way, what do you intend to do when you meet him?"

"Put on the frighteners," Sue answered honestly.

"Mmm, that sounds like the kind of thing that Andrea and I would do."

"Not at all," Sophie disagreed, "we're not actually going to hurt anyone."

"No," her partner smiled, wickedly, "just scare the poor bugger senseless!"

"Sounds good to me. Apart from the appointment, do I need to do anything?"

"Just give us access to your armory; we can get inventory information, but we can't actually get in." Sue sounded annoyed. I'd have bet money that she'd already spent a fair amount of time trying to hack her way into it.

"No, you're currently not cleared for that - I'll sort it out immediately. So, what're you looking for?"

"We've no idea," she laughed, "but I'm sure we'll know when we find it. We'll keep you informed anyway. So, we're off now. Maybe see you for lunch."

I finished my breakfast in a bit of a daze, trying to work out what on earth the women could be planning.

***

It was another swimming-with-Katya morning, although today Di had elected to join us in an unusual display of masochism. Rain was lashing down and a blustery wind from the sea was sending breakers crashing against the beach. We were catching the edge of a winter storm that was building up in the Atlantic, destined to hammer either the northeast coast of the states or northwest Europe in a week or so.

Katya was, as usual, clad only in skin and seemed completely unperturbed by the, by Bajan standards, distinctly cool rain. By contrast, Di was wearing a figure-hugging black wetsuit. I opted for a compromise option, a small pair of swimming trunks and a thin reef shirt.

Our exercise this morning was straightforward, stick with Katya and swim out directly into the swell for about half an hour or until one of us felt uncomfortable, both women smiled in my direction at this point, then turn and coast back in with the surf.

We were lashed by clouds of spray as we waited on the end of the jetty for Katya's signal. Then we were off, diving as far out as possible and fighting quickly through the first few waves to avoid being swept back against the pier. Thereafter it was survival swimming, trying to cut through the heavy swell as cleanly as possible and time our breathing to avoid mouthfuls of brine.

As we got a bit further from shore, the chop caused by the interference of waves with their reflections from the beach died away and it was easier to adopt a regular stroke. As I began to finally relax into a power crawl, I realized that this was one of the few tangible benefits of the Crash, the freedom to swim deep into open water under rough conditions without being in constant fear of being mown down by a speed boat or, more likely, a fuckwit on a jet ski. During my first decade on the island, I had a running battle with some lunatics who constantly ignored warning buoys that

321

designated the swimming area around the Folkestone marine park. I even developed and tested a design for a perimeter marking system that had a monofilament line strung at jet-ski throat height. Probably just as well that Andrea convinced me that the locals were unlikely to be happy at me decapitating the local yobs, for what was considered, by them, to be a minor transgression. In any case, jet-skis had gone the way of formula-1 racing and free-fall parachuting: decadent luxuries that wouldn't re-emerge for generations. As I battled through the waves I made another mental note; ensure that I gain control of any technology relevant to development of jet skis so that I - or my estate - can kill any initiatives in this direction stone dead.

The warmth of belated revenge against ignorant louts, probably long dead, kept me battling against the texture of the sea, going in the direction that anyone with a bit of sense wouldn't. I was so distracted by my daydreams that I almost missed Katya's signal to turn. Now that would be a serious fuck-up, I realized; keep on in this direction and the next landfall is probably Senegal or some other Godforsaken part of Africa.

The good news was that we were now going with the swell; the 180° turn was like cutting in turbos, for the same effort, progress through the water was dramatically faster. The bad news, however, was that Katya had upped her pace; not so much turbocharged, she went off as if powered by nitrous oxide injection. Clearly Di had also been caught out by this maneuver, she actually dropped behind me for the first time as she struggled to adapt to both the changed water conditions and the increased pace.

I've seen Di in a swimming pool; she powers through the water like a juggernaut: unstoppable, tireless. She wasn't too keen on what, to her Caribbean blood, was cold water and hence had little experience in the open ocean. I could have tried to help, but the thought didn't even cross my mind. This was a sign of weakness, blood in the water. I set off as fast as possible after Katya, leaving my aerobics trainer to her fate.

Chop was building up, a sure sign that we were approaching our target on the coast, I could sense, rather than see, that Di was catching up rapidly. I was almost level with Katya's heels, but really beginning to puff as the stepwise increasing speed pushed me closer to a heart attack. It was the worst possible moment to remember Katya's penalty for today's game. The only important factor was the difference in arrival time between the second girl and me. It seems that the option of me coming second wasn't even worth considering. Anyway, the critical measure was the number of seconds that number three lost to number two. This was the number of chest presses for the former, with the bar that the latter would be standing or sitting on. This bar had been especially constructed by me to Katya's specifications. She simply told me that she wanted something that felt like a barbell, but that she could load up with whatever material took her fancy. Naively I set up the program to fabricate it from cheap high density steel so that, on its own, it weighs in at about ten kilos. If I had guessed how often that I was going to suffer under that bloody thing, I'd have ignored the costs and produced a variant from resins, DLC, buckyballs and graphene. Same strength and a weight of around a couple of hundred grams.

My senile moment distraction had been enough for Di to pull level with me. This was now one-on-one. The brain was playing only a secondary role as I strained to stay ahead of the racing black shape at my side, but I had a sudden flashback of my last catastrophic race towards the pier. This time, if I kept just about level but took time to carefully check the position of the jetty and the sequence of waves, it would be easy to set Di up to hit the waves wrongly and end up being battered against the structure, just like me last time, while I took my time to efficiently exit on the ladder.

All went well until we were about two strokes from our goal. As I expected, Di was heading straight in, oblivious to a huge wave that was starting to break immediately behind her. Di was certainly a lot fitter and better trained than me, but here she was suffering from a lack of open water experience. She was probably tough enough to ride it out, but it could be very painful.

Just as she was about to commit herself to a serious mistake, I grabbed an ankle, causing her to break stroke due to the shocked reaction. She had half-turned towards me when I saw that the crest of the wave was lifting her towards the ladder; one hearty push from me was all that was needed to ensure that she made contact with it, unfortunately also ensuring that I slammed into the rubber tyres, used as a buffer for mooring craft, and ended tangled up in a rope as the next monster wave approached. I had braced myself for the impact, filling my lungs with air, when, at the last possible moment, a black hand grabbed my shirt and yanked me clear, almost choking me in the process.

As I lay spluttering on the decking, I glanced up to look for some recognition of my selfless act but, instead, Katya was giving Di a good telling off. "... this training is not only physical, it's also mental. If he had gotten himself a real pounding and spent another twenty, thirty seconds in the water then there'd be a lot less chance of him making the same mistake again."

"But he helped me out. There's no way I'd have made that ladder without him"

"No, you certainly wouldn't have. But he was supposed to be concentrating on getting out before you, not being a good Samaritan." The slim naked blond looked down at me as I struggled to my knees, puzzlement showing on her face. "It's not like Cof, though. He has many faults, but being over-endowed with the milk of human kindness isn't one of them. Usually he's over-competitive, if anything."

"Why don't you girls just talk about me as if I'm not here?" I spluttered, rubbing blood from a split lip that I'd only just noticed.

The women continued to ignore me, so I couldn't tell if they had even heard my complaint or not. "Well, anyway, I think it's only fair that I do the presses." Di was adamant, hands on hips, her black-clad frame almost completely blocking Katya from my view.

"Doesn't work that way." The smaller woman was not going to be intimidated. "However," she looked at her watch, "if you want to show solidarity, you can do six presses with Cof on the bar, then he'll do eight with you on it."

"Look at the size of me, girl! Eight will kill the poor boy. Let me do the eight."

I looked around my defender to see the evil grin that was lighting up my swim-trainer's face. I groaned.

"Eight, nul problemo. You do eight and Cof does ten! Any further bids?"

I pulled Di around and squeezed her arms. "Thanks a lot, Di, but we're on a hiding to nothing here."

The black woman pulled down the zipper on her suit, exposing a very deep, dark, cleavage. A heavy arm went around my shoulder. "OK, lovey, let's get this over with."

Because of the heavy rain, Katya's torture kit was set up in the gym, so we had a chance to recover somewhat during the walk back to the house and while we dried ourselves off. As I sat on the bar, my backside above Di's face as she lay on the bench below, I tried to estimate our relative weights. I come in just below eighty kilos, but Di

326

was about ten or fifteen centimeters shorter than my one-eighty. On the other hand, she was much more muscular, with a big bum and huge tits. How much would those weigh?

With a grunt, I felt myself smoothly lifted up and down. Another grunt and a second lift. By the eighth, there was a definite tremor, but the bar was settled down gently onto the rest with hardly a noise.

While we changed positions, I noticed sweat on the woman's brow and trickling down her neck, vanishing into a black Grand Canyon between her ponderous breasts. Overheating in her wetsuit, I tried to convince myself.

Now I was looking up at the large black bottom perched above me. The suit was so tight that the crack of her bum was clear, as was the trace of a small tanga that she was wearing under it. Concentrate on that tasty chunk of anatomy and ignore the pain, I commanded myself. I inhaled deeply and then pushed up with all my strength. The bar maybe moved up a centimeter before it crashed back into place, sending a shockwave through the taut fabric in front of my eyes. "One," announced Di decisively. I arched my head back to look at Katya who was staring down at me though the gap between ebony thighs. She rolled her eyes, but said nothing. Possibly the slightest trace of a smile on her face. Maybe this wasn't going to be too bad after all.

My new confidence lasted one more press, which maybe raised the bar a full two centimeters.

By the third, I was down to about one centimeter again and after that things went downhill. Most of my attempts thereafter failed to move the bar at all. Any jerk sufficient to even cause an audible click was counted by Di, without any complaint from Katya. When we finally reached eight, Di started to plead. "Eight, that was the original target, couldn't we... " but evidently saw the danger in going further with this line, "... suppose not. OK, lad, only two to go. Then you're done."

The thought of an approaching end to this torment allowed me to mobilize my last reserves. Crash! Must have been about half a centimeter. "Nine!" One last push now, but nothing happened, all strength had completely left my arms. Another grunt and another complete failure. Maybe this is what happens when the brain degrades beyond a certain point, the body has the physical capacity, but not the willpower to break through pain barriers. Why had I delayed the fucking cerebral rejuv? What's the point of having the physique of a Greek God, when there's only mush left between the ears. Fuck it!

Crash! "Ten! Well done! I thought that you had blown up there, but you did it."

My arms fell to my sides like pieces of soggy spaghetti. My biceps and chest muscles hurt so much that I really felt as if I had torn something. Di helped me into a sitting position, but then punched my arm in playful congratulations, causing me to yelp with pain. "Sorry, Cof - I think you need a long hot shower!"

"I think I need morphine and surgery to re-attach ripped muscles and ligaments." I moaned.

"Don't be a big baby!" Katya supported me from the other side and the two women dragged me to my feet. "Remember: that which doesn't kill you makes you strong!"

"If that was the case, I'd be like Superman after the number of near-death experiences you've inflicted on me over the last few years."

"Alcoholic beverages and loose women are your kryptonite," she retorted, dragging me into the shower where I was unceremoniously stripped and, while she gently rubbed my upper arms, a now equally naked Di started to soap my back. "We'll just get you loosened up enough so that you won't seize up over the next few hours. I'll give you a proper massage this evening, when your muscles will be a bit less sensitive."

"Less-sensitive, that's trainer-speak for not quite screaming in agony so much, isn't it!"

"No pain, no gain" Di responded, squeezing my buttocks hard. "How 'bout we try seein' what we can gain from these flabby buns of you's?"

The girls laughed, their little tiff forgotten as they teamed up for their shared hobby of tormenting their boss.

***

At lunch there was no sign of my secretaries, partners, lovers, whatever they were. I munched on a sandwich containing a very convincing synthetic cheddar and Branston pickle, washed down with a local Banks beer, the brewery being now back in production. I was sitting in the conservatory, watching sheets of rain sweep in as the storm built up while I pondered my evolving relationship with the two women. They still, formally at least, worked for me and were supposed to produce my book, so they were secretaries of some kind. In terms of running the estate and the wider Renaissance project, they were clearly much more: partners, co-conspirators, team-mates, colleagues; something along those lines. Maybe even more, considering the lead role that they were taking at present. Would they be my protegees, heirs-apparent?

And then, of course, there had been our night of outrageous debauchery. Had that been a one-off, a demonstration to establish our new working relationship? Or was it more of an indicator of things to come? Would our greater intimacy lead inevitably to regular sexual encounters? If so, was the perversion and kinkiness an inevitable component of our interactions or would that, as with the twins, be an infrequent diversion from more conventional sex?

I had lots of questions, but no answers. Trends were emerging, however. Simply by agreeing to hand over responsibilities, even if only temporarily, Andrea and I had crossed into new territory. I could already feel a weight lifted from my shoulders and this was changing the entire way I behaved. Katya's words, in particular, had been going through my mind since I had recovered sufficiently for abstract thought to swamp out the continuous reassessment of my inventories of aches and pains. She had been really surprised at the way I had behaved with Di, by my uncharacteristic display of human kindness. Although it hadn't stopped her inflicting the penalty for failure, this had somehow served to build a tight bond between Di and myself. We had known each other for years and would probably have considered ourselves friends, but now we had become close.

Maybe this was all part of a new phase change. Originally, my home had been a reasonably straightforward rich man's villa, fundamentally no different from hundreds of others on the island, thousands throughout the Caribbean. It had its eccentricities - my technical infrastructure and my sister's staffing policy - but my interactions with employees had been typical of the norms of the '30s. The chaos resulting from the loss of quantum computing caused a first phase change. I became absolute ruler of an enclave separated from the rest of the world by a barrier of technology. Although my sister and I played different roles in our relationships with specific staff, we alone took all responsibility for decisions affecting the future of our community. In some cases these were life-and-death calls, which we made without asking the opinion of any of those affected. The tacit bottom line was that it was my estate and, if anyone didn't like the way I was running it, then they were free to leave.

This was accepted - and necessary - during the crisis conditions of the first pre-Crash decade.

Normalization was moving forward fast, though, and it was time to change things, certainly at the level of my extended household. I no longer needed to reinforce unquestioning trust by constantly proving how tough I was. I could gain respect by showing a more compassionate side of my character, even if I had to fake it a bit. Then, all being well, we'd gradually end up back where we started in the mid '30s. Or maybe not, I corrected myself; together, my employees, Andrea and I had gone through trauma that caused irreversible changes and the resultant hysteresis meant that the memory of our past would always remain. Nevertheless, this move towards rebuilding more normal working relationships was an internal indicator of the relaxation within our walls caused by the decreasing level of pressure from outside, certainly a result of reduction in the previous huge discrepancy in our standards of living.

Definitely feeling cheerier on the basis of this introspection, despite slowly stiffening joints, I adjourned to my study to set up the meeting with Nigel and prepare the background bumf that would be needed to cover any questions he may have on the girls' proposal. In fact, the more I thought about it, helping re-establish the university seemed like an eminently sensible proposal in its own right and I tagged it for a follow up whenever the dust died down from our planned overthrow of the current Bajan government.

**

By the time I was soaking in the onsen, the storm had blown over and the sky was clear, with only the faintest haze on the Western horizon. I was watching the sun deform as it rapidly dropped into the sea, vanishing with a distinctive green flash, one of the clearest that I'd ever seen, despite having watched thousands of tropical sunsets. I had been so caught up in the view that it was only when the sun disappeared that I became aware that my protegees were silently standing in the pool behind me, watching the show over my shoulders.

I turned and sat on the sunken ledge, draping my arms over the sides of the bath. Sue took a seat on my left and Sophie on my right, both women leaning against my arms and causing inadvertent twitches as they came in contact with tender muscles. Sue closed her eyes with a sigh, but then came straight to the point. "Meeting with Nigel set up?"

"Tomorrow afternoon, his house at three."

"We guessed it'd probably be there. It's got reasonably high security and everyone in the place is completely loyal to him. Or, at least, that's what he thinks."

"I don't think there's any doubt about it," I responded. "It's all his extended family and they're the ones who are living well on the basis of the present regime. Sons, brothers, cousins, uncles: they're all incredibly close. If you're thinking of fomenting a palace coup, then I don't think it would work. They all have too much to lose and too little to gain."

"Yes, well, anyway, we'll see. Can you organize wheels to get us there with some kit?"

"We've got an old biofueled Landrover that we use for lugging stuff around on the beach or less accessible parts of the estate. I haven't had it outside the walls since the Crash, but I think that here are enough vehicles on the roads now that it won't cause too much unwanted attention. Anyway, Nigel's residence is on the other side of Bridgetown, so we ought to leave plenty of time to get there - probably best going around the old ring road to avoid the middle of the town."

"That'd be fine. Can you drive it?"

"Haven't done any driving since Jamaica," I confessed, causing the mood to darken a little. Probably a good thing, I thought, it's important that they realize that this isn't all an intellectual game; here, if you screw up you don't lose points, you may well lose your life.

"Anyway," I added, "I don't need to. We can take a couple of the security folk and they can drive."

"No, we won't need security. In fact, it'll be better without them. The three of us should be able to manage things on our own."

"Well, if I have an active role in this palaver, you'd better brief me on it."

"We'll go over this later this evening... " Sue started.

334

"... just after we shag you half to death!" Sophie finished.

A snort from above caused heads to turn. "Well, based on his present state, you wouldn't have far to go. He's like death warmed up like it is. I suppose I'd better do my best to put him back in working order for you, but I can't promise miracles." My masseuse was patting the table, a clear indication that, after her silent entry, she was ready to start.

"Katya most certainly has a point," I confirmed as I dragged myself from the bath. "In my present state I doubt that I could be aroused by a bed-full of chocolate-covered schoolgirls."

Sophie had followed me and was drying my back while I rubbed down my upper torso. "Well, two schoolgirls seemed to be quite enough to do the trick last night... " she sniggered "... and not even covered in chocolate!"

"Those twins talk too much!" I tried to keep my response to a whisper, although Katya seemed to be completely uninterested in our conversation.

"Don't be silly, they're professionals - in more senses than one. They'd never talk about details of activities with clients unless that was expressly permitted."

"So, how do you know so much? Don't tell me that Sue was able to deduce it from first principles."

"She's not quite that good, but she's now able to access all the house video records after you upgraded our clearance to universal. Very instructive it was too!"

335

I groaned as I was pushed onto the massage table and Katya started to arrange my limbs to suit her purposes. "Well, this seems like a bit of a challenge, but doable," she commented. "I'm afraid, though, it's going to hurt a bit now."

"Not as much as it's going to hurt later!" Sophie laughed, managing to slap my bum before Katya covered it with a towel.

It did indeed hurt, a lot. But not so much that I was prevented from wondering what exactly the evening had in store. Was my next sexual encounter with my new partners going to really hurt more than this and, if so, would I then be in any shape to carry out whatever role was planned for me tomorrow.

***

Despite everything that I had been through, the massage really did seem to have sorted out major muscle strains; or, at least, postponed resultant suffering for a day or two. Sue and Sophie had made themselves scarce as soon as Katya started to work on me. It certainly couldn't be that they were discomfited by my grunts of pain, I concluded; in fact, my suffering had previously had exactly the opposite effect.

Interestingly, Katya didn't seem concerned about my planned encounter with two members of my staff, but more worried that it could be dangerous for me getting involved in schemes cooked up by these women. As she put it "I don't know what's going on here, but there seem to be

336

changes at the top and those two are up to their eyeballs in the new regime. Personally, I don't seem to be much affected by all these strategies and tactics by the deep thinkers, so I can just wait until the dust settled. You, on the other hand, have to watch out for yourself. In the past, I wouldn't have had to even think this, but the world seems to be changing and the alterations are filtering through to our little enclave. You've spent the last fifteen years looking after us, now you've got to think about yourself for a bit."

This unexpected outburst showed my masseuse to be, as hinted at by previous comments, much more aware of the environment than she pretended. Nevertheless, she couldn't really have much of an idea about what we were up to. I accepted this intellectually, but the warning preyed on my mind for the rest of the massage. If the women came up with any plan that I could go along with, then the risks to me should be negligible. Even if the hazard was small, I finally decided as I dressed for dinner, a bit of belt-and-braces insurance couldn't cause any problems. A mental note to myself on this, then down to the dining room to find out what my future had in store for me.

***

At first it looked as if dinner was intended as a replay of that from two days before, the main difference being that tonight Sue was in white and Sophie in black. No schoolgirl uniforms, I was

337

pleased to note. Nevertheless, throughout a very pleasant meal, accompanied by oldies pop from the year 2013, I couldn't help pondering the significance of their dress and the format of the evening. The only other definite information that I had was that the twins had, again, been given the night off.

After listening to an hour of ancient pop trivia, I finally cracked. "OK, ladies, it's been a lovely meal without shop talk but, as we move towards deserts or cheese or coffee or whatever, won't somebody put me out of my misery and let me know what you've got planned for tomorrow."

Sophie got in first. "We've talked about that and decided that you'd be more receptive... "

"... more easily manipulated," clarified Sue with typical bluntness.

"... if we got the sex out of the way first. I mean, you're just about drooling every time I lean forward." Sophie demonstrated by leaning forward and, perfectly on cue, her small left breast escaped the minimal restraints of her low-cut gown.

Sue guffawed. "What my foot-in-mouth partner was trying to convey is that, in the presence of nubile female flesh, you lose concentration."

I couldn't help smiling. "At my age the drooling comes naturally, it just gets a bit worse when a tasty little tit is dropped onto my plate."

"Anyway," Sophie concluded, after stuffing the wayward bosom back into its cage, "we thought you would concentrate better if we reduced the pressure on your underwear before proceeding further."

"So this is nothing at all to do with me, is it? I may be getting blind due to advanced age and an inordinate fondness for masturbation, but the nipple that you presented for my inspection a few seconds ago had the appearance of an acorn. A very large acorn, at that."

"Hoist on your own petard, Sophie love!" Sue was evidently enjoying this exchange immensely. "Or, maybe, your deadly acorns. We'll just have to be careful later or you'll have someone's eye out. I've never really believed that stuff with King Harold and the arrow: probably just a cover up after some pre-battle shag of a randy camp-follower did for him with a nipple like our Sophie's"

Sophie was staring down at the front of her dress, as if force of will would reduce the two prominent indicators of her state of arousal. I suddenly felt a bit sorry for her but, in the same moment, recognized something familiar in Sue's taunting - something that reminded me of myself.

I stood up and walked around the table until I could put my arm around Sue's shoulders. "Can we have a bet now? You told us about how you get turned on by watching others having sex. But I bet you're ready for it now. Going to take the wager?"

Sophie sprang to her friend's defense. "No, Cof, we've been together quite a while. She really can't get the juices flowing unless she's a voyeur to live sex."

"If that's the case, she'll take the bet, won't she?" I squeezed Sue's shoulders.

My captive smiled up at me. "Cof, you know you're not as senile as everyone makes you out to be!" With that, she pulled up her dress and opened her legs, revealing her lack of underwear and a vulva that was, literally, so wet that the vaginal fluid was running down her thighs.

"Wow!" Sophie exclaimed as I hauled Sue onto the dining table, pulled my shorts down and proceeded to get waded in, slurping noises accompanying every thrust. Seconds later she had shed her own clothing and was writhing on top of her partner.

Not like the last time with this pair, more like last night with the twins I recognized, just before my analytical facilities were swamped by animal lust.

***

After a short, but very intense, session in the dining room, we gathered up scattered items of clothing and adjourned to my bedroom. I felt a bit guilty about leaving the place in such a mess for the second night running, but such guilt was minor compared to my burning curiosity about what the dream team had come up with as a plan for handling Nigel.

Sue was taking control of things. She vetoed my suggestion of a shower to freshen up, with the argument that we should get our plans sorted out first, without further potential for distraction.

"Shouldn't we get some clothes on then? The amount of bare flesh on display could get distracting," I pointed out.

In response, she pulled back the single satin sheet covering my bed and patted the space next to her. "Hop in. It's probably as comfortable as anywhere to have a chat. No, over here!" She plumped up the pillows and reorganized us so that Sophie was sitting to her left and me to her right. Then the sheet was dragged up to chest level and she smiled at me "There we are, distractions removed, so you have no excuses now."

"Me? It wasn't me I was concerned about," I retorted. "I seem to remember that an hour at the dining table with me, even fully clothed, was enough to bring you on like a couple of panthers on heat. The place smelled like the changing room at the lesbian love Olympics!"

"And you thought it was just the proximity to your delectable body did that?" Sophie sniggered.

"Well neither of you seems shy as far as girl-on-girl action is concerned, but I have been the focus of our last two encounters. I think it's a safe conclusion to draw."

More laughter to my left. "God, but you're an egotistical bugger, Cof! It's true that we were both turned on, but we were already that way before we even came to dinner."

"Mmm, a bit of pre-prandial lesbian foreplay. Tasty!"

"Christ, no! Well, not on this occasion anyway. We were watching the video of your last

341

performance with the twins. We were surprised that you have so much of your personal space wired for sound and vision and it took us a while to determine that the action took place in the dining room rather than any of the more obvious - and comfortable - locations."

"Twins idea," I responded automatically, while trying to fit in this new information with my other attempts to find a pattern in my changing relationships with these two women.

"Didn't look that way from what we saw!"

It took me a moment to place Sophie's comment in context. "No, not where we had sex last night. The audio-visual coverage. They use it for their own purposes, but they make up compilations of some of the wildest stuff that we often watch at the beginning of an evening together. Does a good job of getting you into the mood."

"I'll say!" Sue sighed. "Anyway, this kind of distraction was just what I wanted to avoid. We have to go through our plans for tomorrow."

"Fine, fire away!" I responded, failing to report that risks of my thoughts veering off elsewhere were being increased by the fact that the sheet had now slipped down to waist level. I closed my eyes in any case; the importance of planning was clear because, as Andrea had emphasized, a fuck-up could have serious consequences for us all.

"OK, Sophie and I have prepared a file with more details for you to look at, but first we want to give you the broad brush picture. The fundamental idea is that we are going to frighten Nigel - a lot -

342

with the threat of a weapon that he has no defense against. We point out that the way that he is building up his little dynasty is unacceptable to us, but give him an option where he can retain some influence. He then has the choice: back down gracefully and retain something or stand up to us and have everything taken away. We think that he is pragmatic enough to cut his losses and go for the former."

"Nigel's pretty well established now and must have considered this type of confrontation occurring at some time or other. What weapons do we have that would be so frightening that he'd meekly give up without a fight? Biologicals?"

"Fuck no!" Sophie interrupted. "There is no way that we're getting involved with those things again."

"Brain control," Sue answered, "the type of thing used for riot control back in the good old days of super-science technology.

I remembered the system that she was alluding to. It was actually a direct spin-off from the wireless systems used latterly for delivering electrical power. One thing that QC-based AIs were very good at was manipulation of electromagnetic fields. These could be fine-tuned in 3D to flexibly distribute power anywhere you wanted it, without the need for any clumsy fixed cabling. The widespread implementation of this infrastructure was, in fact, one of the greatest barriers to recovery when the required QCs vanished.

"Yes, well, the basic concept is fine, but I'm afraid that this needs technology that's been gone for a decade and a half now. You just can't do it."

"Actually, I'm fairly sure that's what Nigel will think as well. So that, when we demonstrate our system, he's going to get very scared."

"Right, I'm all ears. I'm just wetting myself to hear exactly how you're going to pull this little miracle off."

"Well, your medical facilities include a functional superconducting nmr tomography machine."

"... fairly standard bit of kit and, although they got a bad rep because of the nuclear part of the name. Infinitely better than all this PET stuff, anyhow."

"... and you've got a non-QC wireless power distribution system."

"Ah, that. Well, I don't think you want to bother with that piece of shit. I got lumbered with it along with the reactor. I think they were trying to sell poor-man's technology to unsuspecting mugs in the back of beyond. We faffed about with it for a while, with the idea of replacing the cabling, but it was just too unreliable. Actually, I'd go as far as to say fucking dangerous. You just can't move significant amps without the EM field resolution that QCs can provide."

"According to your knowledge base, we can couple these two machines together to replicate the QC crowd control tool. Of course, the range will be extremely limited and we'll have to do the fine tuning manually, but it's doable."

I looked at Sue in amazement. "I guess if the search engines say that it's possible, then it probably is. But putting something like this together is going to take a lot of work."

"Sure, that's why we have teams working shifts on it as we speak. Actually, I guess we should have discussed this in advance, but we noted that our clearance level allowed us to reassign staff, so we did so. Is that OK?"

"Why not - if I give you the responsibility for doing the work, then I can't limit your access to the resources that you need to carry it out."

"Actually, the key resources were your workshops, where we over-rode all the past priorities to put this project at the front of the queue."

I had a momentary twinge of annoyance, remembering how long Andrea and I debated setting such priorities, but this vanished quickly as I took into account how critical tomorrow could be. It was true; all of the other stuff could wait.

Seeing my shrug of resignation, Sue continued. "We will only know for certain when we put the various bits and pieces together, but if all goes according to the plan that we put together - with the aid of your expert systems - then a fully functioning and tested system will be built into your jeep by tomorrow morning."

"This is a bit too technical to assess on the basis of a chat. I assume that you've downloaded all the specs of this Heath-Robinson device," Sue nodded, "so I'll just give them a quick look over. A double check can't do any harm."

"No problem, any comments would be useful."

"But this is all the technical side. From what you were saying earlier, you were going to force him to back down by providing both the stick of your terror weapon, but also the carrot of something left in it for him."

"Yes, indeed," Sue smiled, smugly, "this is the cunning part of the plan. He will need to give up power, but he can still be part of the administration and, ad interim, one of his relations will take over the wheel. This allows him to avoid losing face, as it will look like a very small transition which can be easily interpreted as him wanting to slowly have more personal time after so many years at the helm. In fact, it will be a fundamental transformation of government style that will pave the way towards creating a democratic region that could play a central role in helping to establish a world government."

"Sounds fantastic. There's only one problem: there aren't any of Nigel's relations who're capable of either leading a government or of standing up to Nigel if he has set his mind on something."

"Aren't you forgetting about his sister, Gloria?"

"Gloria? OK, I remember that she was also a politician pre-Crash. But, so far, post-Crash administration has been set up mainly by emergency service types. Not a lot of women."

346

"Exactly! How many women have any senior government positions at present?"

"Well, none as far as I am aware."

"Cof, you're the big one for setting up a new world system that gets rid of the systems that caused or supported inequality in the past - financial manipulation, organized religions, national conflicts. What about the way in which women have been exploited throughout history, right up until the '40s? Your sister worked in this area, so you can't have been unaware of what was going on."

"You're right, I suppose. There may have been reasons for allowing alpha males to take control of things when the shit hit the fan, but these have been long overtaken by developments and hence we should have a proper balance of the sexes in the government, whatever form it ends up being."

"This isn't just suddenly appropriate, it is long overdue. Nigel has been particularly guilty here, so his sister is the ideal choice."

"But she can hardly stand up to Nigel, her brother!"

"Nobody on the island is better qualified!"

"... remember this isn't like you and Andrea," Sophie added. "Unlike you two, siblings tend to be rivals rather than partners, especially brothers and sisters who are of similar age and of high intelligence. Even in the '30s, it can't have been easy for Gloria to compete with her older brother. His is the name that's remembered and he was the one set up to make a big move forward when the world fell apart. Gloria, however, was a lawyer rather than a firemen and established her current political credibility despite, rather than because of, her demonstrated academic abilities."

"Mmm, a lawyer. Just what we need!"

"Don't be facetious!" Sue reprimanded me sternly. "We are looking for an optimum solution for here and now, not just responding to the chips on your shoulder accumulated in the past. Gloria is perfect for us; she can give the impression that this is an evolutionary change rather than a coup and she is certainly capable of standing up to her brother. That's very evident if you have a look at her early political record."

"Even if that's the case, would she be interested?"

"The woman would crawl to Holetown on broken glass for the chance! We talked to her yesterday. She's been prominent in trying to re-establish senior roles for women and has had a lot of success at parish level. At the national level, however, she's been completely blocked by her brother. I'm sure it isn't a coincidence, Nigel really hates Gloria's guts and seems to go out of his way to make things difficult for her."

"I'll admit that it wouldn't have occurred to me to make use of sibling rivalry like this; too close to my sister I suppose. Nevertheless, if Nigel hates Gloria so much, why will he go for a change that allows her to move over him?"

"Ego! He won't be able to accept that his young sister will be able to control him. He'll go for this as

348

an interim option, with the assumption that he'll be able to work behind the scenes to regain power."

"Won't he?"

"After a long talk with Gloria, we're both convinced that all this woman needs is a single toe-hold in the administration." Sue looked at Sophie, who nodded agreement. "She sees the danger of overly powerful individuals at a national level, so she'll devolve as much responsibility as possible to the parishes and then move towards a small, democratically chosen executive. We may not have a plebiscite for some time, but her suggestion of nominations by the parish councils seems like a good interim compromise."

I sat in silence for a bit, impressed by the novelty of the approach. I doubted that Andrea and I would have ever come up with an idea like this. The more I thought about it, the better it seemed: if Nigel responded as predicted. And also, of course, if Gloria lived up to her promise.

"So, you're sure that Gloria is kosher?" I asked. "There isn't a chance that we'll only replace one tin-pot dictator with another?"

"You know, by now, that there are no guarantees in this game. But Gloria has already expressed ideas for a united Caribbean region, based on the same idea as the parishes; the islands would nominate an executive which would coordinate things. We didn't have any chance to discuss your world government ideas with her, but I'm sure this would be completely compatible with her concept ... "

"... except, maybe, they'd be a bit more democracy and less elitism in her model" Sophie added.

"Right, I'm convinced. So, what else do I have to do to prepare for tomorrow?"

"Get a good night's sleep!" Sue laughed, pushing her partner out of the bed. "Go through the files we left for you in the morning and then we can have a last run through things over lunch."

The two naked women left the bedroom with their clothes bundled under their arms. Just before the door closed, I noticed Sophie looking back with a distinctly worried look on her face. I suspected she didn't have as much confidence in this plan as the redoubtable Sue and, in the second that our eyes met, got the strong message that she'd much rather have spent the night cuddled up with me.

After the door closed, I lay for a bit and wondered why Sue had forced such an abrupt departure. It could indeed be that she felt that we should all be fully rested for the morrow, but I had a feeling in my gut that there was more to it. If Sophie still had doubts, then maybe Sue was also not as sure of herself as she made out. In that case, the rapid withdrawal could either indicate that she didn't want me to pick up on this doubt or else that she didn't want me to play the role of experienced patriarch, providing comfort for the worried ladies.

It made sense, I decided, as I headed to the bathroom for my delayed shower. The women had to demonstrate to me that they could do the job alone, without support. If there was any comforting

350

to be done, they'd also have to organize that amongst themselves. I couldn't help speculating on what form such comfort could take, which caused a first tremor of tumescence.

I was amazed again by the ability of even the thought of sex to produce endorphins that can counter even the most extreme physical exhaustion. By rights, I should be out cold by now. Instead I was pondering how best to set up a comparison of the video records from the dining room. In parallel or sequential, that was the question.

Overestimating the power of such brain chemicals, or underestimating the wear and tear on my body, I went for the sequential option. I was thus sound asleep well before the first recording was halfway through.

Chapter 10 - Taking care of Nigel

I was awakened by a movement on the bed, which did the job for me before it was light enough for my normal internal alarm clock to go off. The body slipping up against mine was naked and definitely female. Usually the only person who would join me like this was Andrea, but my sister was not an early riser and such pre-dawn perambulation would be unusual in the extreme. Then a felt a hand grasp my dick and start to gently caress it. Well, then, certainly not my sister.

I had already a good idea of who my unannounced visitor might be when a muttered "Morning, Cof," confirmed that it was, indeed, the ex-Jesuit priest. "Got to be quick," she muttered, "Sue thinks I've just gone off for a drink of water."

At that point her head, which was only a vague shape in the faint illumination permeating the room, disappeared beneath the sheet and oral ministrations replaced the initial manual ones.

Although surprise certainly slowed down my response, it wasn't long before Sophie decided that my erection was sufficient and squirmed up to impale herself upon it with an inelegant grunt. She was so wide open and wet that I was struggling to retain rigidity due to the lack of friction when she forced her tongue into my mouth in a deep, sloppy kiss. Despite the other sensations, the distinctive flavor of vaginal secretions was unmistakable. I had no idea if they were her own, Sue's or somebody else's, but in any case the idea itself was sufficient to restore the blood pressure to my cock just in time for the gymnastics that commenced as the woman started to bounce on top of me, pile-driving up and down to utilize the full length of my shaft.

I slid my hands up the sweaty body until I located the engorged nipples crowning two small conical breasts. I grabbed hold and squeezed hard, setting off Sophie's noisy orgasm, which was so dramatic that it immediately drove me over the edge and I came inside her with a long sigh of ecstasy.

My seductress slumped on top of me and we lay panting, sweat cooling on our flesh. After less than a minute, she groaned and pulled herself up and off, sitting astride my waist. I could feel warm, viscous juices seep from her open vulval lips onto my belly. She then rubbed herself forward, using the hair on my chest as a towel, then rapidly dismounted.

"Fuck, I needed that!" the indistinct shape concluded with a heartfelt sigh and exited the room without a further word.

Well, that certainly stopped me worrying about the adventure ahead for a bit and I hoped that it did the same for Sophie. I rubbed a finger in the sticky fluid on my stomach and inhaled deeply. If that is characteristic of Jesuits, I wondered if maybe I'd been wrong in the past by trying to stay away from clerics as much as possible.

***

I spent the earlier part of the morning going over the files that my partners had left for me, in particular using a range of software tools to check the specs of their terror weapon. The more I got into it, the more cunning I realized that it was.

My wireless power distribution system was completely useless for its intended purpose, it just didn't have the sophistication to manipulate EM fields carrying any significant power; in particular its effectiveness dropped off exponentially with power load. It could just about light a torch bulb at fifty paces in an open field, but anything more needed the computing capacity that could only be provided by QC-AIs. For the neural controller, however, the power requirements for synapse manipulation were orders of magnitude lower than a bulb, so could be easily handled by this system.

The other limitation of a non-QC system was resolution. Even at microwatt power levels, being able to deliver impulses over tens of meters with nanometer precision was no mean task. This would have been completely impossible if the demonstration wasn't being carried out indoors, but was just about doable in a house that was fully cabled for electrical power. The bastardized chimera that my workshops were assembling would piggy-back most of the power supply and target localization onto the existing cable network. The final linkage thus only had to be made over a few meters at most and, in addition, we'd carry SQUID-based location and calibration monitors that would help with detailed location of the chosen target.

All in all, it was a Frankenstein's monster of sub-optimal technology but, for the very specific application envisaged, it should actually work. It was, however, really pushing the envelope, so I hoped there would be time for shakedown testing before it had to be used for real.

Having convinced myself that there were neither fundamental flaws in their plan nor any obvious ways that it could be improved, I decided to spend the rest of my time before lunch getting myself prepared. After a bit of thought, I decided to cancel my planned run and, instead, spent a much more relaxed hour in the gym, stretching and going through a long Tai Chi routine.

On the way to lunch, I detoured via my laboratory and had a look at various weapons that I had cobbled together over the years. The question was should I place full trust in my team or else take some backup with me, risking that, if it was discovered, I would have shown my lack of confidence in their abilities. With a shrug of my shoulders, I postponed the decision and went to eat.

***

Despite feigned cheerfulness, there was a palpable tension in the air over lunch: a pseudo Camembert with a French-style crusty baguette and some crisp apples. I washed this down with a couple of glasses of a synthetic Cetes du Rhone, but noticed that the ladies stuck to sparkling mineral water, which was actually carbonated Bajan groundwater from a well in the grounds of the estate.

By unspoken agreement, the confrontation with Nigel was avoided in discussions while we were eating, leading to stilted conversation and long silences. Everyone seemed relieved when we could leave the table and get down to business.

Sue started by quickly skimming through the content of the files that I had received, double checking that I was in agreement with the plan in all details. She then ran through all the final installation and testing of the kit that had been packed into my old Landrover, along with some heavy duty fuel cells. By the standards of present day Barbados, we were carrying a fortune in hard- and software. If our plan went pear shaped, Nigel could well come out of this with equipment that would help him strengthen his position further. I didn't mention this observation, as I was sure that Sue, at least, would already be painfully aware of it.

Finally, there was a last run through our roles. I would take the lead, in line with the University cover story, until we got into Nigel's office. Then, as soon as it was practical, Sue and Sophie would take over and I would simply provide any support needed to convince Nigel that the ladies were in complete control of this op. Other than that, my main job was to watch for any signs of divergence from the plan and, if anything significant was spotted, let Sue know immediately and provide any support requested. If all went well, I was a bystander and could spend my time making mental notes to help with the subsequent debriefing.

Time flew and the next I knew it was two o'clock, our cue for a last toilet visit, then grab our kit and get moving. The equipment that comprised our weapon was already loaded in the back of the car and we piled into the front, squeezing together onto the basic bench seat.

I was driving and, within minutes, was glad of our robust, all-terrain vehicle. The roads in Barbados had never been particularly good, having evolved organically over time as opposed to logically planned on maps by Roman or Teutonic engineers. The car was so old that it had a manual gear shift, which I abused terribly over the first three or four kilometers, before I slowly got the hang of it. I had actually practiced in advance of this trip by driving circuits of the garden for half an hour. This had, however, done little to prepare me for fighting along potholed tracks that I shared with a huge diversity of other road users; everything from farmers herding cattle to smoky, alcohol-fuelled trucks straining under massive loads of sugar cane.

I drove initially towards Holetown but, before I entered the town proper, cut left up the hill towards the old highway that bypassed Bridgetown and ran south and then east to the airport. Possibly due to the higher number of trucks, the quality of this highway was even worse than the access road and even getting up to fifty kph was a challenge due to

357

the slalom course required to avoid the deepest pits in the surface of the tarmac.

A little over thirty minutes later, after being slowed on a couple of occasions by convoys of crawling trucks, we finally turned off the highway towards Oistins and I threw the heads-up navigation system on the screen to help us find our way towards Nigel's residence.

Although the road was marginally less terrible, it only improved significantly as we turned into the wide drive leading up to Nigel's baronial villa. Two policemen armed with heavy-looking machine pistols waved us through the gates, allowing us to proceed about three hundred meters before we were stopped at a check point. Our identities were checked with a bulky retinal scanner, which seemed to have been ripped-off from an IBC branch office. I made a mental note to check up on how that might have occurred. Meanwhile, a couple of dog-handlers were leading large brutes, which seemed to be crosses with a lot of Doberman in them, around our ancient vehicle. The snuffling dogs and the handlers peering into the windows seemed to be checking for concealed passengers, the pile of equipment chests in the back didn't merit a second glance.

Two armed guards on farting alcohol mopeds led us further up the drive and then through an archway into a circular inner courtyard. All of a sudden I recognized the place - an ultra-luxury villa constructed by a British billionaire just after I arrived on the island in the '30s. I had gone over building plans and all kind of background bumf in the files but, only when I saw the marble-coated walls in real life, were memories of news reports covering the innumerable parties at this house dragged from some cobwebbed deep store. Whenever pop stars, models and actors arrived for these bashes, they were always photographed in this courtyard. Driving into it myself gave me a strange feeling in my gut, which was kind of crazy when the paparazzi fluff of that era was set in comparison to the potential global significance of our present mission.

A liveried butler waited by an open double door of shining mahogany. There was definitely a feeling of visiting royalty as we progressed along wide hallways adorned with paintings and sculptures that looked like they would be more in place in a museum or an art gallery. Probably where they originally came from, I realized belatedly.

Nigel's office seemed almost modest by the scale of the rest of the villa, but maybe this was mainly the effect of the high ceiling and the bookcases crammed with leather-bound tomes which covered three walls of the room. The fourth had obviously been a huge video panel, pre-crash, but now looked like plain grey slate. The effective dictator of Barbados sat behind a modern steel and plastic desk that seemed completely out of place in the classically-styled library. He certainly seemed comfortable in his black leather swivel chair as, without rising, he majestically waved us to three smaller seats on the other side of the table.

Everything deliberately set up for impact, I saw, remembering our first encounter when we jostled for position by radio. He had never really forgiven that occasion, when we first established relative pecking order. Our confrontations since had been softer, vaguer, where there was less clearly a winner and loser. Now he had done his preparation in advance. There were things that he still wanted to get from me, but I had asked to see him and he was the one in the big chair receiving the supplicant. He wanted to make this clear, ram it down my throat, but in a subtle enough way that I wasn't going to be offended sufficiently to leave immediately.

Before I could say anything, his eldest son, Winston, entered the room and moved to his father's side, standing there as an epitome of filial obedience. Nigel had obviously been waiting for this entrance. "Well, it's nice to see you again, Cof. This idea you have about the University seems like just what we need now, to show that we're really moving back to the normalcy of the good old days. I brought Winston in for our meeting because, with the huge amount of emergency service training and retraining going on, it falls very closely in line with his portfolio. I don't think you've met Winston before... "

He looked like he was leading up to an extended presentation of his son when Sue interrupted. "Winston really isn't important here. I think I should start by introducing myself, Susan Latimer, and my colleague, Doctor Sophie Vargas. We will take over now from Doctor Moore."

360

Nigel was sitting with his jaw open and Wilson looked, literally, gobsmacked. In fact I was also a bit disorientated, I hadn't heard anyone address me by my surname for over a decade and it sounded wrong, somehow. As if someone was talking about my long-dead father.

Finally Nigel managed to splutter "Cof, what the fuck's all this about. What're your fucking bitches playing at?"

"Well, Nigel old chap, you're looking at the future, the new wave. These ladies have taken over the helm and I'm just preparing myself for being set out to pasture. You should, therefore, be careful with your tongue as these are a pair of very powerful females, who may not take kindly to being called offensive names."

Nigel was shocked into silence, but this gave Winston an opportunity. "Fuck you old man and fuck yo'r scrawny white ho' bitches too. You don' try to fuck wi' me pa or I tell yo' man, yo'r dead meat."

Sue didn't shout, but the ice in her voice cut through the room. "Winston, you stupid bastard, shut the fuck up!" On the last word she snapped her fingers and the heavily-built black youth dropped to the floor like a sack of potatoes.

Nigel's eyes were like saucers as he goggled at his prostrate son. "What? What the fuck'd you do to him, to my boy?"

"Nigel, you shut it as well! And stay put... " This caused the man to stop his involuntary movement towards his son and sink heavily back

361

into his seat. "Your son is fine, just out cold. Get somebody to clear him out of here and put him to bed. He'll be right as rain in half an hour or so."

The shocked despot mumbled into an old-style intercom and, seconds later, two large guards entered and, lifting Winston's heavy frame awkwardly between them, carried him from the room. The fact that this act proceeded without any appearance of surprise seemed a sad comment on the way that Nigel ran his household.

Nevertheless, the man wouldn't have achieved his present position if he hadn't been tough. He tried one last appeal to me but, following my silence, accepted the new situation and addressed himself directly to Sue, trying to regain his Bajan elder statesman status. "OK, Lady, you got the whip hand here. Don't know how you done it, but seems that you can knock out anyone in this here room just by clicking yo' fingers."

"Not just in the room, anybody in the house, anybody on the island," Sue corrected him.

A look of disbelief showed on his sweating face. "You can maybe use some kind of secret taser shit in here, but all that worldwide voodoo control crap disappeared long time ago."

"Unlike outside, we didn't lose all our technology. While you guys out here have been fighting to get back to the 20th century, we've built back to mid-21st. We've now got universal surveillance and can use all the old em-field weapons technology.

362

Nigel was evidently calming down, convinced that this was some kind of bluff. He mopped his brow for show and then attempted a grin. "You know, Cof, these girls o' yours really had me going for a bit. I really thought they had something worrying, but they ain't no poker players, that's for sure. Overplayed their hand. You may think I'm just a hick politico fom de Caribbean Islands, mon," his accent thickened farcically. "But I'm not so dumb that I don't know that you need them quantum computers and power satellites and all that crap to make that magic work. That all went away on 20th February 2041 and it ain't never coming back."

Sue was completely unfazed as the sarcastically replied. "There's nobody so dumb as the man who pontificates in a field he knows nothing about. As a fireman, you know enough about electromagnetic field manipulation using adaptively-altered, holograph-like constructive interference matrices to tell us what can be done and what can't? I guess my colleague and I wasted our time researching quantum physics, we should have just spent our time playing with hoses and ladders and then we'd have known that it was impossible to build the system that we've just reconstructed."

Nigel's smile widened. "Bluff, Baby Girl, yo'r bluffin'. I may not be no quantum whatsit, but an old politician knows bullshit when he sees it. If it looks like bullshit, smells like bullshit then I guess it's probably crap from a boy cow."

"Well let's see what it tastes like when you've got to eat that shit. EM-control means that I can make machines do what I want... " a snap of her fingers and the wall screen behind Nigel crackled to life, almost causing him to fall out of his chair as he span round to identify the source of the noise, "... and see and hear what is going on anywhere." Another snap of her fingers and a grainy picture quivered on the huge display. Not great quality, but it was clear enough to show three women working in a kitchen, with a horde of children around their feet. "And, of course, I can switch off the brain of anyone I choose." A first snap and the children went down like puppets with cut strings, causing the scene to break into immediate chaos, another snap and the women dropped on top of them, freezing the tableau into immobility.

Nigel's dusky face had paled dramatically and sweat was now running down his cheeks, maybe mixed with tears. "That's my wife, my kids... "

"Yes and a couple of cousins with their kids. Like Winston, they're only going to sleep for a bit and will be otherwise unharmed. Now you, not being dumb," sarcasm dripped from her voice like acid, "will realize that if I can cause unconsciousness, I can just as easily induce epileptic fits or simply stop the victims breathing. Would you like me to demonstrate?"

"Fuck no!" the man was broken. He was physically shaking and sounded as if he was about to burst into tears. I felt a momentary twinge of sympathy. Nigel's entire vision of the world had shattered. He had schemed for years to establish a system where he would have unchallengeable control. Just when it all seemed within his grasp, the carpet had been pulled out from under him and he was exposed as a tyrant in control of swords and flintlocks coming up against an individual with cruise missiles and nuclear weapons. He had absolutely no defense against the overwhelming technological superiority that had just been demonstrated to him.

Sue and Sophie now seated themselves and started to lay out their problems with his administration and their instructions for the change of regime. When Sue mentioned his sister taking over the reins, it looked like he might rebel, but the screen flicked on again to show the hubbub in the kitchen as a number of men and women attempted to revive the unconscious victims. A snap of Sue's fingers and all standing figures crumpled onto the floor. Nigel's opposition collapsed as quickly.

While all this was going on, I wandered around the room, appearing to aimlessly scan books from the shelf. Nigel was paying me no attention, so it was easy to place pin cameras in a few strategic positions that would both provide coverage of the room and be provided with both power and communications via vampiric inductive coupling to nearby power cables. The dramatic demonstration of our ability to monitor anywhere had, of course, been a trick. As soon as we arrived, several moth-sized ornithopter drones had been dispatched to provide surveillance of other parts of the villa. These had, however, only limited lifetimes and would, in any case, be recovered before we left to reduce the risk of our deception being discovered. The chances of the minute pin cameras that I was leaving being detected was negligible by comparison.

In just over a quarter of an hour, the details were laid out and Nigel had agreed to the timetable for transfer of power. Sue finished by reiterating the penalties for any deviation from this schedule and we departed, leaving behind a broken man.

The girls were smiling in relief as we let ourselves out of the building and headed for our vehicle. I had already opened the driver's door when Winston rose from where he had been crouching on the far side of our vehicle and charged round the bonnet, swinging the huge machetes that he held in each hand.

I jumped backwards in surprise, stumbling into Sophie, who was slammed into the side of our car. Off balance, I turned the stagger into a breakfall, which saved me from decapitation but couldn't prevent a slash to the left side of my head that resulted in a trailing plume of blood as I rolled up to a crouch that was outside the range of the irate youth's weapons. Although blood blinded my left eye, I could see that his cut at me was followed by a backhand with the handle of the weapon that crashed into Sophie's temple and dropped her like a log.

Sue had been behind the Landrover when the attack commenced and now emerged to scream at the crazed man. "What the fuck're you trying to do, you mad bugger? Harm one of us and your entire family will suffer."

"Fuck you bitch! Yo' fucking voodoo shit ain't strong 'nuf fo' me. Me I'm up an' OK now in ten minutes and hear all yo' sayin' t' me old man." A vicious swipe at her face caused Sue to scamper back into cover behind the jeep.

Taking advantage of this momentary distraction. I stepped forward on my left leg, pivoting into a low kick that crashed into the side of his knee, my steel toecap causing a scream of pain as his left leg buckled. I lunged back, but not fast enough to avoid his counter, which slashed into my right thigh, cutting to the bone.

Shock was dulling the pain of the wounds caused by the razor-sharp blades, but I had to constantly wipe blood clear so that I could see, at least out of my right eye, and I couldn't put any weight on my right leg. Strangely, I seemed to be able to take the entire scene in at a glance, as Winston limped towards me and I frantically tried to hop backwards to stay out of range. Sophie seemed to be unconscious as she lay, half under the Landrover. The blood on her face and upper torso seemed to be mine rather than hers. I also noticed that her wig had been dislodged, showing a tracery of coppery wires on her shaved head. This must be how she had controlled the drone, directed the EM immobilizer and activated the video screen, I realized.

Sue was pulling at the back doors of the vehicle, clearly unaware that I had locked them from within. I guessed that she was trying to get to the computer that Sophie's link could no longer access with the hope of using it to put Winston out. In any case, she would be far too late to help me. I threw myself backwards to avoid a horizontal swing at chest height and landed flat on my back, only the reflex slaps with my arms and arching of my back saving me from being completely winded as I smacked heavily onto the rough tarmac.

"Yo' see, man, all yo' crap can't stop me killin' yo' fuckin' ass." He stood astride me and raised both machetes above his head as I tried to worm my way backwards.

"Die, yo' ...aaaa!" His intake of breath turned into a combination of a scream and a gurgle as my boot sank into his groin. The power of the blow was greatly limited by weakness of the arch made from my shoulders and wounded right leg, which had allowed me to get my foot high enough to make contact between his legs.

In any case, the shock was sufficient to force him back a step, allowing me to scramble onto my knees to prepare for his next onslaught. In this process, which was greatly hampered by the increasing pain in my thigh and blood blocking my vision, I caught a glimpse of a shape starting to fall from my sliced right-leg pocket and grabbed it by reflex. Suddenly I was no longer weaponless.

Winston was advancing slowly and deliberately, clearly intent on making sure that I didn't catch him out again. He could see that I was losing a lot of blood and only grinned as I fought to get my good leg under me and raise myself, swaying, to my feet.

He raised his right arm slowly, savoring the moment, then stepped forward as the blade flashed diagonally downwards, already calculated for my expected attempt to escape backwards. I saw his look of surprise as I propelled myself directly towards him, raising my left arm to block his attack and swinging my right towards his face.

His reactions were fast, very fast. The right blow dropped a little so that, instead of my arm blocking his wrist, the bottom end of the huge knife carved into my elbow. Simultaneously, the machete in his left hand came up and sliced effortlessly through my right wrist. But not fast enough. I was holding my breath with my eyes closed as I dropped to the ground and rolled sideways for as long as I could before the shock of pain from my arms broke through the adrenalin nerve blocks and I finally lost consciousness.

Chapter 11 - End of the beginning

It was a slow and gradual process as I awoke in the hospital zone, back at the estate. I lay for a moment gazing at the sleeping form of my sister, who was curled uncomfortably in a chair beside the bed. Suddenly she stirred, woken by the noise of running footsteps, and had turned to look at me before the door crashed open and Tina, Sophie and Sue burst in. "Ham, you mad bugger! What the fuck were you doing getting into a bloody knife fight? You should know better by now!" Her harsh words couldn't conceal the look of worry on her face and a trace of tears in the corner of her eyes.

Andrea put her arm around Tina, who had rushed to her side, then turned her attention to the others. "And as for you two! You were supposed to be reducing the amount of bloodshed, not turning Nigel's place into a fucking abattoir!"

"That's not really fair" I croaked, suddenly realizing that my throat was bone dry. Sophie immediately spotted the problem and held a glass of water to my lips, which I drained before continuing. "The plan was OK and it was just bad luck that Winston has the constitution of a mule and the temper to go with it. If he had stayed out cold, the entire caper would have gone without a hitch."

"Well, we can go into the post-mortem debriefing later... " Andrea politically changed the subject. "First of all, though, how are you feeling?"

"I appear to be fine, though still a bit spaced from whatever drugs you've been feeding me," I responded hoarsely. "I'll know a bit more about how I feel if you'd let me know how damaged I am." Both arms and my right leg were sealed within the white sausages of portable hyperbaric oxygen chambers and I could detect no sensations at all from my limbs.

My former secretaries looked at each other, then at my sister, but it was Tina who spoke up in the end. "The good news is that your leg is OK. A very deep cut, but clean and fixable. The bad news, though... " she seemed at a loss for how to go on.

"My arms must be pretty bad. I can't really remember details, but I think young Winston landed a couple of good ones on me."

My calm analysis encouraged my sister's partner to continue. "Left arm almost severed at the elbow, right hand cleanly amputated. If this had happened here in the estate, not a problem for the robotic microsurgery kit." Once again she was having problems giving me the bad news.

"But I wasn't here, I was at least an hour away. There would have been bits of me scattered about on the road and I'd be bleeding like a stuck pig. Actually, bleeding out must have been the biggest risk. We had nothing in the car but a small first aid kit, but there must have been plenty of material for tourniquets."

"Self-tightening cable binders," Sue contributed.

"Ouch! Just as well I was unconscious. They'd certainly do the job of stopping the blood flow, but not easy to manage regular releases of pressure."

"Actually, we didn't know that you needed to do that" Sophie confessed.

"Double ouch! And you'd be driving back as fast as possible on bumpy roads in a car with pretty crappy air con and no refrigeration capability. I think I can see what you're getting at. So, what have I got attached to my shoulders, hooks?"

Andrea smiled wanly. "Not quite as bad as that, lad. After more than twenty-four hours of reconstructive microsurgery you've got two arms that will look pretty normal after the scars heal."

The feeling of dread that had been building up since I regained consciousness suddenly ramped up, sending a shock of fear up my spine. Somehow, the fight with Winston had been too fast for shock to turn into real bowel-churning terror; now it all seemed to be catching up with me. "Look normal?" I silently cursed myself for the tremor in my voice, which was probably making this ordeal even worse for the others. "I suppose that means that there won't be much function; I won't be playing with myself anymore."

"We don't know what functions you may eventually recover," Tina responded honestly, "but the chances of you playing the piano again are negligible."

"Never was that keen on keyboards. Guitar?"

Tina shook her head, then Andrea took over. "Skin, bones, blood-vessels, all that stuff is OK. It's

372

the nerves that are the limiting factor. In the old medical AI days, they'd just have cloned new nerves and rewired your arms using em-field directed axon growth. This isn't an option now. All we can do is use microsurgery to reconnect any nerves we can and hope that, after healing, they'll be viable. Best prognosis is about 10%, but this could well drop below 1%. So you'd be losing a lot of both tactile sensation and fine muscle control. We'll know more within a few days."

"So I'm not going to be enjoying a good Sherman for a while, if ever at all."

"Worry not, little bro'," She smiled. "Just give us a call when the need comes upon you and Tina and I will pop over to sort you out."

"Destroys the spontaneity a bit, but thanks for the offer anyway." I managed a grin as the shock of the news began to wear off. 10% was certainly a lot better than nothing and, at a pinch, even 1% must be survivable. I was lucky to be alive and, when looked at from that perspective, I had come out of the fracas remarkably well.

"Actually, while we're on the topic of injuries, what happened to Winston?"

Andrea glared at Sue, who shrugged and answered. "As you can imagine, he must have been in incredible pain after he got that facefull of concentrated ammonia. He was blindly crashing around the place when I finally managed to get into the car and activate the EM system. First I put him out, then everyone else in the house, as his screams had started to draw attention away from the scene in the kitchen. I first stopped your bleeding and then woke Sophie up. We loaded both you and Winston into the Landrover and then drove back. That's it in a nutshell."

"You brought him back here? Why?"

"We couldn't just leave him lying in pools of your blood: it wouldn't at all support our omnipotent reputation for you to have been carved up by a juvenile thug."

"Yes, well the problem would only present itself if he was able to talk. There are very simple ways of assuring that that doesn't occur." Thinking of my own injuries, I was rather annoyed that the young psychopath hadn't been put down immediately, which is what Andrea or I would certainly have done.

"We thought of a better way of handling it," Sue responded, with typical bluntness. "After we got you back here, we told Nigel only that his idiot son had attacked us while we were leaving. We were forced to hurt the boy and, as an indication of our displeasure, we immediately demonstrated what we could do by putting the entire household out. As we were sure that Nigel had nothing to do with this, our response this time was non-lethal and we would patch up his stupid offspring. If this happened again, with or without his involvement, we would not be so moderate in our response."

"How will that work? He'll just go back and open his big mouth... "

"No he won't. We've already induced chemical amnesia that covers at least the last few days. He

374

won't remember anything at all. He will also have a couple of huge scars, which will look like machete cuts and will explain the blood outside Nigel's house. Of course, if someone typed it, they'd quickly find out it wasn't Winston's, but who'd ever think of doing that?"

"So this actually reinforces your position, showing that you really will come down heavily on anybody that goes up against you. Clever, I suppose, although I'd really like to think that the little bastard wasn't getting off so lightly."

"Well, it's hardly light," Sophie objected. "Due to the ammonia he's blind in one eye with only reduced vision in the other. We've put one of the surgical scars right through his eyes and removed the sightless eyeball completely. Getting beat up with his own machetes will thus explain the damage."

We chatted for a bit more, then I could feel my eyes begin to droop. Andrea noticed and suggested that we call it quits for now. My secretaries promised to come by the following morning so that, while I was laid up, I could work further on the finalization of the book.

After the women left the room I thought over the book project. It really had served its purpose. I could see that my time leading the renaissance work was done and that this could be passed over into the more capable hands of my protegees. Nevertheless, it was probably worth finishing the text off, as there may be other hints that the women could pick up from my past mistakes that may help to make their challenging job easier. For me, before my brain turned completely to porridge, maybe a good project would be helping to set up the new University. This would allow me to introduce some of the ideas that I had for developing new materials within a training course, so that my experience could be passed on to the next generation.

Just before I drifted off, I remembered how Sophie had kissed me before she left, surreptitiously licking my ear before she whispered into it. "Shame that you can't satisfy any urges that you may have at present. I'll sneak back later to help you get rid of any excess pressure." I could feel a slight stirring in my groin. At least that part of my anatomy still seemed to function. I felt certain that, despite tiredness, I would be able to take the woman up on her offer.

My sister had been last to leave. After the others had left the room, she also bent over and gave me a kiss, her eyes glinting in a mischievous manner. "What?" I asked curiously.

"Well, the Winston yob may not be getting off quite as lightly as the others think. He's getting sent home tomorrow, but I've already spiked his drip."

"Something lethal?"

"No, worse!" Her smile was truly wicked. "I managed to get hold of some GM genital herpes. I actually had it synthesized after the Darcy affair. You may have some problems playing with your willy for the next while, but Wilson's prong is going to be covered with bleeding sores for the rest of his life. If he even gets close to a hard on, the pain will drive him mad. Every piss will be like sulfuric acid and, as it goes for the anus as well, every shit will be a porcupine. Seems fair to me!"

We grinned manically at each other as we chanted in unison, "Wha daur fuck wi' us!"

THE END

www.ingramcontent.com/pod-product-compliance
Lightning Source LLC
Chambersburg PA
CBHW011119050726
47495CB00020B/2739